Praise for Marianne Wiggins and *Evidence of Things Unseen*

"Wiggins has created a story as compelling as it is devastating."
—*Los Angeles Times Book Review*

"Marianne Wiggins's talent is obvious . . . a fine stylist who depicts everyday people with sympathy and realism."
—*The Washington Post*

"*Evidence of Things Unseen* is one of the finest fictions I've ever encountered."
—Liz Smith, *Newsday*

"Marianne Wiggins's remarkable new novel . . . is not only a terrific read that should sweep up a sackful of prizes; it's also an important work that merits comparison with the classics of American literature."
—*The San Diego Union Tribune*

"An extraordinary new novel. Rare and startling, shimmering with luminous language and a confident understanding of the capacity for faith and love."
—*The Miami Herald*

"The author can make you weep in a single sentence. . . . The events and relationships are rendered on the page with an immediacy that catches you up short."
—*The Boston Globe*

"A strongly traditional work in the best sense, drawing on the foundations of American literature laid down by Melville and built upon by a later generation of writers, including Hemingway, Fitzgerald, Wolfe, and Steinbeck."
—*Pittsburgh Post Gazette*

"Wiggins' prose is alternately pyrotechnic and luminous. . . . *Evidence of Things Unseen* is the most perceptive novel about America you will read this year."
—*The Memphis Commercial Appeal*

"Another tour de force from a first-class literary novelist."
—*Library Journal* (starred review)

also by marianne wiggins

NOVELS

Babe

Went South

Separate Checks

John Dollar

Eveless Eden

Almost Heaven

SHORT STORIES

Herself in Love

Bet They'll Miss Us When We're Gone

marianne wiggins

evidence of things unseen

a novel

simon & schuster paperbacks
new york london toronto sydney

Simon & Schuster Paperbacks
Rockefeller Center
1230 Avenue of the Americas
New York, NY 10020

This book is a work of fiction. Names, characters, places, and incidents either are products of the author's imagination or are used fictitiously. Any resemblance to actual events or locales or persons, living or dead, is entirely coincidental.

First Simon & Schuster paperback edition 2004

Simon & Schuster Paperbacks and colophon are registered trademarks of Simon & Schuster, Inc.

For information about special discounts for bulk purchases, please contact Simon & Schuster Special Sales:
1-800-456-6798 or business@simonandschuster.com

Photo by James Fraher / Getty Images, Inc.
Designed by Jeanette Olender
Manufactured in the United States of America

7 9 10 8

The Library of Congress has cataloged the hardcover edition as follows:
Wiggins, Marianne.
Evidence of things unseen : a novel / Marianne Wiggins.
p. cm.
1. World War, 1914–1918—Veterans—Fiction. 2. Tennessee—Fiction.
3. Radiation—Fiction. I. Title.
PS3573.I385E94 2003 813'.54—dc21
ISBN 0-684-86969-1
0-7432-5809-6 (Pbk)

Severin and Melville

those two necessary salts

evidence of things unseen

The Material that destroyed Nagasaki was plutonium-239.

Plutonium was the first man-made element produced in a quantity large enough to see. It was created in 1940 at the University of California at Berkeley. The idea of it had for many years been indicated by the periodic table of the elements, where a row of blanks paralleling the rare earths suggested the theoretical possibility of elements whose family characteristics—like the characteristics of thorium, protactinium, and uranium—would be similar to those of actinium. It was possible that unknown elements (with ninety-three protons, ninety-four protons, and so on) had long ago existed in our solar system but had vanished . . .

JOHN MCPHEE, *The Curve of Binding Energy*

white sands

Somewhere in the heart of North America there is a desert where the heat of several suns has fused the particles of sand into a single sheet of glass so dazzling it sends a constant signal to the moon. On a map, this unmarked space looks like a printer's error, an empty region on a page the cartographer forgot. One way or another each of us is drawn to this forbidden place. Like a magnet, this glass desert calls our irons the way the whale's heart used to beckon a harpoon. In our dreams or in our fears we imagine what it must be like to walk upon this surface. We imagine we could balance there, like an angel lighting down on ice, glissade, perhaps, without cracking its thin shell with the weight of our existence. This desert's name is Trinity. One day the sun rose twice there in a single mourning and Man saw his face reflected on the underside of Heaven. When the first atomic bomb exploded over earth that morning, the entire sky broadcast the news. Creation of the universe, that day, was reenacted. This time, God was not the only audience. If birth is fission, then the love we make is fusion; and to make an End is nothing more than to realize a Beginning. Because the end is where we start. Somewhere in the heart of North America there is a desert made of glass. Reflected in that glass there are two lovers, twinned for all eternity, the shape of all their days preserved like history's signature in stone. Their love preserved, like wings, in amber.

. . . when seamen fall overboard, they are sometimes found, months afterwards, perpendicularly frozen into the hearts of fields of ice, as a fly is found glued in amber.

HERMAN MELVILLE, *Moby-Dick,* "The Blanket"

radiance

On the night that they found Lightfoot, the stars were falling down.

All along the pirate coast the lighthouse keepers cast their practiced eyes into the night, raking dark infinity with expectant scrutiny the way the lighthouse beams combed cones of light over the tillered sea.

Over the Outer Banks, from the eastern constellation Perseus, shooting stars like packet seeds spilled across the sky, tracing transits of escape above the fourteen lighthouses from Kitty Hawk and Bodie Light to Hatteras and Lookout.

It was the yearly August meteor shower and Fos had driven out from Tennessee across the Smokies to the brink of the Atlantic for the celestial show as he'd done each August for the last fifteen years ever since he'd shipped home from France in '19, once the War was over. He and fifteen other sons from Dare County had been among the first recruits to go across the North Atlantic in '18 for valor, decency, and hell like they'd never known. Not one among them who survived was proud of it in any way that didn't cast a shadow back across his pride. Fos himself, by accident, had been a sparker in the field, an incendiary artist, and he'd been brilliant at it. He'd always had an interest in what made things light up, made things radiate, but he never knew he had a latent genius like a fuse, a flare for fireworks, until they handed him a uniform and stood him up in front of a regimental officer and asked him what, if anything, he was good at doing. I'm good at making things light up, Fos said. Looking at the open file on the camp table between them, Fos watched the R.O.'s pen stall where Fos's name was written on the page. You mean explosives? the R.O. said.

—um no sir.

The pen still stalled.

—chemicals? the R.O. pressed.

—*radiance,* Fos explained.

They put him in Artillery and shipped him over with the rest of the First Army and on the fifth day in their training camp in France two British officers with more brass than a church organ between them interrupted gun assembly in his barracks. Who's the chap here who's the chemist? the one with more brass asked. When no one volunteered, the one with less brass held his clipboard up and read out, Private First Class Foster? Fos felt the heat rise to his cheeks and took a weak step forward.

—that would be me, sir.

Come with us.

They led Fos past rows of wooden barracks to the quartermaster's depot into the munition stores. Next to a stepped-temple of stacked diesel drums there was a brick hut with a flat roof, buttressed by sandbags. Inside there were four men in blue smocks and gauze surgical masks in a makeshift laboratory. An astringent tinge of sulfur in the air was the first thing that Fos noticed. Speak any French? the British officer asked before he left him there.

—no sir.

—learn to.

—yes sir.

Four pairs of dark wide eyes stared at Fos above the surgical masks. Then one of the men, the short one in the foreground, spoke. A patch of moisture appeared on his mask from where the words emanated and Fos stared at it, uncomprehending, as if a translation would materialize there as well. The tallest of the four untied his own mask and, with a heavy accent, said, He wants to know are you the candlemaker Uncle Sam has sent?

—candlemaker?

Fos stared at the material around them. There were shelves of chemicals in jars, sieves and grinders, meshes, funnels, fuses of all sorts, crates of French F1 pineapple grenade casings. As best as Fos could reckon from the things that he could recognize, the men in the blue smocks were making firecrackers. The short man gave an impatient shrug and seemed to ask the same question again, only this time with more force so his mask made little jumps, in and out, like a pumping artery. Fos nodded, mutely, and then there were *oo*s and *ah*s all around and then the short one asked him something else in a nicer way with what appeared to be a little curtsy. He wants to know where in the United States we come from? the tall man translated for Fos.

Oh, Fos answered. North Carolina.

They stared at him.

Kitty Hawk, he said.

—kiti—? the short one repeated.

Kitty *Hawk,* Fos emphasized. He flapped his arms. *The Wright brothers,* he said.

There was a burst of recognition as all of them flapped their arms and chimed Or-*vee!* Wil-*bear!* That established, everyone turned back to what he had been doing and left Fos in the care of the tallest one among them, the one who spoke the English, a French-Canadian, as it turned out, who handed Fos a mask and smock and began to show him around the little laboratory.

You wouldn't think it, Fos would later tell his son Lightfoot, *but the worst of problems over there was Light, pure and simple.* Daylight. 'Cause there wasn't hardly ever any of it. Almost none. You would have thought the vermin and the brute of noise would have been the worst, but men go crazy without daylight. In the smoke and in the dark. Men go crazy when they have to run out into somethin that might kill them that they can't see right in front of 'em.

So Fos's first job in the Great War was to learn from four Frenchmen, who'd had three years' more experience, how to light the trenches, how to light the field. So that the boys could see what they were shooting at. See death coming, when it came.

Sodium nitrate, Lead tetraoxide, Potassium chlorate, the Canadian recited to Fos from the labels on the bottles on the shelves. Oxidizers, he explained. Hot. *Vurry* hot, he emphasized. Then he pointed to another group of chemicals and read, *Charcoal, Lampblack, Titanium* and told Fos, Make the *boum.* You understand? Fos nodded. All the labels, except the ones for casings and the fuses, were printed in English—all the warnings were, too—and Fos comprehended that all these chemicals must have been delivered from the States, or from England. Somewhere where the native lingo produced disclaimers written in English that warned FLAMMABLE SOLID. SPONTANEOUSLY COMBUSTIBLE. DANGEROUS WHEN WET. The Canadian took down a jar and shook out a salting of powder on a glass slide and said, *Paris green.* Is copper. Makes the fire burn in blue. Blue flare.

Behind them, one of the Frenchmen nodded over his work and translated, *La flambée.*

—*la fusée,* another said.

—*la flamme vacillante,* and Fos was reminded of a drawing he'd once seen of mediëval monks at their tables, brushing color onto pages of gospels, while chanting.

Barium chloride, the Canadian told him. For the green flame. *Barium sulphate.* All the bariums, green. *Sulfur*—yellow. For white, pure white flare—the magnesiums. *Vurry explosif!*

—*foum!* one of the Frenchmen mimed.

—ker-*plouie!* another one joked.

But Fos was transfixed by something else. He wasn't a chemist. He wasn't transported by processes that needed to burn oxygen. He wasn't interested in energy that *burned.* One of the Frenchmen at a small desk at the back of the lab had a glass vial and a paintbrush in his hands and he was painting a sign on a sheet of metal with a liquid that appeared to be water.

But in the dark, Fos knew, that liquid would *glow.*

—rah-*dyoom,* the Canadian said.

I *know,* uttered Fos.

He was impressed.

A gram of radium these days, he reckoned, must cost a fortune. Tens of thousands of dollars.

—*caviar,* Fos said, searching his English for some way to express to the Frenchman that he knew the stuff's value.

Above his mask, the Frenchman's eyebrows went up and he pulled his fingertips together and gestured at his mouth and said, *Mais il faut qu'on ne le mange pas!*

—he says Don't eat it, the Canadian said.

—*don't worry!* said Fos. He knew about radium, about radium's effects on humans. Ever since he'd first seen the light that nature can make without burning air, seen his first vision of bioluminescent plankton in the waters off the Outer Banks, Fos had been fascinated by the kinds of lights nature can produce, the ones not always visible to man, the range of lights radiating just off the edge of human vision at the boundaries of the human spectrum. Infrareds and ultraviolets. Colors only birds can see, in their mating rituals, in the feathers of prospective mates. Or colors only underwater animals can see in the ocean's depth beneath the reach of solar light. x-rays, for example. x-rays fascinated Fos. First time he saw an x-ray image in a magazine when he was still a boy, it captured his attention, totally. He stared at it the way a person stares into an icon during prayer. It was an x-ray of a human leg. You could tell it was a left leg from the way the foot bones were arranged. There was something ghostly in them, Fos thought—in the bones. There was something spectral in the picture. As if the image, in and of itself, possessed a soul. Or captured one. He tore it out and carried it inside his billfold, kept it hidden in his pocket for luck, for prayer, for the same reason someone else would keep a rabbit's foot. Subsequently, he made a point of reading everything he could about the subject—how x-rays are made, how they'd been discovered, who invented the photographic process of fixing them to film. When he was only twelve he wrote off to one Dr. George Johnson of Boston, President of the American Roentgen Ray Society, to inquire how he could become a member of their august scientific circle. Roentgen, for whom the Society had been named, had "discovered" rays emanating from a cathode-ray tube in 1895, five years after Fos was born. One year after that the Frenchman Becquerel noticed energetic radiation emanating from a uranium salt when they'd fogged a photographic plate that he'd placed next to it by accident. Two years later Pierre and Marie Curie discovered radium—a new element—in uranium ore. The radium, itself, owned the capacity to *glow.* Soon after the Curies' discovery, Becquerel went to visit them at their Paris laboratory and asked if he could take a sample of their new element home with him for experiment. They gave him a phial of liquid radium which Becquerel placed in his waistcoat pocket next to his pocket watch. By the time he undressed that night, six hours later, the radium had burned an outline of the phial onto the surface of his skin through three layers of clothing and had irradiated the numbers on his pocket watch so he could read them in the dark. In other words: they glowed.

Soon before he joined up to go to War, Fos had read that a watch factory in Salem, North Carolina, had closed down because a dozen factory workers, watchface painters, had developed a mysterious bone disease, necrosis of the jawbone, and subsequently died. What the article in the local paper hadn't said was why only the painters at the watch factory had fallen ill. But Fos had guessed the reason. Working on a field that small, painting lines the livelong day on a circle half the size of a silver dollar, the watch painters had a built-in opportunity to attract hazard to their bones, especially if the paint contained pure radium. No doubt for precision and to perfect their points, every quarter hour—maybe even every minute-on-the-minute—the painters must have licked their brushes. So Fos understood the culinary subtleties the Frenchman had referred to when he said, Don't eat it. Fos was never one for insubordination but the truth was until he saw the radium he'd been thinking he should come clean to the Canadian and tell him to tell the Frenchmen that there'd been a regimental error and they'd recruited the wrong guy. It would have been a stupid thing to do, Fos knew. Even in so short a time as he'd been in France he'd heard the horror stories about what they could expect once they moved into the frontline trenches. At least if he played along here with the Frenchies he might reasonably expect to stay *behind* the front. When he thought about it he knew he was better off making flares and staying under cover than strapping his gas mask on, arming His Trusty with its bayonet and hurling his entirety against sure desolation, land mines, and the unknown of that hell between the trenches they called No mans land. Still, until he saw the radium Fos wasn't keen on simply playing out his Army time setting loose a load of chemistry into French heaven. But when he saw the radium he knew at once there was before him something he had dreamed of: Chance of a lifetime. It wasn't the last time nature's active miracles would offer Fos A Chance, but they weren't always as self-evident as that one was. That one was a beaut—the first step in a chain reaction of events that soon had Fos sharing a cramped space dubbed the Boom Bunker in the trenches on the American Line southwest of Verdun outside the town of St. Mihiel with an intense fella from Tennessee they called "Flash" Handy who would ultimately change Fos's life. Flash was the regimental photographer and he and Fos were the only boys—other than the mustard gas and chlorine boys in the Chem Corps—who were supplied with active chemicals on the front line. Fos had all the oxidizers, neons, burn reducers, phosphorescents, and fluorescents he needed to create a Light at the end of every tunnel for the doughboys in their darkest hours: Flash had the acid baths, developers, gum-bichromates and platinum and silver powders for his photographs. If the Jerries had ever landed a live one on them Flash and Fos had enough volatility in store to take the whole American Expeditionary Force one way to the moon. Fos, himself, took a nasty dose of mustard gas on the September morning the First Army made their raid on St. Mihiel, and after that his eyes watered continuously. He couldn't see without his specs in daylight, but his night vision stayed the same as it had always been—and it had always been near superhuman. It was legendary, all the things that Fos could see that others couldn't in the dark. Which meant that not only was he indispensible on night maneuvers in the field but he was also an enlightened wizard in the darkroom—a fact which Flash was quick to grasp. Fos could make a photographic print with such resulting subtle nuance and precision it seemed the image that emerged onto the photographic paper had been bled from Fos's hands. When the armistice was called on November 11, Flash's unit was dispatched to Rouen for the Occupation, while Fos's went to Metz, and the two of them were forced to go their separate ways. But when Fos returned to Kitty Hawk in the late winter of '19, Flash offered him a partnership in his studio in Knoxville, Tennessee. Fos packed his x-ray books and tide charts into his Army footlocker and drove his old Ford truck away from the Atlantic Coast on the hottest August morning of that year on record. For as long as anyone could remember, Fos's people had been lightermen in and around the shoals and hoaxing sands of the Outer Banks—conveyancers of cargo in scoop-hulled longboats called *lighters* in those waters—until the family tree had pruned down to a single shoot, *Fos,* like a pot-bound exotic in an orangerie too strenuously pollarded. Tidal salts ran in his blood. As he drove away that blistering morning and the land fell off behind him in the first swell of its Continental self, Fos felt a tightness in his chest and his eyes began to water. Well his eyes were always watering, fogging up his glasses. Blister gas, the boys had called the mustard, because that's what it did. You couldn't see it coming and it didn't hit you right away but several hours after it got to you it blistered every living tissue it had touched—in Fos's case, his corneas and tear ducts. The specs—rimless so he didn't have to view the world through picture frames—gave his face a bookish absent-minded look, and the fact that he was teary most the time endeared him to old folks and certain kinds of women. But the truth was, for that first year after he was demobilized, that first year in Tennessee, Fos eschewed the company of the gentler sex and stayed almost entirely to himself, either in the darkroom or in his rented place above a bakery, studying about light and working on his theories how to capture it. Fos had several theories that first year. One thing that the War had taught him—and that working under Flash's tutelage added to—was how to make a framework for experiment. His experience in the Army had given him a confidence in his ability to adapt and improvise, to think sideways. Fos had no formal education beyond what was handed out to every child by the State of North Carolina in its local schools, but what being in the War and being in the Army had shown him was that people by and large tend naturally toward light, toward its source, as sunflowers do in a field. People lean, either in their dreams or in their actions, toward that place where they suspect their inner lights are coming from. Whether they call it

God or conscience or the manual of Army protocol, people sublime toward where their inner fire burns, and given enough fuel for thought and a level playing field to dream on, anyone can leave a fingerprint on the blank of history. That's what Fos believed. Adapt and improvise—he'd read his Darwin, he was a fan of H. G. Wells, and he spent most his time that first year after the Armistice inventing ways of showing people properties of *light,* how things that they believed were hidden in the natural world could be revealed in unexpected ways. Some of the methods he devised were easy science and mere theater—but he got a kick from holding people spellbound. He rigged his truck with tricks he'd picked up, making showy things like Roman candles, fireworks, and pinwheels, and drove from town to town through the muddy rural landscape of the Smoky Mountains outside Knoxville on his days off, like a one-man circus, picking up a free meal now and then, sometimes even pulling in a dime or two. That first year he worked straight through the summer, running the business single-handed when Flash took off to New York City and Niagara Falls with a grass widow from Chattanooga he was hoping not to have to marry. By the end of Fos's second summer in Tennessee he had earned two weeks' vacation and he knew where he wanted most to spend it. Back on the shining shore where he'd experienced his first miracle of light. Back home on the Banks.

Fos's theory—the one he hoped to be able to develop into a serious research paper, maybe even get it published in a scientific journal—was that creatures who produce their own light don't emit light randomly. Random light emission in, say, a creature like a firefly wouldn't make a particle of sense in Fos's view. He had studied them, the fireflies, keeping them in jars and letting them fly around his rented room. He kept charts and tables of their rates of radiance. He noted their responses to various controlled conditions. He ended up with inconclusive data and gallons of dead bugs but the evidence suggested *moonshine* was a factor. Fluctuations in celestial lumens. When the moon was waxing, full, or gibbous, the fireflies emitted light more frequently and for longer periods than when the sky was cloudy or the moon was new, and Fos's theory was that these two facts must constitute a cause-and-effect relationship. If they did, then the same cause-and-effect might exist between celestial lights and other bioluminescences, between starlight and other light-emitting creatures, between moonlight and the radiance that emanates from breaking surf. Back home on the Banks was the place to test this theory with photographs and observations, Fos believed—and the Perseid meteor shower, peaking as it did, like clockwork, every summer near August 12, was the perfect time. Fos's Farmer's Almanac of 1921 told him that the moon would be waxing through those first two weeks of August, getting full on Thursday morning the 18th—nocturnal celestial conditions which couldn't be more beneficial for conducting his experiments. Not only would there be more lights in the sky as the earth clocked through the arc of cosmic dust in the constellation Perseus, but Sister Moon, our best and closest nightlight, would be unveiling more of her pale face, increasing her surface of reflection, every evening on the very nights the stars in Perseus would be showering down. On the darkest night in August, the night of the new moon, Fos packed his tent and camp bed, Army mess kit, tripod, and his box and pinhole cameras, canisters of water, and some tins of food into the back of the Ford truck, checked and rechecked his equipment, and sipped coffee while he watched the sky and timed the dawn against the Almanac to verify its accuracy. Sure enough the sun rose as predicted from the east on the dot at 5:44 over Knoxville, longitude west 83.9', lat. N. 36 and zero. Fos went back up to his rented room, shaved and packed his razor, and put on a clean shirt, smoothed the thin white bedspread one last time on his bachelor's bed, closed the door behind him and went downstairs to the aroma of baked bread coming from the bakery. Flash was waiting for him by the truck, in a shirt without a collar, cup of coffee in one hand, freshly baked Knoxville cruller in the other. The morning sky had clouded over. Hey, Flash said. Hey, Fos acknowledged. It was their standard greeting. Came to see you off, Flash said. Uncharacteristically for the fashion of the time, neither of them wore a hat. Flash because he claimed it made it easier to kiss a woman, and Fos because he didn't like to shade his eyes.

Weather comin, Flash prognosticated.

Fos nodded. Yep.

Rain, Flash emphasized. An' don't we know too well what *that'll* mean.

Fos pressed his lips together.

Mud, Flash said.

Fos wiped a teardrop from his eye.

Mud without the poetry, Flash observed. It was a reference to their war experience. Fos had once come into their bunker from an open gun emplacement wearing mud up to his shoulders and said, *Every other man you meet here thinks he is a poet* and Flash had answered, Poetry and mud. That's what Thomas Jefferson swore all men are made of. One half poetry. Other half of mud.

Maybe I'll outrun it, Fos now told him.

Flash contained a laugh. Fos was a legendary hazard on the road. He looked around too much.

It starts comin down, Flash said, you won't make it past those mountains.

Fos nodded. Roads in Tennessee were ruts cut against sharecropper earth. Notorious for soil that wouldn't root. Notorious for mud.

I'll be all right once I get to North Carolina.

If you get to North Carolina.

They were standing by the truck that way men do when they like each other, standing about a foot apart, shoulders back and chests thrown out so their hidden hearts could pound at one another.

Well you take care and don't hurry back on my account, Flash said.

Fos opened the door and hauled himself into the driver's seat.

You wait a day the rain will end, Flash told him.

Can't wait, Fos said.

Flash stepped back and cast his eyes along the bodywork.

Well you know I think you're a fool, Foster, for what you are about to do.

I'm always a fool for what I do, Fos said.

Flash raised his eyebrows and inclined his head toward what Fos had painted on the truck and chuckled, Ain't *that* the truth.

So long, Fos said.

Flash raised his chin. Drive careful now, he called. An' don't come back without a woman!

Fos shook his head. Flash spent as much time thinking about women as Fos did thinking about light. In his entire life Fos had probably never thought about a woman half as much as Flash thought about a different one each day. He backed the truck into the street and headed out of Knoxville, east, toward the Great Smokies, the Appalachian Trail, the state border and Ashville. He hoped to camp somewhere between Ashville and Winston-Salem that first night but the sky started to come down on him in sheets right after Gatlinburg and made the narrow Newfound Gap Road into a chuting river. And even over mountains men insist on building roads as if they'd never heard the rumor *Water runs downhill* so Fos was stalled for most the afternoon leeward of Mount Collins waiting for the clouds to shred. Around three a bald sun made a stab at holding the spotlight through a thickening sky and Fos gained some miles but by five the thunder train was on the roll again in the nearing distance. Just before six o'clock coming down the Gap beside the Oconaluftee River near the Blue Ridge north of Cherokee Fos's headlamps highlighted a beached Model-T stuck like a hog in mud, angled something awful, like tipsy freight balanced on a catapult. Bent against its glistening frame and seeming to be strapped to it like prayer to fate were two rain-drenched figures, pushing with all the visible effect of gravity on hills of granite.

Fos pulled the truck in front of them and got out to help.

The wind was something terrible.

I got some rope with me in the truck—he shouted.

The man that he was yelling at had his face turned from him, from the wind, but Fos assessed he was of ample size, broad-shouldered, massive muscled, and with hands like hams.

I think—if we can rock her—we can rock her front wheels loose, the big man shouted—*if you go round t'other side an' push together with my wife*—

Fos took his glasses off and folded them inside his pocket and went around the tilted Ford and took up a position on the right side of the chassis on an axis to the stronger man, behind the narrow figure of a woman with black hair dripping down the pale dress clinging to her spine and bony hips. She didn't turn around to look at him at all as Fos steadied his balance and shouldered to the job. On a signal from the other man, they all three threw their bodies into it and the car rocked forward. Once more they gave a heave and Fos's head and shoulders carried forward in exertion to within an inch of the woman's back and he could smell her. Blinking in the rain he saw her bones smooth as horn beneath the fabric of her dress where it clung flat as oil on water to her form, he saw the flat spades of her scapulae and her ropy spine rising from the meagre compass of her unspanned hips toward the frail width of her slender shoulders. Beneath her hair she had the longest whitest neck that he had ever seen. He could have cracked her like a chicken bone. Not once did she turn her face toward him, even after all their effort righted the car back onto the rutted road. Fos let the Model-T precede him down the treacherous pass and as the Ford turned off the gutted route at the road for Cherokee the last image he retained of her was her pale profile against the darkness in his lamp lights, her elegant neck arching like a fisher's rod hooked by an insatiable hunger into its ultimate submission.

That night he camped under a squally sky in a windswept field ten miles on the Tennessee side of Ashville and harried the odds over in his mind of how many nights he'd have to sacrifice to weather if the rain kept up. Or worse, if there was cloud cover over the Banks during the meteor shower. The rain had bogged his progress and dampened his initial hopes. He was restless and preoccupied and nothing that he touched felt dry. He lit a candle and watched the shadows on the tent and listened to the rain against the canvas. He ate a cold meal of hash and beans directly from their tins, then he lay down on the camp bed under a thin blanket that smelled of damp and thought about the stars behind the clouds. He thought about the woman's neck. It was true, what Flash had said about the mud, Fos thought. About the poetry. Not since his time in France had Fos seen so much mud as he had today. Nor known so many grown men who relied on rhymes and starry wishing for their entertainment. For their salvation. For their souls. Worst night he ever lived through over there had been a night like this one. Rain and thunder running through the trenches sideways. Fos was holed up flat against a mud retaining wall inside a dugout no wider than his shoulders with a boy from Massachusetts next to him while they took a beating overhead. The noise was stupefying but between the rounds there came a hollow silence which was worse because you knew the Jerries were reloading those big guns. Watcha got there? Fos asked the boy during the brief lull. The boy had a book inside his jacket between two buttons on his chest just above his heart as if it might protect him from a piece of shrapnel.

Poetry, the boy said.

They took another round and then the boy said, Emily Dickinson.

Fos remembered now that he'd never heard the name before. Even now he knew he probably would have forgotten what the boy was reading if what had happened to him next had never happened.

He remembered that they took a pounding for a while and then when he got the chance the boy had shouted, *I dreamed last night I was making love to her!*

Fos had kept his silence in the dark, hoping that would end it.

In the dream I could see how white she was! the boy had shouted. *I could feel her bones—!*

Fos remembered that he'd wondered how a boy that young knew what making love was.

He remembered thinking maybe he should ask the boy what making love was like before they both got shot. But then the boy reached over in the dark and grabbed Fos by the shoulder and shouted, *She was so thin and white! It was like flying on a swan with my arms around its neck—!*

Fos turned his head to the darker side of the tent to keep from thinking about what had happened after that. He lifted his arm and made a shadow in the candlelight on the tent canvas. He made his hand into a shadow of a duck. He made his arm into a snake. He made a swan. He arched his hand and moved the swan across the side of the tent, like it was flying.

The boy had died six inches away from him, his hand still holding onto Fos's shoulder.

And Fos had never read any poetry by whats-her-name. Emily Dickinson.

He slipped his glasses off and blew the candle out and let the rain set up its rhythm in his thoughts.

Like flying with your arms around the white neck of a swan, he contemplated.

He rolled over in the dark.

Well, he thought, if that's what all the fuss is all about then I'm not missing much.

Still.

A radiance inside him told him he was wrong.

. . . like showers of silver chips, the foam-flakes flew over her bulwarks; then all this desolate vacuity of life went away . . .

HERMAN MELVILLE, *Moby-Dick,* "The Spirit-Spout"

the glory hole

At noon on Saturday, August 6, 1921, Ray Foster smelled the ocean for the first time in two years.

The air that carried unseen evidence of the Atlantic insinuated itself so completely through his senses Fos could taste the Gulf Stream and his eyes began to weep seawater. He was late—mud and rain had held him up, he'd been three days behind the wheel and he was itchy with frustration. He was not a man who took to slowpoke travel. He liked to set a *pace.* So when he had to decelerate to a dogtrot, stuck for nearly half an hour on the tail of a mule-drawn buckboard on a go-nowhere dirt track he hadn't meant to be on in the first place somewhere west of Manteo on Roanoke Island looking for a shortcut to the causeway to Nags Head, Fos started to get irritable. Fact was, he was lost. Low on fuel, and with that stubborn pride men have when they're absolutely sure they know the territory better than they really do, he hadn't stopped to ask directions to a filling station in Manteo and now he was stalled behind a throwback to the nineteenth century on a dusty trail between the cotton and potato fields leading Lord knew where while what he wanted was to find a pump and set up camp before the sun sank in a blaze of burnished color into Roanoke Sound where he still might have a chance to finally see what he'd driven all this way to see, his haunting noctilucent destination. He hit his hooter but the driver of the mule cart acted deaf to Fos's fussing and slowed the mule cart down. He was hauling sand. Fos knew *sandbags* when he saw them, from the trenches, and this fella was hauling half a ton of them. Who in God's creation would haul sand out to the ocean? Fos tried to figure. Unless he was hauling it back *from,* which meant Fos was driving in the wrong direction. Panicking, he poked his head out the window into the dust kicked up by the mule and looked up at the sun and took his bearings and satisfied himself that he was heading *east,* the right way. When he tucked his head back in and looked at the road again he saw a narrow chance to go around the cart and gunned the truck for all that Mr. Ford's quartet of cylinders was worth and left a gritty cloud of carbon in the heavy August air for the driver and his mule to chew on. Fos's mood lightened and he smiled to himself and one mile down that same dirt road with the first seagulls swooning overhead and the Sound so close he could hear it lapping, the truck lurched abruptly, sputtered, coughed, and drifted to a halt beside a sand track running from the road between the dunes past an unpainted wooden house to a tumbledown barn with a black smokestack on its tarpaper roof, out of which a column of brown smoke was rising into the yellow sky. Fos tried to start her up, tried again, then got out, mopped his forehead with his handkerchief and eyed the house and barn. *Moonshiners,* he reckoned. Who else would be stoking up a fire on a baking summer afternoon? Just the way his luck was running he could get his head blown off by some suspicious local spirit leveler on top of everything else that had gone wrong for him this trip. But then he saw a gas pump by the barn. He got his fuel can from the truck and started down the sandy path in the direction of the house. Nothing moved except a slight breeze through the sea oats on the dunes. When he paused before the house he thought it looked deserted. Then a dog appeared out of the barn and growled. It ran back in again, then out, then in, then set its head down low between its forelegs with a bead on Fos and started barking. It was one of those coondoggie kind of canines that you see down South, all whelped from the same bitch on day one of Creation, all identical and dumb and mangy, their entire breed a single color, their entire corps the color of their teeth. Fos inched forward and the dog retreated and stopped barking as Fos stepped across the shadow line into what he expected would be the cool murk of the country barn.

The heat that hit him was a barrier, just like a heavy curtain, fogging up his specs.

All along the walls and from the rafters Fos could make out floating orbs of color like the colors of cathedral windowpanes he'd seen in France. He took his glasses off and wiped them. Then he peered through them again. Sure enough, there was glass reflecting all around him—green glass, mauve and strident yellow, a red as soft as hearts of beachplum blossoms. Blue that was the pure expression of high heaven. In the center of this color wheel there was a large man in a grimy singlet and a leather apron with his back to Fos, intent upon the substance in the fiery maw of the long came that he was turning, burning bright and molten in that part of the furnace called the glory hole.

—'scuse me, Fos interrupted.

The glassblower turned his head away from the bright furnace and scowled at Fos beneath his dark eyebrows over his massive shoulder.

—my truck, Fos said and gestured toward the door.

Be a minute, the glassblower said, and Fos watched him as he gave the came a deft rotation through the flames then lifted the long pipe into the air and blew through it. The glowing knob on the came's end shivered into life and began to breathe, ballooning. When it had achieved a certain volume the glassblower pried it from the pipe and plunged it in a tub of water, where it seized. Then, unmindful of his audience, he began the process, yet again.

Fos was mesmerized. He'd never seen a glassblower at work and he very quickly forgot his rush to get to the Atlantic before the sun set. He put the gas can down and approached the furnace.

Your colors are—they're really somethin, he remarked.

The glassblower looked him over. You know color, do you?

Well, some. That blue, for instance. Fos pointed to a flagon on the rafter overhead from which a warm azure aurora arose.

The glassblower flashed a look at Fos.

I used t' make a firework that color outta copper powder, Fos told him.

Paris green, he said.

The glassblower annealed a knob of jelly on the came's end, in readiness to fire it, and smiled at Fos. That there one's a ten-year-old. Caint come by Paris green that pure no more these days. Caint come by it a'tall, not since the War.

Fos wrinkled his brow and ventured a step forward. You mean t' say you've run out of Paris green?

I an' evr'y tother glassman between here an' Flor'da.

I have some in my truck.

Say *what—?*

In my truck. He pointed toward the door. See I run outta gas an'— you're welcome to it. You'll make more of it than I ever could.

Son, if you ain't some divil you're an angel dropped to earth an' I'll be damned. Where'd you come by Paris green?

In the War. In France. I was a—

Stand back, boy, an' let me finish this here rod an' then we'll talk. I don't want you gettin scalded.

Fos stepped back and the glassblower repeated the process only this time the molten globe on the came's end was as big as a prize plum, and when it was heated to a point where it was throbbing to be blown, the glassblower swung the came from the hot fire of the furnace into the air in front of Fos and blew. As Fos watched through his watery field of vision an apparition on the came's end inflated like the bloater of a frog's neck and grew into a shining pearl, then an enlarging bubble, a shimmering orb around an expansive heart of nothing but pure air. Then, in front of Fos's eyes, the miracle occurred.

Inside the quivering bubble on the end of the blowpipe there appeared a pale shape like a ghost inside a mirror, a visible and visiting spook inside a crystal ball.

Fos leaned toward it in the heat and smudged his specs with perspiration.

Inside the sphere, like life held in solution in a specimen jar, there appeared a tiny woman with a halo, in a dress the color of pearl, staring at him from inside the bubble, upside down.

Fos tilted his head to set her upright in his vision when, from behind him, there came a voice that asked, That your truck in front out in th' road?

Fos turned and saw an illusion of light in the shape of a woman framed by the barn door.

He looked back at her upside-down image reflected in the glass bubble, then back at her, then took his specs off, cleaned them in a hurry and fumbled them back on.

Keepin out the sandman, Fos thought she said.

—the sandman? he repeated.

Sandman here? the glassblower raised, taking the pipe from out his mouth.

Yeah, Pa, he just got here, she answered. He coulda gone around it, she explained to Fos, but he mighta gotten stuck. So I went ahead an' moved it.

"Moved" it?

Caint go without my sandman, the glassblower confirmed. Not for long.

I only moved it so the sandman—

You moved my truck?

She nodded.

But it's outta gas, Fos said.

It ain't.

It is. It wouldn't start.

Well mebbe but I started it.

She starts things, the glassblower said. Speshly she starts automobiles. He put his mouth back to the pipe. Donja? he said, then he blew.

Your magneto wires were all damp, she said to Fos. So I wiped 'em.

Fos looked at her hands.

Lord knows where he got the courage but he said, Show me.

She shrugged and started from the barn and Fos, transfixed and speechless, floated off the ground and followed her.

Out in the sun they stopped to look at one another. She was really something, Fos saw. Compact, for a woman, and on the short side, but—in his eyes, at least—she *shimmered.* Skin so pale it seemed made in part of air, eyes the size of pigeons' eggs, light green shot through with gold and pink and indigo and lustered like the nacre on the inside of a mussel shell. Her hair was like, well it was like lemonade, Fos decided, and you could hardly make her eyebrows out at all.

On her part, she was noting he was tidy.

She liked his hands, the length of his fingers. They had a yellow stain on them, she noticed, but he kept his nails clean. He seemed a man who wore personal fussiness with ease, someone who knew how to take care of linen. But there was something strange and otherworldly about his eyes. For one thing, they were set wide apart under a flat anvil brow that lent him, straight on, the blunt uncomprehending look of a sheep lost in the woods. And for another thing, he seemed uncommonly tearful.

But in the way that it's said a penguin resembles a dolphin when they both swim under water, then what she and Fos might have been noticing about the other was the pattern of that wake pulsing between them, those measured unseen waves generated from the synchronized beating of their hearts.

Neither one was any beauty, and they knew it. For the times, and at their ages, they were both far enough along in years to think they'd missed the boat for lifelong mating. Fos was thirty-one, or would be in September. She was five years younger.

Whatsa matter with your eyes? she asked him, standing in the sandy yard outside the barn. He could hear what sounded like a donkey braying somewhere near. You got somethin in 'em?

No. Yes. I mean—

He took a breath and tried to straighten out his thoughts.

The way she looked was having an effect on him.

He wanted to ask her what her name was but he couldn't string the words together that would do it, so instead he said, My eyes got burned. I mean, they got somethin in 'em. In the War. That's what's wrong with 'em. Me an' the men I was with got gassed by the Germans.

What kinda? she said. Mustard or chlorine?

She seemed to speak strung out—in ellipses, Fos noticed—like she was hanging out the wash. He could see the spaces in between her words.

Mustard, he explained.

How long ago was that? she asked.

Three years.

Well that ain't normal, is it? You should be over it by now. You shoulda cried it out.

Fos stared at the footprints she'd left in the sand. The thing is, he said. The way I look at it. I'm lucky I'm alive. There were lots less lucky.

I guess you saw it all, she said.

He looked straight at her.

There's some things I haven't seen yet, he answered, and he blushed.

She appreciated that. The blushing.

He was so immobilized by her he hadn't noticed what was going on around them until he heard the braying noise again and he saw the same mule cart that had slowed him earlier pulled up in the shade beside the barn. The half of the mule that was the donkey half was winning out over the half that was its native horse sense and the mule was braying its fool head off, sending up a hellish noise, laughing like the devil with its lips curled back and its rancid teeth exposed.

Fos laughed with it.

Oh the *sandman,* he acknowledged.

Pa's somethin crazy about sand, she said. She put her hands over her ears and moved down the sand track, away from the noise, toward the road and his truck. You can't make your glass without it, she remarked.

Well, these parts, there's plenty of it, Fos observed.

That's what I say to Pa but still he swears it's purer over in County Tyrell than here in County Dare. So he has it delivered. Just goes to prove, I guess. People always think the grass is greener.

She gestured toward the truck.

Where you been you picked up so much red mud?

Tennessee.

That'll do it, she said. Don't get mud that color out here. Pa and I got relations over there. In Tennessee. On Clinch River. My momma's side. But, still. Cousins.

Oh Clinch River, sure, Fos said. That's close to where I'm livin now. In Knoxville.

What's that you got written there? Under the mud.

That's my advertisement.

Fos stopped and dug into his back pocket and brought out his billfold and handed her a card.

What's this? she said.

Read it.

He watched her read. Fos noticed that she didn't need to move her lips to read it, either.

That's me, he said proudly.

He pointed to a line of printing on the card.

Ray, he pretended to be reading. Ray Foster. Well people call me Fos.

Ray, she repeated, drawling what there was to draw all out.

Raaaaaaay. I like it. It has a way about it. Like ray a' hope. Ray a' sunshine.

Fos was blushing.

Well, he said.

—*ray*dio.

What I hear most, you know, from waitresses an' such, is ex. Waitresses, especially, they hear my name they want to talk about their *exes,* you know. Their *ex*-Rays.

She blinked.

Oh, she said. I get it. See that wouldn't work for me.

What.

X-Opal.

Fos stared at her.

But it works for you. *X*-Ray. That's kinda cute.

Did you say your name is Opal?

Yeah. Why areya lookin at me that way?

'Cause you're like one.

Like an Opal?

Like the, you know, the precious stone.

That's what Pa thought when I was born. Coz I was sorta blue. For a while they thought I was albino. You know. Because of my white hair.

It's nice, I like it. Your hair. You get to see what you'll look like when you're old.

She studied his card again.

What's this mean—? Phen-o-men— . . . ?

Phenomenologist, Fos said.

Ray Foster, she read. Phee-no-men-ologist.

Yep.

Is that what it says on the truck, too?

Fos nodded.

I'm not sure I know what a phee-no-men-ologist *is.*

Most people don't. Not until they meet me.

Well I've met you and so far I'm not none the wiser.

Yet, Fos stressed and blushed again at his own brashness. But he'd made her smile.

And when she smiled, he noticed, she raised her chin a little to the left. And he could see a tiny vein pulse in her neck.

So what is it then.

What.

—*this.* Opal pointed with her toe to what Fos had painted on the side of the truck before she folded back the hinged hood and exposed the engine.

Fos let out a sigh.

He hated looking inside Henry Ford's invention.

It's a kind of magic, he admitted. Phenomenology. It's like doing magic tricks. Only what they are is natural science.

So are you a scientist? Opal asked, making conversation, right at home beneath the hood. This is the magneto, she pointed out. It fires the engine. These are the connector wires, here, that join it to the spark plugs. They're the ones that you had got all wet.

Fos had gone completely silent, and she noticed.

—whatsa matter? Opal said.

Nothing.

Yes there is.

She smiled at him.

You don't know much about motors, do ya?

No.

Well that's all right. You don't hafta. They don't run on magic tricks. Just make sure you keep these dry. Wipe 'em down a couple times a day any time it's rainin.

She looked at Fos and wiped her hands.

—understand?

When she leaned across the engine Fos had noticed how her breasts had flattened on the fender like two patties on a skillet under tender pressure from a spoon. Their inestimable softness so close to the dead heart of mechanized invention held him spellbound. This is one of life's Demonstrations, he appreciated. Another incompatible congruity. A cut-and-measured ambiguity. Nihilism coupling with existence. Birdsong through barbed wire. Like being on that street in Metz near the railway station in the postwar Occupation one sharp cold winter morning and finding himself, unexpectedly, outside a makeshift dairy in an abandoned storefront where a warm aroma had arrested him. Safe, beguiling, milk's perfume had drawn him to a dark interior in which a man in wooden shoes and a clean white apron stood behind a narrow wooden plank supported by two milking stools on which, among a nest of green alfalfa, there was arrayed a line of soft white mounds. *Heaven,* Fos had thought. An incongruity. And even as he signaled his desire to the dairyman he saw the veins of chemicals and trench filth in the fissures of his own rough hands and smelled the gunpowder on himself and the soldiers he was with.

With clean fingers the Frenchman placed the frothy cheese on Fos's open palm.

Key-*riced,* the corporal who was with him had intoned. Sink your face in that, boy. All it's missin is its nipple.

Which confused Fos outright.

What's the name-a this-here stuff? the corporal asked.

Les seins des anges, the dairyman had said.

When he saw they hadn't understood, he translated, with precision, *Angels' breasts.*

Ever since then, the way that food found a place in Fos's thoughts about these things only heightened his confusion.

He retreated a few steps from the truck and from the puzzlement of Opal's amplitude and scratched his armpits.

I *um* promised I'd get somethin for your *um*—

—*father,* Opal said, unraveling, at least, that part of his confusion.

I got it in the back, Fos said. The Paris green. From France.

He scowled at her, she nodded dumbly.

He went around and opened the rear doors and climbed in the truck and Opal let the hood down in the front and followed him.

She peered inside.

Gee, she said. You gotta lotta stuff in here.

Fos was rummaging around and when at last he found what he was looking for and turned toward her, he thought she looked like a canary perched there, weighing up the hazards of a cage.

She had her hand on one of his contraptions.

What's *this?*

It was a cabinet about chest high with two mouseholes cut in the bottom and an ovoid tube ringed in rubber at the top through which it seemed likely that if you looked, you'd see something.

That's the main attraction, Fos said proudly.

—oh yeah? What does it do?

Shows things.

Like what?

Things you've never seen before. Back up. I'll take it out and show ya—

You don't hafta.

Sure I do, you'll like it. Hold this.

He handed her a small glass tube with teal-colored powder in it, then he unloaded the contraption and all its several parts onto the sandy ground behind the truck.

Looks complicated, Opal said.

I built it myself.

Well that explains it, she assessed.

If you don't mind goin 'round an' startin up the engine so we can charge the battery a bit, Fos recommended, then you can step right up.

Will it hurt?

No m'am.

Do I gotta do somethin?

Fos stopped what he was doing and took a good long look at her.

Nothin you ain't already doin.

I ain't doin nothin.

You ain't doin nothin you can *see.*

Opal flicked her glance from side to side.

You want me to suspect I'm doin somethin I can't see, she suggested cannily.

You got it.

She considered that.

Like *what?* she said after a while.

Fos didn't blink.

They stared at one another.

Oh, Opal finally admitted.

See? Fos said. Ask folks to think what they can't see an' they come up with somethin every time. I'll tellya—most things on this earth are plain invisible.

Most things?

Until you make them seen.

Oh, she said again. Like wishing.

—*wishing?* Fos repeated.

That's a thing you can't see, she said. Does your machine show people what they're wishing?

Fos found it hard to answer that.

He shook his head.

Well that's a shame, Opal conceded.

She shrugged.

Or maybe not, she said. Nobody wants to see a wish unless they know it's comin true.

Is that what you were doin?

—when? —just now?

Fos nodded, so did she.

But don't think I'm gonna tellya what my wishin was, she warned him.

Then she radiated bashfulness.

Step right up, Fos instructed her. And put your foot in here.

You're sure this ain't gonna hurt? she said as she complied.

Look through there, Fos said and gently guided her head.

Opal drew her face into the viewing tube, closing out the sunlit world with her hands, let out a gasp, then bolted up again.

—oh *lordie,* she breathed toward him.

Fos was beaming.

—are these my *bones?*

Wriggle your toes, Fos said, and find out for yourself.

Opal looked into the tube again and let out a gleeful laugh.

—*glory!* she said, looking up, wide-eyed.

Fos laughed with her and told her, You should see your face!

That *too?* she marveled, and he laughed.

She pressed her forehead to the viewing tube again, then looked back at Fos and said, You take a look.

No that's fine, I look at x-rays all the time.

Not at *mine.*

Fos blinked and moved a little closer.

When he leaned his head into the tube he could feel her warmth against his cheekbone.

Inside, as snow-covered branches are seen through a parting mist, he saw revealed the bones of Opal's foot. Her articulated talus. Instep. Metatarsus. Seven tiny tarsal plates.

She wriggled her toes.

Kinda hard to move them separately, she said.

Unseen by her, he smiled.

She was staring at the way his hair curled flat around the bottom of his ear toward his jawbone when he brought his head up and nearly knocked her on the chin, their mouths just barely missing one another.

Opal took another breath.

Well, she said.

She looked away and turned the phial of Paris green between her fingers.

I reckon Pa would like it if you stayed to supper, she confessed. Nothin fancy. Ham.

—oh.—I—um. Fos was looking at her footprint in the powdery sand.

I gotta date, he said.

He looked at his watch.

Opal went a shade of pink she hadn't shown before and cast a glance down to the ground.

—no, I mean . . . not like that, Fos said. I mean the sun is gonna set at seven minutes after seven.

Opal looked at him.

—*so?* she said.

I gotta get to Kitty Hawk by then.

—oh, she said and looked back toward the barn.

I'd rather stay and talk, Fos faltered. I swear. Nobody's ever come up with *wishing* before. That way you did.

Oh, she said again, still staring anywhere but at him.

Most people, Fos went on, playing for more time, when I talk to them about things that are invisible, they pretty much just think up things that are the obvious. You know. Like *yesterday.* Or like *the future.*

I was gonna answer *music* but *wishing* just came out.

—oh are you, *um,* musical? Fos asked, wishing he could find a way to ask her to come with him.

Not really, she said, wanting, too, to draw the conversation out. I play the jugs. I don't know that that's so musical. You have a father who's a glassblower, you end up with a lotta bottles.

She blushed again, and so did Fos.

The image of her blowing into jugs to make a tune stymied him a little.

And zeroes are invisible, she volunteered. I was going to answer *zeroes.* Since they're in the news so much.

They are? Fos said, even more bamboozled.

Well in Germany, she said.

They're having to devalue all the time, she said like she was talking about weather.

Since the War, she said.

Just last week I saw in the newspaper where the German mark was something like four million to a dollar, she elaborated.

And that's a lotta zeroes, she told Fos, finally looking at him.

Fos swallowed hard and nodded.

An awkward silence shouldered in between them.

I don't often think too much about numbers, Fos finally said. Normally, my mind's elsewhere.

Normally, so's mine.

She had the feeling if she kept on talking maybe she could make her wish about him come halfway true so she told him, I keep the books for local businesses, that's how come I sometimes hafta think in numbers. Zeroes, even. Bookkeeping. I do the books for the Ford dealership in Nags Head. That's how come I knew your trouble was those wet magneto wires.

So you count things, Fos gamely observed.

That's one way of puttin it.

Can you count stars?

Opal blinked at him and mentioned, *Any*one can count the stars.

—no I mean can you keep a total.

—easy.

—in your head.

—you bet.

—of *falling* stars, Fos said.

Seven hours later earth's accumulated heat rose slowly from the beach of Kitty Hawk into the velvet August night as they lay side by side, their bodies barely touching, on the eroded bluff above the ocean, waiting for the stars to fall, while they told each other, shyly, their life stories.

Around midnight Fos pointed to the northeast and told Opal, That's the Perseus radiant over there. That constellation. That's where you'll want to look.

What does that mean, Perseus *radiant?*

It means where they'll be falling from.

He put his wrists together and made an angle with his hands which he transposed onto her view of heaven.

You expect me to cut up the sky like pie? she asked.

I'll make it easy for you, Fos said and got up and walked a ways over to the truck and came back carrying a megaphone.

I use this when I'm traveling around to announce that I've arrived, he told her.

Like a circus.

Use it to look through and aim it over there—

He settled down beside her on the blanket and propped his head up on his elbow and studied her.

Is it too heavy?

Nope, she said.

He drew out a stopwatch and said, Let me know when you first spot one and I'll start to time 'em.

Opal smiled at him and hoisted up the megaphone and closed one eye and focused through its cone at the sky.

The night was calm and they could hear the rhythm of the sea beneath them like a giant's breathing.

After a while Fos told her, You don't hafta hold it there the whole time.

I don't mind, she said. It's kinda exciting.

Yeah, Fos said.

He shifted his weight so their hips were slightly touching and he kept his finger ready on the stopwatch.

How many do ya think there's gonna be? she asked after another pause.

Oh between now and the sunrise—could be hundreds. Couple hundred is the norm. Ten or twelve a minute. Six hundred is the record, for a single night. Maybe we'll get lucky, see that many. Could you count that far? You could tap on the side like this, with your finger, if it helps you count. You want me to help you hold it up?

His hand had rested, accidentally, on her sternum just below her throat.

No I'm fine, she said.

Her voice was thick.

Her heart was beating very fast.

The circle of night sky seen through the cone in all its specificity and mystery reminded her of the vision of her own specific bones viewed through Fos's x-ray machine.

It's like a sorta nother glory hole, she told him.

—'glory' hole?

She started to put down the megaphone to look at him but Fos held up his hand and held it steady.

When he put it down again, his fingers fell on the top button of her dress.

What's a glory hole? Fos whispered and undid the button.

It was round and may have been a pearl.

It slid out easy.

A glory hole is what glassblowers call the brightest part inside their furnace. Where the heat is, Opal said.

Fos undid a second button.

Peeled back the fabric of her dress.

Her skin was shining.

It sounds a little rough, he said.

What does?

—*glory hole.*

He undid another button.

Placed his palm between her breasts.

Why do you say that? she said.

Oh I don't know, Fos whispered.

He moved his hand to test the softness of her flesh.

It reminds me of the trenches, he confessed. A glory hole. Somewhere you would run for shelter.

Fos undid the button that had shaped the bodice of her dress and watched her breasts fall loose.

But *glory*'s such a word, she breathed.

I agree, Fos whispered.

You can follow any word on *glory* and it'll sound all right.

—glory *road,* Fos said.

He placed a palm over her nipple.

—glory *pie.*

He undid another button.

Put his finger in her navel.

—*oh my they're startin!* Opal warned him, counting in her head.

When he found the final button he asked her, can you feel that?

—that and nothing *else,* she said.

—glory, Fos discovered.

Halleluiah.

The question is, what and where is the skin of the whale?

HERMAN MELVILLE, *Moby-Dick,* "The Blanket"

the curve of binding energy (1)

By the time they fell to earth they were invisible, they had burned themselves to nonexistence, combusting on their essence, skidding across heaven like beads of liquid on a griddle, riding their own melting down the fiery avalanche to earth. As fallen evidence they were as plausible as fallen angels, and the curves of their descents over the Atlantic were merely proofs of their evacuating passage.

A curve, Fos knew, is only evidence of motion.

Every particle aspires toward its boundary—the moon sublimes toward earth across a plane of mutual attraction, the earth falls toward the sun. Everything that falls displaces other matter in a frenzy of sublimed exchange, the path of which is always and forever curving. Man's standing ovation, the human spine, like the horizon line on the Atlantic, bows, ever so slightly, under influence of things unseen. The horizon dips toward the Arctic at one end, Antarctica the other. But lines of sight, like rites of passage and the laws that dictate your perspective, are only fixed to where you're heading. The idea that the world is still is yet another lie from the curved mirror. Even time, its pendulum, swings through a curve. In the time it took Fos to slide his hand from Opal's shoulder down her arm into the valley of her waist and crest her hip, the spinning earth had moved them half a mile through space in the direction known as east from their perspective. In that same time the orbit of the earth around the sun had carried them forty miles the other way, back west. The galactic drift within our solar system had transported them twenty miles in the direction of the star Vega, while the Milky Way itself had spun three hundred miles around its center. All these lines of passage, curves of motion plotted on celestial charts by planets and by stars, revolved, unseen, around them while Fos struggled to find words to say what he was feeling as they lay together under falling stars above the churning ocean where history tells the lie that man first flew. And Fos, who used to fly his dreams like kites along this runway beach on no wings and a prayer for elevation, was suspended somewhere between grief and revelation, disbelief and reverence, gratitude and fervor: between his history and his body and his self, and hers.

You asleep?

Yes, she answered.

Dreamin?

Yep.

Me, too.

What about?

Oh about comin up here as a boy an' racin on the wind, dreamin about flyin. Runnin all along these dunes wishin I could leave the ground, insteada leavin footprints. An' I was dreamin back t' yesterday. When you walked me to the truck. I was thinkin 'bout lookin at your footprint in the sand. How small it was. This one word came to me right then. *Lightfoot.* I think that's when I knew.

He held her tight against him. He had about a million questions at the ready.

When did *you* know?

I don't know, she said. It wasn't like at any stroke. It accumulated. Couple things. Not many but enough. First thing I noticed in your favor was you didn't chaw tobacco, I could tell that on your teeth. An' you looked book learnt. That was in your favor. And before that, when I got in to start it up before I'd even laid an eye on you, I liked the way you kept the truck.

Inside the cab was clean. I liked the way it smelled. Like tree resin. Like a cotton gum. Or a catalpa.

It sits beneath catalpa trees most the time, Fos told her. At my place of business.

He watched her eyes grow large.

With anybody else you could have said they raised their eyebrows but in Opal's case her eyebrows were so pale you couldn't see them. So instead, her eyes got large.

Your place a' business? she repeated.

Fos was looking at the way her mouth formed words.

He was looking at her lips make p's and b's.

What place a' business? Opal asked. I thought your place a' business was your truck.

You ought t' know, Fos said, still staring at her mouth. We'll have some money I set by. You an' me. A nest egg.

Why ought I to know that? Opal asked.

Fos looked perplexed and told her, Stay right here. He got off the ground and nearly ran back to the truck and went inside and rummaged till he found his Army rucksack. The wind had dropped and when he came back she was sitting with the blanket bunched against her breasts, staring up into the western quadrant where the red star Al-Dabaran had chased the Pleiades from their crowning place on the ascent. Below, disappearing in the surf, a green feint of bioluminescence glinted.

I guess we kinda got a little sidetracked didn't we, Opal reckoned, looking up at him. From countin stars.

Fos was staring at the moonlight on her. You must be the prettiest sight I ever, he whispered, kneeling down.

You without your glasses, Opal told him.

He put his hands above her and slipped something over her head around her neck, careful not to snare her hair within its compass. It was something on an old worn ribbon. In the moonlight she could see two smooth silver discs the size of quarters on the end of the frayed band. What's this? she asked.

I tried to think of somethin I could put around you, Fos explained.

Put *yourself,* Opal invited.

He placed his hands on her shoulders and loomed up closer to her face until her features resolved in front of him into a sharper focus. He squinted at her and his eyes began to tear. He was holding her so she couldn't move her hands beneath the blanket so she tilted her head to lick the tears from Fos's cheeks as they caught the moonlight. When I was over there, he began to say. He emphasized the *over there* with a short thrust of his head behind him toward the very edge of crested earth from which Orville and Wilbur bested gravity, and Opal flicked her eyes from Fos to where he nodded, over his shoulder, over the Atlantic, and in the instant that it took her to figure out he was talking about over there *in Europe,* she saw a pale green light like a binding sheet unfurl then gather back again into invisibility beneath the ocean.

When I was over there, Fos said again, drawing her face toward him, sometimes we'd bivouac in churches. There are churches there, in France —you should see them. There are pictures on the inside, pictures painted like you've never seen. Like nothin we have here in North Carolina. Art. Painted by old painters. Painters who were alive when saints still walked the earth. Painting with colors blessed by saints, colors we can't see on earth since all the saints have gone. You walk in an' right in fronta you there are haloes like they musta been, haloes painted with real sunlight, not with gold—with *star*light. You walk in and even in the dark with just a single candle you see these painted angels shining from within their skins, from *inside* the walls. You see the Virgin Mary and the other Mary and all the other women not called Mary in the Bible with these glowing skins and you've been inside the earth living in a trench for months and you've seen too many things you don't want to remember so you make a promise to yourself that if you survive and if you get out, then if you ever see a woman in real life who looks as radiant an' heavenly as all these women on the walls you'll tie a ribbon round her there an' then and make her yours.

—a *ribbon?* Opal verified.

Fos blinked.

He traced a finger on the ribbon round her neck. I shoulda planned ahead but I didn't know when you'd be comin, if you were ever gonna come at all. So all I got with me right now are dog tags.

Opal examined the silver discs on the end of the ribbon around her throat with the hesitancy of a raw recruit examining a box of ammo for the first time.

—dog tags, she repeated.

I know I shoulda waited till I got a chance to buy a ring.

A ring, she said.

His talk was going round in circles.

You're makin me a little dizzy, Fos, she started to say but he took her face between his hands and placed his thumbs against her lips to stop her speaking.

He moved his head around to get her into focus, then he told her, Opal. Listen.

The galaxy was curving up above them.

Surf was curling down below.

Fos was tearing and she realized she would never know for certain when, if ever, he was really crying.

I'm tryin to tell you I wanted to marry you from the moment I laid eyes on you.

—because of paintings in French churches, she managed to say under his thumbs.

He looked so helpless she immediately regretted what she'd said, but still. We only jest met up, she argued. Why don't we wait a little while and see how we get on?

They waited till the day before Fos had to leave for Knoxville.

In his future version of it, in the way that he would tell the tale to Lightfoot, Fos would say they had decided to get married that first night.

That was Fos's way with things, looking on the bright side. Seeing glowing haloes where others saw false paragons decaying into chalk inside abandoned churches. The difference between Fos and Opal was the difference between *x* and something absolute. Fos was light; and Opal, matter. Together they were two sides of the same page.

Opal's version of the way they met was that Fos had driven up one day and stalled his truck where the sandman couldn't get his wagon in to deliver sand.

Fos's version was: Love At First Sight. First time I saw your mother she was floatin upside-down inside a bubble, Fos would tell their son.

Then Opal would burst that bubble and tell Lightfoot that the first time they met Fos had made her look at her own bones.

Where was I? Lightfoot would ask.

In the air back then, Fos would explain.

Like a bird?

Like a bird's song.

So was I invisible?

You were where you were, Opal would sum it up and take his little hand in hers. Like now, she'd add. She had the knack of making sense of almost everything. To the unsuspecting child.

For the actual taking of the vows before the Justice of the Peace in Nags Head Fos bought a new suit thereafter called the weddin suit which he never had to have let out up to the day he died. Opal bought a hat which her father said made her look smugger 'an a temperance worker so she didn't wear it. She went around to all the businesses she kept books for and put in her notice and collected her last wages. Fos said she ought to buy herself a wedding dress with what she got but she said she'd rather set it toward the future. She wore her robin's-egg blue dress that she'd sewn herself for the occasional town socials and she carried a bouquet of black-eyed susans and sea lavender that Fos had gathered for her. She wouldn't let him buy a ring, insisting on his prudence, and she pledged her troth to him with her mother's wedding band, instead. Opal's father, Conway Fiske, gave Fos the ring he'd married Opal's mother with on the grounds that when she'd been alive she'd made him the happiest he had ever been and he hoped as much for Fos with Opal and besides, it didn't fit him anymore. I'll miss your cookin, Conway said once the ceremony was over. She's a fair to middlin cook, he said to Fos. You could do worse.

Opal packed her clothes, the quilts her mother had made, her collection of seashells and colored glass from Conway's rejects, the jugs she played her music by, the Singer sewing machine, her adding machine, and a set of linens she'd monogrammed with her initials. *You won't hafta change them,* Fos had noted. Opal Fiske, Opal Foster. Same initials. I suppose there's women who might think like that, Opal told him, but that weren't the reason why I married you.

If he'd had any doubt at all about the reason Opal married him Fos would have never contemplated taking her within a ten-mile radius of his partner, Flash.

He'll make a pass at you for sure, Fos told her.

No one's ever made a pass for me but you.

He will. Caint help himself.

How come you stay in business with a man like that?

He makes a pass at every woman. If she doesn't take him up on it he stops. He's not a pesterer. Fundamentally, he's harmless.

Men like that oughta have the law read to 'em.

Maybe you should meet him first before you judge.

Opal heard a note in Fos's voice which caught her up. For all her guff the truth was Fos had seen more of life, been to places in the world she had never been to, nor, hard as she might try, could even imagine. Behind his shambling hesitancy he owned a greater worldliness than she possessed. Opal felt at home in North Carolina, but she wasn't certain how she'd feel shipped off to France to fight there in the trenches. Fos had seen men bleeding, sick with cowardice and wracked with lust, and all she'd ever seen were men in ordinary situations with their hats on sweating up a storm at summer picnics, twistin toothpicks with their tongues while they considered if July was hotter this year or the last. Compared to them Fos had seen a damn sight more in life and held a damn sight fewer prejudices. He was not so much sophisticated as he was more likely to accept the unexpected than most men in her acquaintance. And maybe that's why Fos had taken to her in the first place. Because she didn't come to him with store-bought goods and packaged notions. What she thought and felt she thought and felt all on her own and not because she'd heard ideas on the radio or had her morals preached to her. Still, as much as she was headstrong, single-minded, and self-made, she could see a vision of herself taking shape in Fos's eyes that she liked better. Without knowing she was doing it—and because she trusted him—as the miles between herself and the life she'd known in North Carolina accrued, Opal's place in this new world went from being somebody she'd invented to being a defection from her former life. To being Fos's wife.

She looked out the window of the truck at the slate of crops slumbering in late August's heat and told him, Let me know if you get tired, drivin. I'll take over.

She turned to look at him and as she did, Fos tried to downshift, ground the gears like they were pepper balls, stalled and pulled on the brake. The rear end of the Ford almost left the front end as they swerved just short of a pack of coondogs raving down the road in disarray ahead of them, braying something awful. Damn if they didn't come just outta nowhere, Fos swore. You in one piece?

Only just. What are they chasin?

Runnin from.

He pointed at the sky.

A zep.

A *what?*

He reached across and opened the door for her. As she was climbing out she heard the humming of a motor like muffled thunder through the panicked houndings of the dogs. It sounded like that drone you hear, monotonous and mournful, from the wailing dregs of bagpipes. It was the sound Opal was used to coaxing from her B-flat jug, but it was coming from the sky.

She looked up.

Lordie.

It took up half the sky.

Well I never, she told Fos.

Despite the coondogs' yapping and even though a hum preceded it, the sense that Opal had as the dirigible loomed over them was one of silence presaging a doom. When the shadow of the airship fell on them she found it hard to draw a breath and all at once the hounds went still and cowered. That's about as big as they come, Fos finally said.

I don't know if it's the shape or jest the size, Opal finally breathed. She had a feeling she imagined Jonah must have had before going in the whale. But it's givin me the wimwams.

That's what they're supposed to do Fos told her. We had 'em, both sides had 'em, over there in France. Scare bejesus even from the dead.

When the dirigible had drifted off and the hounds dispersed, they got back in the truck and Opal let Fos falter with the throttle till he'd made a hash of it then she got out her side and went around the front over to the driver's. Fos got out and she got in and waited till he settled down beside her. Then she played the choke out like an artist and let the truck slip into first as if into a silk chemise. Well here we go then, Fos said, sitting back with a pleased as punch expression on his face. West, he breathed. The sun, like a hot air balloon, hovered, lowering above the earth in front of them. You an' me, Fos said. Arm in arm. And whereas most every other man on earth would have then said, Into the sunset, Fos said *Into the ultraviolet.*

When he was driving, Fos looked like he was trying to climb over the wheel, clinging to the rim the way a man afraid of drowning hangs onto a life preserver. But Opal's steering style was open-chested and one-handed, her left arm permanently out the open window regardless of the weather, fingers of her left hand nonchalantly at the ready with a feathery touch each time her right hand rode the shift. She was by nature the more meditative of the two of them, her conversation getting going only with a push start. Fos on the other hand genuinely relished talking while he looked around—a hazardous combination for the driver's side, but a welcome trait in any passenger. Consequently Opal at the wheel with Fos as lookout took advantage of their natural strengths and struck a balance which sustained an angle of repose between them every time they took to the road. And with Opal driving, they made better time. Already, at the end of that first day, when darkness finally overtook them, Fos was surprised to realize they'd gone all the way across the state to Deep River, nearly twice as far as he had gone on any single day alone. "How'd that happen? How'd you get us out here clear past Raleigh?" He reached over and slid his fingers down her arm. "I was kinda hopin we'd put up there for the night in one of them hotels. Thought we'd try a real bed, now we're legal."

In better light he might have seen her blush, but she drove farther on and after several miles they saw a place in a cleared field adjacent to a farmhouse where some cars had pulled over to set to camping for the night. There were three tents up and a campfire going and the scent of smoke and roasting corn perfuming the soft evening.

If you're fixin to stop here, Fos said, showing disappointment, it won't be just the two of us. I know these tents. Everyone can hear what everybody else gets up to.

Again the War was playing through his words, she heard. She let the engine idle and touched his arm. It's only for a night she said. He squeezed her hand.

Some honeymoon, he said. He got out and went around and opened the truck door for her and lifted her up and over to the ground in a parody of carrying her across a threshold. Then as a couple they went up to where the others were. They were a group of travelers—three men, three women, and six children. Eve'nin, Fos said. Eve'nin, they returned. From the field behind them Opal heard the *pitpitpitpitPITpatput* she recognized as a two-stroke tractor engine. Someone here we can ask permission from to stay ourselves the night? Fos asked. One of the men stood up. He was holding a banjo by its neck and he let it swing a little in an arc like he was scything. "You go over to the house and for a nickel that nice lady there will trade you biscuits an' some hogback an' show you where the pump is. Her name Miz Jessup. That her husband out there cuttin on the field. Fine as people come." He measured Fos and Opal for a moment then said, Lemuel Johnson. This my wife, my children, my brother and his missus, their children, my older brother and my sister. We all been over to Tar River couple days since Friday last, revivalin.

Ray Foster, Fos said. And The Mrs. Foster. He put out his hand and Opal put her hand out, too, and said, Pleased t' meetcha. Name's still Opal. We been married now ten hours, Fos announced to everyone's astonishment, and Opal seriously wondered if she hadn't gone and accidentally married someone raised by elves.

Before she knew it everyone else was all around them congratulating them and the women were fussing over her and making her feel nice and Fos was heading toward the farmhouse with two of the men.

One of the boys came up to her and said, "Momma says to give you somethin for good luck. So here." He placed an object in her hand. It was about three inches long, golden brown, and Y-shaped. "I found this in the field before you came."

Opal looked at it and thanked him. What is it? she said.

Feel it, the boy told her. Go ahead. It's soft.

Don't pay him no mind. He's weak in the head, the old man sitting by the fire called. Opal noticed a worn-out crooked crutch propped on his leg. White whiskers textured his cheeks. The glint of a mouth organ signaled from his pocket. Opal took a few steps toward him, holding out the unknown object. Do you know what this is?

Sure do. Can't but killt so many rabbits an' been a cony-catcher in the felt trade all these years without knowin every furry thang that lives and breathes, he told her.

'Cony', Opal repeated.

The way he'd said it was like *connie.*

Rabbits the man illustrated, leveling his crutch at the horizon and sighting down it. From somewhere in his throat he let loose an explosive blast. It was a noise more like the expressed frustration of a sick old man than of a killing fusillade.

So you shoot rabbits, do you, Opal said.

No m'am I snare 'em. Can't shoot rabbits but you tear they's hides apart. You gotta snare 'em. It's whatya gotta do once you're in the cony-catching trade. I snare 'em fer the felt fact'ry. Fer hats. They make the felt fer hats from rabbit fur. Sure do wish they'd let me use a gun because I sure do love t' shoot. Easier 'an layin snares.

He sheaved the crutch against his side.

You ever been to a revival? he suddenly asked.

Unconsciously she fingered the Y-shaped item in her hand with aroused suspicion.

"People fallin down," he said. "Evangelized. People risin up. Reborn. People left an' right undergoin transformations, and never once has I. Never. Not a one. People havin revelations like the common cold. First one, then the next like a contagion. Never me. Not once. Never does the tongue a' fire reach down an' set my soul on fire. Lemuel there, my brother, he say, '*Bross,* you better study that Bible page. You better pray the Lord will find you.'" The man grew silent and the children ran off after something in the field, then ran back again that way that children en masse move, tidal-like, Opal noticed. The women turned the corn husks in the fire and Opal put her hands behind her back and let her gaze go up to the sky and wondered what was taking Fos so long.

"So I took that Bible in my hand," the old man said, "an' I ran my finger down the page an' I gazed at it, feelin with my fingers like a blind man feelin at a wall for the Lord to show me somethin."

One of the women called out to one of the children, and high above her through a salmon-colored cloud Opal thought she saw the first star of evening and behind her back she slipped her fingers round the Y-shaped thing and crossed them to make a wish on a star for the first time in her marriage.

"An' then it came t' me, right there an' then, right through these fingers," the rabbit catcher said.

He held his fingers up for her to see.

A hickory log sent sparks up from the fire.

"You know about how the felt is made from conies, doncha?" he asked her suspiciously.

Can't say I do, Opal confessed.

"They skin the pelts off 'em an' remove theys fur. Then they pound and pound it till it sorta gets all gummy like a man chawing dry tobacco. Pound it to a kinda pulp."

He fished in his shirt pocket, took out the harmonica, rummaged around, found what he was after and extracted it.

"See this?" he said, holding up a wad of paper in his hand.

Opal heard the men coming from the house. She could hear Fos call goodnight to someone.

Here, the man in front of her was saying. Take this.

He tore a piece of flimsy paper from the wad and held it out to her.

"What's this mean t' you?" he asked her.

Nothin, Opal said.

Take a closer look, he urged.

To oblige, she took it from him, turned it over and examined it, and nonchalantly folded it around the stem of the Y-shaped thing she was holding. It's not supposed to have a meanin, she entertained. It's just a piece a' paper used for wrappin your tobacco in. For smokin. Ain't it?

—*is* it?

Opal shifted from one foot to the other and wished that Fos would hurry up and come.

"What's it made a', do you reckon?" the man asked her.

Opal shrugged.

She was thinking about something else.

She was thinking what excuse to give to walk away.

Paper, she finally said.

"Yeah, but what's the paper made a'?"

Opal frowned.

Wood, she guessed.

He smiled at her and showed his gums.

Flax, he told her. Grown right here in North Carolina. Finest flax around. Finest flax fer makin paper. Take the flax tow from the stems when all the linen and the linseed oil be used up an' they get the finest flax pulp from what's left fer makin this flax paper. Fer like you said. Fer rollin the tobacco. Makin cigarettes.

Opal took a small step forward only so he wouldn't notice that she took a big step backward next.

Well, she said and looked away. I oughta start t' think 'bout puttin supper on.

Betcha never know 'bout this flax paper fore I tolja, didja?

—no sir, Opal said. I'm much obliged.

Feel it.

—what?

It feel familiar?

Opal made another small retreat.

Where else do you encounter this flax paper?

—where else do I encounter it?

—paper that's this thin.

Look, if I don't get a fire goin soon Fos and me'll be all night 'fore supper—

Cigarettes an' Bibles, he announced. "Cigarette and Bible paper. Made from the same substance! That's my Revelation! That the Lord provides fer book and smoke! Holy Book—*an' holy smoke!"*

He rolled back on his bony hips, his mouth agape with sudden laughter, then he doubled over, spitting it into the fire. He started to jack up again and Opal heard Lemuel call out "Where's that bridey Missus Foster at? Step on over here, come see what your bridegroom done gone an' got—"

Fos was waiting for her with his sleeves rolled up, a covered supper, two buckets of water, and a look on his face she'd never seen before, like he was being squeezed on his insides.

She figured out from how they swung their shoulders and strutted that the other men must have been teasing him. You two settle in an' have a real fine eve'nin now, the one who wasn't Lemuel said to her. Then he gave Fos a playful slap between his shoulders. If he was ten years younger, Opal thought, or half th' size I'd pin his ears against his head.

Cold bacon, Fos proposed, when they were left alone. Dressed greens and biscuits. Lemuel offered but I said we'd take our meal alone. It's too hot tonight to be around a fire. That all right with you?

I gotta learn t' talk t' strangers better, Opal told him.

Oh, Fos said. He put the covered supper down. I like the way you talk.

Not to you. To strangers, like I said. I got t' learn t' stand up to 'em. Not just stand there. Hold my end up of the conversation. Maybe you could teach me.

Fos had hauled up a canvas sheet between two poles off the back end of the truck, set up his field cot beneath it and was striking a match to light the wick inside the lamp when he stopped to look at her and nearly burned his fingers. From over by the campfire there came banjo picking. It started singular and strident like it was heading in a godspelling direction but then it gained some less than righteous pain when the older man's harmonica joined in.

Don't the moon look so lonesome, someone sang, *shinin through dem trees?*

Don't the moon look so lonesome shinin through dem trees?

Don't a man look so lonesome when his woman leaves?

Fos pushed the glasses up on his nose and fumbled Opal closer so he could kiss her. Then, "Watcha keepin in your hand?" he asked.

She showed him the Y-shaped thing.

Boy found it in the field, said it was for luck, she told him. It doesn't look to me like it's a rabbit foot but that's what that old man was sayin. That an' stuff about the Bible bein writ on rollin paper.

This ain't a rabbit foot, Fos told her.

Still lucky, though, she said, cause it's my one an' only weddin present.

Fos looked wounded.

You know what I mean, she said and snuggled into him.

It's lucky all right, he said. An' rare as gold. It's a piece a' staghorn velvet.

Velvet?

Opal looked at it more closely.

You find pieces of it now an' then but not often. Male deer, the young ones, when their antlers come in at the start they're velvety. Then as they grow the fur molts off and that's what you've got here in your hand. Staghorn velvet. Guaranteed to bring you luck.

She looked at him then looked again at the Y-shaped object.

Think of it this way, he said drawing her closer. He touched the end of one of the Y's arms and said, This is you. He touched the other end of the Y and told her, This is me. And *this,* he told her, running his thumb along the Y's long stem, is *us.* He ran his finger back and forth along the two arms where they joined the stem and whispered, "Curve of binding energy."

She took a moment then said slowly, Try to talk t' me in ways I'll understand, Fos. "Otherwise . . ."

He took her hand.

Cross your fingers, he instructed, so she did. Now close your eyes.

Over by the fire someone started singing, *Silver moon need no money, fer her journey o'er this earth.*

Silver moon need no money fer her journey o'er this earth.

But no silver in his pocket, be a poor man's curse from birth.

Opal waited.

Whatcha doin? she finally said.

Fos was looking for his glasses.

Lookin for my specs so I can show you somethin.

Howya gonna show me somethin if I got my eyes all closed?

Fos focused hard.

Okay, he said. He took a breath. Binding energy. Binding energy is what the science boys say holds the world together. Same I guess as some folks say faith does. Or god. Faith in the Creation. You with me so far?

She nodded.

It's the force that holds things in one piece, he said. Holds the whole together. Keeps the moon in orbit round the earth. Keeps the earth around the sun.

With her hand two inches from his face Fos squinted, found the shadow line between her index finger and her middle one where they were crossed. Like this curve here, where your fingers bind together.

He ran his pinky gently down the line that joined her fingers, taking care to touch just one. Feel this?

She held her breath and nodded.

Now tell me: How many fingers am I touching?

Opal concentrated. Two she said.

He ran his pinky on the line again. You sure?

Yes. She scowled.

One, he told her. Look.

She opened her eyes and Fos repeated what he'd done.

I don't get it, Opal told him. Are you tryin to explain that with my fingers crossed I feel things *twice?*

Only along *here,* he said. On this curve where they come together.

Her silence spoke her fear of never understanding.

Maybe I'm no good at getting things, she said.

Maybe I'm no good at teachin.

They watched the sky.

Can you see things in th' distance pretty good without your specs? she asked after a while.

I can see the stars if that's what you're askin. I can see Ursa Major up there—see? Those two bright stars there makin that straight line? He pointed and she nodded. That's The Dipper, she acknowledged. No, he told her. She could hear a quickening gladness in the way he spoke. *Two* stars ain't The Dipper. Yet. He guided her hand. What you need to make The Dipper, make its handle, is a—

Third, she whispered. Well I'll be.

She let out a kind of whistle.

Never thought a' that. Can't get the handle without three. Can't make a curve without a third point on your map. Like that star up there. That it's the third that binds the other two together.

Missus Foster, Ray beamed proudly, crossing toward her.

Mister Foster, Opal smiled, reflecting back his pleasure.

And unseen on the ascendant, Lightfoot rose and spanned above them, an inevitable third, binding them to promise.

> Nor can any son of mortal woman, for the first time, seat himself amid those hempen intricacies, and while straining his utmost at the oar, bethink him that at any unknown instant the harpoon may be darted, and all these horrible contortions be put in play like ringed lightnings . . .
>
> HERMAN MELVILLE, *Moby-Dick,* "The Line"

the curve of binding energy (2)

Everything that falls accelerates along the curve of its descent—so like all falling bodies, the river bends and rushes toward its end.

Because its body is a pattern of convergences, it is impossible to point as one can point to the star *Alpha* in the constellation Ursa Major and say this is where the figure of the Dipper *starts.* It is impossible to say the Tennessee starts *here.* She was always what you'd call an ornery disorganized body of water, disagreeable in terms of exploitation by explorers and colonizers—untameable and stubborn in almost every sense—yielding only parts of herself to commercial trade in brief and unsustainable encounters. Flatboats and keelboats could ply her more predictable turns, her less moody depths; but boats could never own her the way the barges and the steamers owned the Mississippi.

From Knoxville to where she submits herself to the more powerful Ohio at Paducah, the Tennessee falls 500 feet along a 650-mile basin, an average of eight and a half inches a mile—except at Muscle Shoals, where she falls seven times faster than anywhere else in the basin, 100 feet through 20 miles of rapids. Like the Big Dipper, which has seven identifiable stars, the Tennessee pours through seven states: from her northernmost tributaries in Virginia and North Carolina she curves south through

Tennessee to Georgia. At Chattanooga, she hits the hardened heart of the Cumberland Plateau and wavers west through Alabama into Mississippi where, at the border, she is deflected north by even more unyielding rock back into Tennessee in a wide cambering parabola until she's stopped cold in Kentucky by the fourth largest river in the United States, into whose encompassing surround she finally surrenders her identity.

Through her arcing course it sometimes seems she runs against herself, as if her mainstream longing is one of stubborn torsion, opposing forces acting at right angles to her downstream flow, wanting to bolt back upstream to her source. Her course through seven states makes an almost perfect semicircle, one so well described by nature's competing impulses that it proves the philosophical maxim that a curve is nothing but an envelope of all its tangents, a line into the future, an infinity of points moving along a path of proximate discontinuities which, without a binding energy, can and will at any given juncture, exceed its boundaries and go berserk.

Which is what the Tennessee does each year, like clockwork. She explodes.

Indiscriminately, she inundates fields and woodlands; villages and towns. The mountain streams that plenish her headwaters north of Knoxville spill down from the most rained-on patch on the east coast, the Great Smokies. More rain falls in the Tennessee's drainage basin than anywhere east of the Mississippi, and ninety-five percent of it drains into the kills and rills, the brooks and runnels that fill the swelling river. The lowlands along her banks which are the first to flood each year are overfarmed depleted lands tabled for quick-turnover cash crops like cotton. What enrichments the topsoil ever held have been sponged up by absorbent cotton or guttered by recurring floods. The bottomlands grow poorer. The gamblers sniff the wind and wend away. With no navigable passage west to the Mississippi and the sea, the towns built on her headlands remain, at best, backwaters. But when Opal first clapped eyes on Knoxville rising from the shore, it might as well have been New York, Paris, or Chicago to her. "I ain't exactly ever seen a city before this," she said.

You've seen 'em in the picture shows, Fos said. Seen 'em when you read.

That's diff'rent kinda seein, Opal told him. Seein with your eyes is real.

As the Ford rolled over the planking on the bridge across the Tennessee she counted thirteen steeples rising from a wash of green on the farther shore.

Lotta churches, she observed.

Midway across the river the air took on a different smell. Fos pointed to the right and said, That part over there was all burned off during the War Between the States. Everything out here was made a' timber so it took to flame real easy. Don't know which side set the fires first but by the time they both were finished there was nothin left, includin this ol' bridge.

Well they put it back real pretty.

Steel an' stone. They learnt their lesson.

Well there sure is a lot of it, she said about the view ahead of her. It's bigger'n I thought it would be.

The thing about this town, Fos said. Just like back home on the Banks —the water always tells you where you are. Back home it's the ocean— here it is the Tennessee. Town rises up from it toward that highland over there that's Summit Hill. The more downhill you are, the closer to the river. You can smell it most days, even in the winter. River runs from north to south. Railroad runs from east to west. Keep those things to mind you won't get lost.

I wasn't plannin t' get lost, she cautioned.

Off the river, on a street that took more traffic than she was used to, Opal felt the full heat of the August afternoon. Her left arm, after four days lolling out the window, was the color of cooked crab and burned her something awful.

Rich folks live up there on Summit Hill, Fos was saying. This here over to the right is Old Town. There's businesses an' all an' people come to market there. Our house is in this part to the left there up ahead kinda in the middle. Nothin rich but nothin poor about it neither. Gaslit but the plannin board says electrification's on the way by winter. That's what all these wires runnin overhead are for. An' like I told ya. We still hafta pump for water but there's an inside tub.

You don't hafta sell it to me, Opal said. I'm already sold.

She pulled the truck up against a wood sidewalk where Fos showed her the front of a bakery on the corner of Clinch Avenue and 22nd in a shady spot beneath mature catalpas and a trio of brown-leaved dogwoods. Above the glass front at street level two clapboard storeys painted eggshell white with bright blue shutters rose beneath a black tarpaper roof. Wooden stairs climbed up the street side to a wooden platform and a second-storey entrance, also painted blue. All the other buildings on the block were red brick, set back a little more, with shaded porches. Opal turned the engine off. Fos didn't move. His face looked strange and even though the truck was parked beneath the trees he was blinking like a man thrust from his nice cool house into the scorching light of day.

It's not permanent, he finally announced. It's only temporary.

What is?

Remember that. When you start to think it isn't what you want. We can move.

I *have* moved, Opal told him.

Her ankles were so swollen it was a trial to get her shoes back on.

Fos put out a cautionary hand to slow her down.

I don't want to disappoint you, he hastened to explain.

She laid her hand on top of his and whispered, *Ditto.*

Fos got out and went around and helped her down and then, Opal a step ahead of him, they climbed the stairs together. Opal stepped aside to let Fos through the door, then she entered on a glassed-in porch with its contained and musty warmth, an icebox, a stone sink with a handpump, and a long pine table with a lantern on it and jars of what looked like blackened rice but turned out to be dead lightning bugs.

Off the closed-in porch, through another door, there was a short railway corridor leading to a single room fronted by three large windows looking on Clinch Avenue. It was square, well lit, high-ceilinged, and contained cross-ventilation, about two hundred books, a writing desk, three chairs, a bureau, newspaper clippings, framed photographs, sundry gadgets and contraptions, and a wrought-iron bed. Draped over the crossbar at the foot of the bed were a pair of gray twill trousers with the suspenders still attached, and on the floor beside them was a brown paper sack filled with clothing with a soiled white cotton shirt on top. The bed, although still made, looked like someone had been asleep on top of it. Fos was confounded. This ain't mine, he said, tidying up. Someone's been in here. I guess it must be Flash.

He stuffed the bag into a corner and turned around to look at her. She was standing in the center of the room with her arms down at her side. Her left arm looked for sure like it was going to blister.

Come here, Fos said, sitting on the edge of the bed and patting at the mattress by his side.

Opal went.

Will it do? Fos asked.

It's smaller'n I thought it'd be.

Fos looked around, nodded in agreement. It's got smaller in the last two weeks.

Opal smiled.

We need to put some ointment to that arm a' yours, Fos told her. His hand made a blanched pool beneath her skin where he was touching her.

Opal lifted her feet in front of her, examining her puffy ankles. Fos stood up and eased her down onto the bed, running his palms along her hips and thighs, stretching out her legs. He pried her feet out of her leather pumps. You stay here, he said. I'm gonna get a cool damp cloth an' some camphor ointment.

That sounds religious.

I hope so, Fos warned.

He walked over to the windows, closing all the shutters, then he disappeared. Opal heard the sound of water running.

The street outside was still. There was the sweet aroma of sugar icing from the bakery down below. A fly was buzzing. On the bureau on the far wall there was a picture in a Bakelite frame of a fine-boned tiny white-haired woman dressed in black, sitting at a black-draped table. There was something on the table she was staring at, but Opal couldn't make out what it was. But she could see the woman's face was delicately drawn and very beautiful. Opal thought she looked like those women in the fancy magazines, doll-like women, who you knew were never going to sweat and always smelled good. On the bedside table next to the paraffin lamp behind the empty water glass there was another framed picture of her. Through the water glass the image was magnified and Opal saw the woman was, indeed, astonishingly beautiful.

She reached for the photograph.

She saw it was a strange and somewhat mysterious picture. Again the beautiful woman was dressed in black—or what appeared to be black in a black-and-white picture of her. She was wearing a hat shaped like a berry basket. She was walking down curved stone stairs arm in arm with a portly white-haired gentleman in a cutaway and shiny shoes. In her free hand she was holding a roll of paper that looked like a diploma. Without even trying, Opal counted nineteen people in the picture.

Fos came back with his sleeves rolled balancing an enamel basin in his hands and set about to start to dress Opal's sunburn and relieve her swollen feet. Help me slip your dress off, hon, else it's gonna smell of camphor every time you wear it, he told her, already intent on trying to guide a single dime-sized button on her bodice through what seemed to him to be its less than dime-sized buttonhole. He'd seen a lot of women through the camera lens these last two years sitting up against the velvet portrait-taking drapery in their picture-perfect dresses, but he'd never seen a woman who had more buttons on her clothes than Opal had, like rows of zeroes in a ledger book.

Be careful of the sheets, Fos, Opal said, rising slightly on one elbow so Fos could slip her dress down off her shoulders. We don't want that camphor odor in the sheets, we'll dream of coroners and mummies.

When in your entire life have you ever dreamed of coroners and mummies? Fos remarked, taking in the way her slip held to her form.

She watched him fold her dress across a chair. She let him place a linen towel beneath her sunburned arm, then she eased back against the pillow as he applied the ointment in careful swirly motions the way you ice a cake. Sometimes, she said, I dream of coroners. The thing about a coroner is you can tell their line a' work from lookin at their hands. People start to take the shape of their professions doncha think? she mused, half dreamy under his manipulation. Specially fishermen and coroners. Coroners pop up, you know, the way the strangest people drop in outta nowhere in your dreams. Coroners show up in mine every time I start to dream about my momma.

Fos hadn't talked to Opal about how her mother died so he slowed his movements down, not breaking contact with her skin in case she was about to tell him something rare and perishable, but instead her attention turned back to the two photographs of the white-haired woman and she asked him, In these pictures, Fos. Is that your mother?

Golly no, he said, surprised.

Teacher? Opal tried.

Likewise.

She reached for the framed picture on the bedside table, the one where the woman was walking down the steps with the portly man, and held it to her face for closer scrutiny. Wait a minute, she said slowly, this fella here with her on the steps is the President of the United States. This fella here is Warren G. Harding for pity's sake, this isn't even a proper taken picture, Ray, you cut this outta a newspaper or somewhere and stuck it in this frame—

Fos was nodding admiringly. It's Madame Curie, he told Opal, his face reflecting an innermost and privately cultivated joy.

Madame *who?*

Curie. Marie Curie when she was here in the United States last fall.

Opal put the picture back in its place of honor and mentioned, teasing him along, Most bachelor boys keep pictures of other types of women, you know, Fos.

He was wiping down her calves and feet with a cloth soaked in cool water and, taking up her playful mood, he said, I never was a bachelor boy like the kind you have in mind. He rolled up the hem of her silk slip and began to rub her legs. I certainly ain't a bachelor now.

Which is kinda a miracle if you ask me, she goaded him.

Do I need to ask you?

He arced over her, rising from her ankles to her thighs.

Ain't we gonna unload our belongings from the truck?

Someday, maybe—why, you need something?

Yeah, she said.

They were face to face, their noses touching.

I need t' know who Marie Curie is, Opal whispered.

Fos began to kiss her even though he kept on smiling.

Hours later when she woke it was pitch dark but she could see the ghostly billow of the curtains at the windows and there were two sources of eerie light, one stable in the farther corner, the other one wavering across the floor.

Fos bolted up before she finished uttering his name.

What's that light? she whispered.

Back against the pillow Fos gathered her to him and murmured, Phosphorus. Ignore it. I keep a hunk of it over on the—

That light, Opal said, pointing out a pale erratic cone focused on the bedroom floor from the doorway to the hall.

Fos was off the bed in a flash, going toward the source of light in his altogether armed with the heavy volume of *Elemental Chemistry,* blinking, calling to the unseen intruder All right there *all right* this is private property no use comin any further I'm an Army man I've fought in the Army just clear off before you burden my clear conscience with some stupid thing you may regret—

Opal watched the cone of light freeze on Fos's naked body as a voice from down the corridor boomed, *You* were in the Army? Shitforbrains. Mothers in the heartland of America with good hardballin noble sons who *died* on the fields of France must have *shat* themselves to learn some half-formed testicle of life as you got out with both meagre balls intact and fully loaded—

Flash—? Fos recognized, and in front of Opal's eyes there tumbled a sourmash-marinate in light-colored pants and a rumpled shirt, carrying a flask, a flashlight, and a pair of buckskin shoes.

"*Fos! Fos,* my bubba big best hubba bubba," the loose form semi-articulated. "When the hell did you get *back—?*"

"Flash," Fos was saying, "you can't be here right at this moment—"

"Why *not?* Hey why *not* my best bubba? Jesus and his brother Christ what's that godawful smell? Smells like you're *embalming* in here—"

He swung his flashlight in a haphazard search across the ceiling down the far wall, the light dangerously close, like a dipsomaniacal moth driven toward the fumes of flaming brandy, hovering near the place where Opal huddled, sleep-disheveled, sheetless, swollen, naked, knees against her chest, trying to compose herself into some decorative lifeless statuary behind a flimsy pillow.

O lordie, Fos breathed as Flash's unforgiving light settled on his wife.

It was not the revelation one expects from pearly light descending on a human.

Opal looked more like the victim of a raid than the vision of a captured angel.

—*smoke my bacon,* Flash muttered as the light licked over each of Opal's imperfections. What have we got *here?*

Fos was on him in a show of force that surprised them both, knocking the flashlight from his hand, which seemed to make the walls slide along a circle like a moving carousel.

What are you doin comin to my place of livin in the middle of the night like it's your business—? Fos demanded, pressing him against the doorjamb to the hall, which was as far as he could push the taller stronger man.

Hey hey take it easy what's got into you—? I been hidin out here these last few days—

—you been *livin* in my place a' livin?

Well yeah. In so many words.

—without askin my permission.

What the hell is *wrong* with you, when was asking born between us? You were outta town.

—well now I'm back.

—well how was I supposed to know that?

—well Flash the truck's out front.

—well I come up the back, Ray. It's this Chattanooga woman. One I took with me last year up to Niagara, she's come to town and I've been avoiding my own place.

Fos took a step away from Flash to try to focus on his face and breathe some less than moonshine-saturated air. He wished he had his glasses on him, and a pair of pants and a blunt instrument.

This Chattanooga woman, he reasoned. She knows where we work. How have you been hidin out durin the day?

Flash turned his head a quarter back toward the bedroom and looked at Fos with only his right eye. I closed the shop, he said.

You closed the shop, Fos verified.

Somehow this Chattanooga woman got it in her head that I was going to marry her.

—somehow she got it in there.

An' I bet that ain't the only place she got it, Opal thought.

Summertime, Fos buddy, nobody works in the summertime. Flash turned his head again so he was looking straight at Fos through the cloaking darkness. So what's goin on? he said. Who's the, ah, the, ah . . . He seemed to reach way up into his brain to find the right description. Who's the *baggage?*

Fos spread his feet like you're supposed to do before you hit a man. He crossed his arms over his chest and balled his fists against his ribs to hold his temper but it only made him feel more naked.

He tried to find a graceful place to leave his arms without having to land a punch on the body of his friend and business partner. Flash, he said, you better go.

Can't good buddy. No where to go *to.* She's got a husband—kids, too. Told the husband she was runnin off with me. Burned her bridges. So can't go, good buddy.

I'm tellin you you gotta.

Why, because of—? Again he searched for the descriptive word. Hell, he said. You won't be getting up to anything I've never seen before—

Fos tried to push him down the narrow corridor, his arms extended and his hands flat against his partner's chest.

Opal heard a lot of muffled grunting like when you catch a loose pig with a dishtowel then she heard some bumps and bangs and fevered whispers. Then there was a clatter and loud knocking at the door and Flash shouting, "What about my flashlight?" Then Fos came in and took the flashlight from the floor and the room got dark again except for a greeny-whitish glow from something about three feet off the floor over in the corner and Opal turned her face away from it so her eyes would get used to the dark. About the time they did Fos came back into the room and stood beside the bed. That was bad, he said.

I don't fault you, Opal offered.

I apologize for his behavior.

Don't you never.

I wish it hadn't happened.

Well it did.

He was fairly drunk so there's a chance he won't remember.

I'll remember, Opal said.

Fos sat on the bed's edge.

Did you tell him? Opal asked him.

Tell him what?

'Bout us bein married.

No, m'am. No. I did not. Not in his state.

Outside, at the street corner beneath the window, Opal heard the sound of a roadster engine revving and she reckoned it was a V-6 Cabriolet. There came two blasts of the distinctive crake-like mating call from the roadster's horn and then she heard the car speed away. Fos touched her gently. Why doncha take a bath an' let me fry us up some eggs, he said. Before she moved she asked, So I guess there's likker for the takin here. In this big city.

Plenty people runnin stills back home, Fos said.

That's the rural people makin somethin on their own. I was askin about cities.

You were askin about Flash.

She could feel her face smart with embarrassment and she tried to look away from him but he cupped a palm along her cheek and swept the hair back from her eyes and made her look at him.

Up to two weeks ago there wasn't anybody on this earth since I was born except my momma ever seen me naked, Opal finally said. Then there was one other person, she said, meaning him. *And now there's two.*

Fos didn't move. There were a lot of reasons why he'd never taken up a gun to hunt after the War but the main argument against any such pursuit was the one he saw in Opal's eyes just then. Maybe there are moments between any two adults in love when the age of one of them dissolves before the other's eyes, when the first refuge of the soul at its creation is laid bare and skinless as a sunbeam through a window. Innocence and vulnerability, two unmeasurable quantities, rose from her and Fos felt their qualities flow through him like an electric charge. He longed to spread himself around her as protection, but the magnitude of his emotion made any gesture he could make seem small. Perhaps that is the essence of protection's intimacy, that it dwells in camouflage and justifies itself in stillness. As a mother and her unborn child are one while being two, so, too, are lovers in their acts of mercy. In a glimpse and by the merest touch, he pledged her all he owned. It seemed unnecessary, then, to swear that he'd take care of her, but because it was a promise he had never sworn to anyone before he needed to hear himself speak the vow out loud. To both of them it sounded wonderful. Even better when, after he repeated it, she finally smiled.

Nothin terrible will come to you, he promised.

Opal lifted her chin. I'd like t' see this crystal ball you have, she joked.

Oh would you now.

She nodded.

It took a while but after twenty minutes Fos had halfway filled the lion-footed tub with buckets that he carried from the handpump in the kitchen, then he boiled a kettle and rained it over, sluicing the water with his hand so the tantalizing heat threaded through it in unspooling ribbons. He set the kettle on the stove to boil again and fetched a chemist's bottle he kept in the truck and brought it back upstairs with her carpetbag and her cube-shaped little vanity case. Just what the doctor ordered, he commented, not wanting to overstate the cleansing properties a ritual baptism might bestow under the circumstances, but knowing in his bones that one thing they had in common was their rooted territory, having both been born and raised within calling distance of the sea, and nobody grows up under the influence of the Atlantic on the Outer Banks of North Carolina undervaluing the sovereignty of water.

She was standing by the tub, wrapped in the cotton sheet, holding the white bar of P&G naphtha soap she'd taken from her toilet case, watching him uncork the chemist's phial and pour a viscous stream of amber liquid into the water. Water's harder here than what you're used to, Fos explained. The amber liquid hung like spawn suspended in the water and when Fos churned his hand through it just below the water line, bubbles of all colors foamed and sparkled up. He cupped his palms together then drew them apart balancing a soapy veil between his fingers which he held up. *Voilà,* he said, inflating it with steady breath. A single bubble, big as a balloon, rose in her direction. *Your crystal ball, madame,* he said.

He held the cotton sheet away from her and not so daintily Opal hitched one leg then the other over the tub's lip and lowered herself in. Among the many unexpected pleasures of her company the last two weeks Fos had been especially disarmed by Opal's seeming unawareness of his watching her. Most people have a perceptual tripwire which registers the trespass of another's focused interest. Maybe because she'd spent her childhood all alone without a watchful mother, she was self-contained. Or maybe it was because she was somewhere in her imagination counting up godknowswhat, the smallest task absorbed her to the exclusion of the other person in the room. Even now, as he came back with the kettle of hot water and a second lantern, she did not look up from her occupation of constructing, like a second skin, an armorial coat of bubbles over both her breasts. How's that temperature? Fos asked, setting the lantern on the floor, casting up a warm aurora on the ceiling. When you brought that light in all the bubbles changed their colors, she noted, not quite answering his question. She went on piling bubbles on her arm while he knelt and plunged his arms into the water and made little waves. Back home, he started to explain, we have what's called 'soft' water, it has that kinda, you know, soft and lardy feel on it between your fingers. But here in Knoxville it's the opposite. All these limestone cliffs and such you saw down by the river. The water has to come through all that rock. It's got that rock in it. Harder the water, harder it is to make soap lather. Worst of all is water that's got iron in it.

How come you know so much about water?

I don't. But I know some about soap.

He began to lather her right arm, the one that wasn't sunburned.

I used to help my gran make soap, he said. Soap an' tallow candles.

Yeah we used t' have a tallowman come by with soap an' all. Lordie that was years ago. I don't believe I could tellya how t' make a bar a' soap if my life depended on it.

English people make nice soap, Fos said. I saw some men with English soap during the war. They make it so light passes through it. They call it transparent but it ain't. Honey sorta color. Translucent. Glycerin, they claim. Howya feelin, any better?

I ain't never had nobody bathin me before.

Good, he smiled.

He left her there, her shoulders soldered with a chainmail of bubbles and he went down to the street and started to unload the truck, eggs and oysters and Opal's china pattern first. On his third trip back he saw a lamplight and smelled the oven fire in the bakery on the ground floor and he put his head in the door and said hello to the Rinaldis. He accepted a large bowl of hot milk and strong Italian coffee from Mama Rinaldi, which he carried up to Opal. I ain't never drunk joe from a bowl before, she said, eyes shining. A lacy tracery of froth above her upper lip complemented the bubbles all around her. *Opal-essence,* Fos reflected.

They took their breakfast at the marble-topped table in the alcove, which Fos had cleared of all its extraneous mess except for a fishbowl full of water with a waxy-looking rock the size of a corn biscuit in it. He laid a white linen cloth over the chemical stains and spills on the tabletop and anchored it in place with the fishbowl as if it were a vase of flowers. He put out the plates and the cutlery and coffee cups and the dish of scrambled eggs and oysters and when Opal emerged pink and dewy, wrapped in a plaid flannel robe, he pulled a chair back for her like a cartoon waiter and positioned her so she could catch the crowning rays of sun above the waking neighborhood. Happy? he asked unnecessarily, and before she had a chance to answer he said, *I* am.

Everything looks different in the light of day she was going to say, but stopped herself because the sentiment seemed commonplace and she was feeling anything but common. She was feeling like the princess in a fairy tale.

I told Mama Rinaldi there's a bride up here so watch out, Fos said. She'd like t' smother you with food.

Opal was listening but staring at the surfaces around her. You sure are clean, she said.

The fishbowl and the rock inside it loomed large between them on the table.

Fos jabbed a black-edged oyster with his fork and said I, uh, I told Flash to meet me at the shop at ten this mornin, you know, so we can talk.

Do I need t' feed the rock while you're away? she asked straight-faced.

Fos smiled. Rock feeds itself. Sunlight.

Uh-*huh,* she comprehended, toying with the edge of the starched linen.

That's the greeny light you saw last night. Phosphorus, Fos said. By day it sits there and absorbs the light. By night it self-luminesces.

—it self—?

Shines in the dark.

How come you keep it in a fishbowl under water?

'Cause if I didn't it would spontaneously combust. It's the stuff we used for fireworks, in shells. They use it in grenades. It's extremely sensible in air.

I wish I was 'extremely sensible', Opal remarked. She chewed her eggs. Whereja get it? I mean—howja find a rock like that an' get it home without explodin? How can something 'sensible' like you say exist out in the open without settin the whole world on fire?

Self-taught himself, he liked to see her mind unscrew the lid off something.

Best I understand it, he began to say—an' if I sound a little simple in the explanation it's because I ain't no expert—even though it's an element the same as oxygen an' tin an' gold an' all, phosphorus, itself, all on its own, exists in nature only inside somethin else. Inside limestones, for instance, inside shales. You have to take the phosphorus outta them by artificial means by boilin or by treatin 'em with carbon or ammonia. This here piece comes from the phosphate deposit down by Muscle Shoals where they found this large deposit of it and built a plant to manufacture phosphorus to make ammo for the War. Didn't get it built in time before the War had ended though. I'm borin you ain't I.

No, Opal said too quick. Not entirely. She was looking round at all the stuff of hers he'd brought in from the truck that needed sorting out.

I get too enthusiastic, Fos assessed.

It's nice you do, Opal reminded him.

No I get too carried away. Over just the ordinariest of things. Like soap. There you are a vision in the bath that I can have the privilege to be sittin there beholdin you and instead a' sayin lordie darlin but you're breathtaking I start yappin all about hard properties of water an' how the English make their soap. It's a fault a' mine, I know it, thinkin everyone gets riled up as I do over how things work and what things are when the simple fact is scientific query wearies folk, it wearies them as fast as bookkeepin, faster than debts an' credits, faster than statistics, bores 'em paralyzed. I don't blame 'em. Best way for me to get along with people is to turn anything I know about the miracle of science into circus entertainment and do tricks.

I like it when you talk your science stuff, she said. Her tone was gentle but still she didn't smile. I like it when you do the tricks you do. They don't explain much, she informed him, but they're interestin. Nothin wrong with that in my view. Kinda helps things seem more fun.

Well if I did a science trick for you right now could I get a smile?

Depends.

She turned away a little.

You don't hafta, she appended.

You're still feelin bad about what happened, aren'tya?

Opal pinched the corners of her mouth into a curve that was a halfway Yes.

Well what if I offer to bend this here knife an' fork before your very eyes using these two fingers, Fos propositioned.

I seen bent tableware before, Opal cautioned, looking disobliged.

Bend this pencil then, he ad-libbed, reaching for a pencil from the nearby shelf. He brandished it between two fingers above the fishbowl, invoking the spirit of True Science in his doughboy French, and set the pencil free to face the fate gravity would infallibly impose on it, and it fell, its profile broken and displaced at the waterline by light's refraction. Ta *da,* Fos emphasized. Ocular illusion. *Bent* pencil.

She was clearly disappointed.

Short notice, Fos apologized. Tonight I'll pull a rabbit from a hat, I promise. Smile?

She gave it half a try.

Please darlin, I can't leave knowin that you're sad.

I ain't sad, she told him.

What then?

Getting anything emotional from her was like, well, pulling rabbits.

Disappointed?

Lordie no. Other way around. I'm afraid a' disappointin *you,* she told him for the second time.

As if the sun could disappoint the sky, Fos told her.

He cleared away the breakfast things and went to shave and dress and when he came back in the room she'd started to unpack and the place looked brighter. So did she.

Go make yourself acquainted with the Rinaldis downstairs, he told her before leaving. Mama Rinaldi can tellya anything you need to know.

He went down the outside stairs with the new sensation that he'd left a piece of his identity behind. Early though it was, there was a lot more going on than he was used to after two weeks' absence. He headed up Clinch Avenue toward the commercial heart of town and at the first cross street a convict crew from the state farm was surfacing the road, part of Knoxville's plan to pave the city. Clinch Avenue was paved, but the numbered streets that crossed it from 11th to 23rd were still dirt. Road surfacing, electrification, and the telephone were the civic issues of the season and the city councilors were determined to bring Knoxville up to standard. *Progress,* Fos considered. Some of the downtown streets were electrified from a hydro-station on the river, but full electrification for the city was still only on the drawing board. On the corner of Clinch and 11th where a vacant lot had been overgrown with watermelon vines, Fos noticed a filling station going up advertising Pennzoil and Dr Pepper. At the intersection with Henley, truck farmers hauling late corn and peaches from the flatlands west of town had pulled onto another empty lot to sell to the local markets and were nearly done, their workday more than half completed. He had just started wondering to himself how married men could bear to tear themselves away from making love all day and go to work, when he made the right off Clinch onto Locust and pulled up outside the shade-drawn storefront window with the words PHOTOGRAPHIC PORTRAIT STUDIO painted on it in flaking gold. *O lordie,* he breathed. The place looked singularly abandoned. The window shade was pulled down across the front and the glass door was papered over on the inside with jaundiced pages from a week-old *Knoxville Journal.* Dead flies and other former insects littered the corners of the window panes. Fos thought he'd wait for the mailman to pass by before he unlocked the door to what he half hoped he wouldn't find inside but Hey Fos, the mailman greeted him and stopped. Where at you been?

Over back to Carolina, Fos explained.

Hot there?

Fos rendered the expected answer. Only in the shade.

Kept the mail back when I didn't notice no one, the mailman said while Fos evaluated Flash hadn't even left a sign up on the door. On Vacation, for example. Temporarily Closed. Gone. Fishin. Ain't like you an' Mr. Flash to fold and disappear like that for nothin, the mailman was saying. He was waiting for the story. Fos fingered the key to the door and cast his eyes overhead like he was searching for a high ball in the outfield. There was a welter of wires, cross-hatched and hitched to buildings from the block's sole telegraph pole. Fos could feel the silence weighing so he turned to answer him. Across the street there was a new sign in the window, YOUR CREDIT'S GOOD WITH US. I got married, he finally said.

Back in Carolina?

Yep.

Chilehood sweetheart?

Easier not to put too fine a point on it, Fos appraised.

Well that's swell, the mailman said. Now all we have to do is wait for one to come along and hogtie Mr. Flash.

Fos saw him off then unlocked the door and stepped into the gloom. There was a stale air about the place like the inside of a disused silo, and routinely Fos rolled the shade up in the window and hung the OPEN sign. From the abrupt look of things Flash must have closed up on the hop. The

Camel cigarette he'd been smoking had burned down to a gray ash where the end of it still balanced, leaving a resinous singe on the counter's varnish. Work lay unfinished on the desk and in the back room baths of fixatives and developers were left undrained and open in the sinks. Fool, Fos fussed. It was the first time he had entertained the notion and he was so absorbed with cleaning up and setting down to work he didn't notice when the designated hour of their meeting came and went. At one o'clock he closed up shop and hung the paper clock on the inside of the door with its hands pointing to one-twenty and he walked to the post office to collect the last week's mail. He stopped in at the bank and broke a ten into five ones and a five because there'd been nothing in the cash box when he'd had a look inside. He had a few words with the teller he suspected was a little sweet on Flash. She was always dropping by the shop and noticeably let down whenever Flash was in the darkroom. Other than his brief exchange with her, a few words at the post office and his dialogue with the mailman, Fos didn't speak to anyone all day and by four o'clock he was feeling lonelier than heck for Opal's company. He spent another half an hour hand-lettering a sign that read BUSINESS AS USUAL NORMAL HOURS, which he stuck inside the window. Then he locked the door an hour early and went to look for Flash.

There was no evidence of him at the rooms he rented and the landlord said he wasn't the only person looking for him, there had been a woman on the scent as well. I ain't seen him since the middle a' last week. You know I'd tellya if I did, Fos.

Fos got back in the truck and headed home, taking streets that cut across the university campus. Five surplus army tents had been erected on the parade ground on Volunteer Avenue for student registration and around them were field tables manned by students in various forms of outrageous dress. Fos pulled over to observe them. The closest he had ever come to being in a herding ritual was in the first days of boot camp and then again on the troop transport across the Atlantic. Line up, state your name, receive instruction. The system sifted you like grain. Still, the sun's rays striking sideways on the steeples elevated the stamping ground to something more illustrious than a threshing floor. He believed in education, he truly did, he had unstinting respect for those who kept to it through life. Had he had the chance, he would have wished some better learning on himself. More on a whim than with a reason, he got out of the truck and approached the milling crowd. Students, some of them not that much younger than himself, circulated among the tables, some of them alone—though not for long—some of them in twos and threes, some with their parents. All the benefits of student life—athletic groups, the chess club, debating society, fraternities, sororities, French and Latin clubs and sports teams—advertised themselves with placards and solicited attention through their vigorous attractive members. Fos found himself before a table for the Science Club, crewed by male and female students dressed up, presumably, as famous scientists. A boy with spectacles as thick as Fos's own and a bedsheet draped in imitation of an Athenian was demonstrating something with a tiny block and tackle to a couple of doubting onlookers while a young woman in a lop-sided peruke which looked suspiciously like George Washington's focused all her salesmanship on Fos and said, Would you like to join the Physics Club? Fos was staring at her out-of-season long-sleeved dress when she explained, I'm supposed to be Madame Curie. All us girls are dressed like her. We argued to be Newton but then the boys argued that we wouldn't like it if some of them dressed up as Madame Curie so they won the argument. Would you like to know about the Club? We meet bimonthly for discussion. Three times a year we go on field trips. Last year we went to Princeton to hear Professor Curie's lecture.

Fos blinked into the face of this young innocent.

You saw Madame Curie? he repeated.

We were way in back so I can't say I *saw* her the girl said. She shrugged and her white wig slid an inch and she handed Fos a sheet of paper and said this is our schedule. Hope you join us. Then she turned away and even though the light was more than generous for reading Fos watched the words printed on the page swim before his eyes as his mind registered the fact that within a half a mile of where he lived, without his having known it, there were people as interested as he was in the unseen workings of the world. For reasons he could ascribe only to a general sense of newfound optimism, he thought of Opal. Maybe soon he'd have to face the fact that everything from here on in was going to make him think of Opal. He thought of her whenever he saw light at play. He thought of her while he was seining paper for a capture in the fixative and he thought of her when he saw buttermilk-colored moths mirror-flashing through the bluegrass of an abandoned lot. He was thinking of her when he ran into a fellow with his head bent into his chest like he was looking for a four-leaf clover. The man was holding a black box above his navel, staring into it, while thirty feet in front of him a woman in a floral dress flanked by two identical grinning boys shouted, Dad don't take it when the sun goes, I don't want my face in shadow.

Then take yer hat off, the man said beneath his breath as Fos smacked into him. *Sorry,* Fos apologized, I wasn't watchin where I was goin. He looked at the man and at the camera and at the man's wife and their sons. Wouldja like me to take one of all a' you together?

Thanks, the man said and handed Fos the Brownie.

It had been invented as a toy box, a kindergarten camera for toddlers, and even after all the years it had been a popular sensation Fos was still amused by its widespread use by grown-up people.

He framed the family, fanning them around one-eighty so their faces would be better lit, then he raised his hand to signal them and called, *This one's for posterity!*

Before the Brownie's owner came back to retrieve it another family asked if he would do the same for them. This one had a Speed Graphic, which Fos openly admired. Flash had all the portables—he was an unrestrained collector of all the latest gear and gadgets in the field. Their partnership depended on Fos being the fixer, Flash the man out front. Most of their trade was in studio photography and weddings, graduations, anniversaries and such for which Flash was the legman, Fos the backup. Flash had purchased three Vest Pocket Kodaks and the single lens reflex cameras for the shop but Fos had never used them, leaving fieldwork up to Flash, who had the improvisational nerve and hair-trigger timing for it. But even halfwits could take mediocre photographs these days thanks to the enterprising team at Kodak. Men and women who knew nothing whatsoever about lighting, framing, and half-tones were turning out whole museums worth of fileable historical records. And whereas in the past you had to have the know-how to fashion your own incising tool to make your own hieroglyph and leave a scratch on the rock of ages, these days all you needed was a couple dollars for a light-tight apparatus and some Kodapaks. It took more skill to lay a concrete road in 1921 than it took to take a picture, Fos was thinking as he passed the intersection where he'd seen the convict crew at work that morning. *Progress,* he considered for the second time that day. He was right back where he started. She was waiting for him in the window.

Opal had been counting up the minutes since he'd left that morning, counting up the hours till she'd see him. Even now the joy that animated her response the moment she spied him in the street couldn't communicate how much she'd missed him even though from where he stood it looked like she was going to fly. He wasn't sure his shoes were making contact with the earth but somehow he got up there through the door. Then he had her in his arms and all he wanted was to make love to her.

Something that smelled good was going on the stove which made the kitchen steamy so she led him down the hallway toward the main room, piping to him the whole time like a nervous little bird, more noise than size.

The place had been transformed.

She'd been careful not to disturb his artless clutter but she'd somehow managed to arrange herself and her belongings into balance with his half of the bargain. It still felt like he lived there but she'd filled in blanks and blurred the edges with her modest frills. She had colonized the empty spaces, added strokes of color and sprinkled fairy dust, it seemed to him, with that same transforming sugaring a first snow bestows on an autumnal canvas. What do you think? she said, the quaver in her voice prompting him to speak his admiration. She looked so swell, the place looked swell, the dress that she'd put on was prettier than anything he'd ever seen, the way she'd made the bed up with her hope chest linen looked like something out of Ward's or Sears & Roebuck's. Kings were meant to sleep on beds like that. Ope, he started to say, too choked up to get the second syllable out. She tilted her head. Fos's eyes were tearing and when she raised her hand to wipe his cheek he pressed his lips into her palm like he was making a plaster cast with them. He swallowed hard and hoped like hell she'd get the hint without his saying anything. She studied him and went a shade of pink then whispered, Well all right but let me turn what's in the oven off before we start.

It was dark and hours later before they got around to recounting to each other how they'd spent the day. Don't start there, Opal told him when he began with the Physics Club, I want to know what all went on with you and Flash.

Fos fell silent.

Oh *no,* she said.

You know, Fos said, gathering her to him under his arm, I should feel betrayed or somethin but I don't. He let down his half of the bargain—I mean he didn't *let* it down he dropped it. Still . . . well I'll give you a for instance. All day I had a feeling like good news was comin to me. Like the best news I ever heard was about to be delivered. On the way t' work just up here on the corner I passed a chain gang layin road and instead a' thinkin what a sorry lot those mens' lives are I looked at what they were doin an' I thought *Now I wonder what's the logic layin road that way?*

Oh I saw them too when I went to the store with the Rinaldi ladies. They was layin slabs a' concrete.

Well exactly. Slabs. And everywhere you go you feel that slab-break every other second through your chassis—why not pour the whole street down in one piece?

There must be a reason, Fos, she told him, trusting to authority.

That's what *I* was thinkin. That there must be an engineering reason I don't know about that they teach you when you go to engineering school. And then not fifteen minutes later I was standin on the sidewalk out in front the store talkin to the mailman an' I look up and overhead I see all these wires, tens a' them, all strung up without a method just hung up like a private's laundry anywhere. Now why is that? What are they there for? Sure we know they're there because that's what hooks folks up to the telephone, hooks them to the wire at the end of their light bulbs, but what's *in* the wires, doncha see. Do you know how a person's voice goes out his mouth and travels into someone's ear sixty or a hundred miles away? Or how a turbo on the Tennessee can make the copper thread inside a light bulb burn so hot it shines? I'll be damned if I know. You can fit what I know about what makes things work and how the world was made into a peanut.

Opal rolled onto her side so she could look at him. What's this got to do with thinkin somethin good was goin t' happen? she said, worried that she'd lost the thread.

Fos lifted her chin. All I'm sayin is I want our boy to go somewhere. T' know enough. I want him t' get whatever's out there in the way a' learnin he deserves.

Opal was afraid to move. Our *boy*? she carefully repeated.

Fos nodded. Eager, she was thinking, as a puppy.

Doncha think it's kinda early t' be thinkin things like that?

Early—? Why?

Well families just don't happen. You know. Kinda like your phosphorus. They gotta be arranged.

They *do?* He stared at her. Is there somethin we ain't doin? *Are we doin it all wrong?*

She shook her head and kind of snorted out a laugh.

Oh *good,* Fos sighed. His stomach growled. I gotta figure outta way to get more business in, he said, so we can buy a place. We're gonna need a bigger place to live. We haven't been exploitin all our opportunities. Flash an' me, I mean. In business.

Opal rose up on her elbow, glad that he was finally going to talk about his partnership with Flash and said, For instance?

Well for one thing we've been waitin for the business to come in instead of goin out to get it. Truth is the days of studio photography are numbered. What I can't figure yet though is this: once I go out an' set up outside the studio at some place, say, the university campus, how do I know that ain't the last I'll see a' 'em?

Well you'll have their picture so it ain't the last, she reasoned.

How do I know they'll come back to the shop and pick the picture up? And pay for it.

Deliver it.

He looked at her.

Take the money on the spot an' mail the finished product to the momma and the daddy, Opal said. Put a little flyer on the inside with your standard Christmas prices on it. That'll bring 'em back.

Fos blinked and tried to focus.

That'd take a second person. All that paperwork.

Plenty kids around the college sure could use a job.

Someone real reliable, he said. To do the sellin. Take the details down. Take the money. Keep the books.

She looked at him.

I'd pay ya, Fos intended. I would match your goin wage.

I'm a married woman now, she told him half in jest. I ain't got a goin wage. And anyway. Don't you think you better ask your partner?

I need to know if you'd be willin first.

Willin to do what?

Work along beside me.

Well ain't that the way we started?

The next morning they dressed and tidied up the kitchen and went down to the truck and went to work together. Fos was wearing a shirt and collar with a blue serge vest and a polka-dot bowtie that wouldn't stay straight and Opal had on square-heeled shoes that didn't pinch. The convict gang was out again and Fos raised two fingers off the steering wheel to greet the foreman. I ain't sure it's right them doin unpaid labor, he confessed.

Pa used t' say they owed a debt to law-abidin society.

Everybody owes that debt.

Opal didn't answer for a while and then she mentioned, Babies don't.

They turned into a street that cut through the University of Tennessee campus, a part of town that Opal hadn't seen before, so Fos could show her where they would be setting out after some new business later in the day. Overnight posters had been tied to the lampposts, and Fos pulled up alongside one to read it. It advertised a fair out on the Clinch River and Fos looked at her and said, Well that's where we'll go Saturday and Sunday. Get the x-ray goin. People stand in line, I'll tellya, just t' get a gander at the inside of themselves. You can look your people up, too, if that'd please ya.

I'll think about it she replied, chewing on the inside of her mouth. They were momma's people. Distant.

He parked the truck on Locust Street outside the shop. Oh my, Opal said. Her face lit up. Don't that look classy, she told him.

She held back at the door while he raised the window shade and hung the OPEN notice. You make yourself at home, he said, while I go get whatall we'll need. He disappeared behind a curtain to another room and Opal stepped tentatively behind the counter, sliding both her hands along the top as if it were a guiderail. She hadn't been there longer than a minute when the door flew open and Flash, in need of a wash and shave, slid in, jacket slung across his shoulder. He didn't notice her at first but when he did he looked at her as if he'd caught her with her fingers in the till and said Jezzy*belle,* who the *hell* are you an' what the *hell* you think you're doin in my store?

He was standing only three feet from her with the countertop between them and she could smell the cigarettes and liquor on him when the movement of the woman across the street caught her eye through the big glass window. Don't look behind but would that Chattanooga lady be the kind who'd wear a muskrat wrap around her on a suffocatin summer mornin—? Opal breathed. *Get out back quick here she comes.*

Like lightning Flash bolted for the floor next to Opal's ankles. *Whatzer name?* she whispered, concentrating all her will on what was soon to walk in through the door.

—uh, Lucy.

Lucy.

—Dulcey?

Dulcey.

Ruby! That wazzit.

He clutched her calf and touched his cheek against her knee and Opal aimed a square heel where a kick might do a stack of hurt while the woman blew in like bad weather. Up close though Opal saw that she was worse for wear and definitely twitchy. Her fingers were tobacco stained as was the hair over her lip and if her chignon had been that color on the day that she was born then Opal's name was santa claus. *Where's he at?* the woman said in an edgy voice that could have sliced up water. I just now seen him come in. You go tell him t' come out. Tell him. Go on. Tell him I wanna—

I *know* what you want, Opal leveled with her. I know who you are, I know your name is Ruby and I know you went up to Niagara Falls with him last year. I know all about the gals he used t' get around with.

Opal splayed her fingers on the countertop and cleared her throat. She made a tapping noise with her gold wedding band against the varnished wood to make darn certain Ruby noticed.

Ruby tried to make her nostrils curl but the face she drew just made her look like she was going to be sick. The lipstick that she'd drawn her mouth on with was doing that thing milk does when you leave it out too long and the fur animal around her neck was losing hair in patches even after death. She tried to summon a derisive laugh but it came out a little growl. You must be *jokin,* she told Opal. How could somebody homely as you are possibly get married?

Well not the same way somebody like *you* could, that's for sure.

Just then the curtain parted and the woman turned around with ripe excitement and there was Fos loaded up with several cameras, packs of film, two tripods and an umbrella-looking thing. He blinked.

This here is that Chattanooga lady I was gonna call the sheriff on, Opal said like it was true.

Oh, Fos said.

If he'd noticed in his chronic teary state his business partner on the floor behind the counter clutching his wife's ankles, he let the sight of it slide mistily by him.

Howja do? he said.

She was just now leavin, Opal told him. Werenja?

Ruby looked from Fos to Opal, back to Fos, and then she raised her hand like she was going to signal something to a person far away and Opal noticed how her hand was shaking. Her fingernails, she noticed, too, were long, immaculately shaped, and ruby-like-her-name and Opal guessed she'd done them on her own, and to perfection. Maybe that was why Opal opened the purse one of the clients she kept books for had given her last Christmas and asked Ruby if she needed money for the train. She held out ten dollars and she heard Fos make a noise like he was stifling a sneeze in the middle of a sermon.

Double that could get me clear to Memphis, Ruby told her.

Double this would be a two-way trip.

A beat went by before Ruby finally snatched it from her hand. Opal shook Flash off her foot and walked around to the door and held it open. Ruby fanned her face with the ten-dollar bill and Opal had to hand it to the woman she didn't skulk she sashayed out, muskrat swinging.

As soon as she was gone Flash hauled himself into a semi-upright slump against the counter and said, *Whew-ee!* Ray boy, didja catch that? I don't know what blew you in here honey but I wouldn't never wanna sit against you in a hand a' poker. Didja get a load of this unlikely she-cat? he asked Fos as if Opal had been his discovery. Still waters, ain't it said still waters are the deep-uns? He wagged a finger at her and clicked his tongue. I owe ya, darlin.

You don't owe me nothin but my ten dollars, Opal told him.

Something in her tone made him alert. One thing Flash had perfect pitch for was a warning tone from women. He decided to ignore it and began to peel the singles from his billfold but whatever cloud had settled down over the others sure as hell was not about to lift. In fact he felt it thicken.

What's goin on? he asked. He looked at Fos. What the hell's the matter?

Fos blinked and shifted from foot to foot beneath his bulky load. He cleared his throat. Finally he said, There's something you should know, Flash. The way he said it sounded like he'd just walked on in a badly written play and blown his single line.

Flash showed all his teeth. Surprise me, he invited.

Fos put down what he was carrying and put his arm around his wife. This-here is Opal, he announced. My Missus.

To his credit Flash fell on the floor again. When he pulled himself back up he'd slicked his hair back and tucked his shirt into the waistband of his pants and hitched up his suspenders. If he remembered ever seeing Opal on a previous occasion then he did a fancy job of making her believe he didn't. You coulda waited till hell froze over and you'd have never found a better man, Flash told her.

Ditto, she reminded him.

Over the succeeding weeks there reigned a fragile truce among them and like all things fragile, once in place, it was regarded as an item to be rarely touched and if so, only with the risk of fracture. *Ditto* was Flash's instant nickname for her, and soon he started calling them *the dittos.* How *the dittos* doin this fine mornin? What's the word in Dittoville?

Someone unacquainted with the fiber of a certain seam of Southernness might have found his sudden good behavior in their presence counterfeit, tin buffed to bluff as gold, but his eagerness to win their favor and approval was made of honest solder: the sight of Fos and Opal coming down the street together absolutely tickled him. The idea that two such strangely unremarkable yet lovable people could have found and met each other reaffirmed his waning faith in anything remotely optimistic about mankind and seemed to be a more convincing proof than all the gospel shit flown from the pulpits of Knox County that life could, in fact, distribute happy endings. Fos and Ope were like two eggs, Flash thought, two undersized blue knobs in a tidy feathered nest which stops you short where you are tramping in your mudboots through an otherwise dun wood. They *looked* like eggs—more round, at least, than angly, with the palest thinnest skin the white race has to offer and a degree of hairlessness that rivaled channel swimmers and would have kept Mr. Gillette awake at night had he got wind of their existence in the gene pool. Looking at them made Flash smile and being in their company was as pleasurable, although of a somewhat purer kind, as being in the company of an unattainable but sexy woman. He was not so much a reformed man in their presence—far from it—but a man on best behavior, and in Flash's case, unbeknownst to either Fos or Opal, the resources for chivalry and graceful manners ran exceeding wide in him, through the finest schools and houses in the South.

But Opal wasn't won at once.

In the weeks that followed on their first encounter she was quiet in his company: suspicious: circumspect. She watched him when she thought he wasn't looking, noting the military crease down his impeccably pressed trousers or the occasional astonishment of lemon toilet water when he took off his linen jacket to roll up his sleeves. There was a sunny crispness to his haberdashery which matched the style of his new manners and except for the playful twinkle in his eye every time he spoke to her she would have thoroughly distrusted it. He kept diligent hours, showing up for work most mornings in advance of Fos and welcomed Fos's new ideas for invigorating their established business with the gusto of a first-generation venture capitalist. When he learned from Fos that Opal had kept books for some commercial enterprises back in North Carolina he was the first to say they take her on as bookkeeper themselves. It was his idea, Fos told Opal that same night. I didn't hafta twist his arm.

For two weekends in a row she and Fos had driven out to the neighboring counties for their fairs and Opal had easily adopted motions of assistance, as if she had been practicing for years. Even if he weren't her husband and even if she weren't in love with him, Fos would still have been the easiest man she'd ever met to work with. He didn't seem to know how to acknowledge skepticism or complain and he earnestly believed that somewhere in every sodbuster and countrywife in the state of Tennessee there was a latent desire to have some element of science laid bare to them by him in layman's terms. When people looked at him a little sideways he turned the other cheek, she saw. When they laughed out loud at a machine he claimed would show them the subtle structures of their bones he persevered and promised them epiphany.

Here, he said, *folks to prove its safety I offer you my wife* and people stood in line to look at Opal's toes.

She got a thrill seeing how Fos worked the crowd for science. Going to an open field and setting up the x-ray from the truck beside the honkeytonk and donkey rides and tent revivals was a lot of fun. But working side by side with him each day with Flash was something different. I think you oughta weigh this over for a time, she cautioned.

Weigh what over?

The consequences.

Such as?

Such as what if him and me don't get along.

Oh, Fos said. *That* consequence. You had me worried. I thought you meant the consequence of what would happen if the moon falls from the sky through the roof and sets the town on fire. 'Cause that's a thing more likely to occur than the two of you not getting on.

Well maybe I don't wanta.

Why would you not wanta?

Well maybe I have diff'rent methods.

Diff'rent methods doin what?

Business. Everything.

I see.

I hope you see.

Well I do.

I hope you do.

Ain't I the trained observer of the things nobody else can see?

Which seemed to win the point.

Nevertheless next morning she showed up with Fos still acting captive and reluctant. Make yourself at home, Flash said, setting her down at his own just-tidied desk in the back room. *Mi casa, su casa,* he said, stacking a tower of account books in front of her. Hereya go, he said. He opened the first volume. Line one, he told her. Eight November nineteen-eighteen. May as well begin at the beginning.

Who . . . um . . . Opal ran her finger down the numbered columns, cleared her throat. Who's been makin all these entries?

I have, Flash confessed.

She looked back at the books.

My handwriting, he attested.

From beginning to the end.

He flared some pages.

Opal took a moment. There wasn't any—? she began to ask.

What?

Someone else who kept the books.

You're the first one, ditto. Only archeologist to visit Troy. So find us a king's ransom willya? Reinvent the place.

Opal settled in and started going through them one by one—each one a sort of masterpiece of tidiness, a product of a tidy mind. Kept in three colors of india ink—red for debits, black for credits, blue for worded explanations—each item was entered with the sure stroke of a mason incising stone: meant to stand the test of time. Ambiguity has no place in death, on tombstones, or in numbers. Precision is borne on this notion: numbers never err. Any proof that's written down that errs cannot be drawn from numbers. Numbers never lie. If they lie they are no longer numbers. If they lie, they're words.

But Opal had seen record books kept like dance cards with entries exchanged and rebalanced like serial beaux in a reel, doseydoeing. Not these. From the first line—a credit entry of start-up capital—in November 1918, the year that he returned from the war, Flash had kept a note of every penny spent. From postage stamps to boxes of matches, equipment purchases and the increases in Fos's weekly take-home, every item was calculated and catalogued. The building was owned by the business, purchased for cash at the outset by Flash who was then sole proprietor. Its current asset value—probably underassessed, Opal thought, given the general rise in the property market—was listed on the most recent balance sheet at only ten percent above its purchase price, and it and all the photographic equipment, depreciating at a rate alarmingly faster than Model-T Fords, she was surprised to note, were the business's only assets. There were no debts. The partnership was in credit, tidily so. There was a document dated August 6, 1919, replacing the original joint stock instrument of 1918, which granted Fos fifty shares out of a hundred in the business in consideration of what appeared to be a payment of one dollar. And according to the record for that month, Fos began to draw his salary right away. Fifteen dollars a week as starting wage, first paycheck issued August 12, signed by Flash. Then a weekly increase of ten dollars March the next year. A bonus of a hundred dollars on the first anniversary of the partnership in August 1920, plus another raise. Another bonus of two hundred dollars paid to Fos at Christmas. Another raise to thirty-five dollars a week starting January 1921. Fos's current weekly take-home pay came to almost forty dollars. Opal leaned back in the chair and put down the pencil. The wail of a noon siren somewhere outside cut through her concentration. Behind her, at the workbench, Fos had been bent over the enlarger for three hours and, like Opal, he seemed startled from a dream to realize it was lunchtime.

Hungry, honey? he said, getting to his feet and stretching. Let me take my favorite girl to lunch.

Where's Flash? Opal asked, then realized she'd sounded almost rude.

Fos yawned and pointed to the darkroom.

In the cave. Probably be there all day. Come on, let's go over to the five-and-dime and get a blue-plate special.

Can't, she said, not looking at him.

Come on, all work no play makes Jill a—

No.

Not looking at him but knowing that she ought to, she said, I gotta go through this one more time. She turned toward him and gave a feeble smile. Gotta double-check, she said. You know. First day on the job. Gotta make a good impression on the boss. The bosses.

She clasped her hands together to hide her nervousness and told him, You go on.

Sure?

She nodded.

Bring you back a slice a'pie?

She smiled again and took the offer just to hurry him along.

When he was gone she walked over to the darkroom door and leaned her ear against it. She raised her hand to knock, then let it drop.

She walked back to the desk, moved the books back into their chronological order, picked up the pencil and started once again, this time with a mission, from the start.

Some time later she briefly noted Fos's return.

At four o'clock she finished and her knees creaked when she stood. The back room they were working in had a single window with nine panes in it next to the door, which gave into a narrow unpaved alley. There was a second source of natural light, a skylight in the slanted roof, and through it fell a cone of sunlight onto Fos, the soul of innocence. He looked up and saw her watching. She was clutching an account book to her chest. He smiled and asked her, Done?

She didn't know how to start to tell him *Toldja there'd be consequences* but Flash, coming from the darkroom, saved her from having to explain for at least another moment. *Bright out here,* he said, raising his arm to shield his eyes. Hello dittos. Why, ditto, look at you! What's the matter, beauty? Why so glum? Santa didn't bring your pony?

I needta have a word with you, she told him in the smallest voice from her Fos had ever heard.

Word away, Flash offered.

Opal couldn't look at Fos, which meant she couldn't look at Flash without feeling like a traitor, so she closed her eyes and said, About the books.

Okay.

In private.

When Flash didn't answer she opened her eyes. He was leaning back relaxed against the bench about twelve feet away from her outside the cone of light streaming from the ceiling. Fos was at the bench in full sun another twelve feet away from Flash on Flash's right. Opal stood equidistant between the two of them—she, too, like Flash, in shade. Looked at from some distant point the three of them together formed an equilateral triangle.

Dit, this doesn't get more private, Flash informed her and made a circle with his hand in the air in front of him from their three points.

Please, she said. She couldn't help but notice Fos was blinking something awful. Ope—? he said, standing up and taking a step toward her.

Come on, ditto, out with it. Flash was speaking gently. There's no secrets in this room. Except of course what goes between the two of you. Speak. You got the vote in '20, use it.

She leveled him a look and took a breath. You keep the best books I have ever seen outside a textbook, she announced. And those were hypotheticals.

Why thank you ma'm.

So you know full well what I got to ask.

Flash tilted his head and said I *do?*

You ain't never once since you started up this business ever taken one cent from it either as a salary or a bonus.

Is that a question, dit?

—you *ain't?* Fos said, turning round to look at him.

He's never, Opal stated. Not a cent.

Fos looked like a person seeing light for the first time. What the devil you been livin on?

Flash gathered himself into a less casual mass and asked, Is what I have been living on anybody's business but my own?

Yes, Opal said. I do believe it is. I believe when you make another person legal for your debts you oughta let that person in on where your money's comin from.

But ditto. Did you find a debt?

You bet.

You *did?*

Flash leaned forward.

Fos's, Opal said.

I'm in *debt?* Fos blinked. I *am?*

Tell him, Opal challenged Flash.

You've lost me, dit, you truly have, he answered.

Tell me what? Fos said.

Opal took a breath.

He gave you this, she finally said. He bought it and he gave you half. He gave you half a fortune for a dollar. Fos, didja ever stop to wonder how you'd pay it off?

Now hold your horses there a minute, dit, Flash interrupted.

—you *gave* it to me?

No of course I didn't give it to you, every day you're here you're in here working like a mule and even if I did decide to trade sole ownership of this, this stinking building for what was worth far more to me—your partnership—who the hell can put a price on that? Can you? That's where you've got it wrong, ditto. I owe this man. *I owe.* Without Fos this business doesn't go. Maybe that's—

He hesitated.

Maybe that's a more enlightened trade than what you're used to seeing back in North Carolina. But I happen to believe our Fos is worth—

I wasn't sayin it was charity.

No ma'm I didn't think you—

I was sayin it looks fishy.

Flash suppressed a smile and repeated *fishy?*

I'm gonna ask it right out now, and Fos forgive me but I toldja there'd be consequences.

She took a small step forward lining up her toes at an imaginary line like she was waiting for a starter's gun to send her off. She cleared her throat and looked at Flash and went full pink despite herself. What is Fos supposed to do someday if he finds out the money that you used to start this business up and keep it runnin—

—business runs itself, dit, you know that, you've seen the books.

What is Fos supposed to do if someday he finds out the money that you used to buy this building—the cash you used—wasn't somehow legal.

—wasn't *legal?* Flash repeated.

Careful what you're sayin, Opal, Fos put in.

No money's ever legal, all money's gotten off some balled-and-chained exploited bastard—

You know what I mean.

No I don't know what you mean.

Somethin that's against the law.

I robbed a bank—is that what you think? Before I came to my Christian senses and marched off to join the War like every other patriot? No offense Fos, you know I don't consider you an idiot.

Well I don't consider you no idiot either from the records that you keep, Opal pursued, but that don't explain where such a large amount of cash came from nor how you manage to maintain yourself in such a high style as you do. Nice clothes an' all, she added. An' a fancy automobile.

She could tell from the sparkle in his eye and his pursed lips that he was laughing at her despite his attentive pretense and she couldn't even stop to think what Fos was thinking of her. One thing that distinguished Opal from all others in whatever fray she'd stumbled into was that once she'd put her foot in it, she created her own quicksand and there was no extracting her as the situation closed around her with its own inexorable censorship. Till that final moment, she would have to go on saying everything she had in mind to say.

I'm sorry if you think I'm buttin in, she forged ahead, but you know as well as I do how easy it is nowadays to make a less-than-honest dollar, even the President of the United States has been led astray and lord knows if a man like Mister Taft sittin on the White House lawn has nothin better on his mind but graft and featherbeddin his own nest, then what are simple folks like you and me expected to be—

You've seen too many gangster pictures, ditto, Flash broke in.

Measuring his moves and milking the suspense, he walked toward his desk and pulled a gold chain from his pocket on the end of which, among the several, was the key to the bottom drawer. Before I offer you my air-tight alibi though, dit, he said, squatting down and picking through a row of files, satisfy my curiosity about what crime it is exactly you imagine I committed.

He turned to look at her.

Fos had come to stand beside her.

I kinda thought you were you know somehow involved in runnin liquor, Opal told him.

Liquor, Flash repeated.

Or somethin worse.

Worse than liquor. Flash shook his head and clicked his tongue while he continued searching through the files. Just goes to prove a point made by a professor I once had way back before the War when I was courting marriage to Philosophy. He told me, Son. You got a set of blinders on. These blinders send you down blind roads. You go down these blind roads chasing secondary phenomena because the primary one is hidden. The primary one's the one that you can't see because you got those blinders on. 'Course in that instance I reckon he was talking about me finding the hidden meaning of Life. Not you finding hidden treasure. Here.

He handed them a file held by a rubber band under which a bank deposit book was lodged.

What is it? Fos said warily.

Read it.

We can't go pokin in your private—

Flash stood up. Oh yes you can—Opal's not that far off the mark saying that you've got the right. I would have told you sooner, Fos, but it didn't seem to matter. Read it, or else she won't leave either one of us alone with any peace.

Fos acquiesced and he and Opal began to read the documents the file contained.

Lord you think you know a person, Fos remarked after a good five minutes had gone by.

They looked up at each other first and then like two barn owls in unison they swiveled their round faces toward Flash, eyes as wide as daisies, Fos irrigating his with tears, the two of them regarding him as if they'd just found out he was the first man to set a record, climb onto the moon or something equally impossible. Split the atom.

Oh now don't look at me with eyes like that, he threatened them, those eyes are why I don't tell people in the first place.

I ain't ever known a person rich as you, was all Opal could bring herself to say. Is that bad manners to confess it?

Being rich? Flash joked. Bein rich is bad behavior.

I mean, she plugged along. I've known families who got land and land is one thing. If that passes onta ya. But I ain't ever known no one who just by bein born has so much money.

Well, dit, don't let the ladies know. What with all my other assets it could make me irresistible.

I suppose I best apologize, she said.

You weighed the only evidence you had, he told her. Now—let's not make a funeral out of this, he improvised. Let's go fishin.

Fish-in? Opal said as if she hadn't heard him right.

Have you shown your bride the joys of boating on our river yet? Flash said to Fos.

Fos started to explain there hadn't been the time when Opal interrupted to confess I'd kinda like t' have a boat ride. If I had some diff'rent clothes on.

Not a drop of water will get near you, promise, Flash assured her. Tell her, Fos. Tell her how I paddle.

He paddles like an Indian with hives, Fos attested.

Opal's spirits rose. She was a child of tidal pools and surf, the first toy she could remember was a bucket meant for clamming. Common as clams was what people said when they meant common as salt. In Knoxville, on the Tennessee, the expression was common as *cats.*

Which meant catfish.

It was said Tennessee River cats would do anything to escape that overpopulated river. The river was so thick with catfish it was said that you could stroll across it from the eastern shore to Knoxville City on their backs. It was said there are more catfish in the Tennessee than there are fish in all the oceans of the world. More catfish in Knox County than there are Christians, more catfish on supper plates than flies. More catfish in Knox County bellies than dreams inside Knox County heads. More ways to cook a catfish than to skin a cat. More meat on a catfish than on a fatted calf. Half the gossip that you heard in town involved the federal government, a married woman or a swindle. Other half involved a cat. There was King Catfish, the undisputed leader of the legendary catfish legion, said to keep a harem that reached from coast to coast, a roe to sow in every port. There was Stonewall, the Confederate catfish who was said to have almost saved the South running sabotage maneuvers against the Yankee boats patroling the Ohio. There was Ol' Glassfish, the catfish who couldn't cast a shadow, skin and bones so old they were thin enough to see through.

Every Knoxville woman had her way of doin catfish same as every Ozark woman had a way of doin hock an' greens. Only difference was that it was rare to find a man north or south who'd argue with a woman over how she did her ham and kale, but every man in Knoxville seemed to have but one opinion that he held above all others. And that was how to cook a catfish. There were those who'd argue to the death that no self-respecting man would batter cats with anything other than a bridal veil of stoneground wheat flour from mother Dixie with a zest of salt and at most a dash of pepper the way the Bible says Christ had it done on that occasion of the loaves and fishes. Others swore by cornmeal, some were cayenne-ites and some, god bless their fundamental souls, faced the fire plain with nothing but their faith in catfish same as every naked soul must face the fires of eternity with nothing but man's natural juices. Somewhere in the South, no doubt, Opal came to think, there'd arise a holy catfish church and develop just as many finicketies and schisms in it as all the other southern churches. There were catfish out in North Carolina, too, because there's practically no inland water in the whole United States this plugugly fish don't frequent, but folks on the coast would eat a shoe before they'd eat a catfish. Not when there were shrimp and clams and crabs and crawfish, oysters, albacore, and sea bass all around. To Opal's mind, a river—or at least the Tennessee—was nothing like the cleansing and dramatic waters she was used to. The Tennessee smelled different than the ocean. It looked different, too. It tasted different, it was different on the skin but most of all it had a different form of life in it. It had more humankind twined in its currents than did any ocean. The ocean, like the sky, was something man could never harness, never dam. A river, like an acre, could be subjugated to man's purpose and you could intuit a river's willingness for service every time you looked at it. Which is the song a river plays instinctively on human hearts. Unlike the rebel ocean, it's mankind's natural servant.

There were things along the river she would have to learn to name before she could begin to trust them. Eventually she'd come to take for granted all the land birds she had never seen—the peckerwoods and flickers and wild turkeys that never summered by the seashore, never left the woods. She'd learn to recognize the meadowlark, learn the names of bankside flora—squawbush trees, the useless sumac, the gumbo tree, the bitter cress. Saxifrage, bloodroot, and dutchman's breeches in the early spring as well as stands of white and azure flag. Yellow flag in summer, waterlilies and the strangling devil's tentacles that insinuated their slimy arms up from the riverbed.

Opal came to love the times that she and Fos spent on the river, she came to love the river's specificity, its changing colors with the seasons, its aspiring vapors in the early mornings, its evening calms. But she was never fully comfortable within its compass the way she was when she was swimming in the ocean. Some part of Fos was always more or less submerged when they were on the river, either his feet were dangling from the boat or his hands were in or he was up to his neck brandishing a net above the surface. Fos was more interested in investigating the optical properties of water and more eager to catch fireflies in the reeds along the banks than he was in catching fish. He rigged the goggles from his war-issue gas mask onto a piece of rubber hose so he could breath and keep his glasses on underwater and he spent most of their time on the river encouraging Opal to take the plunge until, finally, she did. She got along all right, she was a competent enough swimmer, but she was wary of the hidden company the river held. She liked being on the water in Fos's little rowboat. It was an unfussy wooden bucket with cut-down oars of Carolina pine and Opal liked to watch him row, the way he overpulled as if he were still shipping off the Outer Banks. When she started going on the river with him that first autumn, Fos spruced the little boat up with three new coats of paint and lettered Opal's name in bright pink letters on the stern. Oh geez, she told him when she saw it for the first time. It ain't right you callin her for me.

Why ain't it right?

Havin somethin called the same as me that we'd be sittin in. I ain't comf'table with it. You only did it anyway to save yourself from paintin on more letters cause my name is nice an' short.

You saying I'm lazy?

Because if there was one thing Fos was not, it was lazy. Before she could apologize he said, I'll showya lazy and slapped white paint over the letter *O.* It was pink and it was off-center but the name *Pal* suited the little boat and plucky *Pal* soon became a frequent sight along the inner channels. Opal often closed her eyes and listened to the creak of the spruce looms shunting through the oarlocks and imagined she was being lofted by the ball and socket action in the wings of a giant bird. But before then, on that first day on the river with Fos and Flash when she went out in Flash's sleek aluminum canoe, the only thing Opal could imagine when she closed her eyes was the distant muted whisperings of ibises and rushes on the Nile that must have greeted Cleopatra on her barge. Flash's canoe was a shell of bright aluminum patinated a rich navy blue on its hull with lettering on both sides of the bow.

—whatzit say? Opal asked leaning forward, unable to decipher the lettering. Is it Indian? *Yo—urna—me?*

Well if I meet a girl, Flash enlightened her, and she says her name is Opal then I can say What a *fabulous* coincidence. I have a yacht *yourname.*

You are a rascal, Flash, Fos turned to tell him from the bow. But lord knows you sure can fish.

I sure can, it's true.

And you do dearly love this river.

Probably my one and only love. So far. At least, my first. I was swimming in this river before I learned to walk and of all the things I've met in life, this river treats me best. Row half a mile upstream from these two bridges, he told Opal, to where she marries the French Broad or go half a mile downstream and she's as wild and newborn as any river you can find out West.

Opal stared into the water thick with hide-colored silt from the summer's run-off and the ochre leaching of the walnut and the sassafras trees and she decided Flash was talking big. She couldn't for an instant imagine anything newborn or wild about it.

But I betya there aren't catfish in those rivers way out west, Fos argued, startling up some brown ducks from the bankside.

Catfish everywhere, Flash told him, chuckling. You were the one who said we'd find no cats in France, remember?

God they were ugly, Fos concurred. Black as coal, solid black like some kinda hole in night. Scarifyin. Had the meanest eye what ever looked a curse.

You went fishin in the war? Opal asked just as Flash was telling Fos to feint out of the current and drift into a pool beneath some willows so he could drop a line. Not ol' leathermouth *again,* Fos said, guessing Flash's intention. He perched the paddle on his thighs and turned around so he was facing Opal. Flash has got a sick fixation with this ancient carp, he whispered to her. Claims he has been after this same carp for twenty years but just between the two of us it's anybody's guess the dang thing's even real. He's like Captain Ahab over it. Calls the thing his Moby.

Opal turned to Flash and asked him, What'sa moby?

Moby-Dick, Flash said, sighting up his pole.

Is he talkin smut? she wondered out loud to Fos.

He'd brought along the portable Speed Graphic in a knapsack and was fiddling with it to record her first time on the river. *Moby-Dick*'s this longest story ever set to page, he said, that Flash was readin in the war. Bigger'n the Bible. The War went on an extra year into '17 only so as Flash could finally finish readin it.

Whatzit about? she asked in her regular voice but Fos said *shesh!* behind the camera. *You gotta whisper while he's fishin—*

A swarm of dragonflies was breaking up the light above the water into a series of discontinuous images like the ones that used to skip through old-time movies.

Water sure is dirty, Opal whispered.

She turned to Flash in time to see him lift the lid off a tin and root around in it with one hand. At first she thought the tin held macaroni like the kind Mrs. Rinaldi bought by the bagful from the Sicilian grocer but when Flash drew one of the macaronies out and laced it on a hook she could see it wriggle. Darwin says it was water much the same as this, he told her, where the origin of species and life on earth began.

Charles Darwin?

That's the one, he smiled.

Well just you don't forget that you could take all the water in the world, Fos argued, forgetting to keep his voice down, but without that single electrical discharge from the atmosphere at the crucial moment you an' Mister D. an' me an' Ope an' all the panda bears in China would still be formless zeroes in the never never. Even Darwin tellsya that.

Opal turned so she wasn't looking straight into the tin of maggots and asked, What kinda 'lectrical discharge?

Flash dropped the line and settled back and said, Any spark could do the trick. All it takes is one. Right ingredients, right combination—presto. Just enough to start the engine.

You mean like on a Ford? Opal asked. I don't know if I believe that, she deliberated.

He got it right, Fos insisted. A single cell, a bolt of lightning, one jolt of e-lectricity an' sheezam you got yourself some Life on earth.

Well I don't know, Opal pondered. I'd like to think the you know origin of species is more mysterious—somethin like a miracle—than just the engine of a Ford. But if there is that kinda stuff in this here river I, for one, ain't joinin an assembly line waitin to be part of it.

To prove her point she pulled away from the gunwales, gathering her dress in a secure sheath round her legs.

Following his own thoughts Fos said, I would truly like to get me an electric eel, and at that very moment snapped the picture they would subsequently come to call *Flash—with Evidence of Moby.* It was a picture which would fascinate—no, haunt—Lightfoot as a young man because it was obvious it had been taken in a boat from a weird angle somewhere near the prow. At the stern, in sharpest focus, sits a gaunt man with a dark distracted look, staring at the water. Behind him swarm dark insects etched like biplanes against a curdled background which might be sky or might be water. In the foreground completely out of focus looms a foggy spectre with a faintly enigmatic smile. *Moby-Dick,* Fos would halfway try to scarify Lightfoot into believing, *The Whale,* but Lightfoot knew it was his mother. Fos's talent for producing accidental images of scatty genius when he was called upon to take a photograph of his own family was without compare. The work he did professionally was foursquare and faultless, lit with insight and compassion, framed with an eye for line and balance. But when it came to taking photographs of Opal or taking pictures of himself and Lightfoot or of the places they had visited, time and again he produced pictures which might have been taken by a creature with nonhuman eyes, a creature with one eye on top of its head or multiple eyeballs on sticks. Sometimes, accidentally, parts would be in focus, crisp as a rain-refreshed white-clapboard barn in a shaft of pure light—and those focused parts would tease Lightfoot the way that three notes from a song or the first letter of somebody's name can suggest the lost part without ever filling its dimensions. All of them—except for the photographs Fos took of the night sky, which looked uniformly black to Lightfoot; or the photographs he took of bioluminescence in the sea, which looked uniformly milky—seemed wrapped in mystery as if an encoding layer had been imposed between them and the viewer which needed peeling like the shell of a boiled egg. Each captured a place or a moment of heartbreaking solitude. Or so

Lightfoot thought. Who is this? he would ask, transfixed by the man in a picture in the back of a boat. That's Uncle Flash, he'd be told.

Is he fishing?

In the picture, he is.

Can he take me fishing?

No son. He can't.

Can he come and visit so we can take him fishing with us?

No son. He can't do that either.

Uncle Flash was a regular feature in photographs from those years—or some part of him was. A well-muscled torso in a bathing costume behind a fuzzy globular presence which was either Fos's thumb on the lens or Opal's face too close to focus. A dashing dark-haired man in a striped shirt on a blanket on a rock in a river with the nose of a blimp intruding from the left-hand side of the picture which might have been the camera strap flapping into the field of focus or Opal in a wide-brimmed straw hat. Somebody, probably Opal, made sure every photograph had a date, and a word or two of explanation. Lightfoot would never find any photograph of Uncle Flash—or even some parts of him—dated after 1929, but he liked to look at the handsome young man, as handsome as anyone in magazines or in movies. The picture of him that Lightfoot liked the best, because it showed him smiling, was one taken on the rock in the river. It was dated August 1922 with no added word of explanation. Earlier that month, as he'd done the previous August, Fos had loaded up the truck with camping gear to drive across the two states to the Outer Banks to record the effects of the Perseid meteor shower on the incidence of bioluminescence in the Atlantic during the full moon. The full moon that year was at 11:19 A.M. Eastern Standard Time on the Monday morning, August 7, rising at 6:28 P.M. the evening before. Fos figured it would take three days to drive there at a leisurely pace but he hadn't counted on the same foul weather he'd experienced last time. This time it was worse. He and Opal left Knoxville at daybreak Wednesday the 2nd just as the Rinaldis were placing the first loaves in the oven, they hit rain that afternoon, and didn't turn down the sodden sand track that led to Opal's childhood home until early Sunday evening. Even in daylight, Conway had a lantern lit in the front window to guide them in through the gale and he grappled forward toward them in the downpour with another lamp when he heard the truck pull up before the house. Since Opal's marriage the year before, he had been living alone for the first time in thirty years. Pitchy out there, ain't it? he nearly shouted, shaking the rain off as he peeled out of his waterproof. Once he was free of it Opal saw that solitary living was no tonic for his constitution.

Oh Pa, she barely breathed, trying to disguise her worry.

Let me seeya little girl, turn all around, he ordered and led her through a pirouette. Stepping back, assessing both of them, he asked Any news?

Opal blushed and smoothed her dress down in the front, affecting nonchalance and told him, Not yet Pa.

For the last eleven months she'd watched a given day dawn on the calendar. You hold your breath awhile, she'd learned, and wait to see what happens. Then you figure better luck next time. Better luck this month, next month. Anticipation doesn't die so much as start to be a state of being, like a tic that can't relax. It hadn't changed the way they loved. But it made some moments of shared tenderness between them seem more freighted with their silence; weightier; more pregnant.

Looking to change the subject, Opal noted a collection of glass bottles on the mantelpiece and said, I see you're back to blowin long necks.

You know I always liked those long-neck bottles, Conway was telling Fos. I like the shape. I gotta lotta pleasure outta turnin them again this year. That tall one there, why don't you have it, Fos? I made it with that Paris green you give me—but what am I thinkin? Holyer horses you two—don't go anywheres. I madeja somethin, he announced and bolted from the room.

On the mantel was a tan envelope propped against two of the bottles, serious enough to look official, with a raised seal in the upper lefthand corner. The addressee's name was typed in black, all capitals, as was the address. Fos wiped down his specs so he could read it then asked Opal, Who's 'Alma White'?

Momma, Opal told him.

Conway came back into the room with a melon crate packed with crumpled newspaper. Anniversary present, he said proudly, and from the paper Opal unfolded two long-stemmed tulip goblets of the most delicately colored glass she'd ever known her father to produce—diamond-like, with amber hues tinged with pinks of dawn. *Lordie,* she breathed.

They're *opal*-colored, Fos admired.

It's a pattern called Commemorative Cup, I saw it in a catalogue and copied it. Go on, there's more, Conway urged her, there's another in there for the little one.

Sure enough there was, a dram blown from the same prismatic glass like a hollowed egg. Fos wondered how a man with bearshaped mitts could commit an act of such fragile artistry and he looked away, over toward the long-necked bottles, so he could wipe a tear unnoticed.

Opal gave Conway a hug then said, What's that envelope addressed to momma?

Beats me, never opened it.

Whyja never open it?

Weren't addressed to me. Figured if it was anything important someone would show up in person, but no one ever did.

When did it come?

Sometime last winter. You'd already gone.

Opal took it from the mantelpiece and opened it and read the contents while wind juddered the shingles and the rain clattered on the roof. She handed it to Fos and didn't move again until he'd let out a low whistle. Then she said, Pa what's in the envelope is notification of deed registration from the Land Office over in Clinch County, Tennessee. Seems momma's inherited some bit of farm. A house, Opal explained. And—how many acres, Fos?

One hundred forty-four.

That's a lotta land, Conway mused. Fer a dead woman. Well looks like now it's yers.

You think so?

Oh land is one thing always follows bloodlines, Conway said with certainty. You're her only heir, I don't reckon anyone could argue diff'rent. I got her whattheycallit certificate somewheres and you got your birth papers you just used down at the courthouse last year when you was married—

Pa, slow down. Anything of momma's is still half yours.

You're the only thing of momma's still half mine. And now you're half his, too, he said, looking toward his son-in-law. We are talkin about *land* here, li'l darlin, *farmin* land most likely. *Foreign* farmin land—in Tennessee, what the devilsass could I do with a hundred somethin acres of foreign farmin land in Tennessee—?

Well you could farm it, she said feebly.

And give up my career as King of Carolina?

They stayed with Conway six days, sleeping in Opal's former room—six hurricane-in-the-making days occluding into nights of baffling cover with no stars, no moon. Fos stood at the ocean's edge anyway and stared into the sea the way one stares into lost opportunity. He borrowed a lighterboat from a man who'd known his father, took it out a couple times and came back with shrimp and bass and blues that Conway smoked above the embers of the glory hole. And then they left.

I hope you just remember that I marriedya before I knew you were an heiress, Fos told her on the journey back.

I ain't happy with the way Pa looks, Opal said.

What's the matter with the way he looks?

He's lookin scruffy, doncha think?

Conway's got a scruffy job, Fos said. Opal saw him look down at his own soft hands palm up in his lap and flex his fingers. Then he looked at her to see if she had noticed, then he looked back out the window at the sorghum and the fields of indistinguishable silage.

They passed a gray barn standing in the middle of a field, seemingly deserted.

I know what you're thinkin, Opal told him. You and me are thinkin the same thing. That you and me were not cut out to do a life of farmin.

Fos reached over and stroked her arm with his soft hand. Who knows what we're cut out to do, he wondered.

Two weeks later over the last weekend in August, when all the agricultural fairs were up and they were going out to one of them in Harriman in Clinch County anyway, Fos and Opal took a drive to the Clinch River to have a look at her inheritance. She'd gone down to the State Office of Deeds and Land Registry in Knoxville to effect the transfer and pay whatever taxes were entailed and the speed with which the conveyancing was transacted had impressed her. I'da thought I'd hafta be in here for *days,* she told the lady clerking at the Registry.

Oh no ma'm not fer land. Not in Tennessee. Land passes *fast* in this part of the State.

Why is that?

The deeds and titles lady looked at her like she was stupid.

Whyja think?

Opal took a while to think about it.

Well not . . . not land speculation, that's fer sure that ol' river does nothin but *flood.* So land around it ain't that solid. As a thing t' speculate upon. It ain't certain. *Is* it?

What in life is certain?

Well *somethin* must be, Opal hoped.

Then on the morning they were leaving for the visit to Clinch River, Fos was downstairs in the bakery filling up the Thermos flasks with coffee when Opal discovered that her body was still certain, still predictable, two days earlier than the calendar. Even though she tried to take the evidence in stride, her usual tic of optimism didn't kick in as it usually did—*we'll try again next month.* This time the advertising slogan for the future sounded a sad note of disappointment. This time she felt lied to. Sold short. When she went downstairs and slid behind the steering wheel and started Mr. Ford's trusty engine with its trusty random spark she didn't mention anything about the calendar, the time of month or certainty to Fos.

Three hours later the sun had yet to reach its apogee but the immobile air sat on the valley like a laying hen. Tennessee is basically a washboard, valleys between ridges running north to south with three broad scrub basins through which the runoff from the mountains and the overflow from all the streams and tributaries drain. Floods along the valley floor are seasonal, scouring the emaciated dirt off the balding land. Cotton had chewed the fat out of the soil a long time ago and in some places what was left was so thin on the ground that plowing it was useless. But the land Opal had inherited had topsoil which Opal's mother's father had started to replenish with enlightened management back in the days before the

Civil War, before George Washington Carver proved why it's better to farm yams and goobers than King Cotton. Since Opal's grandfather's death, Opal's Uncle Earl, her mother's only sibling, had been farming it and when he died, his son, Earl Junior, took over. When Opal's grandmother died, Alma and Earl Junior were left half of 288 acres each. Earl Junior got the better half, the higher and more fertile land that had the family home on it. Alma's—now Opal's—was the lower half, the acres on the Clinch, and the sorry house on it was a decrepit two-room dirt-floor number built to house a sharecropper. There hadn't been a sharecropper on it for fifteen years and the house, if you could call it that, was overgrown with vetches and bindweed and inhabited by bats.

Opal had sent a telegram to Earl Junior, the cousin she had never met, who was responsible for farming what was now *her* land, to let him know who she was for one thing, and that she and her husband would be coming by the place that weekend. This oughta be an eye-opener, she said as they came within sight of what had to be the house Earl Junior had inherited according to the map she'd gotten at the Registry. The truck sent up a float of chalky dust and Opal slowed then finally stopped some distance from the house so as not to scatter a cloud over their arrival. The house was nothing much to look at, held together by expediency and whatever timber was to hand. Scrap metal was the chosen form of decoration and the barren ground around the house was littered with it. Two mules were chewing through the broken fence for lunch and some scrawny hens were picking through the mule dung for wood splinters and undigested chaff. A whisper of a girl was working a hand pump by a lean-to where garbage was burning and she came toward them through the waves of heat in her bare feet over flat parched earth.

Hidy, she called.

Hidy, Fos called back, going toward her.

Opal didn't move from where she was.

Yawl th' kin from Noxvul?

Howja guess? Fos said, getting in the swing of things to compensate for Opal's silence. I'm Ray Foster and this here's Opal, Alma's daughter.

Opal was standing by the truck looking at the girl, who couldn't have been older than sixteen. She was all bone and chapped skin about as tall as

Opal was and she was carrying a child in her as high and tight and firm as a prize melon.

We gotyer tellygram. Boy carried it out here on Tuesdie all the way from Harriman. First time anybody ever got a tellygram out here. Got Earl godly excited.

She wiped her hands in the hem of her thin dress before she offered to shake hands with them and then said, Call me Karo like the syrup. I'm Earl Junior's wife. Junior's cuttin feed but I can take ye where ye'll find him if ye wanta.

Opal had clasped the girl's thin hand with both of hers and wasn't letting go.

Karo, she said.

Fos thought her eyes looked funny. And she was talking different.

I see you're gonna have a baby, she finally said.

Oh this—heck yes. Caint waita see my toes some day agin.

The way you'd lift your hands if you were going to make a blessing on a crowd if you were pope, the way you'd summon prayer in public if you were Christ's appointed emissary was the gesture Opal made, Fos thought. He watched as her hands came up and she held them there palms out in front her, as if holding out a tiny earth, an unseen world. *May I—?* she said to his amazement, and before Karo could answer, with that annunciating gesture he had only ever seen in paintings on church walls in France—Gabriel's gesture when he brings the news to unsuspecting but expectant Mary—Opal held an unseen life between her palms in an angel's silent penitential laying on of hands.

Throughout the whole of '23 and well into spring planting time in '24, Opal vacillated over what to do with so much land. She talked to Fos about it nearly every day until he threw his hands up and declared Embargo. She talked to Flash about it who said, Sink a cashcrop in it pronto, dit, and get someone to pull your money up in tractorloads come harvest.

I got somebody farmin it already.

A cousin, dit. A *southern* cousin. You know what we think of southern cousins. And anyway, lima beans are not a cashcrop. Does anybody even know what lima beans are *for?*

She talked to Conway about it when they went out to see him for the

Perseid shower at the full moon in August. She sent off for guidelines from the Department of Agriculture and went to Grange meetings and she took notes and collected seed samples from the agricultural fairs that she and Fos attended with the x-ray machine and the new set of lumen tricks and light phenomena Fos had developed. She kept the books for him and Flash and started reading novels Flash encouraged her to borrow from his shelves, which helped to keep her occupied those winter evenings while Fos played with the static electricity he'd captured in a Leyden jar or snapped tongues of buzzing brightness that flickered like a lion tamer's whip between two points of current he rigged up on the little table in their rented room. She listened to the radio and went out to the picture shows every other week with Fos. She played music on the phonograph Flash had given to them as a wedding present, but she didn't like the lonesome sounds her jugs made anymore so she stopped trying to make music through them. Even when she filled them partway up with water for the halftones, it was their emptiness that sang and not their fullness. From the vacuums in the Leyden jars Fos used in his experiments she saw how vehemently nature hates an empty space. Emptiness is nature's strong attractor, she learned as Fos showed her how vacuums attract. She watched the fields of energy subtend between voltaic cells, she watched the way the stars fell through vast distances in patterns of attraction. She learned that attractive force resides in every form of matter, latent, waiting for the single spark to fire it with life. The world itself was lighting up, becoming brighter than it had ever been since the astonishment of its creation. She could see the lights of Knoxville from thirty miles away. At the county fairs and agriculture shows there was so much light and surplus energy in the air that it set the hairs along her arms on end, she could taste it in her teeth and hear it crackle. Batteries and generators worked at maximum capacity to juice the rides and Ferris wheels, to pop the popcorn fry the fat heat the griddles and simulate daylight in the canvas tents. The air conveyed attraction as if paths of movement and direction were laid out like trolley systems along unseen rails and cables.

Seemingly with no conscious motive she found herself drawn more than once to the edges of the tents where there was a different source of powerful attraction—the hucksterism of gospellers and evangelicals, footbathers and berserkers, Bible salesmen, healers, layers-on of hands and snakeoil salesmen, roustabouts and selfmade prophets, exhorters, raisers of the dead, dead levelers. The revelers. The *drama* of salvation. She'd stand on summer nights outside these tents and halfway listen to the preachers preach, it didn't matter what the message was—the message was the same each time—people came to watch the message being *sold.* The events a tent invites, the alibis and cover stories that a tent invents were as attractive as any force in nature, Opal came to realize, as magnetic as any other, every other, vacuum. The preachers raised their healing hands like magnets and the people came, lined up like iron filings to have their pain relieved their cataracts dissolved their sight restored. Fos would sometimes ask her, Whatcha thinkin? on the rides home from these events, and once she said she was thinking about how dark a place the world had been a hundred years ago. Once she said she was thinking about whether or not there was electric power in a human being that could be controlled by something else, like a light switch on and off. Once she was dead honest and said she was thinking about whether or not they were ever going to have a child.

It had been their third anniversary the week before and they'd just come back to Tennessee from their yearly trip out to the Outer Banks for the full moon in the Perseid shower, which had occurred on August 14. The calendar was due to tell them whether or not Opal was pregnant on August 22 and when that Friday came and went without the monthly sign she found, despite her doubts, her hope was rising. *You look happy,* Fos mentioned as they closed the shop at five for the weekend.

Where's the traveling ditto circus off to this weekend? Flash said as they stood together in the half-deserted street. I got a date with Moby in the morning if you want to witness it for history. And Fos, if you say Call me Ishmael again you're gonna fry. No offense, dit, but your husband isn't funny.

Fos was *very* funny, funny-looking at least, bobbing in the water near the canoe next morning for sticklebacks and elvers in his blue-and-white-striped bathing costume and his gas mask with the rubber hose stuck in his mouth. Jesus it's Jumbo the elephant, Flash remarked. He was jigging only half-heartedly. The "Trial of the Century" of the self-confessed teenage murderers Nathan Leopold and Richard Loeb was drawing to a close in a courtroom in Chicago. Clarence Darrow, their attorney, had delivered his twelve-hour closing argument the day before and Saturday's *Knoxville Journal* had printed the entire speech. I can't get enough of this, Flash confessed, arriving at the boathouse that morning with his bait, his line, and three copies of the paper. Now he sat with his pole rigged to the gunwale, the line drifting unattended, while he read to Opal from the newspaper spread across his knees. I love this man, I swear, dit, I'd give up women altogether for a night with Clarence Darrow, listen to this: I quote: 'Kill them? Will that prevent other senseless boys or other vicious men or vicious women from killing? No! I know that any mother might be the mother of a little Bobby Franks, who left his home and went to his school, and who never came back. I know that any mother might be the mother of Richard Loeb and Nathan Leopold, just the same. The trouble is this, that if she is the mother of a Nathan Leopold or of a Richard Loeb, she has to ask herself the question, How came my children to be what they are? Was I the bearer of the seed that brings them to death? Any mother might be the mother of any of them. No one knows what will be the fate of the child he gets or the child she bears; the fate of the child is the last thing they consider. This weary old world goes on, begetting, with birth and with living and death; and all of it is blind from the beginning to the end. I do not know what it was that made these boys do this mad act, but I do know there is a reason for it. I know they did not beget themselves.' . . . The man's a genius! Hey, Jumbo—! Send some fish this way, willya—?

Though she'd never tried before in all her times out on the river Opal had decided to give jigging a go that day. She brought along a bag of baits which she was trying to keep on her hook, but they kept falling off. It sounds to me, she said, tossing yet another piece of ruined bait into the water, all that Mr. Darrow's doin is attemptin to shift blame. That takes a bulldozer, not genius.

Flash looked at her. So you think we're justified as a society to let these boys fry on the electric chair, is that what you're saying? Because they've already confessed, Darrow's only trying to keep them alive, he's not trying to keep them out of jail. All this particular part of his argument says—and godknows he went on for twelve hours so this is just one minor part of a complex argument—is that any society which kills its own citizens as a form of retributive 'justice' is a flawed society, maybe even a sick one. Having trouble there, dit? he asked her, smiling. What the hell are those things?

Spud macaronis. Try one, they're tasty. Mrs. Rinaldi makes them, they're called knocky.

—*gnocchi,* Flash said, correctingly tongueing the *gn* and hooking one for her.

I guess my problem is I don't see how it serves a purpose blamin those boys' mothers, she said, lowering her line into the water.

Well he goes on, listen to this. I quote: 'I know, Your Honor, that every atom of life in all this universe is bound up together. I know that a pebble cannot be thrown into the ocean without disturbing every drop of water in the sea. I know that every life is inextricably mixed and woven with every other life. I know that every influence, conscious and unconscious, acts and reacts on every living organism, and that no one can fix the blame. I know that all life is a series of infinite chances, which sometimes result one way and sometimes another. I have not the infinite wisdom that can fathom it, neither has any other human brain. But I do know that in back of it is a power that made it, that power alone can tell, and if there is no power, then it is an *infinite chance'*—emphasis mine, dit—'which man cannot solve . . .'

—*o lordie* Opal breathed as her pole curved toward the current, line pulled taut. O lordie no—

Lean into it, dit—that's my girl! Now reel! Reel up, easy, keep on leaning, that's right, reel again—jesus christ dit look at this! God bless Al Capone, even fish prefer Italian, I swear! Fish are so . . . they're so *mysterious!*

She was chastened by the colors, by the intricacy of its beauty, its power to struggle for its life. It was a panfish, a roach about ten inches long and it lay there with its rhythmical gills, its eye locked on her face as Flash drew the hook from its mouth without drawing blood. He was laughing and shaking his head, calling to Fos, god*dam!* Fish are *so* mysterious! and Fos was splashing over to them, making strange conversational sounds through his hose. Less than a minute in air and the colors looked duller, she saw, thinking of her own clockwork life, its gill flapping was slower, eye fixed, mouth rigid, light was leaving its surface, retreating, knitting its fishheart into a miniature fist, fleeing the scales and the bones and the fishmeat, rushing into the vacuum of death. Opal reached down and laid her hands on either side of its pumping flesh and felt its life pulse through her palms.

Fos was hanging on the boat, peeling off his mask.

What are you doing, dit? Flash said, working to steady them. She'd nearly tipped them just then leaning over too far setting the fish free under the water, back into its living realm while Fos clambered aboard soaking the papers. *Mercy,* he gasped. What's all the *excitement—?*

That day and the next and the day after that she thought she was pregnant, her certainty increasing with each hour. For the first time in her life, for those three days she thought of herself a different way. She thought of herself as becoming an untested version of Opal, a mothering one. The sun rose and the sun set and she thought about the words of Clarence Darrow Flash had read to her, about the weary old world going on with lordknows how many babies born every day every hour even every minute. Like so many dittos. And she knew while she waited, Loeb's and Leopold's mothers were waiting, too, waiting for another sort of certainty, another sort of sentencing, another verdict.

Two weeks later, on the day that the verdict was delivered, Opal was with Fos at the agricultural fair in Harriman, near the Clinch River. It was the largest fair they'd been to all that summer, almost double in the number of folks who'd gone last year. The number of exhibitors was down, reflecting a general drop in the country's farm prices, but the number of amusement and carnival attractions was way up—reflecting, Fos speculated, that people were spending money frivolously not because they had more money to spend on foolish entertainment but because they wanted to be entertained more foolishly regardless of the price they'd have to pay. They'd begun to notice even the poorest-looking people turning up at these large fairs—some looking for work, perhaps, some for handouts, some for trouble, some for the unknown, some for Jesus or His local version. Fos had been aware of Opal's change of mood when she'd discovered ten days earlier that she wasn't pregnant and he was determined, in his gentle way, to help her take her mind off it, enjoy herself. She was quieter than he had ever known her and maybe that was normal for what she must be feeling. But he was hoping he could get her interested again in the new crop samples for the land or some new farm equipment—something, a new hobby, anything but what was obviously still preoccupying her. She was standing by the truck, nose in the newspaper, reading about the murder trial, when he put down what he was doing and said, Come on, let's take a walk. Let's take a look around.

But doncha hafta—?

We don't hafta anything. Come on. The two of us are always working. Let's enjoy ourselves at one of these-here doodahs for a change. Get us some barbecue or some fried chicken, go look at the prize heifers, taste ourselves some blue ribbon jam and see the bearded lady—

She could see what he was trying so she folded up the paper and said, All right. They're gonna let those two boys go to prison and live ya know, she mentioned.

If you call a life in prison livin.

Better'n bein put to death.

Well that decision will make Flash happy.

—it'll make their *mommas* happy, she reminded him. And I don't even wanta think what the mother of that boy they killed is thinkin of tonight.

They were making their way toward the center of the fair behind some flatbeds with electric dynamos and generators on them, and there were cables running on the ground all over.

Careful where you step, Fos cautioned. Somebody oughta say somethin about this mess, they've let this get into a tangle somethin awful—

They cut between two trucks to make their way to clearer ground and found themselves beside a trailer selling fresh-spun cotton candy.

Doncha dare, Opal warned, you'll end up with a bellyache and spoil your supper, but he told her sorry, Ope. I gotta.

They were standing there, pink filaments of sugar spiraling around the curve inside the drum in front of them when Fos looked over Opal's shoulder and said, Why look, there's whatzername, that girl, Earl Junior 's wife. Opal turned around and saw Karo coming toward them through the crowd looking just the way she'd looked two years before, when they'd seen her last—*exactly* as she'd looked, only this time as well as being pregnant she was carrying a towhead toddler on her hip. *Hidy!* she called to them. What yawl doin way outcheer—?

The toddler twisted in her arms to see who she was talking to and something seemed to fall out of his mouth onto the ground. He swung around, confused, attempting to retrieve it then kicked his mother, fussing. Hesh up, Early—*hesh,* Karo said and moved him to her other hip.

Well my goodness, Opal said. Karo. Look at you. And who's this little bundle?

This is Earl the third—Early for short. Don't mind his fussin he's jest teethin.

The toddler bawled and took a swing at Fos's cotton candy.

But just look at you, Opal couldn't help from saying. With another on the way.

Is Earl Junior. with you? Fos asked. He didn't like the way Opal was staring at the two-year-old. It would sure be great to catch up with him, wouldn't it, Opal? he said, trying hard to change the subject.

He's runnin in the plowin contest later, Karo told him.

She put Early down to quiet him, keeping a tight hold on his hand. The boy gathered his mother's hem into his free fist and put the bottom button of her dress into his mouth and started gumming it. Karo got the button from his mouth and let go of him to rearrange herself and the boy took off with uneven steps over the beaten ground.

It's the mule pull over yonder where those bright lights are, Karo was saying. Starts at six—ifya want I'll walkya over to where Jr. and the mules are getting hitched an' we can get a seat together in the bleachers.

She turned and then they all three turned together to look toward the toddling child.

All life, Fos would consider later, is a series of chance points, connecting in curves. When Early stopped in front of the flatbed beside the cotton candy machine to look at the small object on the ground at his feet there were still infinite chances at play in his life—as many as ever. When he leaned down and picked up the object there were as many chances at play as ever, minus the previous one. All this Fos thought of only later. How the binding curve of fate plots its course. But as Early plotted the next point on his curve, Fos only watched. He watched as the teething boy shook the object in his fist, not even realizing that at that very moment his chances still rolled with the clatter of infinite dice.

There was only one chance left out of all his chances at play at that moment—only one, which would be irreversible.

—*now what's he got holda?* Karo was asking as Early looked at the black plastic knob on the end of the cable.

Still there were infinite chances at play.

Until Early chose the only one that was finite.

He put the plug end of the electric cable in his mouth. To teethe on.

It took three-tenths of a second for the thousand volts in the electrical cable to hit Early's heart through his gums, astonishing it with a power so strong it lit him up like a light bulb, his whole little body excited as atoms in wire as the charged force sent him flying, shocked, seventeen feet high into the air.

And he fixed there, christ-like in his station, as time seemed to stop with his body's momentum.

All three of them knew he was going to start falling.

Karo started to scream.

Fos started running.

Despite herself, Opal started to count.

Like the points on a graph.

Plotting his curve. One two three.

Then for a reason that probably saved her she closed her eyes. And couldn't help thinking. *Too many fish in the sea.*

Consider, once more, the universal cannibalism of the sea . . .

HERMAN MELVILLE, *Moby-Dick,* "Brit"

the curve of binding energy (3)

Fish are so mysterious.

Some are quick and some are silver.

Some are lights inside the glasshouse of the river.

Some are dull as bark.

Some are thick-skinned as the ocean sharks, arcing like harpoons in hunger.

Some are dark.

Some are pikes who hang like uncharged ions before lightning strikes.

Some are minnows. Some are carp.

Some are born to prey on others, some are small as winnowed grain. Some, like comet dust, are stunning only in vast numbers, when they're raining.

Some are mirrored, some are dun.

Some are rustic.

Some have eyes on stalks.

Some aspire to the sea, designed to catapult their bodies toward their suicidal spawn.

Some are meek and some are triggered.

Some are known to seek the depths of cold profundity.

Some navigate by stars.

Some are drawn upstream by water's chemical aroma, some seduced by magnetism.

Some are compassless, possessed by lassitude.

Some are fat, with fins like feathers; some have spinnakers and spurs.

Some are plumed and some are sketchy. Some are fossils. Some are etched. Some are mere suggestions of the never seen. All are captives of the river. Packets of cold blood.

Like the dead, Fos thought.

From where he stood on the bare hill beside the open grave the earth was powdery and he could see the river, the color of a split log, down below.

He was standing on the upper side of the dug grave—Opal and the dead boy's family on the other side, staring down into the open earth. The river was behind them. Opal's face was hidden by the funeral hat that she'd put on that morning. Temperature was eighty-eight at daybreak, but Opal put it on before she went downstairs and got behind the wheel inside the truck. Four hour drive, Fos mentioned, thinking maybe that would carry all the meaning he needed to communicate to her about the hat. It was navy blue and made of felt and fit her like those hats that Pilgrim ladies wear in oldtime paintings. She'd put it on before they'd left and hadn't spoken since, as if her personality had vanished in it. And now the sun was acting like a flatiron.

In Tennessee, along the river, within the limits of the flood plain, the coffins of the dead are known to surface on the flood, rising with the waters like fish eggs, packets of ancestral spawn. The Tennessee at flood is a graverobber, voracious as a vulture in its talent to pick bones. In spring and autumn at the flood along the Tennessee souls rise as fast as griddlecakes only to sink again into the mire farther down the river. Along the Tennessee the dead, like landed gentry, seek high ground—the hills belong to mansions and to mausoleums. If the Tennessee were infinite, Fos found himself considering while the preacher told them all God's children find eternal life in Heaven, then the Tennessee would be like Paradise, souls floating there forever. Except, of course, Fos thought, for all the fish.

Unlike what Fos expected people thought of when they thought of

Heaven, the Tennessee was full of fish. And unlike what people thought of when they thought of Heaven, the Tennessee was a place that ends in time. Unlike Heaven, every river starts somewhere, and stops. Even every ocean stops, somewhere, Fos was thinking. Because the quantity of water is a finite. Like the span of someone's life. There's a quantity of life each person gets to live, and when that quantity's expended, well then, that person stops. A river or an ocean, all the water you can find on earth—all these things and peoples' lives—are finite, Fos was thinking. Unlike love.

Wherever love comes from, whatever is its genesis, it isn't like a quantity of gold or diamonds, even water, in the earth—a fixed quantity, Fos thought. You can't use up love, deplete it at its source. Love exists beyond fixed limits, beyond what you can see or count. It isn't something measurable, something you can say okay, this is love from here to here. But if you take that river down there, Fos was thinking, you know darn well despite the tricks it plays to make you think it's something that can last forever, that river can flood only up to a finite point. Even if you took all the water in the atmosphere, all the water vapor in the clouds, all the ice, the fog and mist and frail evaporates and fat humidity above the belt of the equator and fed them through a mangle, wrung the weather out, twisted the whole sky like a dishrag until it wept, the tears that it would shed in the form of rain would uniformly flood the planet with only one inch of water. One inch in Death Valley, one inch on the Andes, one inch over the Pacific. You could squeeze until the canopy of heaven ran dry, but that is all you'd get. An inch. All the water that we have on earth and in the molten core and in the atmosphere is all the water that there is. It goes up off the land and off the oceans and the lakes in waves of expiration then it sheds itself on earth again. Since time, this planetary time, began, Fos thought. He shifted in the heat. Yellow talc—part dirt, part pollen—lifted from the earth, sifting down onto his newly polished shoes.

What do people think about at funerals? he wondered.

You take this kid we're burying—what are we supposed to think about a child who dies that young?

All morning he'd been wondering what to think, trying to imagine who the boy had been, who the boy had talked to in his own thoughts, what his thoughts had sounded like within his own imagination at an age before his thoughts had words. All the way out here on the drive from Knoxville in the company of the wall of silence emanating from beneath Opal's hat, Fos had tried to reckon with the dead boy, out of respect, but his thoughts kept slipping off to other things. Even now, with the preacher and his bat-wing ears and shiny suit and Adam's apple bobbing on his collar as he tried to guide the group tour through the halls of righteous contemplation, Fos's thoughts were straying from the heard. Maybe he should be ashamed he couldn't think about the child in any way that captured his attention—his thoughts kept rolling down the sunbaked hill to the torpid river, yellow in the distance like washed silk, like the yellow pollen on his shoes. Maybe he was guilty of a lack of rectitude for wondering about the lives of fishes at such a solemn moment, but how could he not? All those fishes down there in the river in the water where you couldn't see them, swimming round living out their lives feeding mating giving birth and dying—if you think about that river as a limit of existence then you start to think about the water of that river and all the waters on the earth and in earth's atmosphere, and then you have to think about those sums of water and they are a limit of existence, too, how all of us are as limited in our native element, captives in our glasshouse atmosphere, as the fish are in the Tennessee. Just as the realization that all of life swims suspended in a thin-skinned bubble in the vastness of the universe began to overwhelm him, Fos saw something fall on Opal's shoe across the open grave from him. For an instant—less than that—something falling through the air caught a ray of light and interrupted the unbroken stillness with a flash against the ochre background. Fos blinked, thinking maybe he was seeing something that wasn't there, that his eyes were playing tricks on him under the grilling sun. But then he saw the glint of a reflection on the top of Opal's shoe. It was a drop of water. A drop no bigger than an appleseed had fallen from the cloudless sky, been caught by Opal's shoe and flattened to a clear refractional lozenge. As Fos watched, it quivered in a tiny pool, sensing Opal's pulse, then sinuously formed itself into a nozzle and dripped onto the barren earth. Fos looked from face to face to see if anyone was watching him, then threw his head back and stared up at the sky. When he looked at Opal's shoe again another drop had fallen there.

He blinked again.

Although he knew it was impossible, Fos saw Opal's face reflected in the silvery drop atop her shoe—not as she had been that morning, standing with the blue hat in her hands and a look of vacant sadness in her eyes—not as she was now, her face unseen beneath the hat, but as she'd been the first time he had ever seen her in another bubble, that other radiant sphere that her father was creating into glass. In another trick of light or mind, he saw not only Opal's face reflected but the scope of her whole being, the way she stood and walked and talked and hugged her arms around her body when she wasn't sure of what might happen next. The way she laughed, the way a smile played on her face, the way her lips moved when she spoke, the dedicated way she had of sitting stock still, staring, as a part of how she listened. His eyes began to search upward from her shoes, her swollen ankles, her white calves, the hem of her crepe funeral dress. His gaze flicked over her clasped hands, her pale forearms, the bodice of her dress. He tried to find the place where her heart was beating, with his eyes he followed the ascending slope of her shoulders to a vein inside her neck and then merely from the angle of her chin, her face still hidden, forehead bent, he could see that drops of water were not falling from the sky: He saw his wife was crying.

What had happened to her in so short a time that made her seem more like a widow than a bride—what had happened to the two of them? Just this morning, dressing, he had realized that the last time he had worn this suit was on the day they'd married—in a blink he'd gone from getting dressed up for his wedding to getting dressed to go to a child's funeral and he couldn't even get the fly done anymore without pulling in his stomach, holding in his breath.

People started to step back a bit from the open grave and Fos realized the moment had arrived for the coffin to be lowered. Earl Junior took one end of the rope in his bloated hands and someone held the other end toward Fos. Fos hesitated and for the first time since the graveside service had begun Opal raised her face and looked at him, her eyes instructing him. He took the rope and looked over at Earl Junior. On his look they balanced the box between them on the rope and Fos felt the button on his waistband go. The coffin, at once heavy and unreasonably light, swung a little, an abbreviated pendulum, then steadied like a cradle in the drop. Fos let go of his end of the rope and, like a fisher hauling in an empty net, Earl Junior pulled his up and stood there, dumbfounded by his fruitless fateful luck. He wore that expression Fos had come to recognize in certain kinds of people of an iron reserve who never cry. They end up looking like they've cried too much.

Fos watched people file to where Earl and Karo stood before they filtered off across the field—he watched their shadows, crowlike and foreshortened under the high sun. When it came Fos's turn to say something he was grateful Earl spoke first. *God's way,* he levied. Fos took his glasses off and made to clean them with his tie as a way of speculating. It wuz what God wanted, Karo said. It must be why He had us call him Earl Lee—*Early.* 'Cuz 'at's th' way he's wint.

Fos twisted his wire specs behind his ears and took his jacket off and took up the second shovel and helped Earl close the grave while Opal kept her head bowed down and Karo watched, her palms spread on the child inside her belly.

The earth, when they had finished, was the color of old newspaper.

When they tamped it gently with the curved backs of the shovels, smoothing it to make it flat, a little cloud of dust arose.

When it settled there was nothing left for them to do.

Still not speaking, Opal started toward the road where they had parked the truck but Fos caught up with her and touched her arm and told her, Come with me, and took off for the river.

Opal watched him go. In a while she called out, Where ya goin? When he didn't answer her she followed and caught up with him beside a willow tree rooted by the silky listless river.

The tree seemed tired, old but graceful, as full of gesture, vertically, as oriental writing on a scroll. Even in the stanching heat all its leaves were green and vigorous as ice. Fos made an entrance for them through its curtain. The only sounds were muted, coming from the river's unseen currents. What are ya doin? Opal finally asked. Whydja bring us all the way down here?

Fos followed her between the parted branches, the leaves scattering a silver light over a hundred mirrored planes. The branches formed a dome around them almost twelve feet in diameter. Fos walked to its farthest side then turned to face her. Light undulated over her, transmitting coded messages across her skin as if ships far out at sea were signaling. Take the damn fool hat off for godsake, Fos finally said.

Opal shrank.

What areya so angry fer?

Fos gently peeled the felt cloche off her head with one hand and ran his other over her damp hair. She looked like she'd been swimming.

What's the matter withya? Opal said.

Her forehead pinched up where her eyebrows should have been.

Fos tried for words but everything he thought to say melted on his tongue like the soul of an intention inside a Eucharist.

Why ya been so quiet all this mornin? he finally managed to say.

Quiet, whadja mean?

Ever since you put the hat on.

It's a funeral hat. We were buryin a child. I don't think you oughta get too talkative when you're buryin a child.

Fos took a breath. He had to ask her.

Whose child did you imagine you were buryin out here today?

Opal's eyes went wide.

What are you accusin me of, Fos?

He tried to take her in his arms but Opal pressed him back.

Don't break my heart here darlin, he finally begged. Don't tell me what we have together ain't enough.

He ran his fingers up the frets of her spine until he found the little hollow in her neck beneath her hairline, then he eased her head against his chest and held her there.

He could hear the river.

It's not like I'm unhappy with us, Fos, she finally tried to explain.

It's just I look around and see these other women. I start to think there must be something wrong with me.

Nothin in the world is wrong with you.

I blame myself.

—for what?

You know what I mean.

I think you better say it, Opal.

It took her a while.

Her voice, always on the breathy side, almost disappeared completely when she finally told him she was afraid they might never have a child.

Well, he said. Listen. Somehow I put it in your head about us havin us a baby far too soon. Truth is we got loadsa time for that. Bushels of it.

Still she clung to some idea all her own. I hafta hope, she told him.

I know you do.

You gotta let me hope.

Fos nodded.

Promise me, he said.

He could see some sparkle come back to her eyes.

Two things, he elaborated.

He drew an imaginary eyebrow on her forehead.

Promise me you won't let all your hoping take the place of all our love.

—and second?

After all the time I spent in trenches, I don't wanta end up in the ground. Promise me you'll never let 'em land me there.

Bad luck to talk such things, she told him. Still, on his look, she promised with a slight nod of her head.

Two days later Fos followed Flash around the shop that way he had when he was trying to engage with something unseen in the ether.

What's the problem, buck-o? Flash was forced to ask.

Well you know those prophylactics that they handed to us back in boot camp?

Flash leaned against a wall and lit a cigarette.

I'm acquainted with them, he relinquished.

Well I put one on one time, Fos confessed.

Flash bit himself to keep from grinning.

It was a struggle, Fos elaborated.

Flash encouraged further headlines by pretending stoicism.

Even though, in Fos's case, wild horses would have made no difference.

And now me an' Opal, Fos announced. We're havin trouble havin babies.

You're serious, Flash ascertained.

Oh yeah we definitely wanta have 'em, Fos verified.

About the rubber, Flash retraced.

Oh yeah.

Fos shook his head.

You don't forget a thing like that, he marveled.

—you used one *once,* Flash certified.

Fos shook his head. No I didn't use it. I just put it on.

You put it on.

Fos nodded.

—*once,* Flash verified.

Like I said. It was a struggle.

Flash could only just imagine.

And by some lone mutant of sophisticated logic you intuit these two entirely cosmically unrelated episodes in the epic of your plot-filled life have some causal connection, do you Watson? On the evidence, I mean.

Fos blinked.

Well let me tellya, pilgrim, Flash conspired with him. When your cat crawls in the oven to give birth, it don't mean those kittens come out biscuits. Understand?

From the look of it Flash could see Fos didn't.

It's not a circumcision, Fos, it ain't a lifetime thing. You use a prophylactic once, it's over. Jesus. Every joe on earth but you is worried sick the damn thing *hasn't* worked. Relax, willya? Read a book about it. Get yourself examined. You trust science, doncha? Have the thing looked at by a pro.

There were times, Fos thought, when, as a human being or a friend, Flash exhibited the delicate compassion of a stoat. But other times, in particular with women, the man could make the troupe of christian saints seem like a trope for grifting truants. Leaving work that evening Flash casually invited Fos to fish with him the coming weekend. Knowing full well Ope would tag along.

Oblique as dawn's first rays, he took a stab when they were alone in the boat to ask Opal how things were. In general, he suggested.

Same, she said.

—how was the funeral?

How *wuz* it?

Lots of people?

Well the deceased hadn't hada lotta time t' make a lotta friends, she told him. An' county folk ain't long on pomp.

You in a bad mood over somethin, ditto?

—*nope.*

Anything you wanta talk about, especially?

Whydja ask?

No reason. You fishin today or merely dreamin?

She stared at him, not taking kindly to this line of questioning.

Because if you ever need to talk to anybody about anything you know I have a high threshold for tolerating other peoples' misery, Flash said. Not that I think you're miserable. But if you were.

Fos's said somethin to ya, hasn't he.

No ma'm. Fos and I hardly ever speak. I haven't heard from Fos for decades—

Either from the sun or from some other source of energy Opal's face had gone bright pink.

All I'm saying is if you ever need advice, this is my backyard. Not only just this here river the whole stinking town. I grew up here. I know a lotta people. 'Case you ever need to talk to a professional. You know. Doctor. Lawyer. Indian chief. *Doctor,* he said again.

Opal turned her face from him and stared at something in the bottom of the boat.

I don't think you need to see a doctor yet, dit, but if the situation ever—

You're one t' talk. I can think of plenty reasons you could use a doctor's help.

If you're talking about drinking, madam, under the current law of Prohibition I consider my inebriation as my striking an heroic blow for individual freedom—

Against big government.

—precisely.

She shot a smile his way, regaining her composure.

You still have family here?

Is this a change of subject, dit? Or do you always think of family—*daddy,* and the like—when you think of government?

Family here? Or not.

Family here, he said without committal.

He settled back, began to fish.

She tilted her head and said, I've never thought of you as someone with a family.

Everybody's got a family. So I've heard.

Only child?

If only.

Brothers?

If you call a snake a brother.

Sisters?

Regretfully not.

Mother?—father?

Rumor has it they're alive.

Where are they?

—*where?*

How come we never see them?

Oh you see them, baby sister. All the time.

They were drifting in a pool, outside the river's major channels under the marble cliff near Dickson Island. The fishing this far upstream in the wake of the effluent waste of the American Limestone and Southern State Asphalt mills was dire, but Fos had pleaded for a chance to try and bag an electric eel near the mouth of one of the industrial outflow drains. Leaving him to chance, Flash rowed the boat into the channel until the skein of Knoxville's skyline unwound above them. Downstream, a freight train bearing blocks of marble stalled and hissed above the river on the trestle bridge, scaring up the shore birds from the blinds. Even on a Sunday there was evidence of industry among the smokestacks in the foreground, making the church steeples in the inner precincts seem cold and unproductive by comparison. A church bell sounded from somewhere up on Summit Hill and Flash shipped the oars and pointed toward the heights. Two houses—mansions, by all standards—dominated the summit above the others. One was Blount Mansion, home of the first governor of Tennessee, said to be the finest Greek Revival house in all the South. But the smaller of the two was the one that people talked about. To it, Flash pointed and said, Home sweet home.

To let him know she was nobody's fool she bunched her fist and hit him. Get off't, she said.

God strooth. Son of a Son of the Confederacy. Scion of a Scion of the South.

But that's the Luttrell place, she argued, blushing in the face of the admission that she knew it. Observing habits of the wealthy, like building zoos, was on the rise in small municipalities across the nation, not only in Knoxville. Still, Opal was a latecomer to the game—the rich, as a spectator sport, hadn't existed where she came from except from afar, at, the movies and in books. Growing up she'd had firsthand encounters with tenant farmers, with working people, with coloreds, poor whites, and the entrenched middle class who seemed to be in charge of her part of North Carolina—the schools, the agricultural co-ops, the shrimp fleet, the party lines, the local Ford franchise, and the sheriff's department. The wealthy were elsewhere. Not until she came to Knoxville did she glimpse inside the self-aggrandizing hall of mirrors of enriched materiality. Hill Avenue, a broad street climbing grandly up to Summit Hill, was lined with the biggest private houses she had ever seen, some with handblown glass in all their windows, she had noticed, being a connoisseur of at least that much. She knew, she could tell, that class distinctions were being drawn, being played out around her in Knoxville that she was unskilled at recognizing. She knew for example that the color line was more strictly enforced in town than in the countryside. No white sat down with a Negro in a public place in Knoxville—not in the street or on a curb or in a jitney or a trolley or a wagon or at a lunch counter or in church. Negroes in Knoxville had their own schools their own religion their own neighborhoods their own ways of living. Their own things. Their own haberdashers, icemen, profiteers, photographers. Negroes never came off the street to sit for their portraits in Fos's and Flash's establishment; their picture men were down by the water on Front Street or over the bridges in South Knoxville in the warren of alleys behind Blount and Servier. Only three percent of the population of Tennessee was ever what the people of Knoxville would call *furiners* and these were mostly Lithuanian and Polish pitmen from the bitumen lodes of Europe who cut Tennessee coal and Italians from Carrera who polished Knoxville's twenty different kinds of fine-grained marble. Several years ago at the request of the Rinaldis Fos had rigged a generator up to light the light bulbs in the Virgin's halo for the feast of the Assumption at Saint Anthony's Catholic Church and since then there had been a steady trade of Italian wedding, Polish baptism, and Lithuanian first communion clients through the shop. Methodically she kept a book of cuttings of all the photographs that Fos and Flash had taken for the *Knoxville Journal*'s society and wedding pages—and methodically she'd noticed that people up to a certain social level came to them to have their pictures taken and then the business stopped. "Society," it seemed, went elsewhere to record its life—they sat, rendered dyspeptic and reptilian, for the "society" picture taker, one Mr. Percy Polk, the ex-President's great-nephew once removed. Up to that moment Opal had found the posturing and posing for society according to society's rules arcane—like the rules for playing Mah-Jongg or quoits—something she wasn't very interested in. Only now she heard herself, surprisingly, ask Flash, For godsake just how black a black sheep are you?

Black as night. The blackest knight.

What did you do?

What did I do? What *didn't* I, ditto. I didn't *do* what was expected of me. I didn't do what was expected of me so well that not doing it became what was expected of me. I became an expert. I excelled at it. Still do. You might even say that it's my only genius.

Why would a family—all the people in "society"—up and turn their backs on one of their own, do you think? Opal mused to Fos that night.

Sounds to me like Flash up and turned his back on *them.*

Well did he ever mention it before?

Nope.

—never?

First time I knew Flash had any money of his own was when you found it in the books.

Why would he make a secret of it?

Sounds to me he is ashamed a' them.

Well I don't believe he oughta keep it secret. His own family life or who his family is.

But family *is* a secret, darlin. That's what family *is.* A secret. From the world.

A few days later, under one of those mid-September noons that throw no shadows, Opal was at the shop door looking for a bit of breeze when a caravan of bunting-festooned automobiles turned the corner at the river end of Locust Street and started heading in her direction, a recording of a marching band playing scratchily from a loudspeaker mounted on the rumble seat of the Chevy at the forefront. GALLAGHER!! an otherworldly voice was shouting through a megaphone. *Come shake the hand of Candidate Lowell Gallagher—the next Supervisor of Knox County! Come and meet your man!*

The noise drew Fos and Flash from the back room. What's all the rumpus? Fos asked, peering through his specs.

It's the *go go go with Gallaghers,* Opal apperceived.

God why doesn't someone build a bear pit and let them go at it unseen somewhere far away? Flash wished.

Coolidge wouldn't go, Fos told him. As a bear, Calvin Coolidge is in hibernation.

As *a man* Coolidge is in hibernation, Flash reclassified.

Well well well Flash murmured, lighting up a cigarette and looking down the street at the approaching bandwagon. *Don't fate just always love the fearless.* Know that poem, dit?

Opal only knew but three poems, that was all, by heart. And two of them were nursery rhymes.

"Fate loves the fearless," Flash began to quote. "Fools, when their roof tree falls, think it Doomsday. *Firm stands the sky.*" This should be interesting, he said and went inside.

Coming toward her at an alarming pace was a pack of people—men—all teeth, all shiny with sweat, all in straw hats and starched shirts with stiff collars, all bearing down on her to get the only thing about her they had any interest in, the only thing she had that made her worth the teeth the smile the eye contact the pressing of the flesh, the word, the nod, the wink—her *vote.* Her hand was clasped and wrung as if she were a saint dispensing sulfa to the lepers and a man with very very neat teeth breathing peppermint said, Bet you're pleased as punch to finally have the vote now aren't you *young woman?*

He thought he was doing her a favor, she could tell, by calling her young woman. He thought he was flattering her, making *his little joke* because what with her white hair and all some people sometimes thought she was a very well preserved *old lady.*

These were stupid people.

No sooner had he finished speaking than he and his entourage tucked inside the shop. Well what have we here—? the candidate for Supervisor asked, looking around.

Progressives, Fos informed him. Mostly. Opal ain't decided yet.

Well I'm Lowell Gallagher and I'm running for County Supervisor. I'm here to ask for your vote, it's that important to me. This-here is Tay Luttrell, my runnin mate for the office of District Attorney.

Opal watched the candidate for Supervisor reach for Fos's hand, shake it, then turn effortlessly along the counter, like a person looking over plates of food along a buffet table. Then she saw his eyes flick from Flash to the face of the young man in the straw boater standing next to him.

If you bent the mirror, Opal saw, Flash and the man in the straw boater could be twins.

Tay, Flash reluctantly acknowledged.

Chance, his brother seconded.

I pass this place most ever'day, candidate Gallagher was saying, looking round at all the pictures. I didn't know you were behind it, Chance.

Yes you did, Flash answered. Don't try to con me, Lowell.

Well you take a mighty pretty picture. I gotta have Mrs. Gallagher bring our Lally in to have her picture took by you.

Lally—is that your dog? We don't do dogs. We don't do politicians either.

Gallagher turned to Fos and told him nice to meetcha. You'll be seein

Mrs. Gallagher real soon. And good-bye to you, *young woman.* Don't you be too absent-minded to get out an' vote now come November.

He handed her a *go go go with Gallagher* banner and a button that said KEEP COOL WITH COOLIDGE and then he marched his parade on down the street.

You didn't ask him anything, Fos noticed. Three months you've been talkin back to politicians on the radio and now one comes and stands in fronta ya, how come you didn't ask him nothin?

Anybody who mistakes me fer a old woman doesn't rate to have his brain picked. She looked at Flash. And I suppose from now on we won't need the radio for entertainment when we can have our own right here in the store thanks to you.

Oh I'd keep my faith in radio if I were you, dit. When it comes to entertainment I might let you down.

Least I can *see* you.

What you see ain't always what you get.

What I get ain't nearly what I feel entitled to, she told him, he thought, a tad too frostily.

In a world where people get what they're entitled to, ditto, what would you need me to say to you right now?

Opal stretched the *go go go with Gallagher* banner out in front of her without realizing what she was doing. I think just explain yourself, she said. I think you have that responsibility to us—to Fos. To say what you can't say to no one else. About yourself.

What do you want me to explain?

Well for one thing, Flash, your *brother* was just in here—callin you another name. Fos an' me wouldn't even know you had a brother in this town if I wasn't such a, such a—

—*old woman?* Flash volunteered.

Really it ain't any of our business, Fos put in.

Except when people turn up and start to call you by another name, Opal countered.

I changed my name when I enlisted.

Okay, Fos said as if that were enough.

No it *ain't* okay. One thing to give yourself a nickname. Call yourself 'Flash' instead of—what was it?

Chance.

Now there's a stretch.

I changed my name from Chance to Charles. 'Flash' came with the job they gave me in the service.

Well whydja change your last name, too?

I took my mother's maiden name—Handy.

Okay, Fos said again.

He nodded.

That makes sense, he added hopefully.

But *how come?* Opal seemed to need to know.

Flash shrugged. I don't much like the family, dit. Nor the family name.

So you went off to war.

I did—off to war as young Charles Handy—soon to be rechristened 'Flash.'

—and then you came back home.

—*alive,* to everyone's amazement.

To Tennessee.

Uh huh.

To Knoxville.

Yep.

Instead of—

—instead Paris, Rome, or Timbuctu? Is that the problem, dit?

In a word. Yeah. Sorta.

Granny, Flash explained. He rubbed his thumb against his fingertips like he was peeling greenbacks from a stack of bills. Stay in Knoxville, Granny wrote. Last will and testament. Conditions to inherit, thus: Set up a business. That was Granny's honeytrap. As long as I stay here, keep a business going, the money keeps on rolling in. Run it at a loss, run up debts—it doesn't matter—just keep up the pretense of a businessman. And the money keeps on coming, that bank draft every month. Nothing to lose by stayin here in Knoxville—everything to gain. A prisoner of my own dependencies. And this whole thing, this setup of a 'photographic' studio was a *joke*—I did this as a *joke.* A way of getting my inheritance. Until the two of you waltzed in.

Fos blinked. And now—?

And now I'm actually enjoying myself.

Enjoyin yourself, Opal repeated.

She started to fold the *go go go with Gallagher* banner into a tidy shape.

How come the only things you do are prompted by your own enjoyment?

Maybe 'cause I'm human.

Mebbe cuz you're *spoiled.*

Fos got that look he got when chemistry experiments began to go all wrong but Flash put him at his ease by saying *Spoiled—?* You bet. My point, exactly. What's a poor boy like me to do since I was *born* that way—?

Why doncha do like your Mister Darwin says low creatures are supposed t' do?

—*low* creatures?

I'm sorry, I didn't mean—

—you mean put a little social Darwinism to the test and make myself *evolve?*

I didn't mean t' callya 'low.'

Well I'm trying like the devil to evolve a halo just for you, Flash told them, flicking his burning cigarette through the open door. But, just like you, I've got a basic unfulfilled requirement so far in life. If I'm ever going to *evolve,* he said, pointedly, Opal thought, to her—I need *a future generation.*

Ouch, she breathed.

Ditto, he said and sauntered toward the sunlight out the door.

Through that same door, five days later, Opal saw a thing she'd never seen before—a chauffeur-driven car arriving at the shop in Locust Street.

It was a brand-new '24 Big Six Speedster Studebaker in white with an ivory canvas top, and as she watched it stop, she started thinking to herself she might just ask the chauffeur, if he had a moment, could he let her have a gander at those jewels beneath the hood.

But as she neared the threshold of the open door she saw the chauffeur get out and adjust his hat and tug his jacket smooth across his belly and go round to the other side. He must be awful hot, she thought, assessing his getup. She watched him open the rear door, and a figure in pale blue stepped out and opened up a parasol. As she came toward her Opal couldn't help but notice she was wearing opaque stockings. And she smelled like bluegrass after rain.

Inside the shop the woman closed the parasol and looked around. Hello, she finally said to Opal in a voice that needed bending toward in order to be heard. I'm Mrs. Gallagher.

Oh yeah the candidate's wife. He said he'd send you by. I'm Opal. That's some car you got.

The woman tilted her head.

She was wearing gloves in all this heat and a pale blue hat to match her dress. And you could only see the outlines of her features under the cloud of blue organza, not so much a veil as a disguising curtain.

What's it like t' drive?

I beg your pardon?

—how's it handle? Heavy?

She had the sense the woman must be staring at her hard.

—your *car,* she prompted.

Still, the woman seemed to stare.

I've never asked, she finally answered.

Her dress was long-sleeved, too, and even though it seemed as light as air it dawned on Opal then and there that there was something scary in the way the woman chose to dress. Or had to.

So what can we do for you today, Mrs. Gallagher?

Lowell has it in his mind that you should do a portrait. He was most impressed by what he saw the day he came to visit.

Visit? Opal thought. She tapped her fingers on the counter. What kinda 'portrait'?

That would be at your discretion, I suppose. The pose. Something Lowell could feature in his office.

Look I gotta tellya, Opal said, leaning on the counter. Regardless what you think you're doin here ain't none of us is gonna vote for Mr. Gallagher. Specially not me, not after how I saw he treated Flash.

Opal saw the outline of the woman's lips part through the veil.

—Flash?

So mebbe you should think again about this 'portrait'.

I'm sorry, I don't think you understand me.

Well *I'm* sorry you don't think I do.

—perhaps there's someone else that I could speak to?

Opal motioned toward the door.

City full.

The woman took a step toward Opal, placing the furled parasol between them on the countertop.

A half an inch of skin showed below the blue sleeves and the tops of the white gloves.

Pink and marbled as raw meat.

You're entitled to your own opinion, but in spite of what you think Mr. Gallagher does not 'buy' votes. Mr. Gallagher and I would like a portrait of our daughter and if you'd be so kind as to allow me to address someone with whom I might arrange a sitting—

What happened to your arms?

The woman pulled her hands back from the counter.

Were you in some kinda fire?

Opal saw immediately her whole body must be that way. Her whole face.

Lally—that's our daughter, the woman said, fussing with her gloves—is away at school. She's—well, she's very rare. She needs looking after. When you see her you will understand. She's *special.*

By which Opal understood her to mean 'burned.'

She's here at home with us in Knoxville only on the weekends. Would you have an opening on Saturday?

Fos an' I are workin the State Fair the next two Saturdays. How 'bout in three weeks' time? That way you an' Mr. Gallagher have time t' change your minds.

Mrs. Gallagher seemed to nod but Opal wasn't sure. She stood there. Should I give you money? she finally asked.

We ain't done nothin forya yet.

Should she dress a certain way?

Does she *need* to?

I beg your pardon?

Opal realized her mistake and asked, How old is she?

She's just turned eleven.

Well what do just-turned-elevens wear?

Frowns in my experience. Should we agree on ten o'clock?

Sure. That way we'll agree on *somethin.*

At the door the woman paused to open up her parasol.

And I'll find out about the Studebaker for you, she told Opal in her whisper before parting with what might have been a smile.

Three weeks later, on the Saturday that Lally Gallagher was due to sit for Fos, the Studebaker came down Locust Street with all the weight and circumstance of a circus elephant leading a procession. It parked before the shop and sat there while a figure in the back seat appeared to have a discussion with the chauffeur. Then the chauffeur got out as he'd done before, pulled his cap down, smoothed his jacket, and opened the rear door for his passenger.

It was a morning graced with that October light that loves proximity to water, and the high sky over the Tennessee bounced the river's shimmer back through every cranny in the city.

Someone across the street was sweeping yellow leaves into the gutter and the mailman who had just dropped off the morning mail with Opal was sorting through his bag outside the shop. Without looking up he turned to hold the shop door open for the figure moving toward him. But then as Lally entered and he saw her face, he stared.

Inside, Opal passed the mail to Fos, getting herself ready for the Gallaghers.

Instead, this lonely figure appeared in the doorway.

—well *hello,* Opal said, so overcome by what she saw that she underwent a rush of strong emotion and had to bring her fingers to her lips to hold it in.

Before her stood a girl her own height—tall for anyone that young by any standard, but of a line so straight and graceful she seemed bound together by a force far more celestial and attractive than mere gravity.

There was nothing openly suggestive of a mature woman about her body—but in her face the full force of feminine beauty radiated its incomparable expression, and Opal didn't know whether her own strong emotion in response to this young girl was the simple relief to see she was not disfigured like her mother or the more complex and unexpected shock of beholding unadulterated beauty in a fellow human being.

You must be Lally, Opal said behind her fingers.

Are you the woman with white hair?

Well I guess I am.

Mother said to wait until we stopped out front to ask about the Studebaker so I wouldn't forget and then go in and tell the answers to the woman with white hair.

Where is 'Mother' by the way?

Don't you want to know about the Studebaker?

Well I do but I also want to know if your mother's—

Something in the child's look made Opal stop and bring her fingers to her lips again.

—do you have the *hiccups?*

—no.

—then why have you covered your mouth? Mother always says to cover my mouth whenever I get hiccups.

Opal labored toward composure and said why doncha come on in, Lally, so we can all get started. Lally's such a pretty name. I don't think I've ever known a 'Lally' before you. It suits you.

I don't like it. I don't think it suits me at all. I'd rather have a name that is something. Like 'Skylark' or 'Daisy'.

My name is somethin. It's Opal.

Lally crossed the threshold and presented Opal with a slim cool hand. Pleased to meet you. Mother said you'd entertain me.

Oh well Mr. Foster is in charge of entertainment. Aren't you, Fos?

She led Lally into the space between the plate-glass window and shaded corner where an artificial backdrop was set up behind the horsehair davenport.

Fos was standing by the counter with a letter in his hand, blinking through his specs at it.

He looked up from it and Opal thought for sure the next words she was going to hear were that her father had just died.

But Fos said, *It's Karo.* And the infant. Both.

Opal didn't realize she had Lally's hand in hers until she reached to read the letter.

It's from the preacher who did Early's service. That Baptist one with the bowtie, Fos said.

He gazed distractedly at Lally while Opal read.

Our cousin has just passed away, he mentioned.

Oh.

Against the disarray she said my uncle passed away in San Francisco in September.

Then she added people seem to pass away in any month.

—true.

Are you the man who's going to take my picture?

—yes.

He waited for a sign from Opal.

Well we hafta go, she finally said. I think we hafta leave right now—Earl Junior's all alone, he must be in a sorry state.

Earl Junior is the dead one? Lally asked.

They looked at her.

No honey, Opal said. But now what are we gonna do with you?

You went and got all prettied up today for nothin.

Lally smiled.

Pretty is no bother, she confessed.

She gave them both a practiced look.

But pretty takes its price, Opal saw inside that look. Something had already been exacted from the girl's childhood. Not innocence, exactly, which still showed in Lally's eyes. It was in her timing, Opal saw. She had aged beyond her years by the knowledge she had gained from watching people look at her, seeing their reaction to a quality about her that was outside her control. She had learned to wait a little, hold back—see if the response was there. No *child* does that, children have a rate of speed that doesn't wait for anything and this girl had built-in pause, an acquired trait, a mechanism polished to reflect, as watchful and as needy as a mirror. The price the child had paid was what existed in that moment that she took to see if the response was still forthcoming. What existed in that moment, Opal saw by chance, was a blankness void of anything but terror.

And she saw it on the girl's face in the instant that Flash entered.

Then, seeing his reaction, like a pool of mercury reshaping, Lally's face, her sense of self, of her own beauty, recohered.

Hello she said, and offered him her little hand.

And for the life of her with everything that happened through the rest of all that day—their hurried departure, the long drive west into the sun—Opal never could recall for certain what Flash had said, what sound had come from him, whether he was funny cryptic mute or *entertaining* that October morning when, for the first time, he laid eyes on Lally Gallagher.

As Opal drove she kept looking over at Fos, sometimes saying I just can't get over it, and sometimes saying nothing. When a while went by without her speaking she'd reach over to him to assure him, I ain't goin quiet on ya, donja worry. I just can't get over it.

The letter had been sketchy but the best they could determine from its contents was that Karo had either died in childbirth or from malaria —*. . . she was taken by the fever and the gleets just while the child was being born . . .* — carrying the unborn infant with her to the grave an unknown number of days before.

What's the matter with that Earl he didn't get in touch with us first thing? Opal fussed out loud.

I don't think he thinks of us as proper family, Fos hypothesized. We kinda only ever show up for postmortems.

He should of written us himself.

Maybe Earl can't write.

The Earl they found was a husk of the man, already decreased by loss, who'd buried his first child little more than a month before. He was a big man whose only understanding of the narrative of life, its shape and substance, was made up entirely of the world he worked with his big hands, not his mind—the world he saw, the one he walked upon and cursed at, sowed and harvested and thanked and ate for supper. He lived a diet and a calendar of crop requirements: things beyond that, things he couldn't see and touch, may as well have been things from another planet. Beyond a farmer's natural cycle of fatality and hope, his struggle against soil and pestilence and unrepentant weather, there was no abstraction in Earl's life. Land ain't land less somethin comes of it Earl was finally able to tell Opal through his haze of incomprehension. Farmin without nobody to farm for, tho, won't be the same. Two mornings in a row he wandered out before day broke and Fos found him hours later standing in a field. Sometimes he'd climb onto the tractor, sit it, start it, and Fos would hear the engine chugging in the barn only to discover after fifteen minutes that it hadn't moved. It was soon apparent, even to two people who knew next to nothing about how to husband land, that in his present state Earl was no way fit to run the farm. Next season's crop was in, the fields cleared and turned before his tragedies befell him but, inexorably, the calendar rolled on and Earl, the man who could not grasp abstraction, had become one.

Calvin Coolidge, another abstract in a pair of pants, took the White House in a landslide on November 4, sweeping with him into office a full slate of Republicans in Tennessee, including Supervisor Gallagher. The days grew short, the nights grew longer, the carnivals pushed south or folded for the winter, and Fos used the hours after supper to practice his experiments on the marble-top table and peruse the chemistry and physics books he'd borrowed from the library while Opal read. She was following a course in reading dictated by Flash but every now and then she'd buy a novel at the drugstore on the basis of the man and woman on the cover and Fos would raise his eyebrows when she wriggled in her chair, engrossed in one of them. She seemed happier to him—a change that didn't happen overnight; but a softening occurred in Opal's attitude beginning with the news of Karo's death. Soon after, Fos had noticed, her record book, the one she counted out her days in, disappeared from where she kept it, a silent clock on the bedside table. She never said in so many words, why should we worry we don't have a baby yet when people who have children have to face the possibility of loss—but Fos knew that was the shape her logic took. She seemed to place her trust in what life still might have in store for her. She visibly relaxed. And wonderfully, Fos couldn't help but notice, even though it might have only been the fallout from the drugstore novels, she became—a word he toyed with, assiduously, through those lengthening evenings—*adorable.*

The autumn rains came late that year; so did the autumn floods. The bottomlands along the river disappeared, their substance liquefied like sunlight on a desert—less land, more mirage. Men who had put down the seed for clover, timothy, alfalfa, soybeans, sorghum, corn, and winter wheat watched their spring drown in autumn flood. Frost came behind the rain, and the resulting scene across the fields was a ponded desecration, frozen like a photograph of ruin, an upheaval painted with the hues of autumn which had bled to mud.

Fos was looking at this landscape from the front seat of the truck, his face against the glass, his breath fogging up the window. They were on their way to visit Earl out on the farm in the last week in November and every now and then—often enough to rile her nerves—Fos would sweep the window with his coatsleeve to wipe it clear of condensation until Opal finally told him, Fos I wouldn't mind the cold. Open up the window if you need t' look.

I'm doin an experiment, he said.

She was driving so she couldn't watch.

What's it about?

I don't know yet. *Time,* I think.

He wiped the glass again.

From the sound the truck was making, from the look of things, she tried to estimate their speed.

You mean you're clockin us? she asked, ready to participate.

No, he said real slowly, I think I'm clockin somethin else.

My life, he thought.

Outside, with the November landscape etched by flood, slow smoke skulking in the hollows around damp smoldering fires under an ashen sky—*it could be France in '17,* he thought. It could be War.

—it could be *what?* she said.

He hadn't even realized that he'd talked out loud.

Pull over.

—yeah I think I *oughta.*

He was acting strange enough.

Fos got out and Opal watched him tread across the seeping ground in city shoes. Fifty feet or so from where she sat he stopped and seemed to take his glasses off. She saw him coming down the street sometimes, moving among other people, but that wasn't the same as seeing him out here, in this way. Out here, he looked more lost than usual. More often than not Fos was lost in thought—and she was used to it, never knowing where his thoughts had led him, what he'd be saying next. But out here with the autumn mist rising off the slate-colored river and the sky so empty, he looked lost for words, or worse. He looked lost for meaning. He was standing straight—that was a thing about his looks that she was proud of—Fos stood straight, but now he had his legs apart, his fists clenched—like he was seeing something out there that was coming for him.

As she walked to him she could feel the cold air labor in her chest and she tried her best to find a sign in anything across that barren stretch that might offer up a clue about what he was staring at. This too—this exercise in trying to see things the way Fos saw them—was something she was used to. Something that she'd learned from love. To try to see through someone else's eyes.

There was no sign of man's invention in the landscape. No human intervention. A blighted peach tree orchard, all the peach trees down. Two mules standing in the orchard's ruin. Hummocks of mucky earth boiled up like a rash. Black and green debris, organic rotting matter. Frozen pools of groundwater, like coins, as bright as dimes.

She thought she'd wait for him to say what it was that was bothering him, instead of asking, and after she stood next to him a while he took her hand in his and she could feel its cold all up her arm.

How can one place and time seem so much like another one? he finally asked.

The way he asked it didn't leave her room to answer.

She looked at him then back at the river.

She looked over at the mules.

A chickenhawk flew over.

The way that mist is layin over there? Fos said and pointed. The gas clouds used to come that way. Only they'd be iridescent, kinda greenish—eerie. Not like anything you'd seen before. Not like ordinary vapor. Then you'd see these figures coming from the German trenches through the mist—men dressed like underwater divers. Big bells around their heads, huge. They looked like monsters. Generators three feet high on their backs blowin out the poison through these ordinary hoses. Iridescent, like I said. It would sorta snake around, the gas, and then it sorta gathered, like a thundercloud, like a curtain that you couldn't part—like that mist over there. Except that on the battlefield it was the air, the air was poison and there wasn't nothin you could do but get yourself inside a mask and pray to Jesus you were runnin from it in the right direction. I mean—*six years* ago for godsake. You'd think I could forget about it all by now. Then you come out here and you see this—

He slid his specs back on and drew her to his side.

This is what it looked like, he told her. He waved his arm over the flooded scene. It just shouldn't happen. This is a destruction of another sort but it's still destruction. Two thousand years after the Egyptians invented geometry to build their dykes and levees on the Nile you'd think we could come up with better science than to let these rivers run right over man. We should be better than all that by now. Our science should. Our engineering. It's like we haven't learned a thing for twenty centuries.

Well that's not true, she answered.

'Stead of using chemistry to make a poison gas, Fos went on, you'd think someone could find a way to stop a piddling river in the heart of Tennessee from overflowin. Killin everything it washes.

It's just a river, Fos. It ain't a dog or somethin like these mules you can domesticate. People here *expect* it's gonna flood just like people out on the Atlantic expect the hurricanes t' come. It's nature's way. You can't control it.

What if it was 'nature's way' t' make you sick with somethin there's a cure for are you sayin I don't have a moral obligation t' get you to a doctor?

A river ain't a human bein, Fos.

—no, it ain't, it ain't a human bein. It's *a thousand* human bein's. *Tens* of thousands. Lord you couldn't even have *a South* if it weren't for all its rivers. Every song you sing, every tale you tell has got a river in it—

Well don't yell at *me* I don't give a hilla beans about this river—

No. I see you don't, he said and stalked back to the truck.

Her hands were blue with cold and before she let the choke out and got the truck back on the road she turned to him and said I'd like to take this trip just once where one of us weren't riled and moody over somethin. You can't *fix* the world, Fos.

No, I know I can't.

He rubbed his hands to warm them.

An' that's what's gnawin on me.

It was pitch dark when they arrived, with not a single sign of life around the farm. There was no electricity that far out into the valley but there wasn't a flicker of paraffin or wood burning anywhere within the house as Opal pulled the truck up and lit the porch steps with the headlamps and gave a friendly hoot to herald their arrival while Fos lit a lantern and tried the door.

Inside it looked like no one lived there, ever.

The stove was cold, no wood was cut and the pump out back was frozen.

They found Earl Junior on a bed upstairs beneath a blanket staring at the wall.

Good lord, Opal murmured behind Fos. Is he—?

Whatcha doin up here, Earl? Fos asked, real chatty.

What day is it? Earl roused himself to ask.

What day do you remember it t' be?

Hog day.

Hog day it is, Earl. Now me an' Opal will be downstairs for the night and in the mornin you an' I will go out an' see how things are doin. Includin all the hogs. All right? You gonna be all right till then? You warm enough?

Earl rolled over on the bed and stared at Fos. What day is it tomorrow?

Saturday.

Earl nodded.

—*love day,* he acknowledged.

In the morning he was only barely more coherent. Fos had found a water pump behind the barn that worked and a store of coal in the cold cellar and Opal found some eggs and flour, saltback, and some coffee. Earl came down unwashed, unshaved, unbidden on the trail of bacon frying and Opal made him wash before she served him breakfast. What the devil has got inta you, she asked him. He was sitting with a Bible at his elbow. *Ecclesiastes,* he said.

Fos and Opal looked at one another.

In much wisdom is much grief, Earl told them. *And he who increases knowledge increases sorrow.*

Um *hmm,* Fos said. He watched and waited.

Opal fidgeted.

He who digs a pit will fall into it, Earl enlightened them. *A live dog is better than a dead lion.*

He fed himself a fork of eggs.

That's in Ecclesiastes, he informed them. As if they were in doubt.

Sounds like you've been readin, Fos observed.

All the rivers run into the sea, Earl recited.

> *Yet the sea is not full.*
> *That which has been is what will be,*
> *That which is done is what will be done.*
> *And there is nothin new under the sun.*

Well what the hay has that t' do with the price of local corn I'd liketa know, Opal chided him. 'All the rivers run inta the sea an' yet the sea ain't full'—?

I'm thinkin I should go away, Earl said. I got nothin left t' keep me here anymore. I'm thinkin I could be a fisherman.

—a *fisherman?*

Like Jesus.

Jesus was a *carpenter,* Opal reminded him.

I'd liketa take up fishin. I think there's healin in it. For my mind. Bein on a boat. Away from everythin.

Have you fished before? Fos asked him.

No.

Well you wouldn't have t' go nowhere t' take up fishin, Earl, Fos said. You could fish right out your window if you want. In that river right out there.

I'm thinkin I could go t' California.

If she'd been a hand grenade Opal would have popped her pin and detonated.

Cal-*ifornia?* What about the *farm?*

Well I'm thinkin I might sell my share.

—*sell?* To who?

To you.

Fos said have another cuppa coffee, Earl, and positioned himself between his wife and her ecclesiastic cousin.

He put his hand on Opal's arm to calm her.

How long have you been thinkin about this, Earl? he said.

Earl seemed not to remember.

The floods had taken out the full spring planting and Fos wondered if they hadn't been the straw that broke the camel's back. I don't think he's in any kinda shape t' be makin this decision, he whispered to Opal.

Well he ain't in any kinda shape t' run the farm so we got a problem either way.

You know with everything that's happened these past months, Fos said, I think he's in some kinda shock.

I think he ain't the *only* one.

I used t' see this kinda thing in boys with shellshock in the War. It was somethin terrible I'll tellya. Like their minds and brains were stolen. They'd just stand there mute and paralyzed. Some a' them couldn't move their arms the mental shock was so debilitatin—

Fos it doesn't help me t' have *two* men livin in the past—if the future's too much trouble forya try an' help me out at least by stayin in the present . . . *Earl!* she said loud enough to wake her cousin from his dream. She leaned across the table close up to his face. *Earl,* she told him, don't you be thinkin of takin off from here. Not with all your history in this land. Not with your whole family buried here. Think of Karo an' your little ones. They're all you got and they're right here.

Their souls has washed away in the last flood, Earl said.

—*what'd I tellya?* Fos insisted. *Shell shock.*

I can't run this place without you, Earl, Opal pressed. I can't buy your half. I don't know the first thing about farmin. An' without you runnin it this place ain't worth much anyway.

The house is, Earl put in.

The house is fallin down. It's hardly worth the thirty nails still holdin it together, she argued.

The land is still worth somethin, Earl insisted.

Not 'less it's sown, she told him.

Ol' man Lusk'll put down clover on it ferya ifya want. I talked t' him already. He wants t' run his herd on it.

Opal looked at Fos.

This ain't no shell shock talkin.

Lusk's the farm just up the road? Fos verified.

Earl nodded. He's lookin to increase his stock by fifty head. Herefords. If he can find another hundred fifty acres.

They drove over to Lusk's place that very morning and the difference in the farms opened Opal's eyes to how shabby her and Earl's smallholding was. Being that much farther from the river's curve Lusk's land was safe from flood and he had half in corn and sorghum, half in pasture. His outbuildings weren't fancy but at least they were still standing, and his house, though small, was newly painted, clean, and warm, and in the kitchen there was brand-new linoleum, an icebox, and an indoor water pump. But like farmers everywhere Lusk had no ready money. He was offering to lease Earl's and Opal's lands for ten percent of what the herd he kept there might bring in for the next season.

Fifty, Opal bartered.

Fifteen, Lusk returned.

Thirty-five's the lowest we could go, Opal advised him.

Twenty.

Opal made like she was leaving.

Thirty-five, Lusk said. Only 'cuz I hada soft spot for your momma.

Before they left Earl turned to Lusk and said I'm headin out t' see the ocean out in California in the mornin. Sunday. Sabbath. *Go-to-God day.*

They took him to the Baptist preacher's house before they went back to Knoxville so someone could look after him. Opal gave him all the money in her purse but still she wouldn't let him sell his half to her till Fos said he could sell it out from underneath you to a total stranger. If you want t' keep your momma's land—an' you ain't said it's that important t' you—then you oughta buy his half. We got the money. An' you can always give it back t' him when he gets better.

I wouldn't know what value t' put on it.

Well try an' think of somethin fair.

I wouldn't even know what's *fair* in this case, Fos.

"Fair" for Earl was money to last him out to California and in exchange for what Opal still thought was a pitiable small amount he signed the deed to her at Christmas.

Where his signature was called for he had drawn his mark. A fish.

On New Year's Day he disappeared, the preacher later wrote to her.

He left behind the money she had given him. As well as anything he'd ever seen and touched. And loved. Or owned.

For months thereafter Opal had the feeling he was going to turn up at her door in Knoxville unannounced but she didn't realize the extent to which his disappearance haunted her until the first weekend the next spring, when she and Fos and Flash went out in Flash's boat—*fishing*—for the first time that new season, on the river.

Well another year of romance between you an' Moby, heh? Fos taunted Flash.

Me 'n' Moby—*yup*. One man 'n' his Dick. Eternal love. Whatsa matter, ditto?

She was staring in the water, wondering if Earl had made it out to California. Wondering if he was even still alive.

I finished that *Other Side a' Paradise* you gave me t' read, she mentioned to Flash after a while. There was a lotta drink in it.

—*and?*

An' now I think I'm ready for the *moby* one.

Well there's a lot of 'drink' in 'Moby', too. It's where they all end up.

—except for Ishmael, Fos told her.

But it is about this man who goes off *fishin?* she needed to verify.

Why doncha read it and find out? Flash offered.

So she tried.

But what with the summer and its boiling weather coming on and those airless evenings and the lure of dimestore novels and the fairs and carnivals taking up her time on weekends with x-ray *phenomenology,* she had only read up to the part where the Indian harpooner whose name she couldn't say falls off the *Pequod* into a whale's head and nearly suffocates in all the muck in there when—starting on July 10—everybody in the state of Tennessee couldn't leave their radios for what was going on in their own backyard eighty miles from Knoxville in a little town called Dayton.

Opal hadn't known a thing about it till one morning at the start of June Flash came racing through the door like she'd never seen him all excited and proclaimed glory goddam hallelujiah, *Clarence Darrow's* on his way to town!

—to *Knoxville?—your* Clarence Darrow?

—not to Knoxville but damn *close*—down in Dayton, defending that schoolteacher—*Scopes*—in the Monkey Trial!

She didn't know what a monkey trial was but she said well Flash. You hafta go.

He stared out through the plate-glass window onto Locust Street where a line of cars was parked. Model Ts and Chevys mostly. Fos's truck and his own roadster. *Go?* he said as if she had just coined the word.

How many times in life can someone get to meet his hero? she urged.

It was the first and only time Flash kissed her.

He left for Dayton in his roadster Wednesday evening after work July 8 under what Fos reminded him was a waning gibbous moon *ninety one percent illuminated.* You better just be back in time for Ope an' me to go to Carolina in three weeks for the full moon in the meteor shower like we always do.

If I'm not back in three weeks, stalwart, you and Ope should *move* to Carolina.

Well ya never know, the way that Clarence Darrow talks that trial could last into the next millennium.

It didn't—it lasted only ten days, the final three so hot and humid that

Judge Raulston moved the proceedings outside under the shady willow oaks beside the Dayton Court House.

Opal listened to it on the radio.

At the start she didn't know which side was right. Men of no middling brilliance, really *smart* men like William Jennings Bryant for the prosecution, were convinced the theory known as Evolution was just that. A theory. Buncha hokum. And dangerous, at that. It undermined the Bible's own account of how the world was made and where man came from. Fos—and Clarence Darrow—stood behind the science, behind the *fact* of Evolution, but that was not the question weighing on her mind. She accepted evolution as a fact of life. The question was which version of Creation should be taught in schools financed with money from taxpayers' pockets. The State of Tennessee had passed a law that spring that said it was a crime to teach that nothing less than "the divine creation of mankind" was the only version of man's genesis on earth. You just can't see some place like France or England passin such a mule-brained law, can you? Fos had groused. Not even *Germany.*

The young teacher at the center of the controversy was as guilty as the day was long. Everybody knew he broke the law teaching Darwin's text in his science class in Dayton, but what Clarence Darrow was trying to put over on the local court was a test to make it legal to teach a version of mankind's creation different from the one depicted in the Bible and the judge was having none of *that.* The judge, from Fiery Gizzard, Tennessee, was not about to let the fancy lawyer from Chicago tell him how to run his court.

Seems like there's some resentment there between the two a' them, Fos observed, listening to the radio with her the evening of the third day of the trial. So much is goin on that ain't about the legal facts it's fascinatin. I feel we're peepin through a kinda keyhole, like we shouldn't oughta hear this stuff, Opal told him.

Good as any dimestore novel?

—*better,* she confessed. Then blushed.

Who's side areya takin?

I don't know. I really don't, she cautioned. Just because a law is bad don't mean you gotta right t' break it. That's the reason people give for drinkin despite Prohibition.

Darrow never loses, Fos tried to persuade her.

Doesn't mean he's *right,* she pointed out.

There was such a ruckus in the courtroom on the seventh day the sound stopped Fos and Opal where they were working in the shop and drew them to the back room where they stood and watched the radio as if the action was about to burst right from it. Someone had brought something into the courtroom and now Mr. Darrow was demanding the Court's attention to it. *Your Honor* (this was Darrow's voice): " . . . before you send for the jury, I think it my duty to make this motion. Off to the left of where the jury sits a little bit and about ten feet in front of them is a large sign about ten feet long reading 'Read Your Bible,' and a hand pointing to it. The word 'Bible' is in large letters, perhaps a foot and a half long, and the printing—"

" . . . hardly *that* long, Mr. Darrow . . ."

"I move that it be removed. Mr. Bryan says that the Bible and evolution conflict. Well, I do not know, I am for evolution, anyway. We might agree to get up a sign of equal size on the other side and in the same position reading *The Origin of Species* or 'Read Your Evolution.' This sign is not here for no purpose, and it can have no effect but to influence this case, and I read the Bible myself—more or less—and it is pretty good reading in places. But this case has been made, a case where it is to be the Bible or Evolution, and we have been informed by Mr. Bryan that a Tennessee jury who are not especially educated are better judges of the Bible than all the scholars in the world, and when they see that sign, it means to them their construction of the Bible. It is pretty obvious, it is not fair, your honor, and we object to it."

. . . There was a long silence from the bench during which Opal breathed *Lordie,* I don't think I'd ever have the courage to stand up an' talk to any judge that way!

"The issues in this case" (that was the judge's voice): " . . . as they have been finally determined by this court is whether or not it is unlawful in the State of Tennessee to teach that man descended from a lower order of an-

imals. If the presence of the sign irritates anyone, or if anyone thinks it might influence the jury in any way, I have no purpose except to give both sides a fair trial in this case. Feeling that way about it, I will let the sign come down. Let the jury be brought around . . ."

Opal gave a little whoop and did a tidy dance around her husband.

Does this mean you're takin *sides?* he smiled.

Two days after the trial ended, in the generous light of the fading sun, Flash drove ceremoniously up Market Street as people came out of the stores and swamped the roadster with requests to hear what it was like to be inside the courtroom. Didja get his autograph? Opal needed to find out.

Flash winked and said, *I got his picture.*

She held her hand up to her heart where it was causing some excitement in her chest. I think the trip did you a world'a good, she told him. You look diff'rent.

I *do—?*

She almost couldn't trust her eyes that he was blushing.

—different *how?*

He ran his fingers through his hair in a new gesture.

Well if you'll excuse the wrong expression, Opal tried explaining. But you look like you're *in love.*

Patent that, she challenged Fos that night in bed. The moon was waxing crescent, its lime light through the open window the only thing that seemed to move in the unmoving July air. If you could patent somethin like that as a tonic, she continued. She took a breath and blew it out to try and cool herself. You'd have people linin up. *Women,* anyway, she finally said.

Fos took up her hand and held it in the milky light.

The effect of hero-worship, Opal said. Put that in a bottle. Lord, I swear Flash looked a diff'rent person. Imagine seein someone who could make you feel that way.

I feel that way when I see you, Fos said.

In the moonlight he could just make out the bones beneath her skin and he began to trace them, recalling as he did how pale and insubstantial the bones had looked each time he had seen them in the x-ray.

But you *know* me.

Inside-out, he marveled, needing to press up to her despite the heat. He did that thing he does that lets her know what he is feeling. That thing he does, built into every man, which lord knows only has one meaning.

Opal went on talking.

He looked so . . . I don't know. Shiny. That way they do in movies.

Ope—

Brand-new.

He lay still, waiting for her fascination with Flash's shininess to tarnish. Waiting for a chance to try again. And as they lay there, Opal in her own world and he in his, a moth flew in the open window, drawn by, of all things, the otherworldly light of the phosphorus inside the fishbowl full of water on the table. The moth, one of those ghostly green tobacco moths with eyes as big as human eyes etched on its wings, beat against the fishbowl. Fos looked at it and recognized a common shared desire with the creature; recognized the frailty of those paper-thin wings that could be shredded in an instant, like man's longing.

It must have been an optical illusion but in the presence of the moth the phosphorus seemed brighter.

The moth beat against the outside of the bowl, then settled on the lip and shivered. Fos, we gotta stop the thing, Opal warned. Before it *jumps.*

In saying so, she finally turned to him, her weight against him in the heat. He began to stroke her. Sometimes I wake up when you're asleep, she whispered, an' I look over at the light inside the bowl an' I think it is the Virgin Mary.

The heat made being close and talking at the same time doubly strenuous.

I ain't never heard you mention her before, he managed. Nor nothin in the least religious.

Well ever since you made her halo outta light bulbs last year for the Catholics, she forced herself to say. You know. You can see how I might think it.

It's a rock.

I know but at night at certain times it has a face. The Virgin's face, like in pictures. And other times . . .

They watched the moth teeter on the lip, explore the inside of the bowl with its antennae.

—and other times? Fos asked, blowing lightly on her skin.

Other times I think it looks like Moby. You know. Flash's Moby. That ol' fish he's never caught.

Fos rolled onto his back and let out a stream of air.

It's kinda like a catfish or a whale, doncha think? Opal continued. Shinin all alone down there inside the water.

Fan me. I'm desperate for some breeze, Fos said.

Well maybe that's the reason, Opal rectified.

She fanned languidly with her whole arm. Not a breath of air reached Fos.

Maybe she was sent to fan you.

She.

The moth. Maybe she was sent in through the window there to stir up air for us.

Sent, Fos repeated. Who would send a moth?

Not so very diff'rent from an angel.

Very different from an angel.

It was one of those *giant* ones, Opal was explaining to the mailman the next morning. The two of them were standing on the sidewalk under the awning outside the shop. I've never seen a thing as big as it before, she told him.

How big *was* it? he seemed to need to know.

Like if you were holdin a magnolia blossom full in bloom.

She used her hands to demonstrate.

About as big as this, she said. Maybe it was one a' those giant butterflies you read about. You know. Whatchacallum.

Butterflies don't fly at night, the mailman told her.

Opal stared at him.

They *don't?*

It was something she had never thought about before.

No m'am, he verified. It's one thing that aids you in identifyin. That an' the fact that moths have feathery ends on their antennae. Whereas butterflies have club feet. You know, little knobs. When you look at them up close.

He seemed to be an expert on the subject. Which should have come as no surprise to Opal, but still. How come you know so much about moths? she asked him.

Hobby, he admitted.

Opal nodded, her gaze lifting from him over the street to the shop fronts on the other side. Directly across from them was Belks the dry-goods store and she knew for a fact that Martin Belk the owner made a hobby out of miniature plants. Next was Campbell's the watchmaker and Cleveland Campbell made a hobby out of digging up rare rocks. Lewis Buckhart, at the drugstore next to Campbell's, sanded down old porthole windows from the scrapyards out in Natchez to make ten- and twelve-inch telescopic lenses for his hobby of stargazing and was always after Opal to bring him any bottle bottoms, concave discards, her father might have on his glass heap by his furnace. Along this single block of Locust, alone, Opal could count up an amateur paleontologist, two sidewalk astronomers, an occasional botanist, one weekend ornithologist, a seasonal rock-hounder, an on-and-off steam-engine enthusiast, and a phenomonologist if you included Fos. It was not unusual to find your average shopkeeper with a dog-eared manual, gazette, or journal open on the counter by the cash register nor was she surprised when neighbor merchants dropped into the shop to consult a back copy of one of Fos's *Science News-Letters.* On those occasions, she noticed Fos would talk to them about some new thing Thomas Alva had been writing about in that week's *News-Letter,* or some phenomenon he had uncovered ("wave mechanics," "the numerical value of *h*") as if "Thomas Alva" was one of them, one of the county's avid amateur enthusiasts, instead of being Thomas Alva *Edison.* It was an age of passionate discovery for his generation, Fos would say to her. Not like the age of geographic exploration when individuals wagered their existence on the mapping of the seen, the known world. This was an age of general rapture with the unseen, with harnessing the unseen natural forces to man's will and his desires. It was an age of burgeoning belief in science as a structure, a place of worshipable icons, a cathedral. An age of hobbyists—of passionate, though part-time, scientists. For men, at least. Women of her generation were enthusiastic, too, in their pursuits. But those pursuits were yoked to responsibilities of hearth and home. Not to raising questions but to raising children.

And there's a difference in their wings at rest, the mailman was explaining. One of those facts of life between two species, he was telling her. Like how to tell between a sheep and goat from the different way they hold their tails—one up, one down. A moth will fold its wings behind itself when it's at rest. Just like a bird, he said.

In the bright light down the street Opal saw a big car round the corner.

Whereas a butterfly, the mailman kept on in his dissertation, will hold its wings straight up or out when it's at rest.

Opal raised her hand to block the sun so she could watch the large car as it came toward them.

So the wings, in relation to the body, the mailman said, look sorta like a sailboat. But both the species pupate.

Opal turned her head and looked at him.

I beg your pardon?

He could tell from her expression she was doubting his civility.

I ain't sure that that's a word that you're supposed t' say in public, she confided as the car approached. It was a Studebaker, she could tell, like the one belonging to County Supervisor Gallagher.

Why ain't I supposed t' say it? the mailman asked.

Well for one thing, Opal started to explain to him.

The Studebaker slowed and pulled up to the curb and stopped.

It sounds like somethin with a hidden meanin.

Pupate? the mailman asked in disbelief.

She could see there was a woman at the wheel.

But it's from the Latin word for *doll,* the mailman told her. Used specifically in referring to what happens to young butterflies and moths. The process they go through in their cocoons. When they change from larvae, hidden-like. In the cocoon. They change and then come out miraculously transformed. All beautiful. Mature. With wings.

Opal had stopped listening.

In the sunlight twenty feet in front of her from the front seat of the Studebaker, a tall young woman had emerged. Beautiful. Mature.

With wings. Opal thought she must be Lally Gallagher's older grown-up sister until, smiling, coming forward, the young woman tilted her head and said, Hello, again.

—*Lally?* Opal verified. Lord is it my imagination or have you grown a good six inches—whatcha done to all your hair?

Like it? Lally toyed, showing off her fashionable bob.

Well I ain't sure. It's very modern. Turn around.

Lally spun and Opal saw how thoroughly she'd been transformed.

Butterfly, she thought appropriately.

Except that Lally Gallagher had always *been* a butterfly.

She was just a stronger more resplendent one right now.

A little bird told me you'd likely get a kick taking the Studebaker out, Lally proposed.

'A little bird'?

With her expression Lally signaled they were in on something, the two of them, together.

The only little bird Opal could think of was Lally's mother.

How *is* Mrs. Gallagher? she asked. I ain't seen her in a while.

'Mrs. Gallagher'?

Your mother, Opal prompted.

Lally looked at her a little funny.

Okay, I guess. The same. She doesn't change.

The Studebaker, that cocoon, seemed to yawn between them.

Come on, Lally urged.

Opal laid a palm atop the smooth and pearly hood and let its heat rise through her skin.

I couldn't, she declined.

Why not?

It ain't mine. In fact, I ain't so sure it's even yours. Where's that man that drivesya?

It's John's day off.

Well does your daddy know you got his car?

Lally tilted her head and asked, Who said it was my daddy's car?

She held the door for Opal.

Get in, she said.

Opal weighed the situation. Well maybe, she considered. She stuck her head inside where it was cool. Only for a minute, she swore.

Inside it smelled like shoe polish mixed with ripe tobacco.

She settled on the leather seat behind the wheel.

She hadn't sat in anything as plush except for one evening when she and Fos had sat down for a stolen minute in the lobby of the Knoxville Grand Hotel on the way to see a picture show.

The steering wheel was grained wood and the gearshift was pearl-handled and engraved with Lally's father's initials.

Start her up, Lally recommended, sliding in beside her.

When she closed the door the world outside went silent.

Opal let the choke out slowly, fed the engine gas, and the horsemen waiting underneath reared up in front like steeds of savior cavalry.

Take her out, Lally urged.

Oh no I couldn't, Opal differed while her hands, despite herself, made ready.

Still idling she depressed her foot and made the engine roar, then before she knew it, like an ocean liner drifting on its anchor at the pier, they were gliding backward, and Opal felt the weight of the car's construction all around her the way a captain must intuit his entire ship. Maybe I'll just try her out in first, she said.

Soon it seemed impossible not to try out third.

As they were coming back up Locust several minutes later Opal said, *I think I've found my hobby.*

Motor racing? Lally laughed.

Just you wait an' see I'm gonna volunteer to Ford an' get a set a' goggles, Opal forecast as she eased the big machine next to the curb outside the shop. Well I enjoyed that, she told Lally. I truly did. You tell that 'little bird' a' yours Thank you from me. It was a real *joy* ride.

I'm glad you liked it, Lally said. I want to be your friend.

With the engine off the inside of the car was soundless.

But I'm old enough to be your mother, Opal said.

She could feel the blood rise to her face when she said "mother."

What difference does that make? Lally asked.

It makes a lot a' difference. You're a child an' I'm a grownup. You're a student, I'm a wife. I'm a workin woman. There ain't a single thing we have in common 'cept we live in the same town—an' what with you bein off at private school for half the time you're not even here for *that.*

I'm going to be a working woman, too, Lally admonished her. Someday.

Oh are you now, Opal said. She sounded peeved and was embarrassed for herself.

I've already chosen my profession, Lally told her.

Opal let the cushioned seat surround her.

Don't make up your mind too soon, she cautioned. You're still a girl. You should be thinkin more about what girls are meant t' do.

Somehow, by her force of will or by something more seductive, Lally made Opal look at her.

Now I *do* sound like a older woman don't I? Opal said.

Lally smiled. You *are* an older woman.

Not so old I couldn't bob my hair, too, if I wanted.

She took Lally's hand in hers, surprised it was so cold.

Not so old I couldn't listen to a younger person's dreams of having a 'profession' like you say.

She squeezed the adolescent's hand.

Although what the difference is between a job and a profession you'll hafta explain to me, she added.

Well I think it's in the skill that it requires.

Oh my, Opal said. How'd you learn t' talk so old?

Lally stared at her and said, By listening.

Opal took her answer as a coded invitation to shut up.

I've decided to become *a photographer,* Lally finally said with fanfare. That's why you and I must become the best of friends. So you can help me.

I don't know a thing about photography.

But you work here every day, Lally argued, pointing to the shop front, where Fos had appeared at the door to inspect the car.

That's the person you should friend up, Opal told her, if you're serious. Fos would love t' teachya.

She let go of Lally's hand.

We're goin back to Carolina for a couple weeks on our vacation in a few days, but after that—

—thank you thank you thank you thank you, Lally said. She leaned across the seat and placed a kiss on Opal, brushing Opal's cheek with her eyelashes like a butterfly.

In the weeks that followed their return from their annual trek to the Outer Banks, the pace of daily life picked up as it always does in any college town every September. Fos and Opal canvassed the arriving freshmen and their families on the campus, drumming up the business there for the fourth year in a row. It was the season of the big fairs in the counties, too, and at the end of every working week throughout September and October, Fos and Opal took the x-ray machine and Fos's other portable phenomena on the road into the hinterland to parts of Tennessee beyond the river. There were ninety-five counties in all, Opal came to learn—and she and Fos, at one time or another, managed to put on a show in all of them. She got to know the names, the relative distinctions, and the position on the map of most of them. Of the ninety-five only one was named in honor of a woman and most of them (she counted ninety-one) were named in honor of a politician, longhunter, or legislator from the first hundred years of consolidation of the state. Crockett, Monroe, Jefferson, Washington, Madison, and Hamilton were names of men from history books most educated people recognized. Giles, White, Fentress, Shelby, Grundy, Bledsoe, Rhea were less well known—but still, she thought. Each one a man. Only Unicoi stood out, the only county in the state with what was thought to be a Choctaw name and no one really knew for sure its meaning. Something about "fog" a farmer from that county told her. In reference to the mists that hugged the ground between the hills. Everywhere else around the state you were reminded where you were by the signposts taken from the names of only one part of the state's entire population. Not just at the county lines or on the maps. Everywhere you looked there was no avoiding it. Kellogg. Ford. Gillette. Pillsbury. Studebaker. Firestone. The world was named for men.

Just on the paved road out of Knoxville before the Carolina line, alone,

Opal counted eighty-six new roadside signs. Seventy of them advertising things named after men; sixteen after women. Restaurants, mainly. And a campsite named for Lorna Doone.

They were on the road driving toward the rising sun and a ghostly August morning had already erased the Smoky Mountains from the background. You're awful quiet, Opal noted. Then under her breath she added *eighty-seven.*

Fos stirred from what was on his mind to ask her whatcha countin?

Signs. Barns, too, but barns remain the same. Each year. Last year I counted Fords. Year before jaybirds.

Yeah I was thinkin that. How we come out here every August an' it's just the same. Each an' every time. Full moon, fallin stars: an' I go home with zero. I've even forgot what the point of this once was.

Bi-o-loo-min-essence, Opal told him grandly.

They exchanged a look that had started to come into play between them. A look that guaranteed that neither one was really saying what was on his/her mind and she/he knew it. They had not yet reached the stage of life where some people congregate to reconfigure their lost hopes. Fos was not convinced yet that he'd never mass the data necessary to support a scientific breakthrough; but he was noticing the summers going by without a single measure of success. And more often he wondered *if,* not *when* his moment of eureka would arrive.

The same way Opal had begun to wonder if, not when, she'd ever be a mother.

They understood with that look, then, what neither dared to ask the other.

Somethin Lally said the other day, Opal was reminded. Made me want to ask. Does bein a photgrapher require 'skill'?

Fos shrugged and said, Depends. Most the things we do I guess require trainin of the kind your average man could manage. Then there's photographs that not even Flash nor me would have the skill to take. Underwater photographs. I reckon I could figure how to do it if I tried, but there's some pictures bein made of things I wouldn't start to know how they've been done. Night photography an' such. Pictures of the surface of the moon. Things you might not see but once in any lifetime. People usin photography almost as if it was a science. Or art. Or a servant of man's history like the wheel. What your daddy does, now *that's* a skill.

Lordie, Opal said.

The skill with which Fos took a simple question and turned it into something like a lens which changed the way she looked at things was exactly why she knew he'd be the person Lally ought to talk to when she showed up at the shop one morning in October with a brand-new camera. Fos took her outside where the light was longing to make shadows of them on the bright pavement. *This light and the light in May,* he started to explain to Lally, is Nature's way of showin us that every surface is illusion. Here, I'll showya. You stand here an' I'll stand over here an' we'll pretend you are the sun. And I'm the earth.

He knelt down.

This is where the earth is relative to you on points of orbit in both October and May. Now stick your arms out like they're rays of sunshine leaving the sun's surface traveling through space to land on me . . .

From where she was watching this performance behind the plate-glass window in the shop, Opal could see that Lally could barely keep from laughing at him, but by the time he'd finished with the demonstration the girl was hanging on his every word. He was good with children, Opal knew, already, from seeing him with kids at carnivals and with the assortment of them paraded through the door by their parents and forced to pose in clothes they felt unnatural in for a stranger who kept blinking at them from behind his camera. Fos's way with kids was more natural than her own. He never bent down over them, he squatted, back erect, until he and the child were eye to eye on equal ground. In Lally's case, however, Opal noted that he spoke to her and treated her as an adult. She brought her pictures to him and he critiqued them in a tone and from a point of view that Opal recognized as pretty much the way he talked to grown-up women. Or the way he talked to her. Soon Opal, too, stopped offering a candy from the mint dish every time Lally came to visit. And in December, over the Christmas school break, Opal didn't even bat an eye when Fos loaned Lally books about photography from his own shelves, some of which had pictures in them that Opal called "artistic poses."

Strange the way her parents seem to have just turned her loose, Opal mused one evening looking through the *Knoxville Journal* till she found the Society Page. There was a picture there of Flash's brother, Tay Luttrell, the city's District Attorney, holding up a pair of scissors just about to snip a ribbon at the new Law Library at the University. Child spends more time with us than she does with them, it seems t' me, whenever she's at home in Knoxville.

No pictures of them, either. If you notice.

Opal looked up from the paper.

Lally's pictures were, in fact, all of objects—a flower in a vase, a book on a table, an apple on a dish.

Well it's diff'rent takin pictures full a' people 'stead a' things. You should know that best than anyone, she told him.

Although with all her veils on Lally's mother looked less like a person than *still life,* she was thinking.

That child is starved for affection I'll say that much, Fos observed.

Whydja think that Mrs. Gallagher wears those scarves?

Fos foundered for an answer.

It's decorative, he volunteered. Lotsa women wear 'em.

Opal looked back down at the ads and pictures in the *Knoxville Journal.* Lotsa women *where?* she collared him.

Bible women.

She was thinking Baptists, Congregationalists. Adventists.

Which Bible women?

For one, the Virgin Mary. She wears that scarf over her head. All those Bible women do.

Opal gestured toward the pictures of the people on the pages of the *Journal* to indicate where Mrs. Gallagher was dressing for the part. Not in the Bible.

I wish you wouldn't read that, Fos said lamely, then regretted that he had. He could see in her, sometimes, the longing of a transplant to assume the coloration of adoptive soil. And he tried as best he could to understand. Tried to summon up a minimum enthusiasm when she mentioned maybe they should go around to one of the town socials, take a covered dish to one of those drop-in potluck suppers, join a club. But Fos was like one of those plants so specific in its nature it's created its own hummingbird. It wasn't so much that she was more a natural joiner than he was: he could join in, joined in all the time when they were on the circus route recruiting penny spectators at county fairs. But like a rare saltmarsh endemic that cannot fix to limestone soil, Fos had never felt he was a "transplant." He didn't see himself a Tennes*seer,* didn't talk like one and had about as much interest in the city where he lived as he had in any other city, which was almost none. He took Opal to a picture show once or twice a month and bought his lunches at the counter at the five and dime and frequented the library, but aside from that city living held no special delights for him. He was indifferent to the social opportunities it had on sale: he didn't drink, he didn't dance, he didn't pray he didn't care to sit around and breathe tobacco while someone in a crowded room banged on a piano and moaned music. Flash was at a music club across the river almost every night and Fos had noticed Opal listened to his stories of that life with more appreciation than she used to. He noticed, too, she liked some things he thought were trivial—she could sing along to lyrics of the songs she heard play on the radio; she knew the names of singers and the names of dances, too. She knew the names of actors in the picture shows and who those actors were married to. Culture—*popular* culture—went by Fos like poultry loaded on a truck, its sights and sounds and signifiers baffled by the mass inside the crates. Not only did he notice that Opal read the *Knoxville Journal* front to back, he noticed that she read it avidly. She circled things. She cut things out. She cut things out of magazines as well. Things that might as well have been written in a foreign language for all the meaning he could glean from them. *How-to* lists. How to look *smart.* How to *dress for success.* How to *impress your husband's relatives.*

That one, in particular, had him stumped.

He didn't *have* any living relatives.

Ten things every bride should know.

How to make a winning first impression.

Ask her what she's readin these days, Fos grouched to Flash one quiet afternoon when nothing much was happening in the shop except early winter twilight.

Oh no, Flash reckoned, wise. No no no no no. Don't drop that bait in there, my brother. Takes more to lure a seasoned fisherman into those disputed matrimonial currents than a line like that. Whatcha readin these days, dit? he asked anyway, deciding out of boredom just to play along. How's that *Moby* comin?

She's not readin *Moby-Dick* no more, Fos betrayed.

I can answer for myself, she bristled. It got a little borin, she told Flash. Over the diff'rent kindsa whales.

So now she's readin about diff'rent kindsa goins ons. Up on that hill where you came from.

Flash took the opportunity to say, One man's hill. Is just another's hell. So watch out where you're grazing, dit.

I think she's given up book learnin altogether, Fos divulged.

So what?

Fos blinked. So *what?* Comin from *you?* He had seen Flash read a book while he was marching. Read while he was fishing. Read, for all he knew, while he was engaged in any method of the highly personal performances men make and do.

She's *young,* Flash emphasized.

A fact Fos sometimes forgot.

She needs to live a little. Have some *fun,* Flash joked. Before she turns into a poached sclerotic picador. Like you.

But if anyone had asked her Opal would have told them *have some fun* was not on any how-to list she cared about. *Fitting in* was there. Belonging. Being part of. Mixing. Milling. Socializing. If anyone had asked her Opal would have told them. She was envious of crowds. In her imagination social sets and social circles ratified a perfect human theorem, a perfect mathematics. Something *more,* something greater than the sum of all its parts seemed to find its proof there—in those rooms, at those cotillions. She looked at them, at the lighted windows in the mansions on the hill, at the pictures of the faces of the men and women in their striped blazers and drop-waisted shifts, their cummerbunds and lavalieres at balls and garden parties on the pages of the *Knoxville Journal* and, like Christopher Columbus standing on a blasted beach in Europe, she wondered how, if ever, she was going to launch her x into that irrational but consummate equation.

Cinderella musta had such thoughts, she chided herself as she stared at a picture in the paper of the dance floor at the New Year ball held at the City Club the week before. When you looked real close you could see some glasses on the tables in the background shaped too fancy to be used for drinking plain iced tea or soda water, Opal thought. She was in the back room of the shop all by herself and didn't want to entertain the thought that there was tolerated spirits-drinking in the higher echelons of this fair city. She felt a chill just thinking it, then realized the frigid air was blowing in through the curtain from the open street door. She got up to pull it shut and found a woman standing at the counter in a fur coat and a wool scarf wrapped around her head. Her face was hidden by a dense lace veil.

Lordie, Opal murmured. It was ten degrees colder out in front than in the back. That's some Northern wind out there—

Yes it is, the woman said in that soft voice she had.

Happy New Year, anyway, Opal conceded. Nice t' seeya again, Mrs. Gallagher.

If *seeya* could describe the situation, Opal thought.

When she was growing up, before she had learned to read, in place of conversation in the evening, Conway would read out loud to her from whatever he was reading—usually the local weekly newspaper, past copies of which he picked up from the general store once or twice a month, whenever he went into town. The first story she remembered from the papers, the one that gave her visions in her dreams both night and day for years thereafter, was the one Conway read to her when she was six years old. The news was five weeks old by the time Conway read it to her at the supper table. A molasses storage vat (he read) had collapsed in Boston releasing a syrup wave thirty feet high into Milk Street, killing twenty-four people. The syrup, oozing in the summer sun, left a sickly sweet thick residue six blocks long like an enormous flypaper. Combining with the sweet aroma (Conway read), the tragedy hung above the scene for days, clotted with flies, like a still life deceptively alive beneath its humming veil of sorrow.

That veil, Opal was thinking, was enough to give you nightmares about what lies beneath.

I was just now lookin at the pictures in the paper of the New Year Ball, she said.

Mrs. Gallagher said nothing; not a thing about her stirred. Not a hair on her mahogany-colored fur nor a breath behind the heavy lace. You could hatch an egg on the expectancy Opal was feeling. You could boil one. Then Mrs. Gallagher moved her arms and placed a book between them on the counter. It was one of the books that Fos had loaned to Lally. The one with some artistic poses in it. *Uh oh,* Opal thought.

I believe your husband is responsible for this? she heard.

Howja mean? she stalled.

Is he here?

Opal shook her head.

She could hear Mrs. Gallagher take a breath like she was going to make a jump. Then she slid an envelope from the book, one of those legal-size ones with a cotton string wound around two paper buttons for a clasp. With her gloved fingers Mrs. Gallagher began to unwind the string. Like a snake charmer, Opal thought. She's gonna serve us up some legal papers.

Before she finished unwinding the string around the paper buttons Mrs. Gallagher stopped and placed a gloved palm flat on the envelope. Before I begin, Mrs. Foster, I should tell you how very pleased both Lowell and I are with the photographs your husband has taken of Lally. And of course we're very grateful to him for his interest in her 'hobby.'

Opal was about to say Fos didn't take that picture last year, Flash did. But her counting mind had heard photograph-*s.* In plural. And she knew darn well she'd billed the Gallaghers for only *one.*

It was a picture in this book, Mrs. Gallagher was saying, that gave me the idea for why I've come to talk to Mr. Foster.

With those gloved hands of hers, she set the envelope aside, opened Fos's book up in the middle and started turning pages.

One or two made Opal blush.

This one, Mrs. Gallagher remarked so softly Opal had to lean a little forward so she could hear her better. She slid the book around so Opal wasn't looking at the picture upside down and almost whispered, Lally tells me Mr. Foster will know how to achieve this same effect.

What 'effect'? Opal was thinking.

You see here, Mrs. Gallagher said, softly running her gloved thumb along a section of the picture, where the details in the skin have been erased.

That's the way it's *lit,* Opal murmured like she knew what she was talking about. Plus Fos would call that part of the picture *overexposed.* He tries not t' do that in his line a' work, she admitted.

Mrs. Gallagher glided her gloved hands toward the envelope.

Yes, she said dismissively, Lally told me there were several ways it can be done. Either through the camera—or like this . . .

She slid a glossy photograph out of the envelope. It was the size and kind Opal knew was used for newspapers.

This was taken at the Deb Ball on my coming out, Mrs. Gallagher explained.

She turned the picture so they both could see it. Seated at a table were four girls in ball gowns and long gloves, all smiling toward the camera. By their sides were four young nip-and-tuckered men with slicked-up hair and airs of casual surliness—except for one of them, caught in profile in a moment of rapt attention, staring past his dinner partner's shoulder at something at the far side of the room.

This is me, Mrs. Gallagher was saying, pointing at the young girl on the right.

Yes but—, Opal interrupted.

She jabbed a finger at the profile of the young man staring off into the distance.

Oh I quite forgot that Chance was in the picture, Mrs. Gallagher observed.

Lordie, Opal breathed. How many years ago was this?

Fourteen. Or thereabouts.

Flash hadn't changed. Longer in the jowls a little, hair a little thinner and a little higher on his crown: but in sum, he looked the same. It was the first time Opal ever glimpsed him as his former self, in his birthright, so to speak: his original milieu. He looks all Rudolph Valentino even way back then, doesn't he? she said a bit too eagerly, like they were girls together looking at a movie magazine.

If you'll just turn your attention over *here,* Mrs. Gallagher put in.

She had her index finger fixed on a certain spot.

Opal couldn't see what was beneath it.

I'm sorry, which one did you say was you?

She felt the woman bristle.

It was like the feeling that she had had that morning when she stepped on ice. When her foot came down and cracks began to form.

This is me, Mrs. Gallagher repeated.

Opal stared.

The moment needed her to say something admiring but that tactic failed her. So did tact. She was expecting, she supposed, a vintage beauty —some trace element from a motherlode of Lally's gemlike qualities. But instead of Lally's dark eyes set in fragile porcelain like a china doll's, her mother's face was an exact inverse—a rounded chin with rounded cheeks and tiny eyes which almost disappeared inside her face. Still, for this occasion, the young woman in the photograph smiled with her mouth open and Opal could see her tongue between her teeth.

It's this person *here,* Mrs. Gallagher was saying.

Again she pointed to a place in the photograph with her gloved finger.

It was a spot beside the table where someone might have stood.

But there's no one there, Opal surveyed.

Well *exactly.*

Opal searched for the woman's eyes beneath the veil.

I don't understand, she said.

He was taken out.

—*out?* Opal verified.

The place in the photograph that Mrs. Gallagher was pointing to with her gloved finger looked different from the rest of the whole picture. Beside the table next to the young Mrs. Gallagher's white shoulder in her white coming-out gown and her escort's black tuxedo was a gray fog that looked like someone's thumbprint on a glass. You mean t' say, Opal verified, where this kinda smudge is—there was someone standin there? Why would you want to smudge somebody from your picture?

This was the photograph that appeared in all the papers. It was the photograph we sent to all our families. To our grandparents, Mrs. Gallagher explained. They did whatever it is your husband will know how to do to take him out. We couldn't have him standing there.

She must think I'm stupid, Opal thought. Still she had to ask it. Take *who* out?

Why, one of those boys from the club. He was *a nigra,* Mrs. Foster.

Mrs. Gallagher went on talking as if hers were the only words that made sense in the universe, telling the speechless Opal how she wanted to engage the services of Opal's husband in the delicate commission of her portraiture, employing whatever techniques of erasure he had at his disposal to discriminate against certain aspects of her appearance, until—and this must have been in answer to her own prayers, Opal thought—the door opened with a blast of frigid air and Fos and Flash came in.

Colder than a witch's teet out there! Flash announced.

He stared.

And how lucky can we get? Here's the very witch to prove it.

Before anybody had a chance to answer him he pushed past Mrs. Gallagher, the cold air in his wake, and disappeared behind the curtain. In a second Opal felt another cold draft coming from the back room and she knew he'd gone back out again and left the rear door open to the alley. If Mrs. Gallagher had heard him or had taken offense she didn't show a sign of it and as soon as Opal introduced her to Fos and explained to him what Mrs. Gallagher was after she excused herself and went out back to shut the door and find that sonofabitch and give him a fair right piece of her righteous anger.

He was hurling snowballs at a brick wall at the end of the alley. Where they landed they left white scatter patterns like stars colliding in the night.

I am a-*shamed* a' you, she told him.

She was shaking more from anger than from cold.

He wouldn't look at her and bent to make another weapon from the snow.

Look at me when I'm talkin! Areya *drunk?*

He turned around and she saw in his eyes something she had only ever seen before in the eyes of people on the covers of her dimestore novels.

She must be onto us, he said. I don't know what I'll do if she is onto us. He looked at the ball of snow in his hand then contracted all his force into a kind of human spring and unleashed it at the wall toward some unseen goliath.

Half the time I think you are the most educated man I ever met and the other half the time I think you are a twisted wreck a' sick intention. How dare you say what you just said t' Mrs. Gallagher in there? I don't care what kinda problems you might have with your own family you have no right to speak to a lady—any lady—that way. *Speshly* not the County Supervisor's wife . . . This business may still be nothin but 'a joke' for you but for Fos an' me it is a livelihood an' we take pride in it, and if you can't start actin like a man who can accept responsibility then maybe me an' Fos would be a whole lot better off workin someplace else. Just the two of us.

She looked most like the gemstone she was named for when she was cold—her fingertips turned violet, her hands turned white, her cheeks went yellow and her lips turned blue. As with an opal, Flash could see the fire in her at that moment. And she could see that look in his eyes again. In another man she would have thought he was about to cry. You haven't heard a word I've said have you? To her astonishment he sat down. Which is how Fos found them—Flash sitting in the snow, his back against the wall, Opal iridescent as an iceberg. Come inside, he said. Flash shook his head. Come on, you're frozen, Fos told Opal.

I'm not movin till I hear a proper apology.

Snowball's chance in hell, Flash said. He seemed to smile.

Come on, Fos urged. Mrs. Gallagher didn't pay no mind so why should you? That crowd of people that she's from have come to expect his bad behavior. Proves their point about him.

Flash got to his feet. Save your pity for *Mrs. Gallagher,* he told her. And give it to her victims. He took his coat off and offered it to her, but she made it clear she didn't want to touch him, or anything belonging to him. Coat in hand, he asked Fos, What did satan's mistress want with us, anyway?

She wants her picture took, Fos said. Without the veil.

By *us,* Flash ascertained.

Well no by *me,* Fos told him. She was pretty clear about all that. I think Lally must've said some things. Anyway she's hopin I'll perform some miracles. He looked at Flash. What was it caused her—whatyoucallit—disfigurement? *Smallpox?*

Flash laughed.

He reached down and made another snowball. Threw it. 'Smallpox' he repeated. Hell no. 'Pox' all right. But there was nothing *small* about it. Except, perhaps, her poxy soul.

He made another snowball. Let it fly. Then looked at Opal. She caught fire one night, he told her. Her clothes did. What she was wearing.

—but that's *horrible,* Opal murmured.

Is it?

Flash threw the snowball at the wall.

Like I said: save your pity, Opal.

She noticed how he hadn't called her *dit.*

People carry torches for all kinds of reasons. Some of them no good. She set herself aflame one night. By ac-ci-dent. Out burning crosses. Black folks' homes.

Opal held herself against the cold.

Men do that, she argued.

And women *can't?* he countered.

That look she'd seen on dimestore novel covers was in his eyes again.

Once more he offered her his coat.

This time, she took it.

Because she had been too young to form a real memory of it, she had either dreamed or she had been told that when her mother died she had clung to her hand. Years later, when she entered school and the teacher went around the classroom asking every child to *Give us an example of something cold* Opal didn't hesitate to mention *Death.*

To which she would now add Knoxville in the winter. And a snowball's only chance in hell.

There was no reason not to believe what Flash had said—his faults were many, but social realism and truth-telling about the upper crusts were among his too few virtues. The Invisible Empire, as the Klan called itself, had been part of the background of her life in the South for as long as she could remember—like bindweed, hookworm, and the other regional contagions. One of them had tried to recruit her father one night at the table in the kitchen and Conway's immediate rejection of the overture established the ground on which Opal judged its gang members thereafter. Her father—like Fos, and like Flash, too—was all front to back in his transparency: what you saw was what there was, there was nothing clandestine in his character, and those few aspects that were disguised or hidden were that way because they were his closely kept emotions. When on those rare occasions he allowed his emotions to be seen, their appearance was all the more surprising. And more powerful. Which taught her early on a thing or two about the power of what's visible—it derives its mystery from what it hides. How many stories had she heard of people sensing ghosts behind the walls, hobgoblins in the woods? People living on the shores of lakes since time began have conjured creatures from those depths. If you believe a thing is something different from the evidence before you, if you believe something is hidden by the wall or in the woods or beneath the surface of the lake, then that belief gives power to the darkness and the depths—power to enchant; to terrify. That was the power—the real power—the Klan aspired to. But, as Conway had told her early on, they were a gang of murderers, not magicians. Despite their names—Grand Wizard, Dragons, Cyclops—they were clowns in pointy hats out to terrify some negroes with their hokum. On the surface of it, she agreed with Conway that they looked ridiculous. But when she saw the bunch of them in Mr. Griffith's movie riding on their horses in that quick-time way the moving pictures have, she had to wonder whether or not it was all the hokum that would scare her if she was woken in the middle of the night by thirty of them standing outside in her yard. It wasn't the regalia that people roused out of their houses found so frightening: it was the evil of intent. It was the fear of numbers. The fear the prey can taste when boxed in by the hungry herd. It was a deeper fear than any costume could inspire or impose, it was the fear that follows on abandonment, the one that shocks and prompts us to ask for evidence of God, the one we have to learn the name of: fear of death.

Some places never freeze, the people there wear robes against the sun and bathe in oil and sand instead of water. Some places never freeze and people there go naked beneath a canopy of green under a melting sun. She had looked at pictures of these places, at the people in them and had thought of Conway's favorite rubric, that the world—and not the Bible—was the only holy book. The world was there before you at each sunrise ready to be read. The man who hired her for her first job bookkeeping in Nags Head had had his portrait as Grand Dragon hanging on the wall and she had looked at it in all its artificial strangeness the way she looked at pictures of the desert nomads in their tented clothes and the pictures of rain forest pygmies in their altogethers. People do strange things, it's the nature of the beast, Conway had taught her—acceptance is the first step toward forgiveness. But as she looked at the picture on the wall in the office of the man who sold Ford cars in Nags Head and tried to see his eyes, black holes inside a pointy hood, her instinct told her there were things, some awful things, that people did that were beyond the strange. Some things, she could only just imagine, were not only strange, but un-acceptable. And you could not forgive them. The man who hired her was a hard-shell racialist. She kept her dealings with him to a minimum of cordiality, and she never saw that black death aspect to his eyes except in the picture on the wall behind his desk. What he got up to in his fellowship with the other dragons she could never know, but she was certain there were men like him throughout the South—not only back in North Carolina. What she hadn't seen before she came to live in Knoxville, though, was the way a city offers up its fabric as disguise. Living in the country you could use the country the way Conway always said you could: like a holy open book. You could know a person's story from the bottom up, from roots, their feet, and from their shoes. You could tell from looking at them where they'd been, where they were from, how much they knew, what flour they were sifting, how far their eyes were shifting from the truth. But in a city, you saw people every day you never saw before or saw again. They passed you with a look or with the notion that a word was being whispered toward you, one word from a complicated sentence. From downstairs, at odd times of the day and night, she and Fos could hear one of the Rinaldis raise their voice or laugh or vocalize surprise or sudden anger and they could smell their food and hear them moving but even after three years living side by side with them above the bakery Opal didn't know their given names, where they'd been born, when they'd started working at the bakery or what they dreamed at night. She could have asked them, they were friendly people, but their daily notice of each other never went in that direction and what was normal conversation in the country sounded busybody when you asked it in a city. She imagined there were people somewhere in the city who were up-to-date and in-the-know on everything and everybody—people at the bank, perhaps, or in the courthouse. Or up on Summit Hill. She wondered what they did at night. She wondered, when she took butter from the icebox, how they spread it on their bread. How they made their beds. She'd look at them in passing cars or going into shops she, herself, had never entered, and she wondered if she'd ever know anybody else the way that she knew Fos. Wondered if she'd ever make a friend again or if, under the rules a city uses to define itself, anyone could appear out of nowhere, a stranger, and change her life the way Fos had. Perhaps, being the country girl she was, she hoped for things from city life that the city, as dispensing agent, was unable to provide. Unlike the open holy book that she and Conway knew the country was, a city is a necessary covenant with secrecy, a system of isolated sancta. You think you're in good company, you're not. You're in a category. You think you have four neighbors, but you don't. You have four walls.

In the days following Mrs. Gallagher's visit, Opal allowed herself to entertain the fantasy of accompanying Fos to Mrs. Gallagher's house, of entering, perhaps, a private room set aside for the picture taking, an inner sanctum. She entertained these thoughts because—in Opal's mind, at least—it seemed more likely Mrs. Gallagher would want to share her secret in the privacy of her own home rather than un-veiling in the shop, in public. She was certain Fos would let her tag along and she went so far in her imaginings as to convince herself that she was actually a necessary part of the transaction—an ambassadress, of sorts. A chaperone. But the truth was she didn't have a clue about the way they'd left it.

Howja leave it? she asked Fos after a week had passed without a word from the prospective artist's subject.

Well she came in an' asked would I take the picture an' I said yes I would. An' then she left. As you recall there was more than the usual polite things bein said that afternoon.

Maybe we should . . . you know. Send a letter. A remind-her.

Fos cleaned his glasses even though he had just done so, so she had an inkling what he was about to say.

I believe we hafta stand by Flash on this one, he admitted. We don't need t' put in with those people. It ain't like us.

By "those people" she took him to mean Klan. And not the better half of Knoxville.

So you think what Flash said about her was true?

I think we have to. What's our choice?

Her critical faculties were not their best when she was judging Mrs. Gallagher, she had to admit, and it was for a more complicated reason than envying the woman's husband's Studebaker. But when a month went by with no further word from her, Opal couldn't help but think something more than just a misunderstanding had occurred. Some offense had taken place. Some line or boundary had been crossed, never to be crossed again. After another month went by without a single visit from her it was apparent Lally, too, had no intention of renewing contact with them. And Fos was disappointed, Opal saw.

It's Flash's fault, she told him.

Then a letter came addressed to both of them, the handwriting on the envelope bold and fluid, though not showy—an educated person's, Opal thought. It was postmarked "RFD Luminary," and she weighed it in her hand and even smelled it before handing it to Fos to open.

Out fell a scattering of deckle-edged 1 1/2 by 2 1/2-inch silver gelatin prints on Kodak paper. *Lally!* Fos fairly crowed even before he looked to see who'd signed the letter.

She was much the same in writing as she was in person—confident that what she'd chosen to impart would be the center of interest to the lucky party receiving it. She wrote to tell what she was studying at school (Latin, algebra, and Greek and Roman history) and to say that she'd been given a new camera, a range finder, pictures from which were enclosed. She signed the letter with her name inscribed within a heart and wrote that she would come to visit next time she was in Knoxville.

Ain't that sweet, Opal admitted, picking up the envelope again to look for a return address. "Luminary," she repeated. Doesn't ring a bell.

Downstate, Fos allowed. Past Big Lick. Down there where Rhea county crosses over into Bledsoe. Strawberry country. Southern Railroad Lines runs through it. Flat. Lots of iron ore.

Fos was looking at the pictures she had sent.

Still can't see it, Opal mentioned. In my mind.

She held the postmark to the light to see if it was hiding something.

Sure you've seen a sign for Luminary, Fos chimed in. Pikeville, he prompted. *Friendship? Slabtown?*

She was drawing blanks.

Well can you see in your mind there where *Rockwood* is? he asked. If you can picture *Rockwood* in your brain then go south there on the 27 down toward Dayton an' Luminary's off there to the west about two mile midpoint between Rockwood an' Dayton.

Dayton? she repeated vaguely.

Where that Monkey Trial of Flash's was—that town where Clarence Darrow was.

Funny place t' put a boarding school for girls. There's nothin there.

He looked at her. That's the *point* wouldn't you say?

He laid Lally's photographs out on the counter for her to see. Each one, though subtly different from the rest, was a study of white clouds set in a darker sky.

Set a school down in the middle of flat farmland, you get nothin to distract from learnin, he pronounced.

But Opal knew the female mind, itself, is a distraction. Especially in girls. Half the serious distractions she had had when she was young had come at moments when there was nothing—*rural* nothing—going on.

In the months preceding the Perseid meteor display in August, Fos was a flurry of activity—*this* year *this* year *this* year Opal sometimes heard him saying to himself. He'd decided to go back to fireflies, he told her. Not that he was giving up on marine bioluminescence but, aware that science as a way of life means pressing all one's bets to overcome the odds, he'd decided to revive his study of glow worms. Which meant collecting them. I'm thrilled, said Opal. She went along, at first, enjoying the drive beyond the city limits to the open fields at sunset on those summer evenings: there was something magical about the process, watching Fos split the rotting logs, peeling them apart like baked potatoes, their floury interiors crumbling on his fingers as he sifted out the firefly grubs which, stirred awake by his intrusion, rose in points of light from the dead wood like souls from corpses. Flash was keeping to himself on weekends—though he didn't state as much, she had the impression he was busy seeing people like himself, people interested in drinking: she had the impression he was seeing women. In the fall that year she realized with almost no regret that the three of them had not gone fishing once that summer, that she had not been out on the Tennessee in Flash's canoe since June the year before. She was happy being an exclusive twosome with her husband once again. They were thinking of looking for a house to buy, come spring. At the New Year, on the eve of 1927, Fos made a determined toast with apple cider that more or less summed up the promises he meant to keep *this* year *this* year *this* year. He realized, not without remorse over the swiftness of the passage of time, that it was ten full years since he'd gone off to war. Seven years since they'd been married. A hundred and three years since the death of Count Volta. He mentioned this last item as if it were equal in personal significance to the former two. All the physicists who he talked about as if they had a hardware store down the street called Einstein, Oppenheimer, Bohr & Fermi were gathering in Italy that year in a place called Lake Como on the pretense of celebrating the centenary of Volta's death, where they were planning to present important papers only they could understand. *Who-was-Volta-anyway?* was a question Opal was not prepared to risk and just presumed he must have been the man who named the volt and not the river, even though you never knew with Fos.

In early June Einstein announced that he would boycott the Lake Como meeting on the grounds that he would not lend himself to Mussolini, who was intending to use the convocation of the world's most famous scientists to give himself prestige. Fos stayed up late one Sunday night writing a letter to Einstein urging him to go because, at least in Fos's view, science—and *scientists*—were, by nature, like the stars in heaven, obliged to share their light.

Bright and early the next morning he went out in his pajamas to walk the letter down to the postman on his morning route and found Flash sitting on the steps outside his door smoking a cigarette. Tapping a jar of firefly maggots balanced on the bannister.

Flash, Fos said.

So is this food or . . . *formicary?* Or just plain Fos-itude. I think they're dead.

Flash, Fos said again. What areya doin here?

Nothing. Cogitating. Waiting for the day to break.

Well Fos said. That's sure t' happen.

So far. Every morning.

Want some breakfast?

No I'm fine.

He flicked his cigarette in a defining arc across the quiet street and said, My car broke down. Thought maybe dit could toy with it.

Sure thing.

Fos stood there for a moment, envelope in hand.

Where is it?

Out the south road. Couple miles from town.

The south road, as it was called by people going south from Knoxville, was a spur of former dirt track that ran roughly parallel to the more major route and had avoided highway-ization by the plaintive fact that it was laid out in the flood plain too close to the Tennessee River. Sometimes it was high and dry, and some times it was underwater.

It was the route favored by the slower moving traffic—horse-pulled drays, day-workers, drifters, and itinerant evangelists. Some put temporary dwellings up or camped around what trees there were, but the river, as landlord, was a cruel evictor. Everything was razed when she was rampant, and the drywash that she left behind once her binge was over crusted up from godknowswhat. It looked like suds. Now in the breaking morning light it looked like snow to Opal. Women in sunbonnets were already working rows with hoes, and she had to wonder where they'd come from, out so early in the morning and so far away from any place of habitation. Then she remembered that the city limit sign was only half a mile behind them, and how the city fell away abruptly into blank country, like a fortress in a desert.

Flash was riding shotgun behind them in the truck, his tall frame folded neatly between the x-ray apparatus and the mobile generator. *Cheese and Rice!* he groused. It's Junior Edison's wetdream back here. He pulled a copy of a magazine from the stack that he was sitting on. *Science News-Letter,* he read aloud. The Week Summary of Current Science. O, my christ.

Don't make fun of it, Fos warned. That's Mr. Edison's own paper. Weekly.

It's kinda Fos's Bible, Opal said. She smiled over her shoulder at him and told him, Fos's *Moby.*

'Falling Meteors Might Wipe Out Cities . . . ' Flash read out loud. 'New X-Ray Menace,' he continued. Holy mary, doesn't T.A. write anything that's not apocalyptic? 'X-ray therapy,' it says here, 'one of the blessings of modern science, can, in exceptional cases, produce feeblemindedness and deformity in human beings . . .'

Let me see that, Opal said, but Flash refused to show it to her. Joking, dit, he said.

But she could tell he wasn't.

It had never occurred to her that anything Fos took an interest in could be dangerous to him—or her. Except, of course, the phosphorous rock inside the goldfish bowl which she knew would catch on fire if it got loose.

Change the subject for us, wizard, Flash encouraged.

Fos swept his arm out the window toward the field beside the road.

I was just thinkin, you know. About these farmers out here. What do you think they do all day?

—*work,* Flash scoffed. That's *all* they do. God knows to be a farmer in this country in this century you've got to be out of your work-ruined mind.

You don't see that much workin goin on.

Sure you do. Someone's got to do the planting and the harvesting and the sorting and the packing—

Yes but . . . well. How many people does it take to plant a field?

That's one of those questions, Fos, Flash told him. That have as many answers as you choose to make.

I think it takes about one medium-size adult and a mule a day to plant a field like that'n there.

With what, Opal asked.

With a plow, Fos told her.

No I mean planted with what. Tobacco takes a whole lot longer 'cause you hafta build a little mound up with your hands to put the seed in.

She had read that in a flyer she had sent for from the Agriculture Department when she was worrying about what to do with the land she had inherited.

Well let's just say then that it is tobacco and it takes a medium-size person *two* days—no, let's say three—*three* days instead of one to plant this field. My question is, What does that medium-size person do with the other three hundred sixty-two days of the year?

Weed, Flash said.

Make clothes, Opal said. Buy shoes. Make supper.

Think, Flash said. Make wishes. Walk to town. No shortage of things to do when you're a human.

So in your opinion people work and when they're finished working then they think away the hours of their days, do they. Makin wishes.

Maybe—there's the cabriolet up there, sweetheart, see it?

Opal turned to look at him. You *walked* from here? All the way to town?

I didn't mind, he mentioned.

And she saw that look again, that otherwheres distraction in his eyes that she'd been noticing.

Well I wonder, Fos continued musing. If that's what people really do.

Opal eased the truck to a stop on the side of the road in front of Flash's car, then they all got out.

He had been coming from the south, she noticed, and the eggshell-colored body of the roadster was camouflaged by a sifting of mongrel Tennessee dust.

She just give out onya? Opal asked, already calculating grit inside the fuel line. She got in and tried to start it. She couldn't help but notice the leather valise on the seat beside the choke. A paper tag tied to its handle read AMITY HOTEL DAYTON'S FINEST. In blue ink across the tag was scrawled *Mr. Smith, Room 309.*

Perhaps hoping for a clue or for an explanation she turned her gaze from the valise to Flash who, at that very instant, reached down to touch a vagrant kitten who had come to beg attention out of nowhere. She watched him bend down, this tall man, and with a gesture of unanticipated tenderness, cup his hand beneath the kitten's belly and bring it face to face with him and nuzzle it. *He's in love,* she recognized. I betcha.

Here in front of her was evidence of the circumstantial kind that supported what the dimestore novels always promised: you can see love, on the lovestruck, plain as day. No use even in trying to pretend it's secret. She looked to see if Fos had seen it, too, but he was already halfway across the field, carrying a bucket from the truck out toward the river, up to god-knowswhat, she thought. She got out of the roadster, rolled the bonnet up, and unscrewed the carburetor cap. Blowing in the line reminded her how long it had been since she'd played the jugs and when she was satisfied that she'd displaced the particles of dirt that were the problem, she climbed back in and turned the engine over on the first try.

In Opal's hands his car purred like the kitten he was holding.

Howdja do that? Flash marveled.

Oh there's nothin to it when you know what you are doin . . . *Mr. Smith.*

Ah geez, he faltered.

His eyes flicked past her to the luggage tag on the seat beside her.

The smoking gun from Monkeyville, he said.

Meanwhile he touched her on her arm. I can count on your discretion can't I, dit.

He didn't pose it as a question so much as naturally suppose it was a secret they would keep between them. Opal didn't keep things hidden from Fos—not her feelings, nor the gossip nor her dreams or irritation over expiring firefly grubs kept in jars inside the house. But to be in on Flash's secret generated an excitement for her. Implicit in the confidence that she was keeping was the promise of forthcoming incremental revelations, more installments to the story, further plot and more detail as in the dime-store novels she'd grown used to reading. But weeks went by and Mr. Smith in Monkeyville on weekends was all she knew. Who the woman was in Dayton Mr. Smith was seeing, well—only the shadows knew. She tried on several occasions to allude to love, in general, and to getting married, in particular, but as the summer wore on, Flash began to act even more elusive, as if he had forgotten he had made a tacit compact with her. *The Jazz Singer* finally came to the movie house in Knoxville in the middle of the summer, which led her to wonder why, now that silent pictures were gonna talk, Flash wasn't. Then, too, on August 2 Calvin Coolidge, who never said a thing to anyone, announced to the whole nation that he wasn't going to run again in '28 and Flash put up a sign in the shop window the next day which said SMITH IN '28.

Smith, Opal remarked on seeing it. That's funny.

Why? he asked.

He watched a repeating pleat form on her forehead where her eyebrows, if she had them, would have been moving up and down suggestively. Well, *Smith,* she said.

What about him?

Again, her forehead puckered.

You know. *Mr. Smith* for president.

—*so?* Flash said.

He was acting like he didn't know the sound of his own name.

You're only out for Smith 'cause he's against the Prohibition, Fos put in.

High time we put some drink back in the White House, Flash affirmed.

Fos's first response was not for Al Smith, though, but for Herbert Hoover on the grounds that Hoover's cocktail combination of a Quaker and a civil engineer was better for the nation than whiskey and soda. Fos's reputation had led to his being invited to become a member of the Knoxville Optimists Club, a social coup as far as Opal was concerned. Their meetings were the second Friday night of every month and that August they were drafting nominations for the club's endorsements in the '28 elections. Fos, himself, had volunteered to make the case for Hoover at the meeting even though being there meant missing the peak night of the Perseid shower over Kitty Hawk for the first time since he'd met Opal. Nevertheless, they were going to leave for North Carolina first thing in the morning. The afternoon had been a scorcher and their place above the bakery would stay hot right through the night, even with the windows open. It was cooler on the ground floor in the back room of the shop, and Opal had some work to do before they left. I'm gonna stay on here, she told him. Writin out these invoices if you can get one of the boys t' carry you back home after the meetin.

He left at six and she wrote bills and addressed envelopes until a little after eight when, with the sun just set, she felt a chill from the back alley and got up to close the door. There was no reason for her to go back to Flash's desk instead of to her own. No reason, either, to start opening the drawers. Maybe she was looking for some stamps in case she ran out. Maybe she was looking for more carbon paper. In either case, he never would have kept them in the bottom right-hand drawer.

He hadn't locked it for the simple reason that, with Fos and Opal being who they were, Flash believed there was no need to.

What a causationist would call forensic fallacy.

All along the pirate coast that night the stars were falling down, the sea was churning white with inner lights, and on the heights of Kitty Hawk, no one was there to keep it all accountable.

She should have been there counting astral trails across the galaxy instead of sitting outside Flash's house in Fos's truck down by the river with the pictures in her hands. She could see him in the house standing at the window in the dark. He'd heard the truck pull up outside. After a while he'd turned the porch light on. Now it was a question of her going in or driving off. He wasn't coming out.

She realized soon enough the extent of her revulsion when she couldn't cross the threshold, couldn't be in the same room with him.

She passed the envelope through the open door but let it go before he touched it.

He knew what was inside and let it fall.

She's only a child was the most important thing she had to say but couldn't get it out.

More complicated protestations burned inside her throat, inchoate anger.

If he had marketed his own defense or slammed the door on her she could have marshaled her outrage into an ordered hatred, but he didn't.

Some former kindness he had shown her, some undifferentiated fairness he had once expressed, kept her standing when she should have left.

I swear to you it's not the way it looks, he said. I didn't even touch her, dit. In the beginning.

Opal closed her eyes.

I don't want to know, she stated.

A car passed in the street behind her, and she stepped into the shadow on the porch.

What do you mean—*in the beginning?*

Instead of answering, he moved across the threshold and slipped into the dark across from her. Moths excited by the brightness danced within the pool of light that separated them.

She could hear him breathing.

Above that she could hear the crickets.

She could hear a bullfrog booming by the river.

She could hear her heart.

You don't hafta answer anything I ask. I didn't come here to ask questions.

No, I want to—

I came here to tellya that I found those pictures. An' that I think what you've done is the wrongest thing I've ever known a man t' do. An' if you don't stop it right now, tonight, if it hasn't stopped already, then I'm personally goin to her parents I don't care what shame an' trouble it'll cost. 'Cause I'll tell you right now as soon as Fos learns about this he an' you are over. Done. An' that's a fact.

She could see his white shirt in the dark, a shade of silver from the moonlight.

Now I've said my piece, she told him.

She had backed herself against the clapboard siding of the house to keep her distance from him.

So now I'm goin, she announced.

He reached to touch her, saying at the same time, but I love her.

Don't you use that word with me—

You—surely you can understand what happens to a person when love like that bursts in on you—

She couldn't see where it would land, so the full force of her swing connected with his face a little sooner than she thought it would. The pain raced up her arm and made the blood ring in her ears.

She made it to the truck not really seeing anything, her temples pounding.

She got in and gasped out loud when his face was there beside hers in the window. He reached in to stop her hand from turning the ignition.

He was stronger than she was, and when he saw that he was hurting her, he eased up.

Don't tell her parents.

—*too late.*

Give me a week.

Why should I?

He released his hold on her and told her, Lally's pregnant.

The weight of all her patient waiting fell on her then, the years of wanting to be pregnant fell the way a boom drops or the way a line of mercury collapses in a glass tube under falling pressure.

She felt dizzy.

We're going down to Georgia the beginning of the week. There's a doctor there I know. Who'll fix it.

—*fix* it, she managed to repeat.

She waited for the explanation.

It came, a wordless shrug accompanied by a simultaneous gesture of erasure with his hand: *you* know: *fix* it: done. The end.

He stared at her.

She's fourteen, Opal.

I know how old she is, Flash.

She wants to go to college in a few years, have a job. You can't do that in this country if you've had a baby when you're fourteen years old—

You're not fourteen. Don't you want . . . don't you want this baby?

Even as she said them she knew her words were falling on deaf ears.

She took a breath. Promise me you won't do nothin till me an' Fos get back from North Carolina.

She gripped the steering wheel, stared straight ahead. An' I'll promise not to say nothin to anyone.

She looked at him.

Probably the smartest man she ever met.

So she knew he knew that part of her was prospecting, already staking claim to his own child.

She knew he knew it by the way he nodded.

The problem was: she could never know what was going on in Flash's mind.

And she knew he knew that, too.

So she hit the horn and kept her left hand on it with the whole weight of her upper body as she drove away, engine racing, the combustion sending out a ghostly cloud of smoke until she could see him growing smaller, distant in the sideview mirror. Then she turned the corner. She had reached the river.

Blue thread through gray woven fabric, the comet trail at night, her conscience tailed the river of her thoughts like a ghost ship.

They'd been driving east since daybreak, back and forth across the traipsing Tennessee three times before it aimed upstream, reverting north, and the road climbed beside the French Broad into the foothills of the Great Smokies, rising from the basin six thousand feet.

They hadn't stopped at noon when Fos brought out the paper bag of hard-boiled eggs and chicken sandwiches, eating, instead, while they were heading east. Now the sun was at their backs at last and they were nearly at the crest of the pitch-and-toss geology from which it was downhill all the way to the state line and Carolina. She wasn't tired, merely bothered by the voice inside her mind that was her conscience.

Read t' me or somethin, she requested.

Fos had cleaned the stack of science journals out while packing but there was a yellowed flyer from the Optimist Club stuck in the visor where he sat.

What is an Optimist? he read.

He sent her a look to see if this was going to meet with her approval.

An Optimist is someone who follows the Doctrine of Optimism. He has a bright and hopeful nature.

Opal sighed a deep sigh and drummed a finger on the steering wheel.

What is the Doctrine of Optimism? Fos continued reading, answering the question in a slightly different voice. For her entertainment:

The Doctrine of Optimism is the belief that we live in the best of all possible worlds. It is the theory that Good will ultimately triumph over Evil.

He stopped to swat a bumblebee with the rolled-up paper.

Settled back again to read.

—*Good will ultimately triumph over Evil.* Read that already. *What does an Optimist do in the event of Evil? An Optimist never loses sight of hope. He*—

I gotta tellya something, she suddenly put in.

Okay, he said expectantly.

I gotta stop. So I can tellya.

There was a clearing in the pines beyond the next switchback. It had a picnic table by the road, where she pulled over and they both got out.

They sat down beside each other on the picnic bench and Fos poured them iced tea from the Thermos. There was a luff of pine branches behind them and some kind of orchids pushing through the pine-strewn groundcover—orchids with those lugs that looked like turkey throats. And there were wild turkeys, too, somewhere, gobbling up the undergrowth with noise like bubbling mud. Through which a bobwhite's music pierced, a silver needle.

Is your hand still actin up? Fos asked, trying to anticipate what was on her mind.

She had told him she had closed it in a file drawer. Not that she had hurt it striking Flash.

I think we got some trouble, Opal told him.

Fos flicked his gaze over to the truck. What is it? Is it the tires?

He started to stand up.

It's Flash, she said.

Fos didn't move.

Flash has taken up with someone.

Fos breathed a sigh that sounded like relief. Well that day was bound t' come.

With Lally Gallagher, she told him.

Nothing happened for a half a minute then Fos sat down and forced a sound out of himself half snort half grunt. I thought there for a minute you said Lally Gallagher.

He waited to hear otherwise.

The optimist, she saw.

This was not a piece of news Fos had a place for in his world.

This was not a piece of news which he had a place for in his galaxy.

This was news from another planet.

How much of it he was equipped to understand she had to take on trust. But she told him everything. Everything, that is, except about the photographs.

If there's anyone that Flash will listen to, it's you. You gotta talk to him, she said.

He nodded, then stood up.

Then he sat back down again and took her hand.

He stared down at the dirt and mix of summer litter at his feet.

I gotta do it now, he said. 'Cause if I don't . . . He stared across the deserted road for words to finish. Couldn't find them.

I know, she said. She squeezed his hand. That's why I toldja.

Climbing back up the eastern slope of the Great Smokies they were driving into sun and then before the sun began to slip behind the mountaintop, a grim cortege of darkening clouds lined up and the first plump drops of moisture, pillows of rain, began to strike the windshield. A summer storm, classic, self-renewing, broke above them in full spate. There was no shelter from its fury, from the lightning, but they battened down inside the truck and spent a sleepless night under its noise.

With the road washed out below the mountain pass and the French Broad threatening the lesser bridges it wasn't until Monday night that they drove across the Tennessee into Knoxville's city limits and turned right along the river to Flash's house. The house was dark, his car was nowhere within sight, but Fos went round the back and found a way in, then came back to tell her, Look's like he's gone.

Tuesday morning she assessed that no one had been in the shop since she'd left it Friday evening and when Flash didn't come to work that day, Fos went over to his house and waited for him.

On Wednesday morning they talked about whether or not he should drive to Dayton and on their way to work, Fos stopped at the Western Union and used the telephone to call the Amity Hotel and ask for Mr. Smith, leaving his name and the message to return to Knoxville because of an emergency. "Crisis in the trenches," as he put it. That would tip his ol' war buddy off. But just in case he also sent a telegram.

By Saturday they'd still heard nothing, which they started to interpret in the always misbegotten spirit of no news is good. Afternoon stretched into early evening and still they lingered in the shop, neither one engaged in anything that couldn't wait but both drawing out the time till they closed up, went home. Sunday would be a day the shop was closed, a day they hadn't planned for, another day of waiting till they heard from Flash and they weren't looking forward to it. They worked on until the light went, then Fos stood up and stretched and said, Come on. We're lettin this get outta hand.

She came toward him in agreement, keys in hand to lock up shop, and put her arms around him where they stood in the shadowy unlit back room. A car drew up outside in the back alley. Then another one behind it. Before either of them had a chance to move a sound like lightning splitting a live oak cracked the silence. Splinters flew. Fos covered Opal's head with his arms and pivoted her away from where steel claws, sharks' teeth, were biting through the door, the rhythm of the axe swings hard and fast, erratic as the sudden pounding of his heart. Three men in trailing robes burst through the jagged breach and stormed the premises with clubs, followed by another three with weapons, all six surprised at the sight of Fos and Opal. Two policemen pulled the split door off its hinges while another with a flashlight pushed them back against the workbench then the lights came on, brighter than they'd ever been and a man in a white suit and buckskin shoes stepped in through the chaos and assessed them with ice-colored eyes. Pull the place apart, he said. You know what you're looking for.

Fos recognized the man in white as the District Attorney, Tay Luttrell. Flash's brother.

What's the meaning of all this? Fos demanded.

The men in the white robes with cloth hoods started breaking into desks, smashing the equipment with their billyclubs.

Stop—what are you doing?

Shut up or I'll land you both in jail longside him.

From his breast pocket Tay slid a photograph and held it up in front of Fos and Opal. It was one of the ones Opal had found in Flash's desk. One of the ones he had taken of Lally.

Fos blinked at it, not comprehending.

Taken in this very place if I'm not mistaken? Tay baited. Found this in my brother's house right out in the open. Where most people keep their Bibles. The Gallaghers ain't seen this yet. I wish t' God they didn't have to.

Opal took a small step forward. Please, she said. For Lally's sake. Can't you just get rid a' that? He didn't mean no harm the way he took it.

It was Tay's turn to blink.

I take it you ain't heard, he rightly concluded.

Lally had bled to death in the back of Flash's car following the abortion by the doctor down in Georgia. Flash had carried her body into a sheriff's office and had been arrested on the spot, pending investigation.

The Gallaghers, beyond consolation, made two requests:

Mrs. Gallagher wanted him strung up like a nigger, his offense dismembered. Mr. Gallagher wanted him strapped in an electric chair.

His death would not restore their daughter to this life but it would be the first installment in what would be, for them, a lifetime of exacting retributions. If they could have redesigned the species so Flash could have died a thousand deaths they would have sold their souls to do so. It was, to a large extent, a credit to his brother that he wasn't liberated from his cell by their vigilantes in the middle of the night and executed. Although he prosecuted Flash more harshly than the letter of the law intended, Tay exercised an extra diligence over his brother's safety before and after extradition for the trial. As he put it, he wanted to make sure he oiled the coondog's neck to make it slicker. For the guillotine. The fact that Tay stood to inherit Flash's share of their family's fortune didn't seem to weigh much on the scales of Knoxville's jurisprudence. As a prosecuting force Tay was after blood, not money. He tried, but failed, to bring the case for murder, then he tried again for manslaughter: in the end it was the Mann Act that convicted Flash: two counts for transportation of a minor, five counts coercion and enticement, ten counts for criminal activity with a minor, ten for publication of pornography. Despite the fact the federal act carried a limit of ten years imprisonment, Tay was asking for internment under the state statutes on all twenty-seven counts—two and a half life sentences. In succession.

I'm gonna write a letter to that Clarence Darrow, Opal pledged.

She did, but the trial was over before Darrow wrote her back.

Fos went to see Flash in the jail and sat behind him at the trial. But Opal couldn't bring herself to do it. Writing Mr. Darrow was all she'd do. And when the time came, she helped Fos pack up Flash's books in cardboard boxes.

Then the moment came when they had to say where they were going.

They stood and looked at all the cartons and Opal wondered, Where we gonna keep this stuff.

I guess we hafta ask ourselves. Where we're gonna go, Fos answered.

She knew he was presuming North Carolina so she told him, I'm not livin with my daddy as a married woman, Fos. Don't ask me to.

They'd been married seven years.

I wasn't thinkin that direction, he confided.

He sat down and spread his hands before him. Not the hands designed to speed the plow, but they'd have to do.

They sent the bed, the piecrust table, Flash's books and Fos's books, and Opal's trousseau to the farm on the Clinch River on a cattle dealer's truck and stayed in the barren rooms over the Rinaldis until the trial was done. The night that Flash was sentenced, they loaded the last things into the truck and went, not speaking, down the stairs for the last time. Opal drove. Fos cradled the fishbowl with the phosphorus in it on his lap. There had been a frost the night before, and he could feel the cold air coming up his pant legs from the floorboards. When Opal came to where they'd turned each morning for the shop he sensed her hesitate and saw her look in that direction. Then she drove straight on toward the bridge across the Tennessee. He could feel the fishbowl getting colder in his hands. Halfway across the bridge he said, Pull over.

What have you forgot?

Just stop.

She pulled over to the right as far as she was able. Turn the engine off, he told her.

What are we doin, Fos?

Somethin that we needta.

No one stops at night here unless they're gonna jump, she said. Or throw somethin in the water.

The night was sharp and bright and she could sense the coming cold in last year's timber burning in the chimneys, in the woodsmoke rising toward Orion. Opal gave a shiver, she could hear the icy river breaking on the black cutwaters of the massive bridge below.

Ready? Fos asked.

For what—?

He hefted the goldfish bowl.

Fireworks, he told her.

He launched the bowl over the guardrail. The luminescent rock ignited like a giant's—like Orion's—match the instant it combined with air, its glow an eerie burning ribbon as it flew.

Flash! Fos called, sadness trailing on his echo.

The phosphorus kept burning, just as he'd said it would, a green unnatural wonder, like a stain of bioluminescence, even as it sank into the water.

It's still goin, Opal marveled.

Other kinds of folks might go to church to light their candles, but not us, she thought.

She watched the point of light still signal, its radiance a race against extinction.

For Flash, Fos said again.

For Lally, Opal added.

For everything that might have been.

For love.

. . . Ahab dropped a tear into the sea; nor did all the Pacific contain such wealth as that one wee drop.

HERMAN MELVILLE, *Moby-Dick,* "The Symphony"

burning bridges

Everything that shines in water is not gold.

Despite what all the boys in Washington will try to tellya.

They'll come down two by two, at first—two by two in their big cars. They'll come down with their charts and maps, and they'll take their jackets off and dab the sweat beneath their hatbands with starched handkerchiefs and mention *mighty hot down here* like they were scouting out some jungle in the New World for the plundering eternal glory of the Old. They come the way those ancient Europeans came, two or three small scouting parties at a time. Men on a mission, armed with shiny glass and enterprise and the belief in wealth of nations.

What good is a river that's not flowing gold, they make us ask. Like land—which they will tell us is plain worthless if it's not producing something we can use—a river going unproductively about its business across plains through valleys from the mountains to the sea is wasted if not brought to heel within the cosmic and commercial wheel of fortune. A river's no mere artery of earth's, no aorta of the heartland, no petty sphygmic system spouting fishies for the hell of it: a river is *a trust:* exploitable: an invitation to a chance to channel, levee, riprap, tax and dam for profit. A river is a goldfield waiting to be panned. A purse. A cursive prayer to fortune. A course in economics.

You watch it one day when it's placid and you tell yourself, I know this angel. She's God's handiwork. She is here to help me. Then you go to sleep and wake up in her torrent, to her rage. You think you know the river, but the river is impossible to know. You think the river is your friend but you discover to your misery that the river has a code of ethics all its own. Ultimately, you resign yourself to trusting it—and even loving it—but it will break your heart. Like other rogues who've left you stranded, a bystander, in their self-constructing wakes.

Like Flash, Fos thought.

You take a man and set him in a landscape and maybe it's his human nature to impose a human narrative on it, to imagine human motive in the turning of a leaf, the falling of a star. He took to starting every day with a solemn trek down to the river as a form of meditation. Maybe even as a form of prayer. He missed his friend, he missed his former life so much those first few months the loss was like a wound to time, a discontinuity in the sequence of his sense of self. And the river, its suffusion, acted like a balm. There were no gaps in it. No disappearances. No losses. As an antithesis to life's dissolutions, it was a seamless promise. It could resurface hope. As an allegory, it was perfect. *Life's a river,* he would think. Time's a river. Love is.

Thus fortified, he'd walk back across the scraggy bottomland to one more day's hard labor.

Fos lost so much weight the first two months on the farm that as he bent down to haul a fallen branch out of the channel one morning his gold-rimmed specs slipped off his face and whirled away from him downstream before his eyes, and in that instant the whole river turned into a cosmic galaxy, a color field, of gold.

Without his specs Fos saw the world as perhaps a fish does from the center of a fishbowl. It was a pleasant world—no depth-of-field, no specificity of form—a world of interlayered color fields like nebulae or gases. It was the other world he lived in half his life when he was sleeping, or at rest. When he was lying quiet, in their bed. Making love to Opal. His *jelly world,* she called it. Where everything, including her, looked like a color gumdrop.

For several minutes Fos stood still, watching with respect how readily the water gave itself to light's illusions. Flashing from a pebble the light looked as solid as his gold-rimmed glasses. A world as real, through all his other senses, as the one he saw when he had his glasses on—but a different one. A world beneath the world. Something known, but unknown. Like a secret kept from your best friend.

He couldn't count the number of times he'd said out loud, You think you know someone.

You think you know someone, he'd start to say. She'd wait for him to press the point: you think you know a man but then you find out he has lied to you. Against your will, without your knowledge or consent, that man's lie has changed your life. Irrevocably. Not for the best. Not even for the better. *You think you know a man,* he'd say. Then stop.

The anger he was feeling—if, in fact, what he was feeling was anger—if, in fact, what he was feeling was so simple a thing as to have a name—call it what she might, whatever he was feeling fell away before it reached expression. Whatever he was feeling stayed inside him.

It was not uncommon as the weeks passed into months, that the day went by without a word between them being spoken. They still touched. Their touch, lingering on contact, lasted through the night while they were sleeping, cloning them into a single dreamless creature. Sometimes, without realizing it, they held hands as they took their meals at the rough table, Fos laying his hand on top of hers, not noticing, as his palm grew callused with farm work how her skin had chafed, grown coarser, too. It was as if a vow of silence, like a marriage vow, held them in thrall. Like monks communing with the sacred: there really wasn't anything to say. Exhaustion, on its own, might have served to silence them—talk, after all, takes energy and concentration. Talk takes work, and they were tired at the end of every day. Still, in the beginning, they found strength. They whispered when they went to bed. They confided in each other. But soon too many things began to happen. One layer at a time—one thing, then another, like quick layers of embalming stoppered their responses, caught them speechless, baffled them, rendered their inarticulateness complete.

The first silencing enveloped them, an atmosphere of soundlessness, a vacuum, on entering the house.

No life had filled it since Early's absence after Karo's and the babies' deaths. Nothing had been living there save funguses and mold, hornets, termites, spiders, bats, and rodents, and if the house had ever had a human soul, it had long ago crawled back down its ladder of evolution. If the house had been a place where she'd etched childhood memory, if its walls had listened to her mother's voice or had witnessed her own birth, then she might have remembered images to disguise its miserable decrepitude. But there was no pretending—even for her mother, this house had never been a home. It was Early's house; and even Early had found nothing here to make him want to stay. If they had had the money they would have torn it down and started from the ground up fresh and new, but money, now, was hard to come by and theirs had become a life of making do. A patchwork life. Anything that worked was old and out-of-date, and everything that didn't work they could not afford to fix. Fos, who prided himself on being able to capitalize on boy scout science to rig contraptions that could run on air, was at a loss on how to mend a fence or get the tractor to back up from where he'd plowed it to a sudden ditch. He was confused by animals, believing, possibly with cause, that they were smarter, in their way, about unscientific things than he was. He liked them too much to justify them to the general train of thought about the food chain. When he accidentally killed a vole beneath the plow it ruined that night's sleep. It silenced him. When she asked him what was wrong he couldn't say I killed a vole. It would sound stupid. He couldn't say I can't figure out how to chop wood in equal pieces. She couldn't say I can't work out how to keep the stove lit. I can't keep the food from going bad. I can't get the yeast to proof. He couldn't say I can't keep myself on godsearth without help. I can't make a simple sawcut. I can't mend a harness, tap a maple, make a table. She couldn't say I can't keep myself on godsearth without products. I can't weave a basket. Can't make a brick wall. Make a broom. Make bronze. I can't smith or thatch or whittle. I can't cooper, thresh, smelt ore, card wool, tan hide, forge iron. Can't render fat from geese. Make bacon. Whistle for the hell of it. Dream of having children. Speak.

The worst of it for Opal was the sense that they were going backward, burning bridges, losing ground. Disappearing from themselves. The worst of it for Fos was thinking they'd become too modern in their habits to succeed in the kind of fundamental enterprise that even Karo and Early had seemed to enjoy with no complaining. *If they could do it* he would think—another monkish exercise, trying to conform to past examples set by martyrs. Then one day, looking for some extra planks to mend the upstairs floorboard, he pried open the stuck door to the unused room. The door cracked open on a dim space where the roof declined to the eaves around a window dormer, shuttered closed. It was that shutter, loose on all its hinges, they could hear on windy nights, and when he prised the shutter off, the chamber filled with ghostly light.

Since losing his best pair of glasses in the river, Fos had started wearing his spare pair tied around his head with a shoe lace. Now he lifted them an inch up to his eyebrows. Then he dropped them down again.

The floor, on close—that is to say *focused*—inspection, was littered with wood shavings piled in curls which stirred around his feet. In the middle of them was a cane seat chair, facing toward the window. On one side of the chair there was a stack of white pine blocks, uniformly cut, two by two, six inches long. On the other side, and all along the dormer wall, was an array of something lined along the floor, covered up with gunny sacks. Fos picked up one of the pine blocks and turned it over. He sat down in the chair and looked out the window. It was facing west. You could see the river and the sky above it and the fields beyond. There was a bucket in the corner with two blocks in the bottom of it, cracked and discolored as if they'd been left out in the rain and then exposed to sun. They reminded him of the skiff makers on the Outer Banks who whittled in their spare time. Pipes and things. Animals and miniature churches. Fos pulled back the gunny sack beside the chair to see what was beneath it: before him was a line of objects, maybe twenty of them, eerily identical. He picked one up and looked it over carefully. There was no mistaking what it was; still, he'd never seen one in its element, he wasn't altogether certain it was drawn from life or if it was a mythical concoction. He would have bet Early had never seen one, either—never seen a whale, especially a white one like this white pine specimen. But there it was, neatly fitted in his hand: a white whale with two beady eyes and a forlornly downturned smile. Fos picked up a second one and compared it to the first: a virtual repeat. Exact in every way except for an almost imperceptible difference in the grain of wood. One of these objects might have been amusing or, in a strange way, even beautiful. But there were *twenty* of them, chillingly identical. He stood up and pulled back all the gunny sacks to see if there were more. There must have been a hundred of the creatures, all facing in the same direction, staring up at him, sinister, like an army, in their uniformity. Sheep on a distant hill, pebbles in the riverbed—nature isn't prone to turning out identicals, the odds are stacked against it. Nature's hand, like man's, slips and trips the light fantastic, errs, improves upon itself and improvises. Even a machine turning spindles on a lathe will oscillate and spit out less than perfect replications but these were all made not on an assembly line but by one man sitting in an attic staring out a window and the grammar of their manufacture did not speak of joy. The grammar of their making announced fear to him; spoke of desolation. They had no context in nature, these objects of conformity, no place in the natural world. They were contrived, like turned and practiced worries on a rosary, not to relieve one's sorrow but to degrade the act of suffering, to humble it, by numbering, through repetition. Numb it. Take the noise and bruit of being human and shutter it, inutterably. Make it dumb.

The way he looked at her she had to speak. *What's the matter withya?* she asked when he walked in. You look likeya seen a ghost.

He put one of the whales down on the kitchen table there between them.

What izat? she said.

What do ya *think* it is?

He placed another one, identical, beside it.

Look like whales t' me.

Me, too.

She blinked at them, a trait she'd learned, unconsciously, from Fos.

Early made 'em, Fos explained.

They hadn't said this much in weeks.

Must be a hundred a' them, he went on. Upstairs in the attic room. All a' them the same.

She scratched her arm where it was riddled with mosquito bites.

Why would he do a thing like that? she wondered. Surprised that she had wondered it out loud.

Fos stared at her. Mosquito bites were on her neck and forehead, too. I think he went plumb crazy, he ventured. *This life,* he said. He gestured toward the kitchen walls. This life is *hard,* this kinda livin. Hard enough for you an' me. Go an' add on top of it for Earl his wife an' babies dyin—you saw the state we found him in, can you imagine how he musta lived here all alone, what his days and nights were like—no one t' share his worries with no one to answer to or answer back imagine what goes on in peoples' minds when they're cooped up inside themselves like that—

It was as if a dam had burst inside of him—he hadn't said so many words in months. She stared at him and stopped her itching.

I mean—you think you know a man, he tried to explain.

He gave another plaintive gesture.

Your turn t' speak she thought it meant.

Well, she started.

She cleared her throat. I don't think neither of us thought we *knew* him. Earl. Except for he and I bein related, he was a stranger.

Yes, but you think you *know* someone.

Fos began to pace, his whole body, now, needing to speak.

It's like that river out there, he pointed. You see it every day you hear it moving in your sleep you look at it and think about it wonder where it's been and where it's goin and you think you've come t' know it pretty well an' then one day you wake up an' discover it's *betrayed* you—

He stopped, staring past her toward the Tennessee.

A river don't 'betray' a person, Fos. Just because it don't do what you want it to. It's just a river. May as well get angry with a tree for coughin leaves insteada money.

It makes you wonder, is all I'm sayin, he continued. How much you can know about a thing, a person. If you can know anything at all. Maybe *no one's* who we think they are. No one. Makes you doubt yourself, wonder if you even know yourself or if you've been lyin, too, along with everybody else.

He heard her take a gulp of air and turned to tell her I'm not talkin about you.

Who, then? she said.

He shook his head.

The solace of not speaking was in never saying Flash's name.

Go see him, Opal said.

Fos shook his head again and looked at her. Maybe if their first months on the farm had been a neat success, if he and Opal had been able to accomplish the transition from their city life to their new one in the country, then perhaps there would have been no ground on which this sense of betrayal could seed and grow. But when they moved onto the farm they crossed a burning bridge between two realms. Almost everything that Fos was good at doing in the former had no application in the new. He was, by nature, more a tinkerer and thinker than a man who in the routine of a day was equally as balanced on a mule as on a fence post. Now he had no time for tinkering—for thinking, even. No time to sit upstairs and whittle life away while his mind roved in ever smaller self-deceiving circles. No time for innovation. None for dreams. Every blister that arose, every strained and aching muscle, each humiliation in the face of unaccustomed simple tasks, seemed to bear the imprint of a name, as accusation: *Flash.*

He's sittin there in prison, Opal said. He's all alone.

So was Earl. So is everybody. So are we.

Go see him, she said.

I can't.

Say at least *'some day.'* Least say 'maybe.'

He knew that it would take another world from this one for him to go and see his friend again. Another world—like the one unseen, that his specs brought into focus.

He put his arms around her for the first time in days and murmured, Cross that bridge if I ever come to it.

But in his heart he knew that bridge was already burned.

Is it not a saying in every one's mouth, Possession is half of the law: that is, regardless of how the thing came into possession?

HERMAN MELVILLE, *Moby-Dick,* "Fast-Fish and Loose-Fish"

ENTER LIGHTFOOT, radiant

They called it *spoondrift* where she came from. Funny word, she thinks, now, when she spots it rising out there where the road comes from.

Spoon. Drift.

*Spin*drift, the other word for it, is the better of the two, describing what it is: cool spray spun back from a wave's curl like blown kisses.

Sometimes she'd see a single one arise, a spume of dust way out there in the field where nothing ever was, a spasm of red powder flaring as if a ghost down by the river, bored with heaven, was pitching quoits to pass the time.

But this one moved.

Moved fast, its trail of ochre smoke parading out behind and she prayed that Fos was somewhere near not three fields away so she didn't have to face this uninvited trouble on her own. *Po-lice,* she is thinking. Because they both sure look like they're policing something when they step out of the car. Not so much the way they're dressed—shirtsleeves, but their shoes say *city.*

Fos had seen them, too, so he's there to meet them on the porch.

Mr. Foster? one of them calls up.

She watches when he takes his straw hat off and mops his brow. Married man, she notices, the wedding band is on display.

I'm Mr. Foster, Fos responds.

One of Opal's chickens comes around the corner, sets to pecking in the dirt in their fresh footprints.

Ray Foster? the other fellow asks. The fella with *the truck?*

Fos lets this pass unanswered.

'Cause it's standing right beside them big as day.

Which they suddenly take note of, inspecting what's still lettered on the side. The paint is fading but the message is still clear: P-H-E-N-O-M-E-N-O-L-O-G-I-S-T.

You've got some reputation in these parts, Mr. Foster, one of them tells Fos.

The other one says, Everyone we talk to tells us you're the man we have to see.

The first one steps a little closer, his attention moving momentarily to Opal.

And I guess you must be *Mrs.* Foster, he says.

She steps forward, too, and says, Are you from Knoxville?

No m'am, he replies.

He goes for his billfold, looks into it like he's searching for his cash and hands over a printed card.

The *Government?* she reads and passes Fos the card.

An atmosphere, material as weather, suddenly arrives.

Fos, clearing his specs, reads what's printed on the card: "Office of . . ."

His voice breaks off and Opal looks at him to see what's wrong.

He looks like he's heard a joke. Ya live long enough, he muses. Ya getta see it all.

The man who handed her the card says, Perhaps you heard the President when he was down here last December? Down to see the dam at Muscle Shoals? The Wilson Dam?

Fos and Opal look at one another. Muscle Shoals is out in *Alabama,* Fos explains.

Well but it's *on the Tennessee,* the man maintains. Implying *So's your farm.* Maybe you heard him on the radio.

Opal says, We used to listen to the radio when we were livin back in

Knoxville but since we moved out here—She gestures toward the barn and fields by way of explanation.

Well then you must have read about it in the paper.

Fos tells him they used to read the paper back in Knoxville but living out here printed news is hard to come by. *Any* news is hard to come by, he adds. Any news that has to do with things outside the Valley.

He doesn't add that he and Opal didn't even vote in the last election. Doesn't mention that they hadn't even heard that Mr. Roosevelt had won until a letter came at Christmas from the Rinaldis back in Knoxville.

The men from Washington exchange a look. Then the married one says, The speech at Muscle Shoals was the first policy address by Mr. Roosevelt after the election. Before he was inaugurated. The first one he gave. We have a copy with us we hand out to people—

He opens the car door and starts to root around while the other man focuses his attention on the truck. Opal watches him, her suspicions rising. She hasn't seen such men as these in quite a while. Hasn't heard such talk since Flash.

May I look inside? the man next to the truck asks Fos. I'd like to see what kind of tricks you've got up your sleeve. And even though his tone is sheepish his hand is on the truck's door handle so Fos comes down the steps and says, Just what is it you fellas want?

The one who gave the card to Opal now gives Fos a pamphlet from the back seat of the car. Why Mr. Foster, he says, smiling. *We're here to offer you a job.* He hands Opal a pamphlet, too. Across the top is printed the same thing that was printed on the card: OFFICE OF RURAL ELECTRIFICATION.

You read this, he says, you'll understand what Mr. Roosevelt proposes. This part right here—he points, then reads out loud: . . . I believe we are charged with the duty of planning for the proper use, conservation, and development of the natural resources of the Tennessee River and its adjoining territory for the general social and economic welfare of the Nation. We have an opportunity to restore the land of the pioneers to its ancient good health, an opportunity to set an example of planning, not just for ourselves but for generations to come—to create a complete river watershed involving many States and the future lives and welfare of millions . . .

Future lives and welfare of millions, Opal repeats. That's highfalutin talk.

We're going to bring prosperity to the Tennessee River Valley, he continues. Water-power. Better living through electricity.

He turns to Fos. And that's where you come in, he tells him.

Opal sees that all his talking has brought the blood to the man's face, like a little fire. It's the quieter one, though, who says, The idea is to take a page from the revivalists' Bible. Spread the message. Preach the future to the people.

"Preach?" Opal wonders to herself.

The lure of maximum possibilities, she sees on his face, is somehow irresistible to him, almost delicious, as if *e-lec-tri-city* is a pleasurable emotion. Sure, she likes what it can do—likes the miracle acts it brings to town—but she's never found it *exciting* like these boys. They were lighting up before her eyes from sheer excitement. They were telling Fos how they could change the course of history if they worked together—route the future as if time flowed on the earth like water and tomorrow was a river they could riprap dam and beautify. *Reforestation,* they were saying. Hydroelectric plants. Lakes stocked with fishes. Eradication of disease and poverty. An end to soil depletion. End to mosquitoes and malaria. They would push the boat out and sail into the future—maybe even sail into the *sky* the wind was so much in their favor. The glow of their excitement was beginning to reach Fos—she could see it in the way he stood, his arms extending slightly toward them like a man before a fireplace. Together they could show the missus how to flick the switches, how to Mastermix and turn the stove on with a finger on a button. Demonstrate the Coolerators and Electroluxes. Round 'em up and bring 'em in to buy the products that would lighten most the burdens of the peoples' daily lives. But first, they had to show them what they couldn't see. Show them things they'd never seen before. *Oh,* Opal heard herself say out loud. That's the nature of a revelation: it makes its own pronouncement. It says: the world you see before you is brand-new. The world you've known is gone.

And you're left there, a hatched chick, to contemplate that broken egg behind you.

You mean you're gonna carry electricity all the way out here? it dawns on Opal. How you gonna do that?

But Fos had stepped in, closing up the group. What kind of job? he wants to know.

She watches both men smile.

Well like we said. We're going to go around and set up tents and take some music people with us for the entertainment. We're going to make demonstrations. Put on a show. Like people say you used to do there with your truck: the *Phenomenologist.* Only instead of doing tricks we'll show them how to wire up a light bulb. How to screw it in the socket. How to earth the plug.

You mean you're askin Fos to travel? Opal focused.

The men turned their smiles on Fos again and one of them said, Why don't you show us what you've got in here?

He touched the truck.

Well, Fos said. He pushed his glasses up his nose. You boys are engineers yourselves I take it.

You got that right.

Then you'll recognize everything in here. Spark coils. Switchboards with some low-watt bulbs. Trickle charges, storage battery, vacuum tubes. Effervescent salts. Your standard chemicals. And oh yeah—

He pulled the rear door open. A kind of chemical presence emerged.

I've got an x-ray here with a fixed plate.

Now you're talking, one of them enthused.

Fos climbed in and started to unearth the contraption. Haven't had this out in quite a while, he mentioned. Not since Caleb Belk came by with that bird.

It was a baldy eagle, Opal tells them. Fell outta the sky into his yard. Thing was five feet across, with its wings outspread. Caleb was concerned it was diseased because he keeps that chicken farm so he brought it here to get a look inside. He didn't want to cut it up, you know. It bein a bald eagle an' the symbol of the nation. You don't open up a baldy without second thoughts.

The men helped Fos unload the x-ray to the ground then one of them climbed into the truck and poked around. She could tell neither one had paid attention to her story. So she starts to use her hands to make the next part of it more interesting. We never put a *bird* inside (she gestures.) Have we, Fos? Usually we just show *feet* (she shows them her shoe.) You should have seen the *bones* in that bird's wing—you think you know a thing or two about birds' bones from eatin chicken but I'll tellya, that bald eagle had more bones in its one wing than a fish has scales. You think you'd see the *feathers* show up, too, but nope, it was just the bones. White *lines,* you know? Inside. Then there were these *dots. White* dots like stars up in the night sky. White stars against dark sky and those were the lead *balls* from where somebody with a shotgun took the eagle down, the shot so fine you couldn't see the entrance wounds through all the feathers. You could see the wing bones with the shot lodged in them and it looked like someone with a piece of chalk had connected up the dots and drawn a constellation called *Bald Eagle* up in heaven.

She could tell they were occupied with something other than her story, so she concentrated on the one who wasn't in the truck and said, Can I *ask* you something?

Go ahead.

She noticed Fos was staring at her with a strained expression on his face.

Is electricity *fire?* she asked.

No m'am.

The reason that I ask is 'cause it *looks* like fire, Opal tried to rationalize.

Yes it does, the gentleman agreed. His lips curled with the beginning of a smile. That's just the kind of question we *expect* people are going to ask, he wagered, trying not to patronize. But fire is a chemical process, as I'm sure your husband knows. And electricity is *not.*

She didn't think this was an adequate reply but still she answered, Oh.

Behind her, in the truck, the other man rubbed his hands together and said, Well I'm satisfied. Let me ask you, Mr. Foster. What's your training?

Fos blinked and said, Well I was in the Army. Chem Corps.

That's where he took the gas, Opal volunteered. His eyes, she added.

Pointing to her own. She was more nervous now than she had ever been. First time his country called on him she hadn't known him, hadn't been there by his side to caution Fos, what are you doing? *What are you getting us into?* her look now begged.

It was an opportunity that he could not resist. Besides: his country needed him. I don't know about bein on the road so much, though, Fos conceded.

Sorry, wasn't thinking, the married one apologized. Are there *children?*

He cast his gaze on Opal. Her white hair.

*Grand*children?

Fos took another step toward them, reaching out to touch the married one's right arm. Anything to draw away attention from the look on Opal's face. It's just Opal an' me have always worked together from the first day that we met, he said.

The men met Fos's look of expectation with blank expressions.

We're *a team,* Fos said.

They looked at Fos as if they couldn't hear what he was saying. As if they were attempting to lip read without a lesson.

What you can't imagine, you can't understand. And these two gents, a working team themselves, could not imagine the kind of team Fos was referring to. Unless—"She's . . . a . . . phenomenologist, *too?*" they asked in unison.

Oh, no, Fos explained: She knows books. She's a genius at 'em.

Opal watched them look at one another.

Books? they repeated. They moved their feet across the ground in front of them, the dust attracting Opal's chickens. Mr. Foster, the one who wasn't married finally said. This is not the best of times to be a farmer. 'Specially not in the Tennessee Valley.

Still one in four Americans *is.* A farmer. In farmin, Opal said. Counting.

That statistic is a little out of date, m'am, he informed her and she turned a deeper color and looked down at her swollen hands. There's a one-third unemployment rate now in all professions, he explained. He turned and looked at Fos again. Which is why you might want to think more analytically, before you turn us down and make us turn to someone else to take this job, Mr. Foster. Not that anyone else would be as good at it as we know you'd be. You were our first choice, naturally.

Farmin ain't exactly *un*employment, Opal argued.

No m'am, the man agreed. But what we have in mind for Mr. Foster is an occupation of his time and skills resulting in *cash money.*

How *much?* Opal said.

The other one stopped turning dust up with his shoe and repeated, *books,* yep, indicating he was still a rider on that other train of thought. What about that program Topie Whatsername is running?

Topie Rothrock, his companion prompted.

A gladness seemed to spread between them.

The lustre progress generates.

The radiant of problem solving.

Lightning bolts and job creation.

Social intercourse and calories.

Make-work in the glow of government: a New Deal.

There's a woman in Knoxville, one of them explained to her. A librarian. Came up with the thought that the people we'll be bringing down here to the work sites, to the construction camps, will need some fortifying pastimes in their hours off. Constructive hobbies and the like. And likewise people down here in the Valley whose standard of living will be rising will need to educate themselves with more sophistication. Some counties down here now have less than eight thousand people in them—less than two or three adults per square mile—no railroads, no schools, no radio, no newspaper—and suddenly we're going to come down here and connect them to the larger world. *Literacy* has got to be a part of it, this woman says. Where they live and work *a library* has got to be there, so she says. She's got something like fifty thousand volumes donated to put in circulation. Trucks of mobile units. Army of librarians. Books on wheels.

Neither of them seemed to notice Fos's pained expression. *Not that kind of books* he was about to say. Book-*keeping* he was going to tell them for her sake, but she was already responding to the glow of progress, squinting at it, tallying up its possibilities. We have a library ourselves already, she confided. Upstairs in the attic all in boxes we were keepin for a friend. I could load them in the truck an' drive around. Follow with you, once you've started.

Flash's books, Fos thought, might not meet the standards set by Mr. Roosevelt. Nor the other way around.

But within the month, Opal and two other women from the region had been drafted by the energetic bibliophile Mary Utopia (Topie) Rothrock into her Mobile Library Corps. They received written instruction on decorum, the Dewey decimal system, and overdue book fines. Opal whittled the synopses of a hundred novels down to taglines she could memorize like advertising slogans and targeted her prospective clients with as much anticipated lather as Palmolive. It took the Rural Electrification boys longer to organize themselves than it took Utopia's spirited library corps—not from a lack of enthusiasm or want of purpose, but because it takes a lot more science and staging to move a river than it does to turn a page. But the boys were up and running by the fall, Fos going out with two engineers and a couple roustabouts: a day or two of traveling, half day to set up the tent: two days and nights of showtime, then a day for breaking down and packing up again. Sometimes Opal followed with him—other times she set out on her own. Fos's range—the reach of the grand plan to electrify the Valley—was greater than her own. The traveling electric show followed the river west to Mississippi, south to Alabama, north into Kentucky, striking its target like a bolt and leaving the barn door open for Hooker's troupe of salesmen and government employees. Opal's territory, which she marked off on a map with a wax crayon, looked like a drop in the river's bucket by comparison: two counties within a compass of a hundred miles. But unlike lightning, the electric show did not enjoy the chance to visit twice, whereas visiting again was Opal's duty. Opal's work was circular: she was in the trade of circulation. Even though the distance on her map between two points was far shorter than Fos's usually was, she was soon convinced the distance traveled in the reading of each book added up to miles that were immeasurable, even by her. She started noticing the different ways that people had of approaching books they never heard of, books they didn't know if they could trust. People carried books they'd been introduced to differently than the books they didn't know, she noticed. They held them with a greater ease, closer to their bodies, as if, on reading, books became a part of them. Men, especially the younger ones, tucked the book into their armpit between their rib cage and their biceps. Women carried books in front of them, pressed against their chests or up against their throats like mustard packs or a cold remedy. The volumes that had been selected by Miss Rothrock for the general circulation were printed on a list and copies of this list were posted at the local points of distribution—feed stores, filling stations or a church. People could place orders to reserve or they could drop off their returned books there, then once a month Opal would come by and set up business for a day with a Thermos of hot coffee, a folding chair and table, an ink pad and a calendar stamp and all the books. What she noticed was that people liked to look before they leaped. Unless it was a book in the 630s (Agriculture) or the 920s (Biography), most people seemed to be enticed into a future read by lifting up a book and hefting it. That's when Opal would say a word or two about it. That would usually start a brief exchange, sometimes even a conversation. Miss Rothrock's list, and her selections, had been compiled, though, along the lines of conventional edification. Nation-building needed granite blocks—Emerson and Tennyson, Oliver Wendell Holmes—not the less dense porous stuff for its foundation, which, like limestone, might erode but sure could shine. The most-often-asked-for book was still the last decade's best-seller *The Man Nobody Knows,* by Bruce Barton, which Opal was advised to call "a modern update in the life of Jesus." She had five copies of it in circulation and even so, it was always on request. She never had a copy long enough to read it, but she'd had a chance to browse it through. It described Jesus as "a young man glowing with physical strength who has pounding pulses, hot desires and . . . perfect teeth. He picked up twelve men from the bottom ranks of business and forged them into an organization that conquered the world." *My,* she thought. The writing put her in mind of reading dimestore novels back in Knoxville. Those kinds of books though weren't on Miss Rothrock's list. Nor were the books by Mr. Hemingway and Mr. Scott Fitzgerald that Flash had given her to read. Nor was *Moby-Dick.* On her own, then, one afternoon at the farm she got the pole with the hook on the end and pulled down the hatch up to the attic and climbed the ladder into its murk.

Flash's books had been stored up there, ever since they'd moved, in unopened boxes. Strange, where the stuff of paper goes to in time, she thought. It disappears. Some of it yellows, some of it browns. Some of it sheds itself like leaves from a tree. Opal had packed them all by herself the week of the trial, but under the circumstances, she hadn't paid much attention to the titles. Under the circumstances, she wanted to get the job done and not linger. Not conjecture about Flash's personal choices, Flash's nature. It took her the better part of the afternoon to bring the boxes down and arrange the books along the floor of the upstairs hallway according to the categories she'd learned from Mr. Dewey's system. When she ran out of floor space in the hallway she opened up what Fos called Early's Whale Room and started stacking fiction in beside his carved white creatures. She thought she was pretty good at categorizing by title—telling a book by its cover—but every now and then a title fooled her and she had to check inside, flicking through the pages. This happened more and more as the afternoon wore on and she got to the boxes containing what proved to be, to her surprise, entirely books of poetry. Some of them were thin as pamphlets that the government sent out about controlling farm disease and weevils. One of them she was ready to put alongside Sciences next to Mr. Einstein's book for Fos, when she opened it by chance and found that Mr. Whitman's *I Sing the Body Electric* was, instead, a kind of poem—though it didn't rhyme—about different parts of different peoples' bodies. Most of the poems in the books Flash had, in fact, weren't what Opal would have called "poetry." Many seemed to have been written in a kind of English language she had never heard or known. Some were starkly beautiful, as sort of songs. There was Mr. Frost of *North of Boston,* of whom she'd never heard. Mr. Cummings's *The Enormous Room.* Mr. Sandburg, Mr. Pound, and Mr. Wallace Stevens. There was Mr. Eliot's *Prufrock and Other Observations* in which she found the lines:

> *Do I dare*
> *Disturb the universe?*
> *In a minute there is time*
> *For decisions and revisions which a minute will reverse.*

How can you identify what you don't know if you don't know it? The great Unknown is not a static. It is peopled. Scattered through with specificity. It's a havoc. Knowledge is at large, for taking, like the air. Still, she thought, there was so much she didn't know that seemed to be the common stuff of other peoples' lives. How to know which books to read. How to read for learning. How to write a letter or a sentence which described the world the way that Mr. Frost described a wood. Or Mr. Eliot the state of solitude. She, herself, could not remember how she'd learned to read—couldn't remember being taught to recognize a word, a letter, or a sound the way she could remember making sense of numbers written on a blackboard—seeing not symbols of the numbers but the actual quantities before her, measurable, alive. Surely she must have *learned* to read, someone must have taught her how to do it, but she had no memory of that process or when or how she had become engaged in it. She knew, by acquired practice, to take in the whole with a comprehensive sweep—pick out the decoding words: *Found: on Tuesday: dead*—then start again, more slowly, word by word from the beginning. News travels at an indeterminable speed. News that's slow in coming is only news when it arrives.

She heard the car arriving through the dormer window she had opened up in the Whale Room. Even before she saw it she could tell it wasn't Fos: she could tell from the piston stroke it was a car and not a truck; a Chevy, not a Ford. And going down the stairs, she was surprised by dusk.

It was young Guy Craigie, from in town, the gravel quarry owner's son. He was standing by the bottom porch step with the honeysuckle-colored envelope in his hand. He looked away and handed it to her. Tellygram, he said.

Not difficult to read, not long, two sentences, her eyes sweeping over the entire text in the time it takes to blink. FOUND. ON TUESDAY. Then starting back, again, each word, slowly, from the start. All those Western Union codes and indecipherable letter series. All those STOPS. What makes the message a reality—having it written down, or reading it?

Sumner at the P.O. said I should wait for your reply, Guy Craigie said after what must have been, for him, a long enough time for her to understand the message. Said if I could drive it back, he'd send it.

No—I'll drive into town myself tomorrow, Opal told him.

Still, his upbringing prompted him to stay and make sure she would be all right.

You go on, Opal told him.

She searched her apron pocket for a coin to give him. Found some chicken feed and an old button.

You tell Sumner I appreciate it. Need some time to think before I answer.

Still he didn't move. Sumner also said that he could send for Mr. Foster. If you needed.

Opal shook her head and fidgeted around her other apron pocket. Found a nickel. Found something in the young man's face that said he wouldn't take the money so she watched him go, iron-colored Tennessee dust billowing behind his car. Sun coming down, the chiggers rising. It was early April and the rains had yet to come. Soon the barest breeze would start to dissipate the stagnant air upstairs and the evening's cooler touch would lift the linger of disuse off the spines and covers of the books. All along the upstairs hallway unseen stories stirred, the tales of people born, made live on pages and in reading, only. Opal drove to town next day and used the telephone at Winston's feed and grain and set the plan in motion she had thought about all night. After that, on her return, the little room upstairs, the Whale Room, became her lookout, her church steeple, for the next three days while she sat in Early's solitary chair and read and waited Fos's homecoming. With her, for the long haul, down the long hall Mr. Hemingway and Mr. London kept the vigil tolerable, the way that Early's creatures had for him. Lined behind her in the hallway like a vigilant procession chanting through a sacred transit, there was Mr. Bret Harte, Mr. Ambrose Bierce, and Stephen Crane; Washington Irving, Mr. Twain, and Mr. Henry James. Gertrude Stein and Sherwood Anderson and Upton, Mr. Sinclair. There was *The Shame of the Cities* and *Main Currents in American Thought*. There was Flash, in all of them. There was her father and her unborn child. Herself. And there was Fos. *Whatja doin up here in the dark all by yourself?* he called from the landing at the top of the stairs when he got home. The house was dark. He held a lantern out in front of him.

I'm not by myself, she told him.

There was something different in her voice he hadn't heard before.

There must have been four hundred books along the hall between them.

What do you mean? he said. He started to come forward down the hall. Not liking she was sitting in that room.

It was their way, since he'd been on the new job, that on the day that he was due home she'd be waiting for him downstairs with some supper cooked. She'd be outside on the porch before he'd stopped the car. And before they'd speak, they'd touch, he'd place his palm against the hollow of her back. She'd rub his arm. This time she didn't even rise when he approached. But reached her hand to touch his, lamplight shining in her eyes.

Guy Craigie drove out here on Friday with a Western Union from Nelson Boggs, that man I kept the books for back in Nags Head.

Fos knelt down and placed the lantern down amid the pale carved figures on the floor and took her hands in his.

Daddy's gone, she told him. Passed away last Tuesday. Sandman found him on the ground out by the glory hole keeled over. Mr. Boggs was wonderin what he oughta do about the funeral.

Fos was staring at her face, waiting till she met his gaze.

She finally did, and told him, I ain't never buried anyone before where I had to be in charge of the arrangements.

No, he sympathized.

It kinda takesya by surprise.

Not a day you plan for, he consoled her.

Speshly since he never said what he'd a wanted.

Well we'll hafta lay him with your mother.

Her eyes briefly settled on his face, then glided off again, searching down the hall. *No,* she said.

No?

Imperceptibly she shook her head. See, I counted, she attempted to explain. He was sixty-one this year, twenty-three when Mama died, so he was most his life without her. On his own thirty-eight full years. More than half. 62 and 1/3 percent.

She looked back at him.

So it didn't seem right, you know? It didn't add up. An' you know well as I do, Fos, I've never been to visit Mama all the time I've known you. If cemeteries ain't constructed to attract the living, what's the use? I'd never go to see him anyway.

Fos began to blink in this confusing light. But they were bound together. Man and wife, he said. Married for Eternity.

He squeezed her hand.

Her words were balancing on threads that wove his chief beliefs together.

Eternity, exactly, she repeated. She looked a little grateful at the mention of the word, which gave him hope. But then she looked back down the shadowed hall. There's this book, she said, pointing with her chin. You'll like it, Fos. I set it aside for you. Or maybe, probably, you've read it. It's by that Mr. Einstein.

Fos's glasses fogged. *Albert* Einstein?

That's the one—an' I was lookin through it before the news arrived an' there were pages turned down, you know, dog-eared by Flash, an' parts that he had marked in pencil. So I read 'em, or I tried to, anyway. Do you know Mr. Einstein says that the atoms in your body are the same—the same, exactly—as the atoms in the universe? The same as all the atoms that make up the stars? It's like one big lending library out there. A piece of what was once a star or something, a flower or a willow tree, when it is finished bein' that might be loaned away an' become a fish or a person's fingernail or evaporate into the sky and be a rainbow. That the—what did he call 'em?—stuff that makes your atoms up an' mine, that stuff mixed up a little different is the sum of all the stuff that's in existence. Did you know that? Fos? That you maybe once mighta been—I don't know—*a star?*

She watched him while he wiped his glasses clean before he answered. When people die on us, he said. We tend to wanta try to make believe the world's a bigger place than perhaps it actually is. That all of life is bigger. So it can include the person who's passed on. We tend to wanta try to make the world a place where we can hope that person is still with us. Some way. Some people call it Heaven. You call it a rainbow or a willow tree.

He wound the wires of his specs behind his ears and focused on her.

The fact remains, he said as gently as he could, that in your lifetime and for some time to come, Conway—your own father—was what Conway was. Not a rainbow, not a star. He was a man. The body of a man. An' now he's dead we have got to figure out what is to be done with him.

I have, already.

Good.

It took some doin.

I don't doubt it.

I drove to Winston's feed store there an' used the telephone an' called up Mr. Boggs. But first I thought about it, mind you. All the previous night.

She looked at him and squeezed his hand and told him, I was wishin you were here.

He put his lips against her forehead and whispered, I'm so sorry.

They took a moment's silence then she said, He did love that fire, Fos. The glory hole. He spent his life in trust to it.

I know.

So I thought—why not? I think he'd made his peace with Mama's memory years ago—I think he didn't have the expectation that layin side by side in that there graveyard was ever gonna be a duplication of their marriage bed. An' I was hardly ever gonna visit, anyway. So I thought *why not.* 'Cept that, wouldn'tya know it, Gould's Funeral—that's the funeral home in Nags Head—they won't ever do cremations. Not a funeral home for miles around will do one. That's the Carolina Baptists forya. An' Mr. Boggs said it wasn't just a case of firin' up the hole—you have to have a furnace hot enough to burn the bones an' that's hotter than the furnace that you need for makin glass. His daddy was in horses which is how he knew. They used to sell dead horses to a factory for glue, he told me. An' they had to burn the horses right down to the bones. So that solved the problem. There's those stockyards there on the mainland. There's that abattoir. I called 'em up from Winston's—Mr. Boggs signed all the papers. An' Mrs. Boggs is gonna go out to the house an' clean it up so we can put it up for sale. An' all we hafta do is sometime soon drive out an' bring back what is left that we might want. An' bring back Daddy's ashes. Bring 'im home to us.

Bringing Conway "home" was on her mind throughout that spring, into the summer. When she scattered chaff and seed to feed the chickens she wondered how the ash was going to scatter: flouring the board to roll a piecrust she wondered what the ashes looked like, what color they were, if they were white and powdery as stone-ground grain. While she drove she looked for places—*heights* from which to send him. She wondered how to say "goodbye"—but then she understood that thinking about what to say was another way of saying it. That thinking about what to say was something that would be ongoing for the rest of her life—the ongoing soliloquy inside one's mind that sounds like talking with the dead.

Throughout the spring and early summer their respective jobs kept them on the road. She would have thought that people liked to read more in the winter, but as the days grew longer and there was finer weather, the circulation on her route increased two hundred percent. They were rarely home together on the farm. Neither one of them had ever been much good at farming and they were glad to lease the acreage back to Luft as pasture for his livestock. With her stipend from the government, Opal paid two tenant families to tend a kitchen garden for themselves and her and Fos, and what with the amount that Fos was paid they were managing to make ends meet, which was more than they had managed farming. Fos seemed more like the man she married, more his former self: affable, unflappable, curious about the rediscovered world around him. And she was changing, too. He never mentioned it to her, but she could tell that he was noticing some changes in the way she did things. She'd seen it in his face that night she told him how she'd made her mind up not to bury Conway. Pride was there—he was always proud of what she did and proud to be with her. Sympathy and understanding, too—that was Fos's nature. But she couldn't help detecting in his manner a slight sense of loss in her not needing his experience and guidance to make up her mind. She had always been outspoken, but in the beginning of their marriage, in their years in Knoxville, she could dither when it came to making up her mind. Part of it was coming from the country and not knowing city ways. Part of it was youth and inexperience; but most of it was a girlish hesitancy in the yoke of matrimony. Fos knew more than she, she thought. Fos was older. Fos was *the man.* And even though he was and always would be *the man,* she had learned that marriage is not preordained, like clockwork, to function only on a fixed established balance. Marriage isn't mathematics. Marriage is—(she thought long and hard about what it could be likened to after reading more of Mr. Whitman's poetry)—marriage is a *scientific experiment,* one of those where you set out to prove something that's already patently obvious, set out to prove what you already know. Perhaps because she was spending more time on her own, reading more, getting out and meeting more people in a month than she had ever met before, she was finding in herself a new strain of determination. The moment that she comprehended she was orphaned, that her family lines and ties were severed for the rest of her lifetime, she felt apprehensive and a little frightened. Lines were forming to her rear and there was no beckoning gesture pointing toward the future—no child; only Fos. She could feel her youth like a hermit growing mute inside her, its passing best expressed and most lamented by the poets she was reading.

I have seen the moment of my greatness flicker

The New Deal rhetoric that was in the air was couched in terms of *do-it*-ness: identify the problem, analyze it, build a better way of doing things, be a part of the solution, make it happen, do your bit, pitch in. The propaganda of the times was aimed at telling her that anything can happen in a nation great as this one is—a man with polio could be the President. A woman could pilot an aeroplane or win a Nobel Prize or dedicate her life to working for the greater good or social justice like Utopia Rothrock or Mrs. Roosevelt. Fos was keeping company with engineers and men from the Bureau of Reclamation and the Office of Rural Electrification—men with schooling, men with different backgrounds than his own. He was sharing in their talk and benefiting from their zeal and general optimism. He was reading civil engineering tracts, trying to ignite her interest in what was going on in front of them in the Valley by telling her about the various problems encountered in constructing dams, in water flow and resistance in the geological strata, but the fact was things that engaged his curiosity for days had never been that interesting to her and now that they were spending far less time together he could actively pursue those interests with other people and she could find things she liked to do. Subtly and without their knowing it, they were growing distant as the branches of an aging oak tree do: from a single root and bound by life together but in thrall to different light. Same sun: two slightly different angles. Which was why, or partly why, when July came to an end and Conway had been dead four months, Fos announced to her, It's been too long. Let's take time off and go and do what's right by him.

Once again they headed across the Smokies the first week in August, neither one completely understanding where the time had gone or how it could have happened that they hadn't made the trip for the last three years.

The task that had been weighing on Opal was now before her and as soon as Fos had said, Let's go and do what's right, it all made sense: *Kitty Hawk* was just the height the ritual required—the launching place Conway deserved: *birthplace of aviation.*

Opal drove and despite his best intentions to keep her company, Fos fell asleep beside her, his eyes closed behind his glasses. His breathing set a tempo on the lonely road, the moonlight etched the foreground silver and the breeze across the mountains was perfumed with pine and honeysuckle. Her thoughts lifted out into the night: she counted stars, the Milky Way. She counted fence posts. Milky cows in moonlight. And she thought *I should make a list.* My parents are both dead and I'm not getting any younger. I should make a list of things I've never done I want to do, things I've never seen I want to see, and I should go and see and do 'em.

Identify and implement—she had read that somewhere in a pamphlet, liked the sound of it, but there were things she might have wanted which she could identify but which were beyond her power to implement.

She doubted she would ever get to see the pyramids in Egypt.

Or visit anyplace where English wasn't spoken.

Still: she'd like to see at least one Wonder of the World.

She'd like to visit a big city.

See the Statue of Liberty.

Learn to dance the foxtrot.

Dance with Fos.

Taste champagne.

Taste a pomegranate.

Hear an orchestra in person.

Ride a camel.

Go up in an aeroplane.

The list expanded, then contracted down to four things, only, that she wanted. Fos stirred and she looked over at him and began to wonder what his list would be, then started to compose one for him. He'd want to know more, that was certain. Go to school, enroll in courses. He'd want to know more people. When she thought about whom she'd like to meet if she could have her choice she couldn't think of anyone of fame she'd feel at ease with. Fos would probably want to meet Madame Curie. He was moody for a week when Thomas Edison died—she was pretty sure Mrs. Curie was still alive or Fos would have gotten moody at her passing. She wondered if the Madame Curies of the world made lists or had unfulfilled desires. She wondered if Albert Einstein did. Fos would want to meet him, too, she thought. Fos would want to have a friend again, she suspected. *Well I'll be.* Fos finally stirred beside her. Looky that.

There was a billboard looming by the road the size of a barn side. You could read it in the moonlight. It was advertising a new motor court five miles ahead.

That wasn't there before, Fos said. Let's see what it's like an' maybe stop.

The paint inside the Pine Tree Motor Court was still fresh, the cabins each had running water and a tub, and outside every unit there was indeed a pine tree, a picnic table, and a fireplace for cooking. Two families with their children were sitting outside in the moonlight by their fires when the owner showed them to their cabin. Someone had a radio on but by the time they'd had a bite to eat and were ready to turn in everything was whisper quiet except the tree frogs and two owls calling one another through the open window. The breeze brought the suggestion of a storm and Fos said, Hope it doesn't rain tomorrow. He rolled his head on the pillow toward the open window but without his glasses all he saw were shades of moonlight. She was lying still beside him and he cupped his hand around her hip. She was wearing a silky thing he liked the feel of that she saved for rare occasions and he smiled and pressed against her. She rolled so she was facing him. Listen, she said. Earlier out there while I was drivin. I was thinkin.

He tried to focus on the fuzzy features of her face, made another circle with his hand across her silky nightdress.

I was tryin hard to make a list, she said.

It seemed, he saw, that she was in the mood for talking.

If you could change things in your life what would it be? she asked him.

He didn't answer for a while, just looked at her.

Fos?

He never knew, when she asked these questions, where they came from. But she was not a woman who made small talk.

My eyes, he said. I'd like to see the way I used to.

She ran her thumb along his eyebrow. No, she told him, I mean things that you could change. Things you haven't done yet. Things you meant to do when you were younger but never did. Promises you made. Things you'd like to do to make you happy.

But . . . , he said.

He blinked a couple times, played with the silk strap on her shoulder.

I *am* happy.

Happi*er,* she said. Something you still *want,* she prompted.

He seemed about to choke on something.

I already *have* everything I want, he whispered.

It took a while for her to take this in.

And for him to wonder what her life was missing.

I guess—well, he finally said. I wouldn't mind inventin something. Did I ever tell you about Faraday?

She shook her head.

Englishman, he said. Built the first electric motor and that lamp that miners carry with them down the shafts. Lamp that operates without a flame to help prevent explosions. He was working on electric light way back before Tom Edison, before anybody even knew what electricity was—whether it existed in the air on the tail end of a kite or whether it was static—whether it could pass through solid matter. Faraday was the first to show how it could be transformed, like it transforms itself from a field of force into the light that's visible inside a light bulb. An' when he was trying to find a filament an electric charge could pass through, he knew he needed something thin, almost like a thread but very strong. *So he used a strand of his wife's hair.* An' that's how I would want it to be if I invented something. That's how I would want to do it. With that kinda flourish of the personal. Half from chemistry. Half out of love.

He could feel her breathing stop, and even though he couldn't see her clearly, he felt that she was thinking that his recipe for his desired invention—half chemistry, half love—was the recipe for parenthood, how two people make a baby and he could feel it in the way her body stopped responding with that latent lament, that old one that never really went away between them, so he tried to save the moment, pull it back before she noticed, through his touch and just by plowing forward with a rapid speech. The boys at work, he said, those engineers by gol you oughta hear them talk about this dam the Bureau's buildin out there in Nevada on the Colorado River. Boulder Canyon Dam, they're callin it. Biggest man-made building ever. Bigger than the pyramids—forty-nine *million* dollars it's costing and they haven't even started to pour concrete yet. Spent the last two years rerouting the Colorado from the site so they could dry it out an' start to build the scaffolding. Just imagine. Here we think we're movin mountains to divert the Tennessee and these boys are out there playin God with the same river that carved out the Grand Canyon. Boy. I'd dearly love to see it. Wouldn't you? I guess that's one thing that I'd want. To see them build the Boulder Dam.

She pulled up onto her elbow and said, We could *do* that, Fos—that's somethin we *could* do—the Grand Canyon is a wonder of the World, isn't it? We could plan a road trip, say, next summer, and drive out an' back an' I could see a Wonder of the World an' you could see the Boulder Dam, what do you say?

She looked so happy there was only one thing he *could* say: *Ditto.*

Several times during the night the thunder woke him and he got up to close the window, thinking that the rain was coming in, but the storm, though close enough to feel, was circling round them from the north and west, driving from the mountains toward the ocean. They followed in its wake the following day, the sky lead-colored above a startled green, tree barks and fence posts black as ink where rain had saturated them. Several times the rain began anew, battled by conflicting winds, and by late afternoon the storm was standing at the door again, as perversely undiminished in its fervor as an untried Bible salesman. Livestock on the flatlands hunkered for protection against anything that stood between the darkening clouds and them. There was no sun—the only way Opal knew that it was getting late was that every now and then her stomach rumbled. Fos missed the turn to Nags Head at Four Corners and she didn't mean to sound irritable in asking *Whereya goin?* but the truth was she was getting hungry.

Lord I wasn't thinkin, he apologized.

He had taken the old road at the crossroads by habit and they were on their way to Conway's house even though they had decided not to go there till they'd finished with the other business first. Land values being what they were, not a single buyer had come forward since Opal had put it up for sale. You want t' turn around? Fos asked.

Well . . . , she stalled.

She made a show of looking at her watch.

Her stomach growled.

No harm seein it, she said. Before it's dark. Get some idea of the shape it's in.

They drove a little while in silence.

Then the sheer familiarity—the recognition of the landmarks—took over for each one as a kind of conversation.

Most of the farms and places looked severely unattended.

Machines sat rusting by the road or stranded in the fields, stripped of anything of worth. The earth, never a natural beauty in these parts without the greening hand of man, looked trashed and wasted: alien. Poverty, that parasite, had taken hold.

The thought occurred to her that Conway, too, must have changed in those couple of years she hadn't seen him—but she put it from her mind. If the land was going to change, if the land was going to revise itself before her eyes and force her memory of it to change, then at least she should be allowed to keep one image for herself of what her father looked like, once.

Because the world is not designed for keepsake.

It's too cruel a place, and most things go to ruin. Name one thing that doesn't.

Lordie, she had to breathe as they drove in.

Fos stopped the truck on the sand track by the road so they could look at it.

Looks like someone's here, he said.

There were fresh tracks through the sand across the hardpack to the house.

A truck with all the world's belongings of a family on the move strapped to it was pulled up on the open ground between the barn where Conway ran his glory hole and the front porch of the house where Opal had once lived. As Fos drove up a bunch of barefoot children fanned out from the field beside the barn and hid behind the truck. A man appeared—shoeless, gaunt, and disarrayed as if he had just risen from a sleep of years. Nonchalant as someone posing for a picture he put his hand down on the rifle where it lay across the hood and looked at Fos without expression.

Opal counted six pairs of feet beneath the truck. And from somewhere in the back of it, above the wind, there was a newborn infant crying.

You stay here, Fos told her.

The hell I will, she thought and slid out from her side as he called *Hidy!* and walked over to the man. You folks need some help?

The man, whose face was scored as much from care as it was from sun and malnutrition, remained immobile, mute. So did the children, Opal noticed. Only the baby cried. And then the cries were muffled.

Are you lost? Fos said.

The man said nothing.

Opal saw some movement between the slats along the flatbed of the truck. A woman's face, more like the vision of a ghost than of a person, peered out at her: two hollow eyes, impossible to tell their age.

You the law? the man finally found the will to ask.

No, no—name's Ray Foster, Fos volunteered. This-here place is where my wife was raised. Her family home, he emphasized.

The man did not intend to move his gaze from Fos to look at Opal.

We were told the place was empty, he put forth.

Well, yeah. It is. But she still owns it.

We ain't tetched nothin inside, the man maintained. We ain't been in.

The newborn in the back began to wail again and one of the children hiding on the far side of the truck said something that made another of them giggle.

What with the storm an' all an' with the woman takin poorly we were lookin for a place to stop, the man told Fos. The woman—his voice trailed off. She was poorly through the night.

There was an awkward silence and the wind dropped suddenly and the smell of them reached Opal—dark and stinging; repugnant.

Does the woman need a doctor? Fos inquired, looking toward the covered flatbed, only guessing what he couldn't see.

She's better now she's over it, the man obliged.

There was a roll of thunder and the breeze picked up and the children scattered toward the barn, at play.

Well, Fos said, biding time. Where you folks headed to?

Flori-da.

No kiddin. Never been. Lotsa oranges down there. Whereya from?

Oklahoma.

Little *lost* ain'tja?

But his humor was rebuffed.

Tellya what, Fos said after another awkward pause. My wife and I have got some business that we're doin in Nags Head that will take a day or two. Night after next we'll be comin back.

He waited for the man to look him squarely in the eye.

I expect you will be gone by then. You understand?

Opal held her breath till she heard the man say *yes sir* then she looked once more at the house before getting back inside the truck. There was a padlock on the front door and the windows were all shuttered. Mr. Boggs had done a fine job, she was thinking. Anything of any value that had been her mother's she had taken when she married Fos. Still the thought of people camping in the house didn't sit well with her. *These* people, especially. Before she'd had the chance to say her finals. While his familiars, his fingerprints and comfortable aroma were still there inside.

If you want I'll get the sheriff to come out and turn them off the land, Fos said, looking in the rearview mirror as they drove away.

One of the girls was running after them—barefoot, that way a young girl runs, arms flapping. Same way, same spot, Opal must have run when she was young, he thought.

He touched her hand. We never used to see so much itinerancy out this way, she said.

No, he agreed.

Except that one day you showed up.

He smiled, and hoped that she was smiling, too. She wasn't.

It blew so hard that night the owner of the guest house in Nags Head came upstairs at nine o'clock and offered them a room away from all the clatter. When they declined he said there's no accountin for what people like and boarded up the window just to show his disapproval, which only made the whole room shudder more. The storm kept at it through the next day and even though they went over and collected Conway's ashes, it was too squally to go out to Kitty Hawk so they spent a second stormy night inside the shuttered room. Conway on the mantel. On the third day it was just as bad but by noon Opal was impatient. Let's just drive out and take our chances, she proposed. She let Fos drive while she balanced Conway on her lap. When they reached the heights the wind was buffeting the truck from what seemed like all directions, but at least the rain had stopped. They sat a while and watched the rollers tear away the coast with vengeance. Was there something special you wanted to do? Fos asked after half an hour.

Not really.

Say a prayer or somethin?

No.—you?

I'm ready, he announced.

She nodded and the wind tore through their clothes the second that the doors were open, whipping the car door from Fos's hand and slamming it before he'd got his collar up around his ears. Spray hit his glasses and he ducked, then spun around the other way just in time to grab her coat and hold her as the wind knocked them sideways. He saw her turn the lid on the flour tin that Mrs. Boggs had put the ashes in and then there was a burst of powder like a homemade firecracker going off but without the noise, and he was gone. Opal's hair was plastered by the wind across her eyes and she cleared it with her forearm then looked inside the tin, shook it, looked inside again then threw it in the air. The whole thing flew a little way, sailed over the promontory toward the raging sea and disappeared far out where they couldn't see it. They fought their way back into the truck and sat in the unaccustomed stillness for what might have been an hour, maybe more, until they knew the time was right to leave.

Think we'll ever see this place again? Fos asked, still staring at the violence of the waves against the stalwart coast.

I don't know, she barely answered.

I used t' dream that I was gonna make my mark on history here, he said. Here where the Wright boys did their stuff. In their footsteps. I was gonna make some history.

He turned to look at her, her milkglass profile.

And the way it turned out—I did. I did make history here. With you.

She didn't move. Flash used t' say *Be careful what you wish for,* she finally told him. 'Cause a version of it might sneak up in ambush when you least expect it.

He tried to think of some forgiving reason she would say that. He put it off to shock.

Her hands were turning blue.

She'd just parted with her father.

He started the truck and drove.

The gale was driving out to sea and as they traveled inland the air grew calm. Stars appeared. The moon came out, bright enough to winnow by, bright enough to cast real shadows. It was several hours after sunset when they reached the sandtrack to the house, and the moonlight on the scene washed the sand dunes clean and made them glisten.

The little house was standing indigo and solitary in the silvery landscape.

Fos cut the lights and cut the engine and they drifted in on quiet.

The itinerants were gone.

A door was banging in the barn and a draft of air whistled through an open flue in Conway's furnace.

Opal climbed the porch stairs to try the key that Mrs. Boggs had given her.

Fos brought their single suitcase from the truck and stood behind her.

I'll get a lamp, he said on second thought.

The moonlight's good enough, she told him.

A loose door or shutter banged again.

Go see what that bangin is, she told him.

She turned the key and took the padlock off and went inside.

He started to walk over to the barn with the unlit lamp. A little cloud, the size of an infant's fist, pushed across the moon and he looked up and oriented his perspective in the sky through the Dipper's handle up and over to the Perseid radiant and there before him, as they'd done for ages, the stars were falling down.

Two stars from opposite directions shot across the sky above him at that moment and he smiled.

Flash was always such a pessimist, he considered as the moon came out and he continued to the barn and stepped inside. *Careful what you wish for*—what kinda person wouldya hafta be to be suspicious of your own true wishes? Life was better than all that, he thought. Life was full of men like Conway, men who went through life not complicating destiny with unattainable desires, but making simple beauty from the simple stuff of sand and fire. *I shoulda said a prayer,* he thought. I should have said his name, at least.

The moonlight found its way into the colored bottles on the rafters and Fos was once more brought to mind how much this place resembled those French churches he had stood in, reverent, in the War. He drew himself together into what he thought was prayer position—upright, with his hands loose, holding the unlit lamp before him—and he tried to form a prayer of some kind in his mind, a benediction, but the lyrics of some songs and jingles from the radio kept surfacing and a noise like a baby crying echoed through the haunted furnace. Behind a pile of unused sand he found a shutter off its hinge, the source of intermittent banging, and he propped it shut, making a mental note to fix it in the morning. Maybe say the prayer then, too, he thought. If he could think of one.

Nesting doves cooed in the eaves, their music blending with the eerie crying from the furnace, and he let himself out into the greater silence of the night and closed the door behind him.

He looked up for another falling star but didn't see one, picked the suitcase up, then stopped on the threshold, not knowing where the sound was coming from or what it was.

His footsteps sounded on the wooden floor. In the bedroom, she was sitting on the far end of the bed facing the window with the blue light coming through the curtain across the white bedcover, falling on her shock of hair, her shoulders, her arms, where she was cradling a form wrapped in a blanket.

The baby cried and its foot poked from the blanket like a bright pincushion, catching moonlight.

He reached out and clasped the child's foot in his suddenly large hand.

It felt like prayer.

He knelt down beside his wife and this strange infant in the moonlight.

He's ours, she said.

She sounded fierce, converted.

They left him here. *We're keepin him,* she told him.

Call me Ishmael.

HERMAN MELVILLE, *Moby-Dick,* "Loomings"

p a t e r n i t y

Well, you can't hatch a boiled egg, son:
That's what his father would have said.

Can't catch a lobster with a sermon.
Can't mend your nets with dreams.
Can't tack hard in Monday's dory.
Can't tend the dead without a story.

With the exception of the one-or-two-word utterances,

fine sky
high time
good catch
you bet
good-bye,

Fos could not remember anything his father ever said to him that wasn't blunt but cryptic.

Well that'll getya a teepee in China, boy.

That'll learnya Polynese.

He was a man who hoarded silence, like there was going to be a run on it down at the store. People would *run out* of it. And he, alone, would have enough saved up to last him through Eternity.

The last time he spoke to Fos was on the morning Fos left Carolina for the War.

Your decision, he obliged.
Can't expect a windfall from an uproar.

Can't plug a leaky tub with promises anymore than you can swallow vinegar to make a dime.

Fos believed, while he was growing up, that most of what his father told him must be taken from a text, owing to the way his words were packaged, neat and stacked. For a while he thought they must be parables and that his father had learned them at the feet of his own father and that one day he would entrust to him the key to their translation and he would come into this overdue inheritance of wisdom. When he was twelve or so and started working around other men on boats, he briefly entertained the possibility his father was insane, but nothing but his way of speaking ever backed that theory up. His *actions* were all sane. But whereas other men could build a bridge between perceived reality and their private inner thoughts with the rudimentary tools of human speech, Fos's father had the bricks but not the mortar. The materials but not the blueprint. The gift of gab but not a clue.

Someday I will ask him, he kept thinking, what the hell he had been saying all those years.

But when he came back from the War, his father had already passed away without translation. Never teaching Fos a language he could live with—never teaching Fos a language that could let him speak of love, a language that could help him pray.

But maybe that's what sons and fathers do.

Wait and wish.
Obfuscate and disappear.

And when you think about it, God, Himself, didn't make it all that easy on His own Son to understand what He was trying to communicate.

Behold, He cometh with clouds; and every eye shall see Him

And maybe you can't hatch a boiled egg (well—you *can't*) but you can sure give thanks to the hen that laid it for you so here goes:

Lord—

Well you sprung this on me,
an' I'm grateful for it,
but I always thought that when the day would come I'd have the chance to ready for it.
But here it is.
An' I guess if there's one thing my father taught me it was how much a son yearns for a father who will teach him things an' talk to him an' show him how to understand the world.
That's what I plan t' do.

High time.
You bet.

The rest is up to You.

Good catch.
Fine sky.

Amen.

'Twas rehearsed by thee and me a billion years before this ocean rolled.

HERMAN MELVILLE, *Moby-Dick,* "The Chase—Second Day"

maternity

Only one thing makes a mother of an ordinary woman, Opal knew:

Opportunity.

It doesn't take a special talent or a set of rules and regulations, qualifying tests or an uninvited morning visit from an annunciating Angel. The only thing that motherhood requires is you have to *be* there. There's no such thing as *absent* motherhood. Absence is it's opposite—she should know. As a child her first encounters with the world outside her father's house included in their social contracts one adult after another leaning down to tell her *Opal.* Look at *you.* You know? I knew your mother.

No you didn't, she suspected.

By the time that she was six or seven she started thinking, No one knew *my mother.* What they mean is that they knew the woman married to my father who gave birth to me, then died. They didn't know *my mother.* 'Cause I never had one.

So for good or bad, she knew, to call yourself *a mother* the only thing you had to do was show up for the job. And stay.

And some are saints and some are martyrs.
Some are victims.

Some are vanished.

Some are walls.

Some emit more light than they absorb, creating their own planetary systems.

Some are sole survivors of the war against themselves. Some are slaves.

And some are furies.

Some are cold, and some are tender.

Few are blameless.

All have names.

Each must answer for her child's existence.

What did she have to do, she wondered—or, more to the point, what was she doing *wrong?* She kept showing up, but biology, that sharpshooter, kept missing her. Still, she kept wishing. For years she'd taken future motherhood, her future in maternity, for granted. Look around—all you see are mothers, women born to it, women who have children just as casually as breathing, women who have babies hanging off their hips like fruit. Every time the electric lights flickered in their house on Clinch Street back in Knoxville, Mrs. Rinaldi had cried out *eh! ancora un bambino:* another baby born.

Once, it happened three times in an hour after supper.

Once, she counted ten between the time she finished washing dishes and the time they went to bed.

One week she counted the lights flickering forty-seven times.

She was good at counting—couldn't help it.

Some have other talents.

Some have daughters.

Some have sons.

So when Conway died it seemed the right time to make a personal accounting. She didn't know where the idea came from but it seemed to make a lot of sense to her. Take stock. Count her blessings. Make a list and take an inventory. While she was driving, then, on the road to her childhood home while Fos was sleeping in the seat beside her and the moon was shining on the highway's silver ribbon, she began.

Some things are possible.

Some things are not.

Some wishes can come true.

Some can only flicker, like the lights, from a shortage, somewhere, in their power.

She wasn't tempted to wish for things she couldn't get. She wasn't tempted to be taller but she'd like to see the sky up close.

1. Go up in an airplane.

She'd like to travel. She'd like to go some place where there are so many people that, like the stars, you can't count them. She'd like to see what that was like.

2. Visit New York City. Or Chicago.

See a natural wonder.

Understand how electricity works, for conversation's sake.

3. Dance with Fos.

Pick an orange straight off the tree.

Find a pearl.

4. Be a mother.

Then *Careful what you wish for,* she remembered.

It could change your life.

What was Poland to the Czar? What Greece to the Turk? What India to England? What at last will Mexico be to the United States? All Loose-Fish.

HERMAN MELVILLE, *Moby-Dick,* "Fast-Fish and Loose-Fish"

fast fish and loose fish

Possession, so they tell us, is nine-tenths the law. Once you've got ahold of something—anything—it may as well be yours; and in a sanctioned land of cousins, coming home with someone else's baby, calling it your own, is the stuff of everyday occurrence.

Hard times don't ask questions. Hard times make familiars out of strangers by the common needs that they impose. People needing work and food and shelter understand each other quick. Poverty exacts a physics on the surface of our lives and stretches limits of existence. Tolerance is everything. Tolerance is key. Tolerance is stressed and, like an atom under pressure or a filament about to break, having less to give we somehow end up giving more in order not to fracture. The calculation of the give and take of poverty is always brutal: someone's give is someone else's take, and in the end the give has always got to be the greater. Or else somebody dies.

How hard life would get along the Tennessee that year depended on perspective. What some people would have called a natural disaster others had to take as daily life. Comparatively speaking, tomorrow came to be the thing you feared the most, every day saw more hard labor than the last, and recent memory consisted only of those times too hard to be forgotten. Not everyone was poor—but everyone was poorer than before. And since farming families were used to persevering on a system of producing children as added working calories, an extra cousin or a nephew or a niece was usually on hand, especially where someone was holding on to something like a crop, a wage, a tractor, or a promise. People came and went in ways they hadn't done before—looking for a thing they could hold on to. A few took off to cities, but more showed up than went. Fos was one of those who thought that every social ill could find its cure in science and the sight of people going hungry on their land or on the move and homeless made him angry. What a waste, he thought. What a waste of possibility, of resources and manpower. What a waste of know-how. Well *his son* would show 'em. Grow up, lead the way. His son would revolutionize technology. Eradicate world hunger. Invent a way to mint self-replicating silver dollars. Capture solar power in his smile.

Only right now his son was meditating on life's mysteries, bundled like a stiff in Opal's arms, his little nose no more than a flat dime balancing between his big brown eyes. Fos was driving—they were on the road again, toward home. How's he doin over there? he asked.

He's a quiet baby, Opal mentioned for the umpteenth time.

So quiet they thought he might be deaf or mute or otherwise insensitive until Opal pinched his little arm and he responded. He was beanpole and scrawny, underweight, with impossibly large sex glands, Opal thought, the color of raw chicken. His hands seemed longer than they ought to be, and slender, and they flapped around whenever he would move his arms in startled spasms. A dark plug like the wax that stoppers moonshine was where his navel should have been and his entire body was a little gamey with the suggestion of blood and crusted fluid. They had cleaned him up as best they could and wrapped him in a towel which he had promptly soiled. He'd slept the night, sucking drops of tinned sweetened milk off Opal's fingers but now that it was day and they were on the road, they needed to provide him with the proper comforts of a well-nursed baby. They stopped in Raleigh and bought a load of gear but even after the infant had been dressed in a clean blanket with his wispy strands of amber-colored hair slicked back behind his ears, Fos feared the three of them appeared a little strange. He doesn't look like neither one of us, he calculated. But when they stopped in

Ashville for the night the woman in the office of the motor court cooed like normal. Skin li'l thang, she said. What's its name?

Fos hadn't really thought about it. Thought about the things the boy would do, the things he would accomplish, but not about the name he'd have as he went down in history.

Foster, Opal said. Ray. Ray Foster. *Junior,* she there and then decided.

You might have asked, Fos cautioned later. We might have talked about it.

But if she had been headstrong and determined in the past on certain things, when it came to making up her mind in all things pertaining to her boy she was implacable. Fos not only had no say, he had no quarter. A prophet in his own land, he learned the art of covert operation: flanking tactics: rearguard actions: and the name Ray Foster *Junior* wouldn't do. It was okay in the plan to lend the boy legitimacy but in the long run the man he would become shouldn't have to shoulder under someone else's name even if that person was his father. Not that being called Ray Foster Junior was a stigma—it was of no particular advantage, not a leg up on the ladder of success. But more important—it was unoriginal. Naming is a shoe-in for invention—naming *is* invention. But these arguments of his were lost on someone who could sum up numbers faster than Saint Peter counting sins, someone whose philosophy of life was manifest in naming things by numbers—first, second, next, and so on. So rather than call the boy Ray, Ray Junior, or R.J. as Opal did, Fos called the baby Lightfoot.

She believed the nickname wouldn't stick and pretended to ignore it. But in the way these thing evolve the name took hold.

He walked before the other babies of his age—and ran soon after. He could balance on one foot and catch a ball and reach for things and pour liquid from a pitcher to a glass, but when Fos tried to interest him in looking through a lens he didn't light up in any special way to show his interest. *Fire* didn't interest him; moths did. He delighted in running after fireflies at night but when his father captured them and put them in a jar Lightfoot wasn't happy till he set them free. At three he could cast a line into the river from the bank and reel it in, but he refused to bait it. He swam at two, rode a bicycle at three, and backflipped off the dock the summer he was four. But he could not, despite his mother's urging, add without his fingers. Could only reckon time from shadows, not a clockface. And he always slept with one whale in his hand and another tucked beneath his pillow.

Fos worked regularly with the Office of Rural Electrification boys through Lightfoot's infant years but by the time the boy was walking the various field offices and teams of engineers and planners consolidated under one big tent—the TVA, Tennessee Valley Authority—and the scale of its administrative power started to come home.

At first, the Authority seemed more hat than hammer—it set up headquarters in Knoxville and bought whole blocks of office space to house its clerks and quartermasters, geologists and engineers. It was, because it touched on the riverine population of nine states in matters more immediately personal than any other governing agency, a bureaucratic monster. But Congress had endowed it with a humanistic bias—it was a bureaucratic monster, sure. But it had a soul. It built thirty-two different dams—some of them small storage dams for holding reservoirs; some of them massive high dams—nine on the Tennessee itself and twenty-three on the Tennessee's tributaries. To build these dams it cleared 1,129,000 acres and forcibly removed at least four times as many people from their land as did the Cherokee Removal. No one knows for certain how many individuals it moved, but although no one won a battle over land against it, it must be said the TVA did everything it could to relocate every displaced person. It paid for archeologists to excavate soon-to-be-flooded tracts, preserved and relocated landmarks. It catalogued the dead in cemeteries and disinterred each one along with the original headstones. It recorded oral histories. It turned a godforsaken ornery bastard of a cursed and temperamental river prone to sudden drastic flooding into a calm and navigable chain of firthy lakes as picture-postcard perfect as an alpine idyll. It was like converting lightning into a string of pearls.

By building storage dams strategically along the river system it backed the Tennessee into its arteries, creating a permanent flood in many of the valleys, locking up the hazard of a natural flood as if it were Rapunzel in her tower. Where corn and cotton, lima beans and strawberries had once grown, there soon were lakes as wide and calm as ancient geological lagoons. The former nature of the Tennessee made the flooding of so many acres relatively guilt free: there had never been a major railroad built along her banks, nor any modern highways, nor any industry developed. The mineral resources were negligible except for outcrops of some marble, and there was really nothing between Knoxville and Chattanooga of any worth *except* the river—no major towns, no industry, no gold or diamonds: only farms. And, of course, potential. To substantiate construction costs, the TVA convinced the Congress of the United States that the profit generated by the dams could liquidate those loans within the decade. In order to amortize the cost of building all the dams TVA needed to create a market for electric power—*Royal juice,* as it was called. The plan, though perfect for the Valley, had never really sprung from its own initiating impulse—the plan, though overwhelmingly personal to everyone that it affected in the Valley, had originated somewhere else. From the Outside. From Washington. From government. And, like all invasions, it grew by what it fed on.

The first dam up and running was the Wilson Dam—then came Norris Dam with its utopian workers' village built on the construction site—a showcase for the visiting stiffs in the House of Representatives who wrote the checks. Five thousand graves were moved at Norris. At Pickwick, three miles from Shiloh, sixty thousand acres were flooded, including the old shipping towns of Riverton and Waterloo. Four hundred families were removed. At Guntersville, in '35, one thousand one hundred and eighty-two families were relocated; a hundred thousand acres flooded. Bluets, redbird, jack-in-the-pulpit, flame azealea, fringed loosestrife, princess tree, black locust, hawthorn hollows, memory lanes—inundated. Not extinguished nor eradicated, but erased. *You get in the way, we move you* was the accusation hurled by troublemakers, but the process for acquiring the land from private owners was, on the whole, a civil one. TVA hired "county agents"—always Southern whites, if not down-home native Tennesseeans—who would fill the role of assessing the land values. Then, as a preventative of privateering and speculation, third-party evaluators would prescribe a price and fix it. TVA would make an offer on your land and you could take or leave it. If you left it your property would be condemned and the fixed price would go *down,* never up. *How much are they payin all those people?* Opal asked Fos when the practice started getting out. *How much?* was the first thing *everybody* asked. Followed by *Where to?* Where are we supposed to live? Where are they movin us?

It wasn't as if the land designated for the relocations was so much different from the land these families had been living on—it wasn't. But it was land that no one had staked claim to in the history of the South, land no one would have chosen on his own: discarded land: a handout. Charity.

Someone's getting rich was the suspicion that arose. But then TVA would haul out its statistics, invite the public in for scrutiny. Even Opal said the TVA could make you think the world had been built by Congress and a batch of boys with slide rules. *Lies,* some people groused. They made the joke there were three kinds of crooked coming at them from the government: Lies. *Dam* lies. And statistics. It became an article of faith preached from the local pulpits in Tennessee that for every politician you send up to Washington you bought yourself another dam.

Not everyone was sourly cynical—the bald eye of cynicism was the cynosure of country lore, but its observations were from the point of view of a close and closed society, not a closed mind. Fos would reckon half the people that he met who were being forced to move viewed the situation with a spirit of adventure—the other half had doubts about the wisdom of the enterprise and a suspicion they were being duped not so much by These Outsiders as by city folk in general. City people were the ones who needed electricity in the first place—needed lights and trolley cars and gadgets in their homes. City people—you could tell from their complexions that they didn't know the light of day. You could tell by looking at their hands that living in a city made them soft. Fos had started seeing skepticism in the way some people would back off at his demonstrations—the initial play of interest didn't hook the audiences as easily as before. What do I need *that* for? people started asking, when I've got *a broom?* When I've got *a washboard?* When I've got *my hands?* A lot of what he did now on the road was a brand of social work instead of showmanship. Instead of juicing up a lightboard in a display of blinding lights or popping corn on an electric griddle, he buttonholed a couple people at a time and talked common sense to them, hands in his pockets, about the benefits of refrigeration and electric water pumps. Only after that would he show off the toasters and the vacuum cleaners. People without money for a meal don't need to know there are five settings to brown bread. Still, people turned up just to see what he was selling, but they were learning fast to recognize the huckster in the bully pulpit or the clownsuit. Fos and the men he worked with were finding it a tougher sale—Fos, especially, wanted people to appreciate the soul in the machines, the miracle inside the merchandise. He was packing up one night after a lacklustre performance down near Chattanooga where ground was being leveled to build the Hales Bar Dam when a man came up to him and said, "Ray Foster—?"

Fos made the quick assessment everyone had learned: hat, fabric of the clothes, and manicure. Yes *sir,* he said. The hat looked like the ones the boys from Washington were fond of wearing—the real McCoy, a creamy Panama. The shoes were soft and clean.

"Ray Foster from *Knoxville?*"

Fos froze.

He didn't want to cross that bridge.

He never knew which side the question might be coming from.

"—the *photographer?*"

That would be me, Fos said, still not offering to shake the stranger's hand.

"Ira Sturdevant," the stranger said. "Maybe you'll remember me—" He withdrew his wallet from his pocket and slid a picture from it. "You took this engagement picture of my bride-to-be. Look here—" He turned the picture over, handing it to Fos. "It's got your name on the back." To his surprise, Fos's hand shook as he took it. He looked at it then gave the picture back and paused to wipe his specs.

"I'm with the Office of Information now," the man explained. He gave a country laugh: "I *am* the Office of Information—Knoxville Branch. They like to place us Knoxville boys out front where people see us—keep the New York boys behind us in the picture, even though they run the show. You should see the changes this has brought to Knoxville. You would not believe it. Stories I could tell. Have you had your supper?"

Ira Sturdevant was quick and to the point and by the time Fos had mopped his plate clean of chicken gravy with his biscuits he had found himself recruited by the government for the second time in four years. Third time in his lifetime, if you count the Army.

This time, though, he was hired to take pictures.

"The men who are deciding all these things," Ira Sturdevant told him. "Well, you know, I think you'll agree they could have thrown the baby out with the bathwater a long time ago. You can't take on a job as big as this and not make some people angry, and I think they've kept the peace and done a diplomatic job nine times out of ten. And they realize something's going to be sacrificed—some four-hundred-year-old oak or some old Revolutionary War Vet's home. And they want those things that will be lost properly recorded so the history in it's not erased. Imagine if Eastman Kodak had been there when the cornerstone was laid for the first Pyramid. I do believe these dams, these reservoirs we're building are going to be among the most beautiful things man has ever made. I do believe that. Although I've never been to Europe and I hear there are some beauties over there that should be seen to be appreciated."

Churches, Fos put in. They know how to build 'em.

Well someday they will say the same of us: "They knew how to build 'em." Glory dams—have you been to see the ones we've finished? Did they take you up to Norris? Breathtaking. You look at it and you are proud to be a man. Proud to be American, proud to be a part of such a forward-looking nation. I think, all tolled, what we're building here at Tennessee will be considered even greater than the Boulder Dam. I do. We have Europeans comin through already just to gawp. That's why we need some pretty pictures. For that, and for recording history.

Well I have to tell you—I don't own a camera anymore, Fos admitted. I haven't touched a camera since—

Ancient history, Sturdevant insisted. It was the first time in the conversation he'd let on he knew about Fos's partnership with Flash. As for equipment, he went on, I'll get you some catalogues, you tell me what you'll need. No expenses spared, he joked. Courtesy of Congress.

Are you hiring me just because I used to come from Knoxville?

What do you mean?

Like you said—are you hiring me just because I'm from around these parts?

No sir. Sturdevant took his wallet out again and withdrew the little portrait Fos had taken of his wife. I'm hiring you because of this, he told him. He rubbed his thumb across her face before he handed it to Fos and Fos noticed how frayed its edges were.

I have that picture with me everywhere I am, Sturdevant told him. And I always will.

Fos turned the picture over and looked at the stamp Opal used to place on the reverse of all their studio portraits—said it gave them "class." She had picked the letter type herself. Designed it. *Happy times,* Fos murmured and gave the picture back.

Happiness had by no means gone missing from his life—he was a happy man, happy husband, happy father—but when the cameras arrived and he uncrated the equipment in the pantry off the kitchen where he was going to set up his darkroom, he remembered being young again: he remembered holding a camera for the first time, how he had realized, as if in a vision, how light entered there and was captured. He remembered what this had meant to him as a young man—that this was an instrument that could stop time, steal time from where it is designed to go, into invisibility.

His first assignment was to document the permanent residents in the area around the Hales Bar site north of Chattanooga. "Permanent residents" was TVA-talk for the dead—Fos was supposed to photograph the cemeteries, the individual headstones, and make a map of them so that every side-by-side relationship could be replicated when the bodies were reinterred. He was issued with a badge which read BUREAU OF PERMANENT RESIDENTS, DEPARTMENT OF REMOVAL AND RELOCATION, and a sheaf of forms to be completed. Along with photographing every headstone he was charged with filing a report on the type and condition of the marker, type and condition of the inscription, name and age and date of birth and date of death of each deceased, name of nearest living relative or source of current information and that individual's address and relationship to the deceased.

I'm gonna need your help, he said to Opal even before he put the papers down.

Something in his voice—some lilt that didn't fit the words—made her look at him. And there it was. That look, that old look she hadn't seen in a long time.

You come to know a person, you live together every day, you're not really conscious of the changes taking place. Parenthood had come to them like a sudden shower or a gust that, unexpectedly, overstayed like climate, and in a blinking of an eye, without their ever knowing it, Lightfoot had become the context of their day, of every word they spoke, of every look they shared. But now Fos saw a way where they could be together again, and what she saw in his expression when he realized this was the sparkle of relief. He'd missed her. When he took her in his arms now he couldn't help but notice where her shoulders were more shapely, less soft, from lifting up the boy. Her whole frame was firmer, surer, and it gave him immeasurable joy to see her run after Lightfoot and keep up.

In the sunshine, once, beside a stream that gave into the Little Tennessee where they had stopped to stretch their legs and have some lunch on their way to Fos's next assignment, Opal hitched her skirt around her waist to wade into the stream to wash the plates and Fos's heart had skipped a beat. He'd never thought of her as someone who could turn heads, but as he stood there on the bank looking at her body, at her legs, he realized what a fragile thing possession is, how no one person ever owns another, how tenuous our hold is on another and when she came out of the water toward him, her skin reflecting light, he pulled her to him and embraced her. Who is this *fine*-looking woman, he demanded and she dropped her head against his chest, demure, but didn't argue. *He's* the one, she said, turning in his arms so they could both see Lightfoot playing in the stream. It was true, people stopped to look at him. Miss Welty at the P. O.? I showed her that picture you took of him an' she said we ought to send it off to magazines or Hollywood. Says he's gonna be a heartbreaker when he grows up.

Miss Welty knows about heartbreakers, does she.

So you'll have to teach him, Fos.

How not to break girls' hearts? I don't think I needed any practice in that category.

Even if you could have done, you wouldn't've. An' that's something he deserves to learn.

What Lightfoot was learning, though, was how to charm his mother and his father into keeping every living thing that he brought home. Frogs, voles, rabbits, crickets, quail chicks, piglets, feral cats—all he had to do was put his hand out and they came to him. And then he brought them home. We shoulda called him Noah, Fos complained. If there was a stray dog for fifty miles around, it would find him—they would find each other. Then one day, moving things around to make more room for his photographic work, Fos uncovered the old x-ray machine and hauled it out to the back porch and set it up and, like both his parents before him, Lightfoot was hooked. He couldn't get enough of the contraption. He would stare at the ghostly image of his toes until Opal was afraid he would go cross-eyed looking down the scope. He would bring things he had found—a stone, a leaf, a feather—and beg Fos to let him see what they looked like in the machine and when Opal cautioned it was keeping him from doing other things Fos reminded her at least he's finally interested in *something* scientific. Fos tried to interest him in photographic work as well, hoping he would find the darkroom an enchanting sanctum, but it was as if the x-ray machine had filed the claim on the existing sum of Lightfoot's curiosity in visual phenomena. That summer when the season rolled around for local fairs, they started going out again on weekends, using the promise of setting up the x-ray at the fair as the carrot on the stick to keep Lightfoot from pestering to play with it all week. But pester he did, and when he started his first year of schooling that September he cajoled Fos and his teacher into letting Fos bring the machine to school one day to demonstrate. Other fathers go, Fos argued over Opal's disapproval. Other fathers take *prize sows,* she told him. We're getting a reputation.

For what?

For bein book-learned. Lightfoot told me. Kids at school were makin jokes about you. Callin you Professor.

Saint could not have pleased him more. Nor *King.* Nor Mr. Universe. He had been experimenting with longer exposures, colored filters, especially degrees of reds and yellows, and when it snowed the morning of the full moon in December, he told Opal he'd be back in a few days and he took the cameras and the filters on a field trip to experiment. There was a cemetery due for disinterment and relocation that he'd been waiting for the right conditions to photograph and he was running out of time. The moonlight and the refractive qualities of the snow were perfect for the effects he sought and on the way home on the second night, he stopped at Guntersville and set up what would become his most celebrated portrait—a very long exposure under moonlight from the ramparts of the dam's spillway, the concrete battlements etched in stark shadows next to the creamy waterfall beneath the ebony sky. Flash would have hated the photograph's forced beauty, its manipulativeness. But when Sturdevant saw the print that Fos made of the spillway he recognized its iconic symbolism. Look at this: a man-made structure standing tall and lone against the universe. A thing of beauty, like the Pyramids. Built to stand the test of Time. He sent the photograph to magazines and newspapers around the country, and through her friends in the library system, Opal started a scrapbook of the press clippings—*New York Herald, Chicago Sun, Denver Post, Illustrated News of London.* It's all the same picture, Fos objected.

Not for long, she knew.

Fos's photographs began appearing regularly in newspapers and *Guntersville Spillway* won a prize in a gallery show in New York City. The following year Sturdevant put together a traveling exhibition featuring photographs of Fos's side by side with famous professionals and photojournalists from the WPA. The exhibition toured six states at courthouses, schools, and county fairs and when it visited their local fair, Fos and Opal and Lightfoot went to see it.

Will there be *animals?* Lightfoot pressed.

Oh yes.

What kinds of animals?

Big ones.

How big?

Bigger'n you, Fos told him. He could tell Opal was fussing in her mind with something.

Giraffes? Lightfoot wanted to know.

Be sensible, his mother snapped at him.

We're not goin there for *animals,* she told him.

There'll be pigs and cows and horses, son, Fos said.

To Opal: what's got inside *your* stockin?

Nothin. This is *your* day.

Yes it is but that doesn't mean we all can't enjoy ourselves.

I was just thinkin that with all the fairs we been to. We ain't been back to this one all these years.

Countin up again are you?

No. Not countin. Rememberin.

Will there be *elephants?* Lightfoot asked.

This was the fair where Karo's Early was *electrocuted,* Opal whispered.

With a start Fos turned around and looked at Lightfoot, who smiled. Those dimples.

Fos found himself holding onto Lightfoot's hand more tightly than was warranted for a boy his age, but once they found the tent where the photographs were on display he let him go. There was a crowd of folks that Fos and Opal knew from the county and Fos was glad to see there were no men in suits from Knoxville, no visiting ambassadors from the Office of Information or any other bureau of the TVA.

Which one is yours, Fos? one of their neighbors asked and Opal proudly pointed out Those three over there.

Well lookee, said ol' Sumner who owned a piece of land two farms over from them, That's Harlan Couter's tombstone. I used t' know ol' Harlan. Fact I know this cemetery—

A couple of the men had gathered round and one of them said, Word has it we're the next.

The ladies, over in the corner, overheard and Opal felt obliged to counter. Fos would be the first to hear, he works for them. And he's heard nothin, have you, Fos?

I hear they're buyin farms already, Creighton said. Over there by Chickamauga.

I heard that, too, someone else put in. It tears me up. Where in the Constitution does it say the government has the right to come an' take your land?

Where in the Constitution does it say you have the right to own land in the first place? Fos posed.

Opal felt her color rise. That was something Flash might have argued, years ago. Fortunately it didn't seem to bother anybody in the room. They were only interested in words bolstering their argument.

I heard they come around an' tellya how high the water's gonna get, an' if that don't scareya they paint a waterline ferya across the top floor of your house.

I heard they paint the waterline on trees.

My cousin Reg they came out to his place down at Nickjack and they told him the water there was goin to go fifteen feet above the weathervane atop his barn an' he said, You must think I'm stupid. This river's never been above that high line right there where my great-grandfather marked it on the barn door when it flooded back in 1847. Never been as high as that in anybody's lifetime since. And never will. So don't tell me no river's gonna come drown out my land, my house. I'm not stupid. An' I have a gun. I told him, I said, whatcha gonna do, Reg? Shoot the water when it comes?

That sure didn't keep the Mississippi back in '27, Creighton noted.

No, but it would keep Mr. Roosevelt and his boys off things that don't belong to 'em.

I would rather set myself on fire than let them take my land, Milo Candy warned.

That got a laugh.

Then Sumner said, you set yourself on fire, Milo, they'll come and flood you anyway an' claim they had t' do it jest to save your life.

More than once as the talk drifted in and out of *what mights*—what might happen if the government came and tried to put a dam down on the lower forty, what might happen if we all refused their offer, what might go awry, anyway, in the natural course of things without the goddam government—more than once as the men and women talked of what could happen, Opal thought to stop them. Fos would know, she wanted to convince them. Fos worked for the *Office of Information,* for darn sake, so he'd be at the source of information, he'd be the one to get it first. But as they spoke, she realized that the *what mights* they were exploring in their talk were little causeways to the future. Any person who could talk about the possibility of an event, whether it was foreseeable or not, might be better off, she thought, than one who couldn't plan for things at all. Better to have *what mights* up your sleeve, she saw, than to believe in false assurances. Still, it seemed a logical preclusion that if the news was going to come it would come through inside channels, via Fos. But the thing about *what mights,* which you forget while you're inventing them, is how, one way or another, they surpriseya. You go about your business paying heed to unseen possibilities, paying lip service to the practice of preparedness, when one day you are sweeping out the front room and two church ladies show up with their clipboards and rap on your screen door.

Well hidy, Opal says.

Spring cleanin, she explains by way of introduction to the broom when she holds the door for them and lets them in and sees they're not church ladies, but both wearing badges that she recognizes.

BUREAU OF PERMANENT RESIDENTS, the badges read.

DEPARTMENT OF REMOVAL AND RELOCATION.

You must be here for Fos, Opal says.

Hon, run and fetch your father, she tells Lightfoot.

Well hi-*dee,* she repeats more formally, wiping down her hands on her apron. I'm Fos's wife—Opal—and I don't envy you *that,* she says, nodding toward the printed forms they have on their clipboards. I used to go with Fos out to the cemeteries, too, when he first started. Down around Hales Bar.

The thinner of the two, the one with a white blouse with a ruffle at the neck looks a little pained and says, well actually. We're here t' talk to Earl White Junior.

About Karo White? the other one reads off her clipboard. And Earl White the Third, known as "Early." And a child just by the name here of "Newborn Baby White."

Opal looks from one of them back to the other and says, Say again?

Earl White Junior, the first one repeats. Husband of Karo White?

Earl, yes—*Earl.* I'm his cousin. What about him?

You're his *cousin—?*

Opal. Opal Foster.

One of them starts turning pages, seems to look for Opal's name somewhere.

Is Earl here, by any chance? the other says. We'd like to ask him a few questions.

Earl hasn't been in these parts since before Fos and I came down here to live.

Well do you know where we can send him one of these forms to fill out?

No. An' anyway—Earl can't write. What's this about?

Well maybe you can help us. You say you're a cousin?

Opal nods.

How are you related? Through the mother's family or the father's?

My mother was Earl's father's sister.

And her name was—?

Alma White—why are you writin all this down?

And now *Earl* . . . he was the husband of Karo? Karo White who's buried up there on the hill?

Opal nods but doesn't speak.

And would you happen to be able to verify Karo White's "d.o.b."—date of birth?

No, Opal says.

Or her other "d.o.b."—date of burial?

This is some mistake, Opal realizes. They've sent you to the wrong place, she finally says.

She reaches out and takes the clipboard from the woman as Fos comes in behind them, led by Lightfoot. *Ladies,* he acknowledges, like a rooster in the foxes' den.

You're not going to start diggin up that hill, Opal says, reading down the list of names on the piece of paper. There's no need to. There's been some mistake. Tell them, Fos. My kin are buried there. My mother's mother. People from my family for as long as we go back. People who've been here a hundred years. People who were born here, maybe right here in this room. So this list of names is wrong. You have got the wrong place—come on out here let me show you somethin—

She keeps talking as she moves, holds the broom in one hand, leads them out the screen door down the porch stairs, across the chicken yard into the open space beside the pasture where the land begins the slow slope upward toward the height where the cemetery stands, half a mile away.

See? she points. That cemetery is on *high* ground. No one's gonna come an' take away some land that high are they, Fos? An' anyway: no one's plannin any dams around here or we'd have been the first t' know it. Wouldn't we have been, Fos? Because you work for them. See how high that is? How high would you say that land is, Fos?

He was standing there beside her with Lightfoot and the ladies from the Bureau, squinting in the sun and looking up the hill to where two boys and a wagon were stopped under a stand of old oak trees.

Who's *that?* Opal wondered more out loud than she had meant to.

It looked like they were totin buckets.

Lightfoot, run an' see what those boys are up to, Fos instructed.

Back in no time.

They say they're paintin *trees,* he told his parents.

High-water lines, one of the ladies said.

Oh glory, Opal breathed. Glory holes and glory dams and *glory halleluiah* TVA was comin to their neighborhood, a bureaucracy with soul, all right but a bureaucracy, nevertheless: Because two weeks after she already had the news, the official letter came informing Opal that the land she had inherited was required for the greater good, for the glory of the nation.

Well, she said, trying on an irony which wasn't natural to her. I said I wanted to know *how much* they were payin. Now I do.

Now the only question left to answer is *where to?*

. . . others, shading their eyes from the vivid sunlight, sat far out on the rocking yards; all the spars in full bearing of mortals, ready and ripe for their fate. Ah! how they still strove through that infinite blueness to seek out the thing that might destroy them!

HERMAN MELVILLE, *Moby-Dick,* "The Chase—Second Day"

fishin

A LITANY. It goes like this:

No flood, no TVA.
No TVA, no cheap electric power.
No cheap electric power, no factories.
No factories, no aluminum.
No aluminum, no long-distance bombers.
No long-distance bombers, no atomic bomb.

No atomic bomb, no Oak Ridge, Tennessee.

When the War broke out and before our boys were really in it—before Pearl Harbor—everybody thought the critical material that was going to win it for our side was going to be aluminum. Aluminum, aluminum, aluminum—the whole combatant world was trading in its gold to get some and there was only one country on earth that had the resources the energy and the manpower to manufacture it in quantities to satisfy demand. Whichever side could out-aluminize the other first was sure to win the War.

Until, that is, the demand for something else became more critical.

Until the critical material that was going to win the War turned out to be something that, until 1940, even the smartest men could only guess existed. Since the earth was formed, it remained disguised—a thing that *might* exist, if only. If only something smaller than a particle of dust could be made to travel like an eight-ball aimed at tiny targets in an atom of uranium then, like billiard balls caroming on a mirrored table, you might begin an action where one thing strikes another which ricochets to strike another in a self-sustaining chain reaction. *Fission* was the name the smart boys gave this process. Fission—in the nuclear family the power that binds it all together is multiplied a thousandfold when things begin to split apart. The more fissionable the substance is—like a legendary breaking heart—the greater the destructive force is when it explodes.

To make a big explosion, the scientists went looking for a breaking heart in matter.

A fissionable substance.

And that fissionable substance became the critical material that was going to win the war.

Plutonium.

Ploot.

Don't try to find it on your own—you won't. Even God didn't recognize it at Creation.

To make it first you have to make artificial elements extracted from uranium. From, say, two tons of uranium, and at the cost of, say, several hundred million dollars, you might extract a button of very fissionable material the size of a dime which eventually decays into a relatively stable metal the color of a chicken liver: *Ploot.* Because of the activity in its atoms ploot is always warm. The first woman to hold a pellet of it told her husband it had felt like holding a small rabbit in her hand.

Whole eras, Fos knew, had been lived by man when not a jot of history had been written. Whole ages had gone down in history when not a single army overran the land, no marauding horde attacked the gates, no miracles of science were revealed, no savior was foresworn, no prophets born. In all the ages into which he may have been born he might have coincided with those empty times. Those unwritten pages. Or the Plague. Or Pericles. Or

Christ. Instead, he got two wars. He got the Kaiser and the Hun and mustard gas. He got Mr. Hitler. Mr. Hirohito. He got Albert Einstein.

In the 1930s graduates from engineering schools went to work for the United States government because the government was the most exciting place to go to work. The government was building engineering miracles. But by the 1940s the government was attracting talent from a different scientific field—*physics.* Fos had read an estimate that in 1916—the year he had signed up to join the Army—there were approximately two hundred physicists in the United States. By 1942, there were five thousand. Five thousand physicists—and half, he reckoned, had at one time or another in the last six months come through the security gates past the armed guards of the top-secret compound twenty miles west of Knoxville near the Norris Dam where he and tens of thousands of other Tennesseeans worked.

The place was called Oak Ridge—or "Site X," depending on how much you were allowed to know, depending on the level of your clearance. With "Site Y" at Los Alamos, New Mexico, and "Site W" at Hanford, Washington, Oak Ridge completed the nuclear family known as the Manhattan Engineering District—the Manhattan Project.

Purchased by the government in September 1942, the 59,000 acres that comprised the site had no paved roads and no rail line connecting it to anywhere, but it had two advantages: it was remote, and it sat beside a dam, a colossal source of cheap electric power. Like the desert at Los Alamos and like the wilderness at Hanford, the valley at Oak Ridge was a strange unsettled place and the people hired to work there couldn't help but feel that they were pioneering in a legendary way—invading an inhospitable landscape and making it productive. A thousand families had been eking out a meagre living on it, but the government evicted them and within a month sixty miles of railbed were put down, and the ghost trains started coming in.

People miles around could hear them, shunting, in the night.

Lotta stuff is goin' in, folks said.

Even in the daylight you could start to see it—trucks and flatbeds, motorcars, a lot of traffic. A lot of stuff was going in.

But nothing seemed to come back *out.*

"Top secret" and "War effort" were phrases people used when they tried to figure what was going on. No one—even the people who worked in the gaseous diffusion factory where the uranium was separated—had a clue what they were making. No one but the top brass and the physicists. And even they knew only partial truths—knew that the objective was to isolate plutonium but didn't know what for. Knew that the process was potentially destructive but not exactly how. Knew that there were levels of radioactivity involved but not how much was harmful. They're makin planes in there, people who saw all the traffic speculated. They're sewin parachutes. They're makin somethin that'll make our boys invisible. They're makin Pepsi-Cola. A call went out for workers and to work "at the plant" got you deferred from active duty—still, more workers were needed than were in the local area. Carpenters came from as far away as Minnesota and took the Oath. Steamfitters came. Chemical engineers, mechanical engineers, electrical engineers, stenographers, cement fitters, plumbers, pipefitters, millwrights, masons, mess-hall cooks, waitresses, nurses, clerks, secretaries.

The physicists.

A bookkeeper, hired as much for her age as for her skill with numbers.

A photographer, ditto.

It was thought by the people who extracted your Oath and your Allegiance and required that you take a Pledge of secrecy, that the older you were the more you could be trusted.

Only the physicists were very young. And the boys in privates' uniforms.

A Veteran of the Great War was what was written at the top of Fos's file. A Vet. A man whose life had coincided with two global wars. *They're taking Vets,* Sturdevant had told him in the call-up after Pearl. They're giving them priority. If you want to go.

They wouldn't take me, not with these, Fos had answered, polishing his specs. I think I'm probably officially disabled. And too old.

They're taking fellas older.

And I have a family.

They're taking husbands, too. And fathers. Case you didn't notice.

I noticed, Fos said.

Maybe there had been generations before his who had had to face two wars, he didn't know. His knowledge was a little patchy when it came to dates and combats which, let's face it, constitute nine-tenths of the historical record. The generation which had fought the Civil War might still have been alive at the start of the Great one. But there were fifty years between those two—less than twenty-five between the last one and this new one. He had lived, it seemed to him, a goodly lot in those few years. He had lived the story of his life. He had had his finest hours. A few of them alone, with his inventions and experiments. Or with the sky, at night. A few of them with Flash. But most of them with Opal.

He couldn't think what it would do to him if he ever had to leave her.

When the Great War began Opal had been living with her father, walking three days a week a mile and a half to the road where she could hitch a ride to town to clean the local doctor's office and do chores for him. The doctor's wife was chronically ill and sometimes Opal helped her in the house as well. When the doctor's wife became too ill to do her husband's paperwork, she taught Opal how to do basic accounting. Sitting in the doctor's office Opal got to see nearly everyone in town, she got to meet everyone she thought she'd ever meet. "The War," so far as it was real to her, came through the printed word in the newspaper, accompanied by maps of places with strange names and otherworldly photographs of groups of men lined up in uniforms with bayonets fixed on their guns. She remembers thinking to herself that most of them were probably her age or younger. One of them, in other circumstances, might have passed through town, walked into an office where she worked. Whenever a picture of young soldiers in a group appeared in the local paper Opal would set aside that page to look at later, while she ate her midday meal, alone, scrutinizing all their faces for some clues to what she might have said to any one of them if she had ever had the chance to meet him. What he might have said to her. If he had even noticed her. The War, for her, was boys away in foreign places, more boys than she had ever met, more than she could ever hope to meet, collectively, a roll call of unspoken names, an invocation of so many possibilities, lost. Later, when she remembered looking at those photographs, she wondered if Fos had ever been among them, standing there, unconversant with his future as the rest of them. Youth never sees its shadow till the sun's about to set: and then you wonder where the person went who you were speaking to in all your thoughts for all those years.

When the Germans marched on Poland, Fos was nearly fifty, living on the farm and taking pictures for the TVA. The night he learned they marched on France he went outside with Lightfoot on his shoulders and stared into the sky and didn't come back in when Opal called and didn't eat his supper. After Pearl he told her, There's a chance I'll be called up.

She weighed the possibilities.

An' there's a chance you won't.

They waited, and the first thing to arrive was their notice of eviction from the TVA.

Uncle Sam, it seemed, was showing them his sense of humor.

Not for a minute did they contemplate going back to Knoxville—for Fos, that bridge had been burned, he lost no love on those who governed there; no love on the city, either.

For Opal, the argument against returning to Knoxville was something different. She didn't want their son to grow up like the only city people she had ever really known—like Flash. Or Lally.

They were still in the process of deciding where to go when the decision—like most the things that shaped their life together—found the two of them.

Colonel Bud Overmarker was the Army Intelligence Officer detailed to Site X in charge of granting clearances and hiring the key positions. He had been in Belgium in the Great War and had never left the cloth. He spoke as if all life was taking part in a dress drill. Everything was H.C. (Highly Classified). On a NTK basis (need-to-know). Fos was going to be one of the few people trusted to go everywhere within the Site at Oak Ridge—*almost* everywhere. To take pictures. Army needed pictures. Bud never said "the" Army, only Army. Pictures would be H.C. Fos would be one of the few to get a Q clearance.

What's the Q stand for? Fos asked.

Nothing. It's just Q. That's what it is. It's the highest clearance that there is. You want to hear something funny? I'm going to tell you something funny. When you're working undercover and you're in the field and people ask you what you're doing there you say you're a photographer.

I say that?

No—*you.* Everybody. Anybody in Intelligence.

Intelligence, Fos repeated.

Spy work. Army.

Oh you mean *you* say that.

Yeah, me—*you.* Everyone. You say, I'm a photographer, it means you're undercover.

Well I don't think we'd do that.

Who?

My wife an' me. If that's what you were askin.

What wouldn't you do?

Spy on other people.

It wasn't *spying,* really. But you couldn't enter through the gates at Oak Ridge without the sense that you were entering a scrupulously watched world, a prefabricated Eden necessarily exempt of any serpents. It was impossible not to feel that you were doing something charged up and important—urgent. Anybody acting any differently stuck out like a sore thumb. Anybody acting any differently soon disappeared. People on the whole got in the swing of things and helped each other out as people do, but they were careful how they spoke. And they watched to see that everyone was on the up-and-up. The pay was great, there were women on the site as well as men and even though the social circles tended to adhere to job divisions, when you pinned your badge on in the morning you knew that you were doing something for your country that might win the war. Most people there were working harder than they ever had—working double shifts and overtime—and they played with equal effort. Opal reckoned the average age on site was twenty-two and when these younger people played they threw their youth and their exuberance into it. There was always a ballgame of some kind going on somewhere—the women throwing just as hard as all the men. There were biking groups and hiking groups, men's wrestling, square-dancing, jazz groups, archery and calisthenics. There were bingo games and card games at the weekends and in leisure hours there was fun—these were *young* people—but you didn't question Mr. Roosevelt, you didn't even question Mr. Truman. You did your bit and kept an eye out but you didn't talk too much, you didn't share your tales with others.

When Fos and Opal came to the site in the fall of '42, there were still no streets and only prefabricated houses put together along raised wooden boardwalks so people could get around through all the mud. Mud was everywhere—mud yards, mud parking lots, mud "trees" sculpted in the mudfield beside the workers' huts. Their house, and all the others like it, had been put together with such haste that you could see the daylight through the seams, but Opal took pride in its newness. It's modern, she explained to Lightfoot. It's not the city and it's not the country. It's in between. It was certainly a step up the social ladder, by her thinking, from the way they had been living. There was carpeting in all the rooms, for one thing—wall to wall. The kitchen and the bathroom had linoleum. *Tile,* she liked to emphasize. Linoleum *tile.* There was a built-in stove and a built-in electric oven with a dial for setting different temperatures and when you stuck your head in you could see a separate heating coil on top for "broiling." There was water from the tap and the heat came out of vents cut in the carpeting. It didn't bother her that every house on the muddy avenue was identical to theirs, a replica—she liked to visit just to see how the other wives, the other families had fixed things up. She was the oldest woman on the street by at least a decade, but Lightfoot paved the way for her to meet the younger mothers and soon she'd been in every house where there was a child that he could play with. Some of the younger wives had paintings on the walls and lined curtains that hung below the windowsill and record players and nearly all of them wore slacks. The girl next door, Janet, smoked cigarettes and came from Chicago and talked faster than Opal had the skill to follow, often. She and her husband, Robert, had a boy named Billy, Lightfoot's age, and soon after they became neighbors, Janet asked Fos and Opal over for "a drink" one Friday night—Opal didn't know that meant real alcohol. It wasn't long before Fos and Opal became the honorary godparents of an entire den of younger cubs. Part of

Fos's job in the beginning was to take the ID pictures of everybody on the site. *Live people,* he joked to Opal. There were still plenty of what he called "studies of mysterious things"—Site photographs—but it had been a long time since he had taken photographs of anyone outside his family. Because he'd taken their pictures, people on the site called hello to him. And those who didn't recognize the Mister definitely knew the Missus—Opal was one of the *pay ladies* from the Cashier's Office. Must be nice to be so liked, Fos kidded her. Glad I don't have to walk around next to the *hypodermic lady.*

Inoculations were part of living on the site—so were the regular blood samples. Opal nearly fainted and had to sit down when the hypodermic lady came to take a sample of Lightfoot's blood for the first time. What's this for? she asked when it was her turn.

Records the hypodermic lady said. You know how Army works. Has he had the chicken pox?

No.

—measles?

No.

—and, oh, I see here we don't have a copy of his birth certificate on file.

No.

Why is that?

I—it was lost. In the flood. When they put us from our farm. I lost it. In the move.

Well that shouldn't be a problem we can get one from the county. Where was Ray here born?

On second thought I'll have another look. I think there's one more box it could be in.

Maybe it's in the Box of Clues, Lightfoot volunteered and went off to get it.

"Box of clues"? the lady asked.

It's what we call it, it's from when we had to move. A box that Lightfoot—*Ray Junior*—found at the bottom of a closet we were cleaning out. It's just a box of old pictures I kept meaning to put up inside an album some day. I told him it's a box of clues. He thought that was better than a box of old-time photographs. 'Cause, you know, we were movin, like I said and everything was all unsettled—

Well when you find that birth certificate you'll bring it to the Health Office won't you?

Why didn't you just tell the truth? Fos questioned later and she had to *shushsh!* him.

The walls were very thin in these prefabricated houses.

So thin that when the ghost trains came you thought they were delivering a boxcar to your door.

Janet next door says she always heard trains crying through the night back in Chicago, Opal whispered.

We're not talking about Janet.

Well what was I supposed to say?

Tell them that we never got around to registering his birth. Tell them we were country people. Tell them that was normal.

I'm a country person and I have a birth certificate.

Well lotsa people *don't.*

Name one.

Through the walls a ghost train whistled.

I don't know why that should remind me of those mules, Fos said.

It would break his little heart to know the truth. It's bad enough he doesn't have so many animals to play with now. *What mules?*

The ones with bells around their necks who used to come out when they gassed us, when the ground was thick with all that poison fog an' lead us back into the trenches. I still hear those bells. The trains at night remind me of them. Things moving on the ground out there that you can't see. Things that you can only hear.

Maybe this will end before they ask again about the birth certificate, she whispered.

Maybe.

Maybe this will end soon and we'll all go back to normal.

And maybe fairies dance on rainbows, Fos attested.

Do you play chess? Janet asked one day.

Goodness, no.

The question took her by surprise. Was chess a woman's game?

Does Fos?

I don't think so, Opal told her.

Would you mind if I gave Ray Junior some instruction? He seems to have a gift for it.

He *has?* Is that—is that something that you only get if it's inherited?

You'd think so, wouldn't you, but I played chess in children's tournaments and neither of my parents plays. Before Billy was born, I was going to make a go of it, career-wise. I was still competing up until the night I went into labor. I was sitting in a tournament ahead by seven pieces when my waters broke. You should have seen the look on my opponent's face—! I'm sorry, Opal—did I say something to offend you? You seem so young with Lightfoot I forget, sometimes, you're from a different era.

No I'm not offended.

—good.

I just never heard that term before.

—what term?

"My waters broke." I just never heard it.

Well what did you call it? When it happened to you?

—to *me?* When would it have happened to me?

A look, as fleeting as a guilty guest.

Oh *that,* she bluffed. She wasn't sure what she was pretending that she knew. She cleared her throat. She hoped she wasn't signifying she knew something she shouldn't.

She never realized to what extent other women talk about their bodies. The single women talked about their experiences with men in language Opal never dreamed existed. Not even in the days when she was reading dimestore novels. They smoked and drank as freely as the men and didn't shy away from their own athleticism. The women who had children talked about their pregnancies among themselves as if they'd been on a trip or on a holiday somewhere. On a bus. And were describing what went by outside the window. Once, when she got up to get more cake from the kitchen she heard Janet whisper to another mother, "Opal doesn't like to talk about the birth."

—really?

At her age. My guess is that there might have been some *problem.*

—gotcha.

But at least the younger women talked a way she *understood.*

When it came to making conversation with a physicist she was not only in a foreign land, she was on another planet. At least when she'd been working with the mobile library and she'd stop to lend out books to engineers at campsites where they were building dams, she could understand the things they told her while they were making conversation as they chose their books. *All things being equal,* they might start to say, *the water-to-cement ratio determines strength in your concrete.*

Oh like *coffee,* she could comprehend.

But with the physicists you couldn't see what they were talking about. You couldn't even hardly start to try to imagine it. For fun one evening at a party at a neighbor's house all the physicists tried to work out what was the smallest-size bureau drawer the total mass of everyone in the room could fit into. The *smallest* size. And one of them kept saying no, *mass of the elements, mass of the elements,* which she kept hearing as last of the elephants. *Do you ever dream that you're locked inside a room without a door?* the man beside her asked.

His breath smelled like rising yeast.

Do *you?* she asked.

He nodded.

Let me ask you something, she got up the courage.

People let you ask them things when they'd been drinking.

The so-called upper "limit of acceptable discourse" went down as the blood alcohol got higher.

Do you think that it is possible that people way way back in history, back around the time of Jesus Christ, do you believe it's possible that ordinary people way back then had haloes?

He thought about this and then said, Is it *possible?* Oh, yes. Absolutely.

Opal was extremely glad to hear this and added it to her reserve of scientific certainties.

That tides are pushed by angels.

Trees are what moves the wind.

And fairies dance on rainbows, Fos repeated.

For Christmas, along with a new set of carving knives and a bathrobe that Janet helped him order from Chicago, Fos bought Opal a beginner's book about the elemental principles of atomic structure.

He bought Lightfoot a sled. And a *Boy's Own Book of Large Warm-Blooded Mammals.*

Opal kept her book about atomic structure in pride-of-place on her bedside table and every night, for months, she picked it up and sighed and tried to start all over. I'll never understand this, she finally lamented.

She was getting tired after work, he noticed. Looking drawn. And thinner.

Let me read it to you. Out loud. Bedtime story.

Better if you read to Lightfoot.

I'll read it to the both of you.

Wait a minute here, she told him some weeks later.

Lightfoot was asleep in the next room.

Do you mean to say that it's *a fact* that the whatchamacallum elements that make up the stars are the same elements that make up a human bein? Is that what you're sayin this is sayin?

Yes m'am.

There were little crescent moons beneath her eyes. Bruised opals.

That my finger here might become be a star someday?

Yes m'am.

That me—that I—that you an' me an' Lightfoot all of us could have been up there as a star?

Yes m'am.

She stared hard at him.

Well that's just ridiculous. That's just about the most ridiculous loada nonsense I have ever heard.

He stifled a smile.

But I thought for sure you'd like that. I thought that would be one of your favorites. Tides are caused by angels sorta thing.

Then explain to me what kinda star my father was that night we threw his ashes offa Kitty Hawk.

Fos needed to wipe his eyes but he sat real still instead.

You're upset, he noted.

No I'm not.

You are.

Well we got another note sent home with Lightfoot from the school about the Health Office. About them needing his certificate of birth on record.

Well then, Fos said. Time we just come clean.

An' tell 'em what?

Tell them that the baby was a foundling.

No Fos, I won't do that.

Ope, this is the last place on god's earth we should be trying to be less than honest.

But it's just the war. Otherwise—

He's goin t' have t' get some papers someday. One way or another. Some day he's going to want to vote and go to college. And you know as well as I do it's the way the world is going. You don't pay a single person here each Friday without first inspecting his I.D.

That's exactly what I'm saying—it's the *war* that's made it all this way. Badges. Oaths.

She couldn't look at him to say the next thing that she had to say.

She put her head against his shoulder, hid her face away from him.

What if we tell them what you say and it makes them take Lightfoot away from us?

It won't. Nothing's going to make them want to take Lightfoot away from us. Who would do a thing like that—?

He reached up to stroke her hair and was surprised to feel it come away between his fingers in wisps, like fur.

Just because you *can* do somethin doesn't mean you should, she told him as he laid her down against the pillow. So tired she was barely making sense. Running to keep up with women half her age.

Tell me again tomorrow what you said about the stars.

I will—

What she needed was that tonic everyone was taking. With that extra iron in it.

Check the boy then come to bed, she whispered, half asleep already and he kissed her. Turned the light out, closed the house up, stepped inside the boy's room and pulled his covers over him.

Then in the bathroom in the stark light at the sink he saw her white hair on his fingers and was too moved by love to rinse it.

She, too, noticed she was losing hair. Not in her comb or in a normal way. But on her pillow. It just *comes out,* she tried explaining one afternoon to Janet. I must be doing something different, using the wrong hair shampoo. You know I've used the same shampoo for years and maybe it needs changin. I thought maybe it might be somethin in the water out here, but your hair looks nice and full. You're not havin any trouble with your hair, are you?

Go see Nancy, Janet told her. She's set up a hair salon in her dining nook. She can tell you what the problem is.

Age, was Nancy's diagnosis. I've seen older women go completely bald but I think I've got a cream that will help you stop it.

The cream smelled like ripened fruit.

Rotting cantaloupe, Fos approximated.

It made her pillow smell like rotting cantaloupe as well so she gave up using it.

I'm not *old,* she argued.

Still, they started cutting back on parties at the weekend. Opal didn't like the smell of liquor anyway and she and Fos were usually the only people never drinking in the room except for Methodists and Mormons. Workdays, she started taking naps when she got home before she fixed their supper when Lightfoot was outside or playing at a friend's house. But if he came home earlier and found her still in bed, he'd tiptoe in and start to play The Sleeping Game with her.

The Sleeping Game was his favorite game to play with both his parents—the only game he'd not outgrown, the one they'd played the longest. The summer he was four, back on the farm, he had found a baby bird on the ground beside a sedge where it had fallen from its nest. He had picked it up and run straight to his father, who was chopping wood beside the barn. By the time he reached Fos tears were streaming from his eyes.

The death of animals was something every farm boy knew but for Lightfoot the death of any animal was a defeat, a blow struck against the side of fairness in the world. He made elaborate burials for the dead animals he found, digging holes for them up on the hill until his animals outnumbered the humans resting for eternity up there and Opal helped him find another place and Fos leveled some ground for them down by the river.

Fos had braced himself for another solemn episode when he saw his son come running but when Lightfoot showed him what was in his hand Fos said a silent prayer of gratitude for the way life can hand a father a random chance to be a hero in his young son's eyes.

The bird was a bound jewel, green and red and amethyst—*not dead.*

You know what you've got here, son?

Dead was Lightfoot's answer.

He could tell the bird was dead. It wasn't breathing and its eyes were closed.

This is a hummingbird, Fos told him.

He sat down on the log he had been cutting and drew the boy in closer.

Look here at his beak—it's like a needle. That's how you can tell them from the other birds. That, and the way they fly. They sorta hang there for a long time—wings so fast that you can hear 'em buzzing. Like a top. Or like a motor. They hang there for a while outside a flower and they stick their needles in and they drink out flower nectar. They use up so much energy that when they rest, their body stops—like a bear in hibernation. Go ahead and touch this little fella—here, I'll showya.

Fos cupped his hands over his son's and breathed warm air around the bird.

He's just sleepin—here, you try it.

Lightfoot brought the bird up to his mouth and gently blew on it.

From your throat, Fos showed him. It needs to be warm air.

On Lightfoot's third attempt the bird revived, opened its eyes, and flew straight up as if to peer into the boy's thoughts, then darted off.

That night when Fos was putting him to bed Lightfoot held one of the carved whales in his hands the way he'd held the hummingbird and breathed on it. Are you sleeping? he asked the whale. Wake up.

No hon, Fos tried to warn him. It doesn't work that way.

One day it will, his son maintained.

Next morning and on certain mornings for years thereafter, whenever Lightfoot woke before his parents he would tiptoe in and ask them are you sleeping? and then blow on them. *Wake up.*

The first time he played this game Fos made him blow five times while he kept his eyes shut and on the fifth breath Fos sat straight up and raised his arms and roared like a grizzly bear. Sometimes he pretended to wake up at once and other times he made Lightfoot wait and wait, milking the suspense. Opal was never good at roaring like a grizzly bear but she found a way to scare him just as much by making him peer closely at her face and then springing her eyes open in a rigid stare without a warning.

He loved the game.

The Sleeping Game.

And it was always his to play with them, never the other way around. Always his to play with them. And with his whales.

When they had moved to Oak Ridge from the farm the whales were left behind. Lightfoot had lined them up for one last time, talking to each one, then chose only two to go along to the new house. Opal chose two boxes of books from Flash's collection and gave the rest to the library service. Fos had difficulty parting with his old machines and rickety inventions but when the time came for them to flee the flood the only two prized objects he took with him were his son and Opal.

And Opal took the Box of Clues.

And the colored glasses that her father made for her.

She placed them on a shelf in their new living room and the women that she had to visit always noticed them, admiringly. She put some of Fos's pictures up, the ones that she'd had framed, the ones that had been in the magazines, and once, while she was pouring coffee she overheard somebody say it seems *artistic* sure runs in this family.

Sometimes she'd find herself staring at the other parents and their children, cataloguing qualities that ran on family lines: a boy who had his mother's eyes; a girl, her father's smile. When she looked at Lightfoot she could see he was as different from the two of them in his appearance as any child could be—one look at the three of them, she felt, and anyone could tell the truth: the fruit had not only not fallen from the tree, the fruit was from a different orchard. Whereas both Fos and Opal had a shyness to their coloring like something growing in the shelter of a rock on frozen tundra, Lightfoot's skin was dark and smooth, his hair a mass of curls like a lamb's before first shearing. He was quick and they were cautious. He ran like the wind and they proceeded by the rules. He sang, they hummed. He laughed, they grinned. But when he stopped to think about a hidden meaning or a depth beneath the surface, Opal noticed he would blink, like Fos, as if his eyes were tearing up. He would mimic Fos's habits, Fos's gestures. Like the cuckoo in a robin's nest, Opal thought. Pretending it was bona fide red-breasted. But, for all that Lightfoot knew, he *was* the baby robin in the robin's nest, Fos and Opal *were* his natural parents, the world *was* their oyster, he *was* theirs. Once—what seemed now to be an age ago, when they were still so new to each other's company—Fos had asked her, "*Happy?*," as if her happiness were hidden or not certified, somehow, by her smile, her every gesture. It had struck her odd that he couldn't see the size of it spelled out in giant letters on her forehead like a place name on a road sign. Welcome to My Face. Home of America's Most Happy Woman. Had he missed the signs? What was she doing wrong that he felt so obliged to *ask* if she was happy?

Remember when you used t' ask if I was *happy?*

Oh dear, he thought. That kinda question with the multiple wrong answers. He blinked a couple times and chose a look of pensive memory retrieval.

I've been thinking about that, she clued. How come you never ask if *Lightfoot's* happy?

Another tricky question, Fos appreciated. But he answered, Well it's obvious. You look at him, he's always smiling. He runs around like every minute is the best damn time he's ever had, no end to wonder or to joy. Every kid who knows him wants to be his friend, every animal he comes across he tenders up to, every person he encounters ends up just a little brighter in his day. The only time—and you know this—the only time the slightest cloud encroaches on his aspect is if he thinks another living thing is troubled or in pain. He's the carefree-est boy I've ever seen—in fact I think he doesn't have an ounce of worry in him except for when he's worried for another. Couldn't ask for someone happier. Everybody knows it.

She was looking at him like she was going to crow.

We did that, she told him.

Yes, we did.

I don't bet there's anybody would suspect he was an orphan. Even if he don't look like us in any other way there's no mistaking we're alike in that. We're *happy.* As a family. That's our family like-ness. An' that's somethin. Don't you think?

He might have said, You have to stop this worryin, but he knew embedded in those worries were doubts and fears that were the defining parts of Opal's motherhood. Every parent has those worries—he struggled with his own each time he saw Lightfoot embrace a stray or clamber up a tree or skate on what appeared to be thin ice. He was afraid the boy would do a careless thing the way all boys are prone to do but he was not afraid the boy would come to harm from some unexpected stranger or that someone would show up at the door some day with a greater claim on Lightfoot's future than Fos and Opal had. Those kinds of fears had never been a part of Fos's psyche, and that was maybe why things had happened in the past that Fos had not foreseen. A reasonable man might have kept his gas mask by his side or might have seen the gas cloud coming. A reasonable man might have guessed that someone with a character and history like Flash's might end up the way he did. But Fos believed that some things happen for no reason. He believed there was an order and a method in the ultimate design of things but he believed that that design was the end result of a lot of trial and error. Trial and error as a fact of life was the first thing Fos expected every time he put on his shoes, turned the tap on, lit a match. Statistically he knew the odds were in his favor that his shoes would fit, water would come out the tap, and combustion would occur—but he also knew that *for no reason* there existed chances that the opposite might happen. No use asking why or how: why and how were part of the design. As soon as you construct a thing you give its opposite a license to exist—you build a tower then you also build the chance it will fall. You fall in love with safety then you also fall prey to its failure to prevent the necessary trial and error. To think of life as foolproof is a fallacy of fools, he thought. Things *happen,* he believed, and there's nothing you can do to keep them from occurring without taking out the magic spark plug, the genius of invention that ignited the adventure in the first place. Fos's worrying about Lightfoot being bitten by a stray dog seemed within the reasonable range of worry: once a week or so, he reminded Lightfoot of the dangers of wild animals. Told him to approach with caution, use his voice and not his hands to try to tame them, told him not to place himself in unnecessary danger. Told him not to climb above the lower branches of a tree and not to reach into a hornet's nest or place his head inside a lion's mouth. But to caution him against going hatless in the rain or running in a way that might lead to a fall that breaks his bones—Fos couldn't do it. Maybe it was wrong of him not to credit the unknown with danger, not to have those kinds of worries, not to grant the fears of living full and fatal due. Opal's fears, he felt, were due in part to the unlikely way that Lightfoot came to them—one improbable event might lead to another, he could understand her reflex to remain alert. *Alertness* on the secret site at Oak Ridge, anyway, was a state of being, the required climate. Signs in the men's rooms, in the mess halls, at the gates and at work stations heralded the dangers of letting down one's guard or letting loose with gossip. ANTICIPATE, the sign outside his darkroom said. IF HITLER KNEW YOUR NEXT MOVE YOU'D BE DEAD. Fos could try to save his son from rabies and from falling out of trees but all the worry on the planet couldn't save him from a world designed, along with all its majesty, to give birth to Adolf Hitler. Could Hitler have been stopped if *he* had been anticipated? The physicists, some of whom practiced sleight of hand and card tricks as a hobby, argued that the signs were there, like the history of earth in stone before the advent of geology, the signs were there for seeing and for reading. THE EYE WILL SELDOM SEE WHAT THE MIND DOES NOT ANTICIPATE, a sign in the men's room in one of the top-secret buildings warned. Above which one of the physicists had written "Isn't this The 1st Principle of Magic?" Fos thought it was. Even though he knew he ought to worry more, he knew that if he harried every motive, guarded every move, that he might be safer, sure. But then he'd miss the magic—wouldn't he?

Which may have been the reason why, when Bud Overmarker, out of the blue and out of uniform, rapped on the door one Sunday evening after dark, Fos greeted him with pleasure, unsuspecting. Fos shook his hand and sat him on the sofa in the living room while Opal came in from the kitchen, turning the last water glass from supper in a tea towel even though she'd finished drying it before Fos let Bud in.

Bud had brought the hypodermic lady with him.

And she had her bag.

Sorry to barge in on you like this, Bud said.

He looks like he's been bowling, Opal thought. He had those kind of shoes on, with white socks.

He and the hypodermic lady must have walked here 'cause she hadn't heard a car.

I wanted this to look like we'd just dropped by on a social visit, you know—spur of the minute, Bud said next.

What can we get the two of you? Fos offered, still without a clue. Would you like a beer, Bud? I think we have a bottle tucked away inside the fridge for an occasion such as this—

Bud held up his hands to indicate refusal and the hypodermic lady pursed her lips and shook her head, declining, then Bud looked around, then looked at Fos and said, The boy in bed?

Oh lord I knew it, Opal said. You've come about the birth certificate, haven't you?

She was so convinced that was the reason for their visit she didn't notice Bud's adjustment to this development. Skilled interrogator, he was ready to deploy a practiced tactic: he sat absolutely still, said nothing, looked at her and waited.

We don't have it, Opal volunteered.

The hypodermic lady didn't seem to know whether she should let Opal go on talking or put in a word to set the record straight.

She took her cue from Bud: sat still and listened.

The truth is, Opal started to explain.

Truth is, Fos said.

They looked at one another.

He doesn't have one, Fos declared. He was born out in the county there in North Carolina where we'd been to settle Opal's father's things after he had died. We weren't living there, just on the visit so we never went to file the birth. Didn't know the parents' name. Took him with us to the farm we had there on the river before they built the dam an' flooded it.

Uh-*huh,* Bud said.

It took a while.

Well, he said.

He looked at the hypodermic lady then he said, Well that answers things. There *has* been talk. But that's not why we're here.

He looked at Fos, and then at Opal.

Opal noticed that her heart was beating fast.

I'm going to need another blood sample from you tonight, Opal, if you don't mind, Bud said. And one from you, too, Ray, if that's all right. Boy's, too.

Our son's asleep, Opal told him, keeping her voice low.

Well that's all right, we can catch him up tomorrow. It's mostly yours we need to have another look at, Opal.

Why? Fos asked.

The hypodermic lady had the rubber strap out of the bag and was standing up.

Oh nothing, Bud said. Nothing much. Precaution.

Against what? Fos asked. He watched the needle enter Opal's arm, then turned away.

Well, you know, Bud said. He, too, stood up and turned away. Chance is, there's an error somewhere. One of those things that screw up your results for no damn reason. I mean, we run these blood tests once a month on every person on the site so you have to figure once in a blue moon something's going to go haywire with at least one of them.

Haywire how? Fos said.

Test positive for something that we all would rather no one here tests positive for.

Fos blinked.

Nothing you should give a second thought to, though, Bud said, slapping him once, militarily, on the back. Believe you me, he said. Nothing's going to make me prouder than to come back here tomorrow night and have that beer and have a little laugh about this mix-up.

Still, although he didn't question Bud about it further, Fos lay awake that night and ran the conversation back in his thoughts while waiting for the nightly music of the coming of the ghost trains.

Opal had been so tired lately it was rare she was awake by the time he finished turning out the lights and looking in on Lightfoot so he was surprised when she rolled over, slid under his arm and put her head against his shoulder. Wish the trains would come, she whispered.

I thought you were asleep.

I've got so used to listening for trains at night I miss the sound.

Me, too, he told her, pulling her in close.

. . . then there's all this business.

. . . yeah.

Bud Overmarker doesn't seem to me to be the sort of man who credits the existence of a "mix-up."

No. But he's the sort of man who can believe in any story if he has to. For his country's sake. He's an Army man.

At least he seemed to take your story about Lightfoot at face value. Which I thought was pretty good even though I don't much like him getting us all worried we've caught somethin. What kinda thing could they be lookin for? What is it, do you think?

Don't know.

Janet says back in Chicago she and Robert had to have the blood tests to get married.

Some states, they do that. Guess it's law in Illinois.

Why would it be law? Make you have a blood test to get married?

Syphilis, Fos said. We had to have the blood test in the Army, too.

Janet says they're probably makin sure that none of us is Typhoid Mary. That none of us can go an' kill off all the others just by breathin the same air. What do you think Bud meant when he told us "There's been talk—"?

No idea.

Janet must have said something.

Put it from your mind.

Always thought she's been suspicious.

Sshh . . .

They can't tell if you're a German spy by taking blood. *Can* they?

Go to sleep.

What if Lightfoot's parents had some German in them—could they tell that by his blood?

Ope—

Well what else could it be?

Probably them doing what they're meant to do: protecting citizens like us from danger. Real or not. Anyway—this time tomorrow it will all be over and we'll know.

He heard her sigh.

Then he heard the distant singing of the night's first ghost train stealing in.

Next morning, timed almost to the moment Fos had driven off and she had the key already in the door to walk Lightfoot down the block to school and get to work herself, Opal was surprised to see a van pull up and three gentlemen in coveralls get out and come toward the house with their equipment.

Mornin, she said, taking Lightfoot by the hand.

Mornin, ma'm.

Next door Janet was just leaving. Gave the van a look, then gave a cheery wave and called, Have them do mine when they're done with yours!

Opal turned her full attention on the man closest to her who said, Here to clean the carpet, ma'am.

She had never seen this man before, not that she remembered every face of every person on the payroll. There was no name sewn on his coverall but the paneled van had the words CARPET BRITE painted on its side.

Bud Overmarker sent us, the man said and gave a dazzling smile.

Bud didn't say, she started to object.

In and out by lunch time, he projected. Picture perfect for you by the time you get back home.

Well I guess—she deferred.

If you want we'll lock up after, put the key under the welcome mat, he told her.

Isn't that nice? she mused to Lightfoot as they headed down the street. Bud Overmarker's going to clean our carpets.

The job they did was pretty thorough, she could see when she got home. They'd moved the heavy pieces, not entirely lining up the legs where they had made their little craters in the rug, but the place felt cleaner, looked it, too, the wall-to-wall as bright as new. When Bud dropped by that night an hour after Lightfoot had gone to bed the first thing she said was Thanks. I didn't half expect it but thank you, anyway.

—for what?

—the carpet cleaners.

—oh.

He was by himself this time, in uniform, carrying a briefcase. I could use that beer, he said to Fos. In fact, let's all go in the kitchen.

He didn't seem so eager to explain himself as he had the night before, Opal noticed.

Fos served Bud the beer and they all sat down at the kitchen table and Bud opened his briefcase and unfolded a map.

Even looking at it sideways Fos could see it was a site plan of the Oak Ridge complex—the perimeter drawn in, the railroad tracks, the roads, each building. It was like looking at some plant life etched in stone—only lines where life was meant to be. Lines, no language: no explanatory words.

Now Opal, Bud began. I have to ask you a big favor.

He handed her a red wax crayon.

I need you to mark an "X" on every building you've been into since the day of your arrival. It doesn't have to be an X, just make a mark, he told her. She was hesitating. Also, if you could, he added. Draw a line on all the roads and streets you've walked on, all the buildings you've walked by. Even if you haven't gone inside.

The map was oriented so that Opal saw it right way up, western reaches to the left, eastern and the Main Gate on her right. Fos watched her locate the little box that was their house, then marking a red starting point outside the gate, drawing a red line straight through the perimeter and down the street around the corner up the driveway to their door.

That's pretty much where we went the first day we arrived, wasn't it, Fos?

He noticed that her voice was tight.

What'd we do next? Let me think here . . .

He could see the knuckles of her hand around the crayon had gone white.

. . . I guess the next place that I went was to the office—

She drew a line along the streets between the boxes that symbolized their house and where she worked.

No—I think I went over *here* to the grocery first.

She drew another line, doubling back across the previous one.

Um, maybe, Bud cut in. Let's forget about the lines for the time being and concentrate on buildings. Have you ever been in this one?

Opal stared at it, an empty box.

Is that the building with the tall oak out in front?

It's the one we call Building 24.

Opal looked at Bud. What has all this got t' do with my blood test?

Well, he said.

He poured the beer into the glass and watched the foam rise up and settle.

We got the same results back that we got before.

Fos took his specs off and cleaned them with the corner of a tea towel.

You never told us what those were, he said.

He put the specs back on.

Everything was slightly sharper but no brighter.

Bud gave a nod, which resembled a salute, Fos thought, rigid with authority, and delivered what he had to say real quick, without inflection, so the words came out newly minted, clean.

Opal's testing positive for radiation exposure, he told them.

They hung on his words as if receiving new theology.

I've had the boys in here—they came through this morning with their Geiger counters and swept every nook and cranny for any trace of radioactivity and didn't register a tick. Not one. Which means that somewhere in our community other than in this house, there's a radioactive source, a leak, that Opal's been exposed to. And bygod, I have got to find it and I've got to find it quick.

Fos was staring at the map.

The physicists, the secrecy, the isolated buildings—the sum of what they added up to was in his kitchen.

—radioactivity? he said.

—but those men were here to clean the *carpet,* Opal tried to understand.

Bud tilted his head toward her as if he was explaining moonlight to a child. That's what I call good espionage, he said. If they could fool a woman smart as you.

He stood up, the beer untouched.

Work on this tonight, he said, and I'll stop by and see you both tomorrow. Walk me out, why don't you, Ray?

Outside, they stopped beside Bud's car beneath the stars, their fissionable radiance visible through space.

Bud had said *radioactivity* and even Fos knew what that meant.

It's a weapon, isn't it? he hazarded.

Don't ask me questions I would have to say you asked me when I write up my report. I tell my boys to tell the folks in town we're out here making parachutes.

He lit a cigarette and pocketed the spent match like he was in the field, a recognizable habit of who he was, as identifying as a bishop's mitre. Or a doctor's stethoscope.

You're going to need to get her over to the infirmary first thing in the morning, he told Fos. Use my name when you go in, they're expecting you.

He reached toward Fos and took his arm, a shipmate's gesture in a storm.

Believe me, I'm going to cover every inch of ground until I get to the bottom of this thing. We've worked a miracle here, Ray—men and women working double, triple shifts and not a single breach in safety or security. I'd pledge my life to every person on this base, I feel that strong a loyalty to them for what they've done. Future generations will look back, I promise you, and say these men and women were the ones who finally won the war. These men and women were the ones who made a victory possible and saved thousands of lives. The sooner this war ends the more boys we bring home alive. We knew that there were risks here, something might go wrong, but I refuse to let that happen on my watch. One person comes to harm here, then I haven't done my job. One person comes to harm we all feel it and that's why you have my word that I won't rest until I find out how it came about and kill it at the source. You have my word on that. My personal word. As an officer and soldier.

He gave Fos another of his military slaps across the back then opened his car door.

About the boy, he said as afterthought. I'm going to do my best about him, too. So he can stay here on the site, with you. Against the regulations but you have to show some heart, sometimes. We'll get the paperwork originated, see if we can get around the rules somehow.

What's the plan when people get exposed? Fos had to ask before he let him go.

There isn't one, Bud told him.

Is she the only one?

No, Bud said.

He slid into the seat and closed the door and exhaled smoke out through the open window.

It's both of you.

Fos felt the night fly down on him.

—and Lightfoot?

You mean the boy?

Bud shook his head. *Not yet,* he told him.

The infirmary had been one of these boxes on the map that Opal hadn't marked in crayon, one of those buildings she had rarely even walked by in the twenty-odd months that they'd been living here. Deceptive, as most buildings were at Oak Ridge, the entrance and receiving hall offered the new visitor no reference for what lay beyond the initial cozy sense of small town doctor's office. She had trained in one herself, her first job. But beyond the friendly waiting room, the water cooler, the magazines and comfy chairs, there were halls where you could hear a pin drop, batteries of closed mysterious doors. Years since she'd been looked at by a doctor, years since she had had her clothes off in front of anyone but Fos. They didn't let him go with her and it was hours later, nearly time for supper, before they let him visit her in her solitary ward. With sixteen beds against two walls it was laid out like all the Army hospitals Fos had known and it reminded him again of how the Army wrote the book on institutionalization. Same food for everyone, same mess, same hour of reveille. Even the wounded were denied the comfort of their individual suffering—except in Opal's case. Alone in a hospital-issue gown on a bed in a room designed to minister to a platoon she looked especially exposed and unprotected. It was a shock to him to see her in these circumstances. Shock to measure in a room this size how thin she had become.

—Lightfoot all looked after? was the first thing on her mind.

Janet's, Fos assured her.

I've had more needles stuck in me today than the Pentecostal Ladies' quilting frame, she tried to joke.

Me, too, he was going to say but decided not to try to share the spotlight. Instead he said, I guess they got what they were looking for because they sent me here to take you home.

She held out the nurses' call button and told him, I don't know where they've put my clothes. I've been buzzin but nobody comes—

Fos found a nurse who found another nurse who directed him to the examining room where Opal had disrobed and there, in a narrow cubicle behind a curtain were her things, all neatly folded. When he bent to lift her shoes he was so unaccountably overcome with grief he had to lean against the wall to compose himself. Her shoes, he realized, triggered the emotion. The fact that they were empty, that he so rarely touched an article of clothing of hers that she wasn't wearing. And her shoes triggered the memory, sudden, clear as daylight, of the first time he had seen her, the first time he had seen her footprints in the sandy track that led to Conway's furnace and the house she'd lived in then. The house where they'd found Lightfoot. It was a while before he pulled himself together and by the time he got back up to the ward with Opal's clothes she was sitting with the sheet tucked tight across her chest, embarrassed to be seen that way in front of the person standing by the bed, even if he was a doctor.

Fos, this is Major Markham—

I've met your husband, Opal—I've examined *both* of you today.

Oh, Opal said, looking like this bit of information made him even *more* improperly familiar.

Fos found his manner reassuring—businesslike, but warm, as a doctor should be; as a professional Army man rarely is. It's going to be a few days till we assemble all the data, the Major told them, and in the meantime I'd like the two of you to go on the way you'd normally do as if this hadn't happened. That's asking a lot, I know—but the one thing we don't want to do is make you feel alarmed or give any of our neighbors or our co-workers any reason to suspect there may be something wrong. Opal, we might want you back for further testing in a couple days—that depends on what results we get. What I *can* tell you is that whatever the two of you have been exposed to, Ray, your body's handling it better. Whatever symptoms are acute for you, Opal, seem to be manageably chronic for your husband. That's why we want to monitor you both very carefully. I can also tell you, Opal, that your red blood cell count is abnormally low, and that's why you're so tired. The white cells are multiplying, as I told you and today's tests are going to tell us more about that. If they don't tell us everything we need to know then I'm going to want to take what's called a bone marrow aspiration but I'm not going to go into the details of that procedure until I know it's necessary. All right? The best news is your son—or foster son, I guess we have to call him—isn't showing any signs of abnormal white or red cell levels and his blood platelets are fine. This leads me back to what I told both of you individually earlier that we can't totally discount inherited factors, although the coincidence of both of you inheriting a condition of surplus leukemic cells would be extremely unlikely. Still, Opal, if you can provide me any details of the cause of death of both your parents I'd appreciate it. Ray, I believe you told us yours.

Fos nodded.

Drowning and old age.

He didn't want to have to think about the different ways that people die. He wanted to keep thoughts of death as far away as possible. As far away as Germany. Japan. The Philippines. Rumors had been circulating that the War in Europe was about to end. Our boys were closing in on Berlin and the fall of the Third Reich was expected any day. The general feeling in Oak Ridge was one of cautious optimism, optimism overdue, and Fos wanted to appropriate that optimism, have a thing he could look forward to. A future with his wife. His family. Happiness. Long life.

The morning of May 7, two days after all their tests, they still had not heard back from Major Markham or from Bud, and Fos started to relax and trust in that old adage that no news means the same as good. Keep a camera with you—*loaded,* his immediate superior advised. The news could come at any second. And when it does—well, *h-i-s-t-o-r-y,* my friend. Oh and by the way. Some brass is here to have his picture taken. Ten-fifteen. All yours.

When Fos arrived at the appointed room at the appointed time he found only Bud and Major Markham waiting for him. He couldn't read their faces well enough to anticipate what they were going to tell him, so abandoning all protocol he sat down before he was invited to and asked them,—*well?*

No easy answers, Ray. No easy answers, Bud informed him. Everywhere there could have been an *alpha* or a *beta* ray discharge from the substance—you know what I'm talking about here, Ray, I'm not going to mince words with you—anywhere there could have been a trace on someone's clothing or from spent material, we've had the boys go over with a fine-tooth comb. Clean. Every building on the site Opal said she'd walked past or said she'd gone inside—same thing. *Clean,* again. If there had been a leak somewhere, say, even a year ago, the ground would still be ticking. And it's not. Unless Opal's intercepted *pi* rays, *sigma* rays—rays we don't even know yet if they exist, rays we're not equipped yet to detect.

Or . . . Markham prompted.

Or she came in with it. A carrier, Bud said.

Well not exactly a *carrier,* the Major argued. She, herself, is not the source of the disease. Her cells' mutations aren't contagious. Except to her own system.

Bud was watching Fos and saw he needed help.

The Major here has made a diagnosis, he said.

Fine sky, Fos heard his own voice praying in his mind.

clear day
good sign

Leukemia, Markham was explaining.

It's in its final stage, he said. I had thought we'd do the marrow biopsy tomorrow but the cell disintegration has already reached a level where it's spread out from the bone to her blood and spleen and liver. The nucleii of Opal's cells are mutating, spontaneously, to copy the abnormal cell. At this stage it resembles an uncontrolled series of division—well, like *fission,* really. Just as a chain reaction is originated when a uranium atom's nucleus is split and releases a neutron, some *thing* triggered this mutation in Opal's blood. Bud here argues that it has to be genetic, but I would stake my reputation that it's not. I'm ninety percent certain that she's been exposed to some material that's altered her cells' function. She wouldn't, by any chance, have handled or had exposure to something, like, as I've mentioned, *uranium* in the recent past? Her father was a glassblower, she told me. Sometimes they have uranium around—

I don't understand, Fos interrupted. What are you trying to say to me?

He began to blink as if blinking could hold back this new interpretation of his world.

Neither Bud nor Markham spoke.

Are you saying Opal's *sick?* Fos asked.

Opal's *dying,* Markham emphasized.

Fos stared at him.

Please god, he began to pray.

Believe me, Ray, Bud started to assure him. We wouldn't tell you this if we weren't certain.

But there's something you can do to make her well again, Fos said.

Whatever this is that is making her this way. You know how to fix it. You've figured that part out.

Well, Markham started to explain, keeping his voice calm. We have almost no experience with controlled exposure. We're still working on it. Nine times out of ten, so far, it's fatal.

"Exposure," Fos repeated.

Exposure to a radiation element, Markham continued to explain. He started to recite them.

Radium.

Thorium.

Uranium, of course.

X-ray.

—*X-ray?* Fos repeated.

His hand shook as he took his glasses off to rub his eyes and there seemed to be a sudden decompression in the room, as if a great mass had exploded, its shock wave sucking out the oxygen and keening like the ghost train as it drowned out every other sound.

First one, then every air raid siren on the site began to blare.

A door burst open and a clerk ran in and shouted *On the wires! It's official!*

Bud and Markham were both on their feet and the room filled up with people.

Outside, there was cheering, and the sirens wouldn't stop.

Bud's face came into close focus and Fos could see Bud's breath against his specs, his hands on Fos's shoulders, shaking him, *History has arrived, my friend! The Germans have surrendered!*

Somehow Fos got up and stumbled through the people racing down the stairwell, out into the open. A couple of the science boys had hooked up a radio to bullhorns blaring the news across the campus. As he made his way through the crowd outside on the street he kept bumping into people wanting to latch onto him. *Great day,* everyone was saying. Great hour for America. Great to be alive. *Great news.*

He had probably looked at all these faces through the camera at least once—probably met most of these men and women sometime in the last two years, but until this moment he had never seen the way a shared emotion transforms every face. Despite their differences—the different widths between their eyes, their different coloring—their common joy transformed them, joined them in a single family. Elation, like a dominant gene, turned them into kissing cousins, every one resembling every other.

Except Fos.

If a creature had arrived just then from another world into this midst, even it, equipped with its alien instincts, could have noticed that one among the many bore no resemblance to the others in the way his face was pinched with care, like another alien transported from another foreign world. *Happiness* ran, abundant, all around him. People swam in joy, and nothing makes a man feel stranger to his kind than to feel profound emotion which the others cannot feel. He thought his heart had stopped inside him, 'cause he couldn't feel it beating. The crowd was like the Tennessee at flood, annihilating anything or anyone who wasn't part of it, and he struggled on against it, like a drowning man, toward the only person he wanted to be near. When he saw her through the crowd, saw her white hair, saw her wave to him, he prayed to God that when she saw his own face transformed she wouldn't see what he was feeling. Grown men were crying right and left, but still she was surprised by the force with which he clung to her.

As they embraced, the crowd fell silent and the President began to speak over the radio, confirming the glad news and cautioning that there was still a battle to be won against Japan in the Pacific and that America was still a nation at war. At the end of his speech there was a solemn moment then a rousing cheer, then somebody put some Benny Goodman on a record player hooked up to the loudspeakers and the place began to swing and the entire site turned out to celebrate.

Fos and Opal sat outside the house on lawn chairs and greeted people and listened to reports from other cities' celebrations on the radio while Lightfoot played, and then, as darkness fell, they moved inside. Lightfoot was too obedient to argue when his father told him, Time for bed, but Fos could see he was too engaged in what was going on outside to go to sleep. I thought it was a birthday party, Lightfoot told him as Fos tucked him in. Are you sure it's not a birthday party?

I'm sure.

How did we beat him?

Mr. Hitler? We . . . like when you play your chess. We captured all the pieces on the board. We captured all the men.

Did we beat Mr. Hitler's children, too?

I don't know what you mean, son.

—his sons and daughters. Did we beat them, too?

Mr. Hitler doesn't have any children.

Everyone has children. Everyone *we* know. If they're married, he amended.

Well Mr. Hitler wasn't married. There's your answer.

Did he have a dog?

Fos kissed his son's head and told him, Go to sleep.

Everyone should have a dog, Lightfoot lobbied.

Goodnight, son.

Are we going to beat the Japs, too?

Good*night.*

Do the Japs have children?

Do you want the hall light on tonight?

No, I'm not scared.

That's good.

I'll talk a while.

I'm sure you will.

I won't be loud.

Fos left the door ajar and leaned against the wall. He took his glasses off and wiped his eyes and for the second instance in that day he wished he had the power to halt time. He could hear tap water running in the bathroom, then he heard it stop. He heard Opal in the bedroom, then he heard the mattress springs. Behind him, in his bedroom, he heard Lightfoot talking to his whales, relating to them everything that happened in the day, telling them the tale of how the sirens started, how he thought it was a birthday, how, instead, it was a party about beating Mr. Hitler who lived across the sea in Germany and didn't have a wife and didn't have a son or daughter and didn't even have a dog to call his own.

Soon after they had moved here from the old place, moved into this smaller house, Fos and Opal had begun to hear faint whispers in the night. Along with the ghost trains, the otherwordly murmuring lent an eerie thrill to their first nights until Opal, ever practical, got up and tracked it down. What she found was Lightfoot curled up with his whales perched on his pillow, telling them in whispers the same story Fos had told him earlier that night. Over time they heard him tell the whales about his school, about his teachers, about sounds the letters make and how the earth is round and mostly water. How tomorrow he would ask if he could have a dog. How the dark was something that you had to make your friend or else you spent the night afraid of what it might be hiding. Sometimes he repeated things out loud that had been told to him. Sometimes he practiced arguments he planned to make. At stake each night was his success at being able to make into words his thoughts and feelings, to find a pathway of expressing his own secrets. Listening to those whispers, now, coming from his room, Fos wished he had his son's facility for verbal gambles, gambits: what to say: and where to start. How to tell the secret that was going to break his heart.

Lotta noise out there, Opal mentioned when he came to bed.

Should I close the window?

No I like the sound. People havin fun. I thought I heard Lightfoot a while ago.

Yeah, he's in there talkin up a storm.

What's he sayin?

Oh the usual . . .

Fos eased down beside her, kept his glasses on.

. . . stuff about the dog.

I suppose we oughta just give in an' get him one. It's too hard to keep on sayin no.

Fos stared at her, then asked her, What's the hardest thing you ever had to tell someone?

She squinted at him, trying to define what she saw in his expression through the dark.

I don't know, she faltered.

What's the hardest thing you ever had to say to *me?*

She could see that this was leading up to something so she took a breath and thought about it, then let out a stream of air. I suppose, she started, on reflection. I suppose it was that day I had to stop the car and tell you about Flash. That was somethin terrible t' hafta say.

Why was it something terrible?

—because it *was.*

—but why was it hard to *tell?*

Because I knew that it would tear you up. That it would hurt you somethin awful. That what I had t' say was goin to make a difference in our lives. An awful difference.

He knew he had to go for it right then and tell her what he'd learned that afternoon. He leaned in close and put his hand behind her neck. *Angel,* he said softly. It was the word he said, if he said anything at all, when they were making love, so Opal thought he was about to kiss her. Instead, he hesitated and then said, I saw your Major Markham earlier today. Bud, too. They called me in to talk to them. They had the diagnosis from your tests. The results of the blood count . . .

Before she let him say another word she placed her hand across his mouth. Listen, she conspired. There's the ghost train, hear it? Even on a day like this.

He blinked and listened, then he moved her hand away. Ope, he started to explain again.

Again she raised her hand and put a finger to his lips.

What's the one thing I do best that makes you proud of me? she asked him in a whisper.

He pressed his lips against her finger, then gently moved her hand down on the bed.

You make me happy, he responded.

No, in general, she maintained. Something that I do you always brag about to other people.

You take care of Lightfoot.

No, come on, she teased, and put her finger to his lips again.

He stared at her, wide-eyed.

I *count,* she prompted. Pennies, falling stars, fish in the sea, you name it. I count them up, not even trying. Seconds in your timed exposures. Miles between the signposts. Jellybeans in jars at Woolworth's. Starlings on a wire. Buttons. Ants. Kernels on an ear of corn. Sunday church bells tolling. Votes. Apples in a barrel. White blood cells . . .

Angel, he repeated and began to stroke her thinning hair.

A person knows when she is sick, Fos. The body knows it, no one needs to tell me that I'm not myself.

They say it's something called—

She put her finger on his lips again.

You don't need to tell me, she confided.

Yes, I do—I *do* need to. For both our sakes. Because I think I did this to you. With the x-rays—

Our x-rays?

He nodded.

Is that what Bud and Major Markham said?

Well no I haven't told them yet—they still think it's something from the camp you've been exposed to—

—oh Fos, she said, tilting her head.

Oh Fos, she repeated, rubbing both his shoulders.

He looked so pained, she drew him to her.

I don't know how to tell you this, she started to explain. I guess I should have told you sooner, but it never seemed to matter and it always seemed like you were having so much fun. But . . .

She pressed his head into her neck so she wouldn't have to tell him to his face.

. . . sometimes, Fos—I hate to say it. It's been years, and I've let it pass for all this time, but sometimes, Fos, even I can tell that some of the ideas you believe are scientific are plain *wrong.*

He looked at her, his face now more despairing than before.

I'm sorry, Opal told him. I mean, all those years with all those light bugs in those jars. What on earth was that *about?* The phosphorus, the Leyden jars, the diving for electric eels in places eels have never even *been.* I love you and I love that you believe in everything you do but in this case we have to trust the experts, don't you think? I mean, my gosh. We x-rayed half the limbs in Tennessee with that machine. We x-rayed Lightfoot, too. How could something that we trusted like that be of harm?

I exposed you more than anybody else. I didn't think it added up to what they call prolonged exposure—

She placed her hand across his mouth again.

They're the scientists, she said. Not you.

She saw his tears well up.

I'm sorry if I hurt your feelings, Fos.

He shook his head and blinked and took her hand in his and kissed it. Outside their window someone laughed. A band was playing on the radio. They could hear a pop and see the sparkle of a Roman candle through the sheer white curtain. Fos put his head back down against her in the niche above her collarbone. She could feel her blood pulse where he pressed against her neck and she thought she felt him crying, so she patted him and said, If they can find a cure for Mr. Hitler, they can find a cure for what they say I've got. Don't worry, Fos, we've got the army of the greatest nation on our side. At its greatest moment. Can't go wrong.

She rubbed his back and soon she was asleep not even knowing he was staring at the shadows on the wall and counting every heartbeat until morning.

In the days and weeks that followed, Oak Ridge felt the added pressure to end the War definitively, end it with a weapon whose purpose was no longer to outrace Germany but to destroy Japan. But Opal grew progressively more ill, the change in her condition becoming noticeable even to the people in the street. By June she was too weak to work and was receiving regular transfusions which made her face, according to her son, the color of a puppy's tongue.

On the night before the first transfusion, an early heat descended on the site, and nothing stirred, stunned by the early reminder of the Tennessee summer. Even Lightfoot was too hot to whisper and the trains seemed stalled on molten rails. Markham had consoled her that the process wasn't painful—but, still: she wanted it to be behind her. For one thing, she didn't take the needle well, the sight of its approach made her stomach turn. And for this, the needle would be in too long to pretend she could ignore it.

When I was young and was afraid sometimes of the dark, she told Fos,

Conway used to say it's a waste of time to be afraid of something you can't see. He said the things you have to be afraid of, like black bears and rattlesnakes, present themselves in front of you.

You had a lot of bears and rattlesnakes back in Carolina, didja? Fos kidded, trying to inject some humor.

I wish I hadn't given all those books away, she said. All those books of Flash's.

—how come?

Keep my mind off things. Keep me busy. Readin doesn't tax your strength the way most pastimes do. I wish I'd read more in my life. I wish I'd read when I was younger. I'd probably be better for it. I don't think Conway was right, anyway, now that I look back on it, about the bears and rattlesnakes. I think what you can't see is *always* what you should be frightened of.

He stroked her shoulder. Skin so dry, and mostly bone.

Then the remedy is *seein* it, he said.

Death, too?

Death, *first,* he answered.

It was the first time they had mentioned it.

Thereafter, after each transfusion, each new blush of health, Fos allowed himself the luxury of thinking that she wasn't going to die. He worried for the boy, how Opal's dying would affect him, this child who wept when bunnies died, who buried animals with all the mourning of a poet keening over love. None of the other mothers of the children that he played with ever seemed to be sick beyond a headache or a cold. Opal was unique among them, anyway, by virtue of her age, but Lightfoot never seemed to notice. If he did, Fos thought, he never asked about the obvious differences between his mother and the other mothers that he knew. And listening at night, outside his door, Fos could hear him talk, as normal, to the whales, never voicing any worry.

The worries came, instead, from someone else.

In the middle of July Bud called Fos into his office. Since the end of the War in Germany and the increased activity around the site, Fos had seen Bud only on the move, hurrying from one staff meeting to another—cordial, but distracted. He'd lost a little weight, Fos now observed—and he seemed very tired. The cigarette, which he had seemed to smoke only for his pleasure in the past, was now a permanent necessity. *Sit,* Bud told him when he entered. He didn't look Fos in the eye at first, arranging papers on his desk. Then he gave a weak belated smile with the regimental charm that Fos remembered, but his manner seemed to indicate he wasn't there to chat. I hate these bastards at state level, Ray. I really do. They've got the vision of some tunneling shit eaters.

He hesitated, seeming to assess his pitch like someone tuning strings, as if he suddenly recalled the melodic key Fos played in. More attuned, he said, I've got some bad news for you, Ray.

Fos stretched his hands.

It's about the boy, Bud said.

He lifted a file, as if he held it accountable for what he was about to say.

Hard to reason with them once they've got a bureaucratic bullet up their ass, he said.

He brushed an ash from his starched shirt sleeve.

I'm sorry, Ray. I tried to get them to initiate a legal guardian procedure—file for an adoption—but the nature of Opal's illness, well—it rules that out. And unfortunately your lab results aren't looking that good, either. Your last tests have come back with no increase in the white count but still with every indication the disease is in development. Markham tells me you're still treatable at this stage, but neither one of you is fit enough to meet the health criteria the state requires for adoption.

He paused again, this time to tap the edges of the papers in the file into a neat conformity. He dropped his chin and looked at Fos like someone peeking from beneath a rock. You understand, he said, more as a directive than a question.

The boy is all we've got, Fos answered forcefully.

That's not a good approach, Bud warned.

—the boy is all we've *got.* To live for, if you take my meaning.

That's not true, Bud argued, shifting in his chair.

I'm begging, Fos insisted.

Bud was listening, but remained impassive. He had scheduled half an hour for his morning's meetings. Half of it was already gone.

What if we weren't a part of all this, Fos proposed—this military operation. What if we had gone about our business and stayed away from military service. Gone ahead and lived our lives, not for our country but ourselves. No one would have come along and asked these questions, stirred this kind of trouble up and I think you kinda owe us something for that service, owe us the full weight of your influence, you should stand behind your people, make things right for them—

Bud had heard this argument before, from veterans, and he warned Fos. Choices that you made are yours to answer for, not mine. You want to make me your scapegoat for things you went ahead and did all on your own, that's fine by me—makes you feel better. But finger pointing never works as a strategical defense—

All I'm sayin is we could avoid all this if we were off the site. If Opal and our son and me were somewhere else—

Bud looked at Fos as if he'd caught him with a shovel by a tunnel in the jailyard.

Opal isn't working, anyway, Fos argued. And you don't need me here just takin pictures . . .

Fos could see he'd crossed a line, see the indignation working in Bud's face. He had made light of the security precautions on the site—people couldn't come and go, he knew it—but he had nothing left to lose, he knew that, too. He had to try everything that he could think of, anything to stop them taking Lightfoot away.

I'm surprised at you, Ray, Bud was saying, speaking in a tone Fos had never heard before. No one leaves here—no adult that is, he amended. Especially not someone in the final stage of radiation poisoning. The War will end and when it does you'll be free to go and visit him—

Fos leaned forward in his chair.

What if someone here adopts him—someone that we know who'd fit the bill on paper, who could do the paperwork but leave the boy with us . . . what if *you* adopted him so he could stay with us—

The idea seemed to outrage Bud on every level.

Christ sake pull yourself together, Ray—remember what we're doing here. I have a million separate goddam details to attend to so we can win this goddam war, bring home a half a million servicemen and restore peace and safety to our nation, and I ask you, Ray, to tell me where your family problems might fit in to that ennobling scheme. I am very sorry about Opal—you know damn well that I can't sleep at night if I think I haven't done my best to make this site as safe to live in as the front pew of a church on Sunday, and despite the fact that the statistic boys were telling me that one half of one percent of everyone on site would probably come down with evidence of radiation in their tissue, the truth is I've damn well kept it safer to work here than on any of the lines Mr. Ford and all his flunkies have created—

She didn't get it here, Fos interrupted. Her leukemia. It didn't come from anything she was exposed to on the site. She got it from exposure to the x-rays that we used to do.

He paused.

So you could let us leave, he argued. You could let us go because you're not responsible.

X-rays, Bud repeated, and Fos nodded.

You're wasting my time, Bud said, but seeing Fos's look he added, I understand you want to clutch at straws, but x-rays are a part of modern medicine. They save lives. Everybody gets them with the greatest confidence. So put that theory back inside the can of nuts it came from.

He looked abruptly at his watch.

Bud . . . Fos tried to plead again.

Ray, I have to bring this to a close, Bud told him.

He has a birthday coming up, Fos said. My son does. He wants a puppy. Maybe you could . . . maybe you could shuffle papers for a while, give us time for that to happen, make him happy while we can.

Bud rolled the ash tip of his cigarette into a contoured bullet shape against his ashtray.

When's the birthday? he asked Fos, taking up his pen.

Eleven August, Fos told him.

Bud looked at him and said, That's more than a month away.

Fos met his look, then watched Bud nod and jot a brief notation in the file.

Done, he said and looked back up as if he half expected Fos to thank him. What he saw, instead, was Fos rocking on his feet, his glasses off, his face distressed with his unexpressed emotion.

What would you do if I drove my wife and son damn through your barricades? In the middle of the night—what would you do if I drove straight down the train tracks leading out of here? Would you shoot us? Would you shoot at a sick woman and a helpless child? Would you kill me? Lock me up in jail—?

Bud leaned back and let the cigarette burn down.

No I wouldn't, Ray, he finally said. I wouldn't have to call the M.P.s, I wouldn't have to send them out to round you up, they wouldn't have to fire warning shots. Do you know *why?*

He sat there, giving Fos a final moment for his fantasies.

Because you're not the kind of man who has that kind of daring, he assessed.

Walking from Bud's office the heat hit him so hard he had to sit down on the ground beneath some temporary bleachers in the shade to catch his breath. The bleachers had been put up for the Fourth of July fireworks and now they stood there, grandstanding before a barren field. He and Opal and Lightfoot had come out for the fireworks and halfway through them Opal had thrown up from some medication Markham had given her, creating a scene among the people close to them. *My hero,* she told Fos when he got her home and out of her soiled clothes. And even then the words landed like a harpoon in his heart. Heroic was the farthest thing from what he had been feeling ever since the day in Markham's office when he learned that she was dying, but she'd called him "hero" with a smile and said it with the tender sweetness she said everything with these days. At some point in her inner dialogue with the pain that was now a living organ in her body, Opal must have resolved to keep herself intact and dissolve the pain through her like a pack of sugar in hot liquid. Sweetness was the result—her fundamental sweetness. Two things strip the character right down to the bone—pain and fear. Fos had seen it in the first war—nothing exposes fundamental character the way pain does, the fear of pain, the fear of dying. And what the progress of her disease was etching on her skin was Opal's character—sweet, self-deprecating, and courageous. Her physical courage shamed him, often—and his shame inspired him to action. They were going to lose Lightfoot because the disease that was killing her would kill him, too, eventually—and the cause of the disease was his fault. His stupidity had caused this—his bad science—so he pulled himself together, wiped his eyes, and went to search for someone whose science wasn't flawed.

When Markham saw him standing in the corridor of the dispensary he withdrew from the bedside of the sleeping patient he was watching and came to Fos's side and led him to a sunlit alcove where they both sat down. Markham laid a hand on Fos's arm and discreetly calculated Fos's pulse.

I need to know some things, Fos said.

The Major nodded.

How long has she got?

I didn't think she'd go *this* long.

Days—*weeks?* Fos asked.

No more than that. I'm being honest with you, Ray.

How will it happen. I mean—

Markham kept his hand on Fos's arm.

Sometime soon we'll move her in here, he said, so I can monitor the—

No, Fos told him.

He looked around the empty corridor and said, She stays at home.

Ray, that's not—

That's final.

I don't want to argue with you, Ray. But the fact is we're equipped to make her much more comfortable in here.

So that means she'll be in pain, Fos deduced.

Yes. Most likely. But I'll give her something that will help her manage—

What else will there be? I need to know what to expect. I want to know how it will happen.

Markham shook his head.

I wish I could tell you, Ray. I wish I had the answer, but the casebook isn't written yet. We're writing it right here, right now. The history of exposure's pretty patchy, you know that. We had a guy at Los Alamos last year, accidentally mishandled a bomb core and started a chain reaction, and he was dead in sixty hours. A physicist. He dictated a description of his death, minute by minute, for as long as he was conscious. Lower exposures—the different cancers they engender all develop over time. You look how long the cancers took to kill the Curies. We don't know how radiation kills the human body—we have to learn—we *are* learning. I mean, look at this facility. It's a hospital, all right, but it's built for research, as a lab.

Fos blinked.

You want Opal in here so you can study her? Is that it?

That's not what I'm saying, Ray—

We're your research specimens.

Ray—

Is that why you keep poking us for samples of our blood?

Ray, I'm a *doctor*—

—then find a *cure.*

There is no cure. A cure for one or two of all the cancers, maybe. Sure. A cure for the immediate effects of radioactive exposure? Not yet. Maybe never. Maybe all we'll ever do is learn for certain at what level it is fatal, at what level it destroys on contact, at what level it engenders cancers and what level human beings can survive with no late-developing metastases. Right now there are too few models to establish any norms. I can't tell you how she's going to die, how it's going to happen. Only that it will.

And you say Lightfoot's safe—?

—"Lightfoot"?

Our son.

—so far, yes. Every indication is he hasn't been exposed. Or if he has, then his exposure was at lower, safer levels.

Because—well I know this will sound twisted. One way we could keep him would be if you said he had to stay here for your research.

—"keep" him? What do you mean?

They're going to take him from us.

"They"? Who's "they"—I don't understand.

The state—we never finally . . . we never filled out any papers. He's not "ours" in the normal way. Some people left him to us. And now, because the site requires all this paperwork they told the state and the state says that we're too sick to adopt him, so they're going to—

Now I understand.

Maybe you can pull some strings or something. In the system. In the—whatever they call it. Social welfare. I'm worried where they'd send him, if they take him. I mean, what are those places like?

What places, Ray?

Orphanages.

Here in Tennessee? Golly, I don't know. I grew up in Baltimore and things were pretty rough. I mean not as bad as back in Dickens's day but pretty grim I should imagine.

He must have seen the anguish his answer was producing because Fos saw him purposefully trim the sail and change his tack.

I'll make some queries, Markham told him. Find out more about this for you.

He patted Fos's arm.

I couldn't face it, Fos admitted. If we lost the boy. I don't know how I'd break the news to Opal.

Maybe you won't have to, Markham said—meaning, Fos apprehended, maybe she will die first.

When he got home the house was silent and he placed the box of ampules of the liquid opiate Markham had given him for Opal's pain on top of the refrigerator behind the toolbox, hidden and well out of Lightfoot's reach. He could see the boys next door, Lightfoot and Billy, through the window above the sink as he washed his hands and dried them on a tea towel. The tea towel had a dog stitched on it and the words *Man's Best Friend,* and Lightfoot had bought it at a church sale with the savings from his allowance and given it to Opal last year as a Christmas present. The thought of Christmas this year made Fos turn away and try to compose himself before going down the hall to check on Opal. He presumed she was asleep, otherwise he would have heard her welcome him when he came home, but in the hallway he heard her moving. How's my girl? he called.

There was an acrid scent filling the room, the bedding was damp, and Opal was convulsed on the far edge of the bed, her body tightly curled, her teeth clenched on the corner of the pillow.

—*pain,* she breathed when he took her in his arms. So severe there was no trace of sweetness in her gaze.

I'm calling for the ambulance, Fos said but she clutched his arm and shook her head. He held her, rocking slightly, and in a little while he felt her shoulders relax a bit, and then her breathing came more steadily.

—where's Lightfoot? she asked when she could speak.

Outside in the yard with Billy.

Don't let him see me, Fos. When I get this way. I don't want to scare him.

Her lips were cracked and her face was bloodless. There were dark hollows around her eyes.

Well you're pretty scary lookin that's for sure, Fos told her, but we're pretty brave around here. We don't scare so easy, he joked, and he could see her start to smile. There's no reason for you to suffer this way, though. Markham gave me medicine to take to ease the—

I'm not takin anything that makes me sleep all day.

Opal—

I started thinkin, when the pain began, I finally understood what those younger women have been sayin this whole time about goin into "labor" having babies—it's *hard work,* this business of the pain . . .

Well it doesn't have to be, and if the medication sends you into dreamland we can cut the dosage. Anyway, you need your sleep.

—it's a waste of time. I'd rather be awake. I'm *afraid* of sleeping . . .

Fos coaxed her to take a few drops of the sedative, anyway, mixed in a glass of Coca-Cola while he changed the sheets, and by the time that he was finished, she was dozing peacefully on the davenport. He tucked a summer blanket over her and walked outside just as Janet was coming out her screen door with two Popsicles in her hands to give the boys.

—they get dehydrated these hot afternoons and don't even know it till they complain of headaches around suppertime, she said.

Lightfoot complains of headaches? Fos was surprised to learn.

—well, no. Billy neither. But Robert does—

She laughed at herself.

—but I'm his wife and not his mother and it's too late in his life for me to change his habits so I do what I can do and choose my targets.

You're a good mother, Janet.

Why thank you, Ray. You're a good mother, too.

She must have seen his face cloud with confusion.

I don't mean to say that Opal's not, she added. How's she doing?

Not so good.

Oh, I'm sorry. Have they—have they found out what it is yet?

They're still runnin tests, Fos said. He was under orders from Bud and Markham not to talk about the illness. Nothing contagious, though, he added.

—oh I'm not worried about *that.* Not the way this place is run. If they thought there was any chance of that they would have had her quarantined before she had a chance to blow her nose. Why don't you let Lightfoot stay the night with us again? Robert said he's going to put the tent up when he comes home—the boys can sleep out in the yard, what do you say?

I say I'm *jealous . . .*

. . . oh there's room in there for you, too, Ray, you haven't seen this tent, yet—Robert got it at the PX, it's big enough to sleep a whole battalion.

Fos looked at the ground and packed a clod of loose sod into place with the toe of his shoe.

Listen, Janet, he began to say.

—oh, top secret, she interrupted. Not supposed to know, but you *are* supposed to know. Lightfoot wants a puppy for his birthday. He made a point of telling Billy when he knew that I could hear them. I guess he's too afraid you might say "no" if he just comes right out and asks.

Oh he's *asked,* all right.

—and?

And we say he'll have to wait and see.

Most children take that as a "yes."

—they *do?*

Anything that's not a definite "no" can be interpreted as "yes."

Where do you learn these things?

At Parent School.

Fos stared at her.

—just joking, Ray. There's no such thing.

I wish there was.

Well if there were the two of you would qualify as teachers.

Well that's nice to say.

I mean it.

Fos looked down and kicked the sod loose that he'd just packed into place.

Speaking of being afraid to ask things, Janet—

He hesitated.

Shoot, she urged.

He took a breath.

If somethin happens to me and Opal, he began. I was wondering if you and Robert could look after Lightfoot for us. I mean, he and Billy get along so well they might as well be brothers—

What kind of "something"? You mean if the two of you are in an accident?

Well, yeah. That kind of thing.

Well, of course, Ray—I mean, we look after him already, sort of.

I mean . . . more permanent.

What kind of "permanent"?

I mean . . . if something happens to us. If we die.

Oh don't be silly. You're not going to *die.* You're just saying this because you're worried they don't know what's wrong with Opal yet.

No, I'm not. I'm serious. I'd like to know if you'd adopt him.

"Adopt" him?

Her hand went up to her hair, a flustered gesture, Fos had seen it many times in women posing for their pictures.

We're very *fond* of Lightfoot, surely, but "adopt" him? I mean, Ray—that's what families do, not neighbors. Surely you and Opal must have family? I mean, in our case, Robert has a sister who'd take Billy and of course both our parents are alive and I have my brothers and their wives down in Texas. And anyway—

She sort of chucked him, good naturedly, a girly punch halfway between his elbow and his shoulder.

—you're not going to *die,* stop talking nonsense. Robert and I were talking just the other night about what we'll do when the War comes to an end and we'll probably go back to Chicago, he can teach or maybe get an offer in the private sector, and, I mean, we might never see the three of you again—know what I mean? You're from around here, you'll probably go back to where you were before the war, right? You know how it is with these wartime relocations, you were in the Great War—how many of those men did you ever see again?

I just thought, Fos wavered, Lightfoot being an only child and getting on so well with Billy—

Well that's true *now,* but once we're back in peacetime Robert and I will be thinking about adding to our family, having more kids of our own.

Of course you will, Fos nodded, staring straight ahead.

But it was sweet of you to ask. I'm touched, I really am, she told him, finishing the conversation with a slight tilt of her head and a pat—dismissive in its brevity—where she had punched him.

Fos stood there awhile when she went back inside and wondered how he might have put it differently, what he might have said to get, if not a definite "yes," at least something, a "let's see," that he could pin his hopes on.

But hope is not a strategy, Flash used to say. You can't just *hope,* without a plan to back it up, and as the days went by, the weeks, he knew he had to tell Opal the truth—then the two of them had to tell the truth to Lightfoot. He knew he could tell Opal anything now, in her current state, and she would be forgiving. The pain was nearly constant and sometimes in her eyes he could see that she was hoping, too, for everything to finally end. I can't take too much more, she confessed to him one night in the first week of August.

—you're only taking half a dose, he argued, taking her thin hand in his.

It takes more strength than I can muster, she started to explain, then used up all her energy.

Lightfoot shouldn't have to see me this way, she continued in a while. It can't be good for him. It's only going to get worse—

I think we have to tell him, Fos said slowly. I think we have to tell him everything. I think we have to tell him how we found him. That we're not his natural parents. And I think we have to tell him that you're dying.

She didn't say anything but he thought he felt her squeeze his fingers.

Sooner the better, Fos, she finally found the strength to whisper.

He curled around her tiny frame, needing to embrace her but so terribly afraid that he might hurt her, and wept.

In the morning they were still like that when they woke to a strange silence on the site and the sound of someone running past their window down the street.

Fos rose and pulled his trousers on and went out to the living room and opened the Venetian blinds. A few more men, unshaven, in their shirtsleeves, ran down the street and then he saw Robert join them from next door, running with his shirt unbuttoned, Janet standing in their doorway in her housecoat and her slippers.

Fos opened the door and yelled across, What's happened? What's going on?

In the backyard, he could see the boys in their pyjamas playing in the tent.

Turn your radio on, Janet called. Yesterday—Japan—middle of the night back here—we're in the news!

For the first time in days, Opal made it down the hall on her own and sat down on the davenport just as Fos was turning on the radio. What they heard didn't make sense to her at first—but Fos reacted to the news at once.

—oh my god, he said.

She was trying to understand each word the broadcaster was saying, but he had a Northern accent and was speaking faster than a man whose house had just been set on fire.

"Hiroshima"? Fos repeated. Why not Tokyo? What the hell's in Hiroshima—?

I don't understand, Opal said slowly. Our boys dropped a bomb?

Fos sat down beside her, paging through their atlas.

—*here* it is, he said, squinting. He put his finger on the dot beside the name.

—*one* bomb? Opal was still trying to grasp. For an entire city? Musta been a pretty big explosion.

It was. You and I have no idea. Mass destruction.

Children, too?

Everything.

And they didn't have no warning?

They didn't give us any warning at Pearl Harbor.

Yeah, but we're not *them.* We don't go to war with children.

Well as of yesterday I guess that is *exactly* what we do.

One by one the sirens on the site began to sound, and more people came into the street, running toward the mess hall and the auditorium.

Fos stood up and stared out of the window and she could see that he was angry.

Japan hasn't surrendered, though, has it, Fos? Why are they blarin all the sirens?

Before he had a chance to answer, Janet came out in a pair of slacks, running toward their house. Fos held the screen door open and she asked him, Can you watch the boys a while, Ray? I don't want to miss this.

Miss what, Janet?

—are you kidding? Can you imagine what this does for everyone's careers who worked on it? Through the roof, I'll tell you. There'll be dancing in the streets of Oak Ridge, Tennessee, tonight—!

Just then her gaze landed on the figure on the davenport. Oh, hi, Opal, she said, feigning cheerfulness, but Fos could see that she was shocked.

—my god, she whispered, close to him, so Opal couldn't hear.—*What's wrong with her?*

Fos stepped back.

Janet wants to know what's wrong with you, he announced to Opal from across the room.

Janet's eyes danced wildly for a second.

Opal's feeling the effects of radiation, Janet, Fos announced.

Janet giggled, but her face registered alarm.

That's not funny, Ray. That's a horrible thing to say.

Well you think about it while you're celebrating.

Opal had sunk back into the cushions, seized by pain again and too distracted to comprehend what had just transpired. Fos was angrier than she had seen him since the night those Klan boys and the police had broken in the back of the old shop hellbent for evidence to use against Flash and put them out of business. Now she wanted nothing more than some relief from her existence and the man she loved was standing over her with something in his eyes she couldn't understand. He could read her pain, though, see its shadow on her face, and he lifted her with one swift motion, so light, and carried her back to their room. When he placed her on the sheet she curled around herself for shelter, like some larval form dislodged from where it incubated by runnels in a storm. He went into the kitchen and got a teacup and a jar of jam and a spoon and brought the whole box of medication back with him to the bedroom. His hand shook as he cracked the glass phial and poured the liquid in the cup. *Medicine,* he told her as he stirred it with some jam and fed it to her. Medicine, he repeated as its bitter fragrance filled his nostrils. He licked the spoon and felt the sizzle on his tongue as the aftertaste of the latent opiate blossomed on the glaze of sugar. *Secret weapon,* he kept thinking—the hidden side of science. You take all the genius in the world and pack it into one delivery for mankind, what could you expect? A cure for all man's ills? Palliative for human suffering? No, what you get is what you pay for—science for the sake of science, regardless of the human cost. Split the goddam atom 'cause you *can,* because chance and circumstance have brought us through the goddam Dark Ages to this pinnacle of time, unscathed, our wits about us, hell let's chance it—that's what man is all about even if there's hell to pay, *especially* if there's hell to pay somewhere down the line. Out of Eden, into Hiroshima, boys, come on, let's go. Let me show you my contraption, darlin', step right up an' slide your foot in here, let me show you what your *bones* look like, what a nuclear explosion looks like in the atmosphere, even though the unseen devils that'll set loose will unleash minuscule adjustments in the fabric of your tissue, in the air you breathe, that may or may not kill you. Of all the things we could have done, of all the things that we could do with the natural wonder we call science, he was thinking. Of all the goddam things. Make a goddam killing weapon. Lord, if he were more like Flash, more cynical about the fundamental nature of mankind, maybe he might have seen this coming. It was good that it would force a quicker end to war, save lives in the end, perhaps, but where was the council of wise men, the counsel of the sages, when the decision was enacted to shift war from formal combat to noncombatants? He hadn't made the bomb himself, but he had been a part of the group effort that comprised its manufacture. So had Opal. Janet, Robert—all of them. But the physics boys must have had a good idea what was going on, what the sounds of midnight ghost trains meant. They must have had it figured from the moment they were hired. But not once was Fos consulted. Never, not at any time, had anybody asked him if he objected to the inevitable application of this science, if he had any qualms about putting all this physics to this kind of use. Truth was, he probably would not have known how dangerous it was—he didn't have the foresight, even, to see the danger in his traveling x-ray show. And that was why he felt the fool, the butt of life's cruel joke right now—no one had consulted him at *any* turn his life had taken, Flash hadn't when they'd lost the shop, the TVA hadn't when they'd come to take the farm, the State of Tennessee would not when someone came in several days to take his son. If he had been a man who foresaw consequences—if he had been a *scientific* man—he could have changed the course his life had taken, but instead he'd gone along, oblivious, not even participating in events that shaped his life, a spectator. *What would Flash have done?* Fos asked himself. What would Flash do now in Fos's circumstances? Hell, Flash had mixed it up with anybody—Flash, the troublemaker. Flash, the talker. When he remembered Flash from those days, in the war, Flash was always angry, getting drunk and getting into fights. Getting into heated arguments about life's meaning, what the hell the purpose was to life, whether there was something in it, a ghost in the machine, or a ghost train, that would deliver The Divine. Instead of drinking with his friend or stripping down to fists and sweat in the arena, Fos had always stepped aside and disengaged. The passive voice lasts longest, *good for you,* Flash would jeer from his hangover. Not Biblical, but definitely Constitutional. To hell with We the People. Too Declarative. So much cleaner to stay passive, he would mock Fos from the drunken depths of his nonpassive voice. *When in the course of human events,* he would recite. *It becomes necessary.* And *et cetera.*

There was one night he remembered in particular back in the trenches when a minister in uniform—a *padre,* Flash had called him—had visited before a run against the German line was supposed to happen the next day, and Flash, sober, Fos thought, but you never knew, had turned on the man of God and told him, Don't come in here peddling Christ to us tonight, *padre,* asking us to ask ourselves *What would Jesus do* in these circumstances because Jesus ain't the man I want to have as my example when I'm fighting for my life—*comprenday?* Correct me if I'm wrong, but Jesus *died* for us. Great with loaves and fishes, cured the sick and smeared forgiveness on a prostitute but when it comes to fighting for my life I'll take some other mother's son, thank you very much, to lead me through because you and all the other halleluiah boys are only here to use Him as a model for the afterlife and that's one place I'm not ready, yet, to visit . . .

Fos could almost hear the rhythms of his speech—that rat-a tat-a fueled acceleration as he hit his beats, but then he realized there was a real sound coming from the hallway, echoing the cadence that he heard in his imagination, a fevered whispering, and as he turned his head to look, a small carved whale appeared, hesitantly, around the barely open door.

Fos pulled the door from where he sat and found Lightfoot, still in his pyjamas.

—hey, Fos said. Hidy.

—hidy, Lightfoot smiled.

You all alone?

Nope.

Where's Billy?

Janet said he had to go with her.

Well, then, who ya talkin to out there?

Spot.

—"Spot."

There were two whales in his hands.

Which one is Spot?

Lightfoot pointed to a dark eye in the pale wood in the belly of one whale and told him, simply, "Spot." This other one's called Rover.

Spot an' Rover, huh? Fos acknowledged.

He reached for Lightfoot and lifted him onto his lap.

Sounds like two dogs' names to me, he said, and Lightfoot grinned. You hungry? Fos asked him, smoothing back his hair. Would you like some breakfast?

Lightfoot's eyes rested on the jam jar by the bed, then examined Opal. He leaned to Fos's ear and whispered, Are we playing the Sleeping Game?

No, son. Not now. Mommy's really sleeping.

Is it someone's birthday?

Why d' you ask that?

Sirens.

Sirens aren't for birthdays, son. How 'bout some eggs an' bacon, would you like that?

The boy's eyes went back to the jar of jam, then back to Opal.

Are we going to play the Sleeping Game when she wakes up?

We'll see.

He saw the trust in Lightfoot's eyes.

I mean, *yes,* he emphasized. Absolutely.

But when Opal woke it was late afternoon and Fos could tell the only reason she had come to was because the drug was wearing off and the pain had roused her. He fed her soup and gave her a sponge bath but he could see the pain was really all she knew and he gave her another, stronger dose, which she accepted passively in the early evening while Lightfoot was still playing outside, without his ever knowing she had been awake.

Somehow, when he had tried to imagine how the end might come, weeks ago, Fos had thought she'd keep her personality intact through all the symptoms, and he'd never let himself imagine the disease would steal her from him right before his eyes, while she was still alive, but that was what was happening, and happening too fast. His own pain, which he had hidden from her and tried to hide from Lightfoot, was catching up with him, despite the tiny sips of medication he was feeding to himself, as well, whenever he fed her. He had discovered a lesion on the shinbone of his right leg, and though he wrapped it, he couldn't staunch the suppuration, and the pain that it produced seemed to come, he swore, from deep inside his bones.

He was hoping for the least reprieve, the slightest reversal in the need for more sedation, the steady increase in her hours of unconsciousness—the sudden and irrevocable fact that she was no longer there for him to talk to. On the morning of the tenth, news came that there had been a second bomb over Japan, targeting a place called Nagasaki. As angry as the news of the first atomic bomb had made him, this news made him feel almost inconsolably alone and sad, his only consolation coming from the act of tracing the bones of Opal's hand while he waited all day for her to wake, while the light outside grew brighter and then fled. Tomorrow was the date they'd reckoned Lightfoot had been born, and Fos knew it was the last chance they had to tell him what he needed to know before the State came to take him from them. Fos had found it hard to speak at all when he'd cooked Lightfoot his supper and he could hear the boy talking to himself and to his whales as he eased himself onto the bed beside Opal and turned out the light. Sometime after midnight he was surprised by something moving in the room and he thought he was dreaming when he saw her standing at the foot of the bed, strong and young and healthy as she'd been when he first knew her. He watched her walk across the room and open the closet door, then he heard something fall and he knew at once he wasn't dreaming and got up and turned the light on. She was slumped on the floor but her eyes were shining and she smiled at him and he could see she was in possession of herself.

The box, she told him, lifting her arm toward the closet as he put her back in bed.

Which box is that, hon?

You know the one. She smiled even more engagingly. Box of Clues. Get it for me, Fos. Lightfoot needs to have it. It's in the closet. And put the book inside it, too . . .

The book, he knew, was *Moby-Dick,* the only book of Flash's that she'd kept. Why she wanted it inside the box he couldn't guess, but he wasn't going to argue. He got them both and put the book inside the box and placed the box inside her arms and sat down on the bed beside her feet.

There was much he seemed to need to tell her.

You look so beautiful, he said.

She did—she looked so young.

He held her hand and after a while she said, I need you closer, and he moved up on the bed and stretched himself beside her.

She leaned against him, staring up into his face.

After a while he asked her, should I turn the light out?

He had always loved the brightness but now its color seemed all wrong.

Yes, she said, resting on his shoulder. I don't need it any longer.

Then, before the other silence, she asked him one last time to kiss her.

In his room Lightfoot found it hard to wait for morning, and when he finally fell asleep the next thing that he knew a thrilling light was streaming through the window, evidence the big day was finally there at last, his birthday. He got up and made his bed and tiptoed past their room and washed his face and combed his hair, then tiptoed past again and listened. He could hear the clock tick in the living room and tiptoed into the kitchen. He opened the refrigerator and took out the milk and stood on a chair and got a glass down from the cupboard. He poured himself a glass of milk and drank it, then went into the living room to check the time, then sat down and waited. He went back into the kitchen and got a plate down from the cupboard and spread some butter on a slice of bread and folded it in half and took it outside on the back stoop and looked at Billy's tent in the yard next door while he ate. Some ants were crawling near his toes and he fed them crumbs and wondered if they ever slept. He put some bread crumbs on his feet and let them crawl across his toes and then, the way it happens when you're thinking about something else, he came to the realization that they were *playing* with him, playing the Sleeping Game, of course. Because it was his birthday. They were *waiting* for him. Even though Fos had said he wasn't supposed to go into their room while Opal slept he figured out that that was part of what they had in mind for his surprise. He wiped the ants off his feet and put the plate into the sink and tiptoed with elaborate suspense down the hall and turned the doorknob to their room and giggled at the sight of them. Opal had a box that she was holding and both their eyes were closed and the only sound inside the room was some buzzing near the open jam jar on the table. Some flies were dead and on their backs and two of them seemed nearly dead, trapped in something sticky near the little bottles of cracked glass.

I *see* you, Lightfoot breathed, unable to contain his glee as he crept around the bed to Opal, first, and breathed some warm air on her neck and said *Wake up.*

He climbed up on the bed and breathed on Fos.

Puffed on Fos's cheek.

Puffed on Opal's.

Said *Wake up* each time he did.

Breathed again, and even shook them.

They had never played this good before.

He breathed again on Fos's cheek and studied him.

Placed his hand on Fos's heart where there was evidence of warmth.

Nothing moved and in a while the flies stopped buzzing.

The same light that had announced the day soon filled the room.

He was nine years old.

And for the second time in his short life, he was unrescuably alone.

Careful not to touch him, or be noticed by him, he yet drew near to him, and stood there.

Ahab turned.

"Starbuck!"

"Sir."

HERMAN MELVILLE, *Moby-Dick,* "The Symphony"

the incognito

When they told him he was going to a foster home, Lightfoot thought they meant a home for Fosters, for children like himself. Named Foster.

That was just the first in the series of hard knocks which, like a hammer striking iron, shaped his childhood, pounding it into a thin defensive shield, a constrictive skin-deep armor.

He had realized something wasn't right when the warmth finally fled from Fos's chest. Lightfoot had put his head down there on that part of Fos that still felt warm, and he tried to listen for the sounds that that embrace had always held. It was so quiet, though, that he could hear the ticking in the living room and his own rapid breathing sounded large and out of place. Something in the way they didn't move frightened him. And something else—a warning sense, a premonition—made him take the Box of Clues and put it on the shelf above his bed beside his whales before he ran next door to get Janet. She was in her housecoat, frying eggs, but she ran over right away and then the next thing Lightfoot knew no one would let him back inside his house and he stood outside in his pyjamas and watched the cars and the white ambulance pull up.

After a while more people came, a man he recognized, and the hypodermic lady, and they tried to get him inside Janet's house but he wouldn't go.

Then, after that, Janet and the hypodermic lady came and led him to his bedroom, past the closed door. There were people in the hallway, and through the walls he could hear more people in his parents' room. The man he'd recognized was sitting on his bed, and there was an open suitcase and a carton on the floor beside him. The man asked Janet and the other lady to leave the two of them alone, and when they were gone, he put his hands on Lightfoot's shoulders and asked, Do you remember me?

Lightfoot nodded.

The man was wearing bars on his khaki uniform which meant he was an officer.

Good, the man said. Now there's a couple things you're going to have to do today as a good soldier. Are you prepared to follow orders?

Lightfoot didn't know, but still he nodded.

The first thing is: you mustn't cry. Good soldiers never show emotions. Second, you must do as you are told. No questions. Understood?

Lightfoot didn't understand at all—he didn't understand what was going on around him—but he could barely move, much less speak, through all the fear he was experiencing.

The man told him to get dressed and to pack up everything he wanted to take with him for the trip and wait in his room until someone came to get him.

If you need anything, you call me—my name is Bud. I'll be outside the door.

Am I going on a trip?

Yes.

Where?

Someplace nice.

It was the first time he heard *Foster* home.

He got dressed and folded all his clothes and packed them in the suitcase, then placed the Box of Clues and Spot and Rover and his storybooks into the carton, then waited. He waited a long time, and when someone finally came to get him, the door across the hall was open and someone had pulled a sheet up over both his parents.

In the kitchen Janet was standing in the corner by the back door, still in her housecoat, and there was another lady there with some papers on the table which she laid out in front of him.

Now let's just see if we have all this straight, the lady said, touching the edges of the papers. Can you read—?

Lightfoot nodded.

The lady pointed to the paper.

Is this right—? Your name is Ray—?

—yes.

Ray . . . *Foster?*

—yes. Ray Foster *Junior,* Lightfoot told her.

—oh.

She kept her pen poised above the paper and looked up at the hypodermic lady, who was standing by.

Leave the 'Junior' *out,* the hypodermic lady said.

The other lady asked him, Can you remember what month it was you had your birthday, hon?

This morning, Lightfoot said.

No—the *month.* Is he *simple?* she turned around to ask the other women.

Goll *darn,* it dawned on Janet. It *is* today, she said, and ran across to her house like she'd forgotten something baking in the oven.

The lady with the papers put them in a leather case, then stood up, and a soldier with no bars on his shoulders picked up Lightfoot's suitcase and the carton, and the hypodermic lady took his hand and walked him to a car parked on the street outside the house. Lightfoot sat alone in the back seat next to his suitcase, and when the car began to move he felt sick and he rose to his knees so he could see out the back window and hide his discomfort from the women in the front. He saw Janet come out of her house carrying a box wrapped like a birthday present and he saw her look up in surprise as the car went past, then Billy ran to follow, jumping in the street and waving, and Lightfoot stared at them in disbelief and then put his head down in his arms to hide his tears as the car was cleared to exit at the gate. The road was ruler straight, and soon the gate and the guard tower vanished in a single distant point and disappeared. Breeze reached him through the open windows and he let it dry his tears before turning back around. He leaned his head against the seat and watched the wavy line where the tops of trees met the summer sky, punctuated, like a periodic heartbeat, by the passage of electric power poles. After a while, there were more power lines, then more buildings, and then there were fewer trees than there were buildings. The rhythm of the line between the sky and earth became less predictable, and when they crossed a bridge over a wide river, Lightfoot saw a city for the first time. He had memories of smaller towns but he had never seen a place with streets like these, with so many people and so many cars. At the end of a wide boulevard there was a driveway flanked by two stone pillars, where they turned in and stopped before a large foreboding red brick building with black shutters.

The lady with the leather case went inside and Lightfoot waited in the driveway beside the car with his suitcase and his box and the hypodermic lady, who took a deep breath and let it out and said, You can always smell that river, here in Knoxville, can't you?

The sun was in his eyes, slanting from the west, so he couldn't read the sign carved in dark wood above the door, but he could hear a sound he recognized as children playing, and that made him feel a bit more confident as yet another stranger came out of the building and asked the hypodermic lady. This the new one?

The stranger looked him over and concluded, Small, for nine. That's good—they like 'em small.

She squatted down in front of Lightfoot and investigated him up close.

What's your name, boy? she inquired.

Ray. Ray Foster, Junior. Is this the 'Foster' home?

Never answer more than just your Christian name if anybody ever asks you, this new woman cautioned. Never speak unless you're spoken to. Never ask a question.

She told Lightfoot to pick up his things and follow her and when the big door closed behind him he found himself inside the clamor and disorder of an institutionalized life that would become what he was expected to call home until he was "fostered" or adopted or reached his sixteenth year, whichever happened first.

That first night inside, the older boys rumbled his possessions, tossed the contents of the Box of Clues on the floor beside his cot dismissively. Fos's dog tags on their fragile ribbon flashed bright among the curling photographs, as something possibly worth stealing, but their worthlessness was soon assessed. One of the boys riffled through the pages of the copy of *Moby-Dick* and asked him, Don't you got no *money?* Another of them held up the whales and started banging them together.

—*hey!* Lightfoot warned, surprised at his own courage, but if the boys knew anything at all, they knew how to recognize the ties that bind. *Never show you are attached to anything,* he learned too quickly. Never show you need something. Never show emotion.

Even under the cover of night, under cover of the darkness on the ward, after the lights were out and the order had been given for silence, no expression of emotion was safe among the other boys—if they heard you crying they would parody you, tease you the next day. If they heard you whimper, they would beat you up. Toughness was the order of the cult, and they brandished it like a material weapon. Some of them had been there all their lives—some had come in the years before the War when times were rough for everyone. Some were bouncers and repeaters—in and out of foster families like recycled clothes.

On his first night Lightfoot was too frightened to undress in front of all the others so he waited until after the lights were out, then huddled on his cot beneath his sheet and clutched his whales. The pillow smelled of camphor and the mattress smelled of urine and he covered up his nostrils with his pyjama sleeve to try to capture the familiar scent of home. No one had offered him an explanation for what had happened, why he was confined to this terrifying and strange place—and when he started to recount the day's events in a low whisper as he always did each night to his trusty whales, the boy assigned to the cot beside him hit him on the side of his head and told him he would murder him if he wasn't quiet. He whispered, anyway, and cried because he couldn't help it, but as the days went by, and people told him not to ask unwanted questions about his parents, and the bruises he was getting began to hurt too much, he stopped making any noise at night. He stopped talking to his whales. He stopped showing other people he was feeling sorry for himself. He didn't toughen up so much as batten down for his protection.

And no one called him Lightfoot anymore.

Not all the boys were bullies—most of them were just as confused as he was by their luck, or lack of it, and to that end the regimen imposed on them by the Home's administration was one of strict Christian observance: suffering went hand in hand with ultimate redemption. As did hard work and reward. Payoff was the order of the day—if you behaved yourself, someone would eventually want you as a friend, a son, a team member, a brother, a companion. Consequently, he was taught to make his bed with hospital corners and excel at Bible learning. He and the other boys endured inspection every morning, like farm animals at auction—clean scalp, clean neck, clean fingernails—and daily they were reminded the value of real money. *Money* was a constant presence as a motivator. With *money* they could each create a different life. They could own their privacy. Buy food. Buy things they only dreamed about. Escape.

Every Sunday, after Worship, all the boys were brought downstairs in their "dress" shirts and gathered in the Hall for mandatory Visit. Visit was when prospective foster parents, local people, came by The Home to look at them on their Sunday drive home after church. Under-threes were in a separate building, but even in the age group four to twelve the four-year-olds got the most attention, the most second visits. Most couples wanted children they could raise, not children who'd been raised by others. Once, he got a couple who came back to see him for a second time. When they told him that they had no children of their own, he answered *Oh, like Mister Hitler,* and after that he was told to never repeat Mister Hitler's name again—a reprimand which was unnecessary since the couple never returned and after that he spent Sunday Visit on the sidelines, waiting for the ritual to end, watching, with the other older boys. And anyway—by the time the first frost bit into the ground in late October, he had shot up a good three inches, almost overnight, and none of his own clothes still fit him. His own clothes, though not expensive, had been nicer than any of the other boys' and they had given him a slight advantage at the Visit, enough to get the visitors to notice him. But by November he was wearing other people's hand-me-downs, clothes with former signatures and mended seams. Worst of these growing blues, though, were the shoes. He outgrew the shoes he came with almost immediately and didn't know how to go about getting new ones, didn't know how to complain. And within a week of finally getting new ones, he needed a larger size again. If the shoes were *nice*—if they were proper leather and hadn't been resoled—boys would keep them even if they didn't fit. Hoarding *nice* things—a cotton shirt with all its original matching buttons, a pair of gloves with no holes in the fingers—was a cottage industry on the ward and Christmastime was the time of year to score some nice possessions. As businesses and charities made their annual donations and the boxes of clothes and toys arrived, it was like watching the arrival of a newborn fawn into a den of wolves. Some of the boys had a distant relative, or an appointed sponsor, who would send a yearly Christmas package or a card with money in it. Lightfoot was surprised one day to hear his own name called and to be handed a square envelope with his name and the address of the Boys Home printed on it in a stylish hand. The notice *Please Forward* was handwritten and underlined in the left hand corner. It was the only card he would receive that year, not counting the anonymous corny stuff the Home, itself, turned out for all of them. It was the only Christmas card he ever received, and it came that year and every year after that from Chicago, from Janet. Inside there was a single sheet of glossy paper with a picture of them sitting in front of a Christmas tree with red balls on it and beneath the picture were the words Merry Christmas and Happy New Year—Robert, Billy & Janet. Every year, it was the same—the same kind of picture—only the next year Janet was holding a baby and the year after that she'd dyed her hair and the next year Robert had unaccountably lost weight and gone completely gray. Janet wrote a little note on the reverse side of the card—but that first year all she wrote was "Hope you're someplace nice!" The words, the picture, hit Lightfoot like a punch. There they were, the three of them, looking exactly the way he remembered them, except shinier. And seeing them brought back the *need* to see them, and he could not afford to have that need, to show it. The only Christmas gift he got that year was a free book—all the boys got one free book to read—and a Hershey's chocolate bar. Lightfoot broke his chocolate bar in two and traded the two pieces for two books from boys who didn't like to read as much as he did. The books lasted him through Christmas into January—but their tales of boys captured by Indians, boys marooned on desert islands, only incited the restlessness in him to find more avenues of escape from his imposed isolation, his silence.

What you can't envision, he eventually decided, you can't need.

He didn't need, in the beginning, to look at Fos's and Opal's photographs to see them, but as time wore on he began to peek at pictures of them in the Box of Clues. At the start, he hardly recognized them, hardly recognized their younger selves. His father had been thinner, then—his mother fatter. After time the image that he kept of them in his imagination shifted slightly, became less and less like he remembered them and more and more the way the camera had portrayed them. The mystery of their disappearance became the mystery of *his* disappearance, too, the longer his own past stayed hidden from him, the longer he stayed hidden from himself. The questions that a nine-year-old might ask are not the same ones that an older boy must ask himself, and as the months and years went by, Lightfoot's memory of their final parting posed more questions than he'd had the courage to ask that fateful day. More and more, once a week, at least, he sifted through the items in the Box of Clues for exactly that: a *clue.* There was a man in many of the pictures, the man that he remembered Fos had told him was called Uncle Flash. Gradually, as Lightfoot passed through birthdays and got taller he saw nothing of his own features in Fos's and more of a similarity in his physique to Flash's. Who he was, though, or why his parents kept so many pictures of him, was a mystery.

The book held a mystery, too. He had tried to read it, searching through it, too, for clues. It was already worn, from someone else's searching, someone else's previous devotion to it. The Bibles that they used in Bible class were newer to the touch than this—but Lightfoot liked that it was smooth to touch and worn in. He just couldn't understand the words inside. He tried reading it from the beginning, from the middle, from the end—but nothing in it made much sense and the words, themselves, were difficult. He didn't even understand the title, *Moby-Dick.* The only thing he understood was that it might have once belonged to the mystery man in the pictures with his parents because written in bold ink in a bold hand on the inside cover were the words *Property of Chance Luttrell.* Then in parentheses, in pencil: "Pvt. 1st Class, Tennessee Overseas Division." Lightfoot stared at this inscription a long time, with the tugging suspicion he had seen the words somewhere else, before he finally remembered where.

On Fos's dog tags.

"Pvt. 1st Class, Tennessee Overseas Division" is what was written under Fos's name.

It was a clue, all right—but one he couldn't understand until one winter morning four years later, when he was thirteen, out on the streets of Knoxville, on his morning paper route.

There were Boys Homes all over Tennessee but his Home was Boys of Knoxville—oldest, biggest, most historical of all. Boys there from the age of twelve were encouraged to take part-time jobs, apprentice themselves to one of many Knoxville businesses which gave priority to orphans in their hiring. So when he turned twelve, Lightfoot had a weekend paper route and by the time he turned thirteen he was a full time paperboy, up at five each morning with the other Boys delivering the *Knoxville Journal.* The delivery truck dropped him off to walk his route then picked him up two hours later and took him back for school. One morning he was walking down the block and coming toward him was a man dressed in his coat, his pyjamas, and his slippers, walking a small dog. Mornin, said the man.

Mornin, Lightfoot echoed.

He missed animals something fierce, he realized, and on the third morning in a row of this exchange Lightfoot told the man that for a quarter he'd walk the dog for him.

Quarter for the week?

Quarter every morning.

Dollar for the whole week and we've got a deal.

As they shook on it the man said What's your name, son?

Ray. Ray Foster.

How 'bout that. I knew somebody called Ray Foster once. Years back.

Lightfoot was speechless—and, as such, started blinking.

Blinked just like that! the man continued. Wore those wire glasses—

—here in *Knoxville?* Lightfoot tried to piece together.

—'course here in Knoxville, where else would I be?

Lightfoot felt his heart beat faster and the next morning when he came to pick up the dog, he brought a photograph with him from the Box of Clues.

Damn! the man said when Lightfoot showed him the picture. That's ol' Ray, all right—went by the name of Fos. Are the two of you *related?*

He's my father.

—well I'll be darned! Whatever happened to him? I was in the Optimists with him—he took my picture. I lost track after that nasty business there with Chance Luttrell.

Chance Luttrell—? Lightfoot repeated, not believing he had heard it right. It was the name inside the book.

Sure, your daddy's partner, the man told him.

The next morning he gave Lightfoot the picture Fos had taken of him and on the back of it was the name of Fos's and Flash's studio and its Knoxville street address.

This information, thrilling as it was to the extent that it brought his parents back into a realm of shared experience, confused him—shamed him, unexpectedly. His orbit of travel through the city was circumscribed by circumstances—few children travel widely, even when they have the comforts of a happy home, but a ward of the state, as he was, had hardly any time, at all, that he could call his own, to go adventuring. The only time that he was free to leave the grounds of the Boys Home was on those rare occasions when a supervised excursion had been planned, and when he had permission to be out to work. Even then, after he'd turned the age to get a part-time job, two things limited his chance to go exploring in the city—his lack of free time, and his lack of transportation. Still, before this news, whenever he had had the chance, he had been drawn down to the river. Its morning fogs, its evening colorations had encouraged contemplation of the sort he had grown unused to in the ward. In winter, when he looked at it, the suggestion of its churning volume underneath its frozen crust reminded him of his own disguised and unexpressed emotions. Now to think that he might have stood somewhere his parents might have stood and never realized it—looked at things his parents must have seen—made him feel stupid. Had they talked about the city, mentioned ever living here? He searched his memory, but came up with no remembered detail. Now that he knew it, though, it seemed impossible that he had missed the obvious in all those early photographs of them in boats on water—it was the *Tennessee,* and when he looked again at them with this previously missing piece of information in his hand, suddenly he could identify church spires in the background, railroad trestles overhead. He began to carry several of the photographs with him, whenever he went out, asking people if they recognized the landmarks in them. His best source of information in this pursuit was Daniel, the man who drove the *Journal's* delivery truck. It was Daniel who recognized the boathouse in the background of one of Lightfoot's photographs and told him where he had to go to find it.

Who's the cool-lookin cat? he'd asked, pointing to the well-dressed man at the oars in the stern of the boat.

I think it's someone that my dad once knew called Chance Luttrell, Lightfoot told him, and Daniel let out a low whistle.

Big name in this town—*Luttrell,* Daniel confided. Rolls a' money. Big ol' pile up on the hill. I'll showya, he volunteered.

They pulled up in front of the biggest house Lightfoot had ever seen and this time it was Lightfoot who let out the low whistle.

You got connections in there, boy, be sure to mention ol' Dan in your will.

The house was as big as the Boys Home itself, and sat back off the street behind ten grand magnolias. On the door, though, just barely visible under the white porte-cochere, there hung a black wreath of mourning.

—who died? Lightfoot mused.

Someone always dyin up here, Daniel said, easing the truck past the mansion. Always some kinda trouble on all of these families.

He smiled at the thought.

Praise Jesus! he sang.

Then he said, You want to really find out what goes on in this city, you need to come down to the *Journal* and listen to the stories they all tell.

But Lightfoot already had three part-time jobs and was studying late every night, keeping his grades up. The grades were important to him—as a way out. Earning money was important, too, because he would need to have enough to find his own place to live when he turned sixteen, so every dollar that he earned, he banked. Still, when the chance came that spring to buy himself a secondhand bicycle, he couldn't resist. One afternoon he took it down to Locust Street, looking for the building where Fos and Flash had had their photographic studio. The old address was no longer there—the building itself had been torn down during the War, but he stood across the street from where he imagined it must have been and tried to reconstruct it. He didn't think it was so farfetched to invest a place with shared experience—that's why people build monuments, after all. He didn't know *what* he was looking for, only that it felt like he was on the trail of something that he had to catch. He rode up to the Luttrell place a couple times, too, but there was never any sign of life there—it was always dark, even at night. He found out, at the end of the school year, that he'd won early acceptance and a scholarship to the University of Tennessee, and the local Lions Club had awarded him an annual stipend for as long as he stayed in college, to cover his expenses, room and board. The day he turned sixteen he strapped his suitcase and the Box of Clues to his bicycle and moved to a room on the second floor of a boarding house several blocks off campus on a street lined with catalpa trees.

He hadn't had a room to call his own for seven years and he spent the afternoon arranging his few books and few possessions with great ceremony. He placed his two whales on the top of the bookshelf and put his newly purchased novels on the shelf beneath them. Then he sat down on the bed and opened the Box of Clues. As he lifted the lid he realized with a jolt that it was his birthday, again—the anniversary of the day it all began, and he still was no closer to understanding what the contents of the Box could mean, nor why he had been left by Fos and Opal with no code to the past, no keys to his future. If we are the sum of all experience, if every moment lived weighs on us to shape and form us, then perhaps, without his knowing it, the imprint of his first abandonment had already left its mark—its precedent—on him. There were things in the Box that he had never understood—empty seed packets with dates scrawled on them in

Opal's hand. He found a pale green lima bean in one, dry and shriveled, and he wondered what would happen if he planted it, if even in its desiccated state it held potential for another generation. He realized he didn't even know Opal's maiden name, what she had been called before she married Fos. Maybe if he knew it it would explain the Y-shaped thing that was in the box, too, brown and petrified, that could have been a slingshot or a piece of ancient coral. Inside the Box now, too, were the seven Christmas cards from Janet. Laying them all out, he was struck by the changes he could see between the years—Billy had grown up defined, if the photos could be trusted, by his Adam's apple and a pair of horn-rimmed glasses. Janet had remained thin but had gone through several tints of blond before achieving her latest state of platinum. She'd included an extra friendly-sounding note on the last card and now when he turned it over he remembered she'd written their telephone number for the first time, a detail which had been beyond his means to act upon last Christmas. *I'm going to call,* he suddenly resolved. He'd never made a long distance call but there was a drugstore on the corner with a pay phone—it might mean he'd have to skip some meals for a couple weeks but what the heck. It was his birthday.

He was feeling unprecedently grown up, speaking to the operator, when, suddenly, there was another female voice, fatigued and husky, answering—*Hello?*

—Janet?

—yeah, who's this?

It's Ray. Ray Foster. From next door.

There was a silence and Lightfoot was afraid he'd lost her. Then he remembered that his voice had changed.

—*little* Ray, he emphasized. Ray Junior. I'm calling you from Knoxville. You sent me the number on your Christmas card.

Well holy christ—Ray Junior. How the hell are you?

I'm swell—how are you? How's Billy?

Let me just get my drink a minute, Ray—

Lightfoot could hear footsteps receding, then approaching, and the rattle of ice cubes.

Isn't this one big coincidence, she resumed, back on the line. I was just thinking of the Oak Ridge gang a couple days ago—now why was that? Oh, I know. August 6. Anniversary of the goddam bomb.

He could hear what he thought was the sound of her taking a sip of something.

So, she said. My goodness. How long has it been—?

Seven years, Lightfoot told her.

Just flies, doesn't it. When you're having fun.

I was hoping maybe you could tell me—

Where did you end up, Ray? Somewhere nice with some nice family, I'll just bet. Billy couldn't get a grip the day they carted you away. They made such a *scandal.* God forbid they should have to deal with *suicides* at their blessed Army base—

Lightfoot didn't know what she was talking about.

—did you say . . . *'suicides'?*

I told that Bud Overmarker, I said—they didn't *kill* themselves—that's what I told him. Right in front of Billy I said—they were too nice! Your stinking *bomb* is why they died . . .

What . . . 'bomb'?

The atomic bomb, Ray! That's what we were building there. What'd you *think* we were all doing there—?

I didn't . . . think . . . anything. I was nine years old—

—and let me tell you something else that you should know. They weren't the only ones. Lotta blood left on the carpet at Oak Ridge, I'll tell you that.

—are you saying . . . the *atomic* bomb . . . killed my parents?

Just to name a few. What about my marriage, Ray? D-i-v-o-r-c-e, she spelled out for him. Who's paying for *that* funeral, I would like to know—

Maybe I should call back later, Lightfoot offered.

This *is* later, Janet told him. And the bombs are falling everywhere.

He heard her drop something then—maybe it was the telephone—and then he heard her swear and then the line went dead. He held the receiver in his hand a while and then the second that he cradled it the phone rang and when he answered, the operator told him to deposit six more nickels.

He bought a Babe Ruth and a Coca-Cola at the drugstore counter and went back to his room, where the Box of Clues was where he'd left it, open, on his bed. He put everything back inside, staring at the contents one more time. Then he took out the worn frayed book and opened the cover. *Moby-Dick,* it said. *Or, the Whale.* His gaze lifted to the two carved whales he had placed on top of the bookcase. How come he'd never registered till now that this story was about *a whale?* he wondered.

He turned past the beginning notes to the first sentence. *Call me Ishmael,* he read.

Until he started taking Bible study at The Home he hadn't known who Ishmael was, that Ishmael, in the Old Testament, was the outcast son abandoned by his father Abraham. Five years ago, even two, Lightfoot would not have known that *Call me Ishmael* means Call me Outcast. Now, when his eyes locked on that sentence something ran through him like light through a sheer cloth, like lightning: a realization. Some longing part of his identity connected with the first words in the story, those first three written words. *This book is about me,* he realized.

Which is why most people read books in the first place, he remembered his mother saying.

To find out about themselves.

To find out about the world.

He stretched his legs out on the bed and started reading and didn't stand back up again until he had to go to work next morning.

It took four successive nights to finish it. Not only did he think he could have been the character called Ishmael, he thought he could have been the character called Ahab, too—Ahab, the *light-foot,* the one-legged Captain of the ship, obsessed with searching, driven by his quest for the White Whale.

It was approaching dawn when he finished reading—and it was a Sunday, his day off. The birds were gathering and there was the aroma of a privet hedge in bloom as he walked up the empty street toward the heart of Knoxville. Daniel, the delivery driver for the *Journal,* had told him that if you want to see a newspaper at work you had to visit by the back door, not the front. Up front you got the advertising and the desks, he'd said—out back you got the deadlines and the sweat.

Trucks were idling in the breaking dawn beside the loading platform and Lightfoot walked among them till he heard a voice call out, *Well how you been—?* It was Daniel, drinking coffee with some other men. It was "half" day at the paper—half the breaking news and half the work force—and when Daniel asked if he would like to have a look around Lightfoot told him, I was hoping you were going to ask me that.

They went inside and Daniel showed him the huge printing press, now still, like the engine of a ship in dry dock. They went into the room where the type was set, then they emerged into a kind of morgue with rows and rows of steel shelves and steel filing cabinets—then they came into a general area with desks and the saturated ochre of cigar smoke. Some men were sitting in their shirtsleeves with their feet up on the desks tossing cards into an upturned hat. Daniel introduced him to them and after some talk about Lightfoot's scholarship to the University, he asked if the paper had a library of back issues.

Sure, he was informed. What areya lookin for?

I want to find out more about the bomb.

—the *bomb—?*

The atomic bomb, Lightfoot elaborated.

Only *but* one bomb in Tennessee, son—we built it!

—yeah, I know. I was out there at Oak Ridge. My dad and mother worked out there.

—*no kidding,* one of the men said, swinging down his legs and straightening up. Well come on, he said, and led Lightfoot and Daniel back into the other room. He showed Lightfoot how the filing system worked—cross-referenced chronologically and by subject—then he left the two of them alone.

Listen, Daniel mentioned, while Lightfoot started opening some drawers. May be none of my damn business, but—what were you doin in the po' boys Home if your folks was out there with the Army at Oak Ridge?

—what do you mean?

Well, son, I guarantee they had some money put by—pensions. Trust me, I'm a union driver and I know my compensations. I'm just lookin out for you, you know—not pryin. Just makin sure you got what's proper and what's comin to you.

Well actually . . . Lightfoot said. My parents died out there and no zone ever told me how and no one ever even told me where they're buried. And it's—it's kind of like a *white whale* with me, if you know what I mean—

Daniel stared at him and then let out another of his low long whistles.

Boy, he finally said. We gotta get you some fine *help.*

The legal editor at the paper thought the first thing Lightfoot should do was write a letter to the newly formed Atomic Energy Commission listing all the facts as they pertained to his dilemma, and then take it over in person to their offices, which happened to be located, conveniently, in Knoxville.

Classes had started at the University, so it took Lightfoot a while to draft the letter, and it wasn't until the middle of October that Lightfoot first entered the offices of the AEC with his statement of what he thought were his simple facts.

On the wall of the Commission there was a large framed photograph of an atomic detonation, the white gigantic mushroom-shaped cloud of gases and debris looming up into the atmosphere like a gorgeous freak of nature from the bottom of the deep.

People *luv* to look at that, the woman who was dealing with his application noted. Don't know what it is about it. Maybe just its shape. Man came in and said that it reminded him of God. That's takin' it a bit too far. But, still.

She made a file with Lightfoot's name on it and attached his letter to it and handed him some forms and told him to come back when he had filled them out.

I'll do it now, he volunteered and stepped aside to start. Father's date of birth, he read. Mother's maiden name. Time and Place of Death. *Supporting Documents.* Birth Certificate of Claimant. Death Certificate of the Deceased.

He started to explain his situation to the woman but she told him if he couldn't fill in all the blanks then he had to sign the form, at least, and write another letter to explain his failure to comply.

She saw him look up at the photograph again before he left so she called him back and handed him a brochure with the same picture on its cover. It was a brochure called "Civic Uses of Atomic Energy," and Lightfoot cut the title off and taped the picture of the cloud to the wall above his bookshelf. Sometimes, with the streetlight shining on it, he could imagine it was moving, like a living thing, growing, like a bloom of bioluminescence under water, glowing in the dark.

At first he went back every week, and then he started going every other week. *Yes,* they finally told him after several months, they had, in fact, traced the employment records of a Mr. Foster and his wife. And after several more months they verified that there was pension money in reserve in both their names. But after a year of correspondence, and another year of waiting, no one could come up with any proof that either Ray Foster or his wife Opal had ever died. There was no record of their burial. And no recorded evidence that they had ever had a son.

Almost two years to the day after his first call to her, Lightfoot put a call through to Janet in Chicago, hoping she would write a statement for him, but the number had been reassigned to someone else who didn't seem to understand Lightfoot's spoken English. He didn't care about the pension money—that had never been the point. He wanted to find out what happened to them, why they died, where they had been laid to rest so he could visit there and make his peace with them. But every avenue he explored came to a stark dead end. He wrote to the Army, and he wrote to the TVA, asking for Fos's records and for proof of his legitimacy. And then one day he showed up at the *Journal* again, where the guys were still tossing cards into an upturned hat.

—*now* what, Einstein? they goaded him.

I need to find somebody and I don't know how to do it.

All depends who this 'somebody' is.

Chance Luttrell.

—*laughed,* they looked like they were going to lay some eggs, but one of them led him to the morgue and showed him where the L's were and said, "You sure you don't want Tay, not Chance?"

—who's 'Tay'?

Taylor, Chance's brother . . . Knoxville's own D.A. nigh these thirty years. Chance is the one I'm looking for.

—you sure?

I'm certain.

—it's your funeral.

—what's that supposed to mean?

Read for yourself.

The headlines shocked him. He didn't know his father's partner was a convicted felon—the trial had run for two weeks, a front-page headline in the *Journal* every day. And then there were more headlines about the sentencing—in total, there must have been a hundred articles about the case, and it took him two whole days to read them all. There were earlier articles about Chance, too—and pictures of him from the Society Page at summer balls, and a picture of him in his uniform when he enlisted. There was a fairly recent obituary of Taylor's son, killed in the Korean War, and of Taylor, too. But the last mention of *Chance* Luttrell was an article about the sentencing and it didn't say which prison he'd been sent to.

Lightfoot asked the legal editor where someone who had been convicted of a crime in Tennessee would be sent.

What was the crime?

Transporting a minor and . . . I think they called it contributing to the corruption of—

—oh yeah, that would have been the Mann Act. Federal. You need to write to the Bureau of Federal Prisons.

Lightfoot got a letter four months later from Washington, D.C., informing him that Chance Luttrell was still in the minimum security facility at Fort Pillow, Tennessee. He wrote to the Warden asking what the Rules for Visitation were and he got a letter back saying all he had to do to visit someone there was show up, ring the bell, and pass the guard's inspection.

Exams were coming up and it wasn't till the start of the spring break that Lightfoot found himself on the bus out to the prison with *Moby-Dick* in his hand and with the Box of Clues inside his knapsack.

Well, this is *a first,* the guard who was in charge of letting people in informed him.

He asked Lightfoot to write his name down in a visitors' book.

Are you from his lawyer's office?

No.

—the bank?

Uh-uh.

—reporter?

Nope.

Well you're the first to come to visit him in twenty years. What's in the box?

Lightfoot handed it to him and he looked through it and gave it back. He looked through the pages of the book, too, then patted down Lightfoot's torso and his pants pockets.

Take a seat, he said. We'll go let him know you're here. He may not want to see you. Prisoner's rights, you know.

Half an hour later another guard called out *Ray Foster?* Lightfoot followed him through two locked gates into a room with a dozen plain wood tables with two wooden chairs at each one. Three men who were apparently prisoners were seated across from three women visitors under the casual scrutiny of the guards. Lightfoot was instructed to sit down at one of the tables and he placed the Box and the book in front of him and waited. He stole a couple glances at the prisoners and noticed that their hands were free—two of them were holding hands with two of the visiting women, and the other one was smoking. He heard an iron gate swing on its hinges then another, then a door opened in the far left corner of the room and two guards led in a gray-haired man in blue jeans and a white T-shirt.

The man stepped forward, looked around the room, his gaze eliminating Lightfoot, then he turned, said something to the guard, and then another guard raised his arm and pointed back to Lightfoot.

The gray-haired man shot a glance at Lightfoot, shook his head, and began to turn away when Lightfoot rose and held up the worn copy of *Moby-Dick*.

He was still handsome, this man who hesitantly approached. Skinny —hard through the upper arms and forearms, ropy through the torso. He'd lost most his hair and what was left was white—but, nevertheless. A ladies' man. A heartthrob. A real killer.

Lightfoot took the lid off the Box of Clues and laid one of the photographs out between them on the table.

This would have been the best goddam blue-ribbon day if you were really Fos, Flash said. Voice all shot to hell with smoking.

Still not sitting.

You must be the kid, then.

He pulled the chair out and sat.

I'd sit down, too, if I were you, he mentioned.

Lightfoot and the guards were now the only people standing.

They're packing .22s, he added. And that's their I.Q.s, not their weapons' calibre.

Lightfoot sat down slowly and held his hands together on the table so the older man couldn't see how they were shaking. When he spoke, his voice came out sounding strange.

I'm . . . I'm a bit afraid to be here, he admitted.

Flash continued staring at him, never blinking.

—afraid of *you*, Lightfoot added.

Well I only kill the things I love, kid, so relax. I don't know you well enough to hurt you.

Lightfoot thought he saw a glint of something funny in the man's eyes but if he had meant his words to be a sort of joke, Lightfoot didn't understand that kind of humor. It confused him, adding to his nervousness. Flash leaned back and watched him, and Lightfoot felt a tightness in his throat that made it difficult to speak. He parted his lips and tried to find his voice, but couldn't.

Deck's yours, Flash finally said. You brought the cards to the table. You gotta name the game for me to know what rules we're playing.

Lightfoot swallowed hard and tried again to say why he had come. The guards were staring at him. Flash leaned forward. See those guys behind me? If we don't start exchanging pieties they're going to think we're up to something.

Lightfoot blinked a couple times.

Still couldn't speak.

Okay, christ, I'll start, Flash finally said. Twenty Questions. Question Number One: Why did they send *you?*

—who?

Who do you think? The 'dittos'—how come they sent you instead of coming here themselves? Question Number Two: What the hell is all this *crap* they sent you with?

He gestured toward the Box of Clues.

Lightfoot's expression clouded, his eyes welled up and he turned his face away.

I'm sorry, he said, after a moment, pulling himself together. I *never* cry—you're not supposed to. Sorry.

Now it was Flash who seemed to be having difficulty forming words.

—aw geez, he finally said, putting it together.—*both* of them?

Lightfoot nodded, sharply.

Flash looked away—then looked back at Lightfoot.

—*when?*

Ten years ago.

—*ten . . . ?* —both at the same time?

—yeah.

—*how?*

I think it was the bomb.

—the 'bomb', Flash repeated.

I think so, yes. Our neighbor said she thinks it was the bomb that killed them.

—*what* bomb?

The atomic bomb.

—the . . . ?

Again, Lightfoot saw what might be a kind of humor enter the older man's expression.

Fos built it, Lightfoot explained.

There was no mistaking—Flash began to smile.

—*Fos,* he verified. Fos built the atomic bomb . . .

Yes, Lightfoot told him.

O sweet Mary's bastard son, Flash laughed. O christ—I haven't laughed since Hitler, and . . . this . . . *hurts,* he sputtered. Lord have mercy Fos built the bomb—so *that's* why it exploded, then—*ac-ci-dental-ly!*

He shook his head and wiped his eyes and realized, from Lightfoot's expression, that he'd been laughing at his old friend's funeral.

Sorry kid, he said. But you had to know him as I did to get the joke. Ol' Fos—

He shook his head again and his hand came to rest on the cover of the book. He picked it up.

I was reading this the day I met him . . .

He took a pair of glasses out of his T-shirt pocket and when he slipped them on his eyes got big as rubber balls behind the lenses.

I was in my bunk and this strange character appeared—well, you know what he looked like—and he said, *What are you readin?* and I held the book up like this so he could read the title and he said, *What's it about?* and I told him It's about a kind of love, and he just stared at me so I said, It's about obsession, and he kept staring so I said, Well, actually, it's about a big white whale and he said, Did you know you can take a fish heart and squeeze it and make ink out of it and what you write with it will shine in the dark—?

He turned the book over in his hands and laid it back down on the table, but kept his hand on it.

First thing he ever said to me. That you could make ink out of fish hearts that was phosphorescent. Well that was Fos. You just had to love him . . .

He took his glasses off, then put them on again to inspect the photograph Lightfoot had taken from the Box of Clues.

—*holy,* he said.

His hand shook.

—I remember the day he took this picture. Jesus. Like a little window of Time just opened up—like I could just walk right back into that day through the window of this picture. What else have you got in here—?

He reached into the Box and pulled out a photograph of Opal.

—aw gee. There she is.

Lightfoot watched as he beheld the picture.

When you came over, Lightfoot found the courage to begin, you said I must be 'the kid.' How did you know—?

She wrote to me, Flash told him. I should have known something must have happened when the letters stopped . . .

He put the picture down where they could both look at it.

She got real thin toward the end, Lightfoot explained to him. She didn't look the way she does in this picture. You could see her bones beneath the skin—

—so she was sick?

Lightfoot nodded.

Listen kid, I don't know who put this nonsense in your head about the bomb, but it doesn't sound like—

—it's not nonsense, Lightfoot told him.

Well I think it has to be.

Well you're wrong.

Flash took his glasses off and stared at him.

I was there, Lightfoot insisted, and you weren't. The sirens had been going off and everyone was happy 'cause everyone had made the bomb and then a couple mornings later they were asleep and I couldn't wake them. I tried to wake them up but they just kept on sleeping so I went next door to Janet's. She's the one who says it was the bomb. And then they put me in the Boys Home and all I had was *Moby-Dick* and what's in this Box and I wrote to the Commission to find out why they died and where they're buried but the Commission says there aren't any records and even if there were I'd have to prove that I'm their son before they'll show them to me and I don't know how I'm going to do that. I can't find the proof I need to do that anywhere and all I've got left are these pictures and your name inside the book so I came here hoping you could tell me something. Anything—where were they living when they had me, the name of a doctor or a county, anything at all—the place where I was born . . .

Flash was looking at him with an expression Lightfoot couldn't read.

You don't know . . . where you were born?

—no.

—they never . . . told you?

—no.

—they never said . . . anything about it?

No.

Flash rubbed his forehead, looked away, then looked back at Lightfoot.

How old are you now, kid?

—nineteen.

And how do you spend your time?

I'm at college. 'UT.' In Knoxville.

—jesus, Knoxville. And how's that going for you? Happy?

Lightfoot shrugged.

A person knows when he is happy, Flash insisted. Are you happy? Or are you not?

Lightfoot shrugged again.

What are you studying to be?

I'm taking Veterinary Medicine.

Flash whistled, approvingly.

A *scientist*, he assessed.

Well a veterinarian, Lightfoot conceded.

And how 'bout books—you read?

—yeah.

—poetry?

—not really.

—novels?

—sure.

—*this* one?

He put his hand on *Moby-Dick.*

—yeah, Lightfoot said.

What did you think?

I didn't like the part about the killing of the whales . . .

—that was the whole entire book.

—but I liked Ishmael. And I identified with Captain Ahab.

Flash smiled.

You understood him, did you?

Understood him? No. But I could have *been* him.

See, this is where Fos and I were different—much as I loved him. And where Opal and I were more the same. Fos didn't read—fiction, I mean. For his own enjoyment. He didn't see literature as an ongoing exploration of the human tragedy—man's condition. He never saw it as an ongoing conversation with the future, with the past. I think Opal was beginning to—I think she was surprised by what she found when she began to read . . .

—she *was.*

I know. She told me. But Fos . . . here's an example. We'd been over there, in France, in the war, about four months and one night they laid on the artillery, jesus christ—the gas. Fos was caught out in a hole near the front line of fire and when he got back in he said this boy had died right in his arms talking about Emily Dickinson and right before he died he put this volume of poems that he carried with him into Fos's hands as a dying gift and Fos comes back in with the little bloodstained book of poetry—I mean fucking poetry-itself, or what? Me, I would have had that baby burned into my frontal lobes before the night was over but I don't think Fos even ever opened up the book. See what I'm getting at? There are people for whom the past is important, in all its many thousands of versions, its poetry, its pictorial art, its narratives—and then there are people who take their meaning of life from completely different sources. And I'm wondering which kind you are. Whether the written word has that kind of interpretative meaning for you. I mean—Fos's fish heart story. There's the prime example. Let's suppose somebody *did* write something in the ink made out of fish hearts . . . I mean, isn't that a kind of *miracle* in and of itself? But here's the difference between Fos and me. Fos would want to know *how long the words would glow.* And I would want to know just what in god's delight they had to say . . .

He touched the book again.

If they left you this on purpose, it was *her* idea.

Lightfoot nodded.

It was in the Box, he said. She was holding it.

Let me ask you something, kid—what do you want?

I told you.

—no, I mean . . . what do you *want?*

—what do you mean?

Flash spread his arms.

What do you fucking *want?* Pretend I'm the goddam genie in the lamp—

Lightfoot shrugged.

I don't know—

—you *have* to know. That's the contract that you make with Life. You have to hold up your end of the deal and know what you fucking *want*—

I guess—

—no guessing.

I want to know the truth.

—the 'truth.'

—yeah. I want to know the truth. I'd like to go and visit them one more time, wherever they are buried. And . . . I want to see the bomb, just once, so I can understand.

Flash began to laugh again, but then was seized with a fit of violent coughing.

Goddam weed, he eventually apologized.

What would *you* want? Lightfoot asked. —if you ever could get out?

—who says I can't get out?

Lightfoot looked embarrassed.

My crime was falling in love, kid. That's a lifetime sentence. But the Mann Act only has a mandatory ten. And I've been in for twenty-three.

I don't understand—

I don't expect you to.

He looked down at his hands, then up at Lightfoot.

My brother died last year, he said.

Yes, Lightfoot said. I read about that. I'm sorry.

Oh, he was a royal pain in the ass to everybody, don't be sorry. But as long as he was still D.A. in Knox County there was not a snowbird's chance in hell that I was going to get probation.

I read his son died, too. In Korea—

—now that *is* a crying shame. Because that makes yours truly the very last of the Luttrells. All that fucking money . . . But you asked a question. What do I *want . . . ?* I'd like to be able to drink again without puking up my guts, but that's not a life-ennobling quest. I'd like to smoke, but what the hell, the lungs are shot. I'd like to see my love again but that is too damn maudlin.

He picked up *Moby-Dick* again and riffled the pages.

When I was reading this and we were in the hellhole there in France I realized one night that most of this plays out in the Pacific, and I had never seen that ocean. So I asked Fos if he thought an ocean is an ocean anywhere on earth or if he thought each ocean is distinct from all the others.

What did he say—?

—what did he say? He said . . . because light travels to us over distance, everything we see is an illusion. And that the whole purpose of existence is to *cut the distance* between the source of the illusion and our perception of it. And if we can do that, then we can see that every particle of matter is the same.

. . . Fos said *that?*

Or something like it.

—golly.

Or maybe I'm confusing him with Einstein. Anyway, it didn't change my mind about promising myself that when the War was over I would go out west—go see the Pacific. Can you drive?

—what?

Can-you-operate-a-motor-vehicle?

—me? —yes. I mean, I don't have a license yet. But I can drive.

Is there a girlfriend?

—what?

Is-there-a-woman-you're-involved-with?

No.

Why not?

It just . . . it isn't . . .

All right, we'll need to work on that. Now here's the proposition. You will get the truth, and I will get the Pacific Ocean. And in the bargain I'll throw in Nevada for you, where they test the bomb.

Lightfoot's hands were folded and his eyes were round.

Mr. Luttrell, he said.

Oh cut the crap and call me Flash.

—I don't even *know* you.

—so?

I can't just up-end my life—

—your 'life'?

I'm on a scholarship—I can't just quit and take off—

—why not?

Because.

—because, why?

Because you're a . . . you're a . . . *felon.*

Bravo.

I mean—

But Flash had pushed the chair back and was on his feet, walking toward the guard and never looking back.

Lightfoot's face was burning and he could taste his sour shame at the back of his throat as he gathered the book and the Box and stuffed them in his knapsack. The guard let him out and he passed through the two iron doors, one after another, but at the final post the guard there told him that he had to wait. He stood against the wall and waited, then, after nearly fifteen minutes, another guard appeared and handed him a leather case and said, You're going to have to sign for this.

Engraved in gold above the case's clasp were the initials "C.L."

Lightfoot signed the form the guard presented him, then walked through the outer gate into the sunshine. He sat down on one of the benches by the outside wall where people waited for the bus and undid the clasp and brought out one of the many bundles of neat envelopes tied up in string.

In blue ink three lines were written on the one on top:

> *Chance Luttrell*
> *Federal Penitentiary*
> *Fort Pillow*

Lightfoot's eyes filled with tears but he still recognized the words in the upper left hand corner.

Opal Foster, he could see.

RFD, Clinch River,

Tennessee.

"Hast seen the White Whale?' gritted Ahab in reply. "No; only heard of him, but don't believe in him at all . . ."

HERMAN MELVILLE, *Moby-Dick,* "The Pequod Meets the Bachelor"

the whiteness of the whale

He looked much frailer on the outside of the whale than he'd looked inside.

When Lightfoot pulled up outside the prison gate in the brand-new Oldsmobile and saw Flash standing there, he realized he had bought the wrong-size clothing—Flash looked like an emaciated chicken in the new sports jacket Lightfoot had picked out for him. He had no complaints about the car, though—the Olds was a made-to-measure beaut.

It's easier to buy a car in this country than it is to buy clothes that fit, Lightfoot joked.

—since when did *you* get a sense of humor? Flash teased him.

It was easy to tease "the kid"—as easily rewarding, in its way, for Flash as it had been when he teased Fos and Opal. But what he couldn't tease the kid about was exactly that—his parents. On that subject Lightfoot maintained an almost eucharistic purity. On that subject there was no pulling his leg. No pulling the wool over his eyes, either.

Flash had kept Opal's letters in the order they had been received, so the first thing Lightfoot had searched for when he got them were the letters written near the time that he was born. Although she'd written regularly, she hadn't written them like clockwork. One a month, sometimes two, was her established practice—except for the month Lightfoot was born. "It's like I'm not there, and then, suddenly, I am," he outlined to Flash on his next visit.

Well welcome to the Facts of Life, tadpole, Flash teased. That's the way it happens on the other end as well: You're here, and then you're gone.

—she doesn't even write to say she's, you know . . . pregnant.

Well she wouldn't, would she. Can't we *leave* this, pilgrim? You wanted truth, I gave you all the facts I owned.

He stared at Lightfoot. Lightfoot stared right back.

I'm sorry but it seems like there's a letter missing, Lightfoot maintained.

—'missing,' Flash repeated.

I mean I'm not there at all and then in the next letter two months later there I am. Already born.

You and Jesus, kid—two miracles. Go explain. Maybe you should start your own religion.

The letter Opal had written to announce Lightfoot's unexpected appearance in their lives had been written on blue paper, the only one of its kind, easy to pick out among the others. And Flash, whose conscience hadn't known the solace of a quiet moment in more than twenty years, had experienced the balm of absolution in destroying it before he turned the leather case with all the other letters in it over to the guard to pass to Lightfoot. If Fos and Opal had kept the secret from the boy for all those years, who was he to break it to him? Without the illusion of that natural line between himself and Fos and Opal, what did Lightfoot have? *Nada,* Flash assessed. But if he thought Lightfoot's inquest into his past would be relieved by the glimpses of daily life contained in Opal's letters, he was wrong. Lightfoot became more like Ahab on the bridge of the *Pequod* than he had ever been, steering only for a course in the direction of the thing he couldn't see.

In the weeks after his first visit to the prison, Lightfoot took his mother's letters to the County Registrar to try to prove the registration of his birth must be somewhere in the county records—nothing came of it. From the point of view of the various bureaucracies, he did not exist before he entered the Boys Home, the early details of his life had been written in invisible ink—his life with Fos and Opal had never occurred. And while, under the boredom of the prison guards' trancelike gazes, Flash would build a careful existential argument for Lightfoot to start living in the present, start cutting the distance between the illusions of his past and the realities of every day, Lightfoot wasn't willing to relinquish his desire for a verifiable history. What he did relinquish, though, was his initial fear of Flash. His language shocked him, sometimes—but he was still the most engaging talker Lightfoot had ever known. His stories, alone, made his company enjoyable. And he made Lightfoot laugh, which was overdue. And when he had those bug-eyed glasses on he looked less and less like someone who was repaying society for his crimes and more and more like someone who was wide-eyed in the world—more and more like Fos.

Certainly there were times when Flash realized he was striking a paternal posture, a paternal tone in his advice to Lightfoot—and he shied away from it at once, peppering his talk with enough off-color blasts to raid the premises of any familial-sounding platitudes. But once they were on the road and he was lost inside the oversized sports jacket in the passenger seat of the Olds convertible, if Flash appeared to be Lightfoot's relative at all, it was his cloistered grandfather out for his last joyride. Until, of course, he started talking. Then he seemed more like Aldous Huxley on an undocumented drug—or Ernest Hemingway impersonating Elvis.

Mother's *milk—!* he would exclaim, look at this smooth-assed road!

Even after they were clear of Nashville, across the Mississippi at Memphis, out of Tennessee and into Arkansas, Flash kept shouting, Shit!—look at this road! I think I must have dug the roadbed for this mama—! Every time they passed a road gang, whether they were prison boys or not, Flash would stand up on the front seat as they sped by and hoot and holler and expose his rear to them, then sit back down and say to Lightfoot, It's just *amazing* the things that you can do without a single worry once you know you're going straight to hell no matter, anyway . . .

They made a stop in Memphis at Schwab's Drugs to buy a case of "the pink stuff" Flash seemed to need to take a sip from every half an hour to keep from gagging up some blood—*prison ulcer* is what he called the hole in his stomach lining that the Pepto-Bismol soothed every time they stopped for coffee and fried donuts, chili, biscuits in red gravy, beans with dirty rice and fricassee of crawfish. They were on no time clock so they stopped and talked and shopped and ate and listened to live music, and soon the trunk was filling up with books and weird folk art and phonograph records on top of the three suitcases full of hundred-dollar bills Lightfoot had cashed out from the Luttrell accounts in Knoxville the day before they left. Lightfoot had agreed to this adventure with no particular objective in mind except a vague determination to end up at the atomic testing grounds in Nevada at the moment a nuclear explosion was occurring in the atmosphere, and whether it was because Flash thought that idea was unadulterated ka-ka straight from la-la land or whether there was some other motivating reason, he put in two requests right from the start: first, that they travel west on the great mother road, Route 66—and second, that he get his first view of the Pacific from John Steinbeck's neighborhood. Looking at the map, Lightfoot argued that if they took Route 50 instead of 66, they would cut right through the heartland, through Nevada, too, and meet the ocean at Oakland just west of San Francisco, close to Steinbeck's hometown of Salinas.

Oakland is *Jack London*-ville, Flash protested. And anyway, I don't crave Nevada. You can pursue your fantasy if you still want to after you have dumped my happy carcass on the beach at Monterey.

They could join Route 66 in Oklahoma City, but before that, wherever they stopped in Tennessee or Arkansas, Flash would play the jukebox and eat enough for a whole chain gang then pull relief from the Pepto-Bismol bottle and lament his bygone drinking days. They spent the night in separate rooms in Memphis and separate cabins at a motor court near Little Rock, but even so, Lightfoot could hear him coughing through the walls at night. Flash had peeled a hundred from his bankroll and told Lightfoot when they had started out, You see something you want, you buy it. You need to get to know what money feels like, he tried to convince him, but Lightfoot wouldn't take it. When he came out of the diner where they ate lunch in Fort Smith, Arkansas, though, Flash found Lightfoot standing in front of a storefront, staring in the window.

What do you see in there, kiddo—?

—a tent.

—a *tent.*

My friend next door back at Oak Ridge had one. Billy. We used to spend the night outdoors.

A *tent*—how am I *ever* going to make a proper dilettante out of you—?

He bought a Coleman stove to go along with it, and an oil lantern, and a sleeping bag and kept hissing *fucking Boy Scout* while Lightfoot picked out the canteen and the hatchet and an air mattress.

They stayed in a hotel that night in Oklahoma City and when Flash left after dinner to explore the streets Lightfoot claimed he was too tired to tag along. But when Flash checked in when he got back, Lightfoot had laid the tent parts out across the floor and was putting them together.

I can use this when I go out to Nevada, he enthused.

Next day they hooked up to Route 66 and before noon, a hundred miles from Amarillo, when they passed the first bar that was open Flash told Lightfoot to pull in.

Inside there were some long haulers and a few local boys and while Lightfoot was still looking at the menu Flash whispered something to the waitress and soon two plates of steak and eggs appeared before them, and a beer.

What's *this?* Lightfoot wanted to know.

Well it ain't a bunny wabbit, Mr. Fudd.

I don't drink, Lightfoot reminded him.

No, and we don't know how to play with girls, either, I see, but we like to set up tents in hotel rooms and pretend that we're still nine years old.

The waitress came by to check that everything was fine with Lightfoot and when she left Flash said, I rest my case. That woman was flirting with you and you were gawping at your eggs like they had nipples. You're a handsome boy, for christsake. Now watch this—

Another waitress passed and Flash said, *Darlin'*—?

She turned in time to see him smile and somehow he made his face light up and suddenly he looked a decade younger. That thing you've done there with your hair in back, I don't know what it's called, he said. That must have taken you some time. I just wanted you to know it hasn't gone unnoticed.

Thanks, she said and raised the coffee pot suggestively. It's called a shag-*non*.

Flash picked up his cup and held it toward her. When she began to pour he said, Please tell me you're not married.

You look for a point of contact, he explained to Lightfoot after she had gone. You don't so much *look* for it as let her know it's already there—let her know you *understand her.* The second thing is—you must *imply futurity.* Imply you'd like to stick around. Imply you're *going* to stick around. Next, display one glaring, but never fatal, fault. Women like to fix things in a man. They need that. Sure, there are some dreadful women out there, some bitches and some harridans, but—and this is the god's honest, you can ask each s.o.b. around here—the first rule about women is that no matter how repulsive you might be as a man, however reviled by society you are, there's a woman out there somewhere waiting to adore you. Men you wouldn't trust to feed your dog were getting letters on the inside from the nicest kindest women who had read about them in the papers. Hell, even *I* got letters. Sometimes I think they are their own worst enemies. Because in her heart every woman's got to know that if she doesn't stay the course, if she doesn't do her man up right, another woman's out there waiting to take over. Any man who can't find a loving woman, it's his own damn fault.

Why are you telling me all this? Lightfoot needed to know.

Because I did *a lot* of thinking on the inside, kid. A *lot.* Built a lot of fucking roads for the state of Tennessee—even built some dams. That's when my hair turned white—working on the gangs. But then some days it would rain and some days it would snow and we'd be locked up in the inside with not a thing to do but think and read and read and think and think again. I even started to appreciate that kind of life—I thought I could become a monk. Well—I should have started earlier. For everybody's sake . . . because way back before you were even born there was this girl, you see. And I fell in love with her. It was something that I wanted—love—not because it was expected of me, but because I found it out myself—that happiness of wanting to be only with that other person. A lover's gaze is like having your portrait painted by a master and then being able to look into it, stare at it for as long as the love lasts—or for the rest of your life. And it's time you got to know that. I *want* you to know that. *They* would want you to know what that's like, to be in love. Because they had it, kid. They really did. The real article. Like no two other people I have ever seen . . .

Something as important as learning to blow warm air on a hummingbird to revive it was being taught to him—Lightfoot could feel it on the skin at the back of his neck the same way he had felt it the day Fos had taught him his first life-saving lesson. This was another life-saving lesson, he could feel it, but he could also feel that the object and its resolution were far more subtle and abstract than a seemingly dead bird on a hot summer day brought back to life by a timely helping hand and a steady exhalation. Flash's face had changed so dramatically while he was talking that Lightfoot, for the first time, saw the man his parents knew. Animated by the subject he was trying to explain to Lightfoot, Flash's face had taken on a glow, a youth—and Lightfoot had seen some of his words float above him in the air, incised in different colors in the ether, the way he had sometimes seen certain passages from the Bible rise out of the preacher's mouth and float above his head during the Sunday sermon at the Boys Home. The word *salvation* always floated—and the word *Halleluiah.* But now when Flash started to speak about *love* the word floated in the same sort of way, only closer in and brighter and with far more mystery, but also with the smell of eggs, and other men, and beer. He didn't know what he was supposed to say as a response. At certain points during the sermon at the Boys Home the annunciation of *Amen* was acceptable and he wanted to be able to rise up, like a Christian knight or a miraculously sighted blind man and shout *yes, thank you, I have seen the way!* to Flash but he didn't wholly and completely understand what Flash had said to him. He *wanted* to, he felt it was his duty—but he couldn't grasp it. And he didn't know what to say or do, how to show Flash that he had his own strong intuition that—sooner or later—he would understand the lesson that the older man so fervently believed was worthwhile learning.

Faith, Lightfoot remembered—that was another of those words that seemed to write themselves in air during the sermons at the Boys Home. And now Flash was looking at him as if he hoped Lightfoot would demonstrate his own.

I guess, Lightfoot started haltingly. I have to . . . take your . . . word for it, he said. About . . . this stuff. Until I understand, he stammered.

The first waitress came by again and asked, Something the matter with the beer?

No, the beer is fine, Flash said and raised a toast.

To love, he said, and drank.

—well we don't hear *that* too often in here, the waitress said.

Flash drained the glass then let out a long and hoppy breath.

First drink in over twenty years, he marveled. And either I'm going to find out that beer won't kill me. Or you're about to have one godawful mess to clean up pretty soon.

At first Lightfoot thought it must have been the beer that put the shine on Flash's mood—it didn't kill him, didn't even make him reach for the stuff in the pink bottle. But Flash's expansiveness lasted through the afternoon and evening, into the next day and kept on going. Lightfoot thought maybe it was Texas, in general, that was cheering him up—Flash seemed to like the music on the radio better than what they'd had to listen to through Arkansas; then again, maybe Flash was responding to the territory—open Texas plain and panoramic Texas sky. But on successive days he realized that Flash's better mood might indeed be affected by all of these things, but its true cause was, in fact, Lightfoot's own education—Flash's daily Tutorials. The man, Lightfoot realized, did like to talk. About what he called the "existential" stuff. About life. About the love thing. About the girl.

Amarillo, Albuquerque, Gallup, Winslow, Kingman, Barstow—they could as easily have been the names of Flash's lectures as the names of towns on Route 66. Outside Albuquerque they passed a place that Lightfoot took to be a pawnbroker or a junk shop but Flash spotted a sign by the door that read EPHEMERA FOR SALE.

—O lord, he told Lightfoot. What a Fos-ism—remember his old truck, the 'Phenomonologist'—?

They pulled up in front and when Flash walked through the door he called out, We're here to see the *Ephemera-logist*— A Santa-like man with a long white beard dressed in faded jeans appeared from the back and said, That would be me.

His name was Ephraim—Ephraim, the ephemeralogist—which tickled Flash pinker than his Pepto-Bismol. His collection was a dog's breakfast of leftovers and unwanted junk—and his specialty was things designed never to last—magazines, newspapers, peoples' photographs and letters, documents of every ilk and empty chocolate boxes. But in a glass case in the back were some vintage cameras and among them was a little Leica that caught Flash's eye. He bought it, and on their way out, Lightfoot stopped dead in his tracks. Hanging on the wall between a paint-by-numbers still life and a calendar from 1944 was a framed black-and-white photograph of the spillway of Guntersville Dam in the moonlight, which he recognized as a copy of the one that used to hang in the living room at Oak Ridge. Flash recognized it, too, and asked, How much is that?

Oh you can take it if you want it, Ephraim told them. It's just something I tore out of *Life* magazine and set into a frame.

Flash took it down and handed it to Lightfoot. There you are, kid. You can hang it in your tent.

That night he titled the Tutorial *Friendship and Ephemera,* and started off by telling Lightfoot how, even in prison, things would happen that would remind him so strongly of Fos—or Opal—or his lost love—that he had to close his eyes and make a fist to bring himself back to reality. There was a show on television, he told Lightfoot, called *Mr. Science* that he simply couldn't watch.

For me, it was the river, Lightfoot confessed.

—the river?

The Tennessee. In Knoxville. It reminded me of him, of them.

Well we spent a lot of time together on that water. Fishin . . .

How come you recognized the photograph?

—why do you have to ask? It was in one of her letters.

—well I haven't read them all.

—why not? What are you waiting for?

I don't know.

—jesus, kid, I'm going to have to start to ask you about *bowel movements* if you keep this up.

—keep what up?

—holding so tightly to the past. Let it go.

You haven't let *her* go.

—who?

The girl. The one you never name. You still hold on to *her.* Why can't you understand if I hold on to them for the same reason?

Because it's *not* the same. Because you're twenty years old and your life is ahead of you. When you're *my* age you can fill your nights with beers and backward longings. At *my* age it's preordained. At *your* age it's pathetic. The past doesn't hold the answers for you about who you are—the future does. Life doesn't progress the way a story does, each chapter leading neatly to the next. Life is a series of collisions, for fucksake. It's not a narrative experience. My advice to you is to stop trying to make it one.

Well what kind of experience is it, then? If it doesn't tell a story?

Flash looked away, out the window of the diner into the Texas sky.

Okay—why I bought that Leica today. Toward the end, he started to explain, I got to really love the job—taking pictures. *Love* it. I'd never loved the job before I met this girl. And then I started taking pictures of her—printing them—probably to capture the experience, conserve it, capture the beauty of it, *her* beauty, before it faded. And I'd stay there in the darkroom, hours, proofing out the negs, tinting, cropping, burning in and shading. You know what I discovered? I discovered what I loved. I loved *the light.* On paper, through the lens, reflecting off her hair, her skin. I loved the light. Still do. Know why? Because it travels.

Lightfoot squinted.

If there was a lesson here, he didn't get it. So does sound, he said.

—*fast,* Flash finished. Light travels *fast.* What's the fastest thing in the universe?

The fastest "thing"? Lightfoot tried to comprehend.

Light.

—you sure?

Well can you *hear* the stars?

Fos would say with a big enough eardrum someone could.

—and with a big enough dick I could pole vault all the way to Mars. What I'm telling you is it would not be wrong to venture that light *defines* the universe. Because it travels at the speed it does. It defines the way that we experience the stars, this galaxy, this earth, our life. And as we know since the thing that we perceive as this experience has *traveled* to us over distance, even the distance as small as the one that separates the two of us right now, then we have to acknowledge that everything we know and sense of this material experience is already in the past by the time we see it, a fract of light, two beats behind. Not so much an out-and-out illusion as the Buddha postulates. But a house of mirrors, nonetheless.

So you're saying . . . Life . . . is . . . like a photograph?

—like *moving* photographs. Moving pictures.

Life . . . is . . . like a *movie?*

Flash laughed.

The visual experiences are similar. A series of still lifes strung together running past the eye at a speed which produces the illusion of movement, of reality. But the light that's bouncing off you right now has to reach my eye, my brain, before I can create an image of you in my mind. So you're *there,* you're *then,* but what I see of you I see as *now.* I just need to think that real experience, what life *is,* is the attempt to cut that distance, like I said before. Cut the distance between where you are, over *there,* and where I am in my *now.*

—*then* what? If I *could* cut the distance between my past and now—*then* what? What's it like?

Flash blinked a couple times.

I don't know how to explain it, he admitted. The ultimate. A kind of *glory.*

—like the *bomb,* Lightfoot couldn't stop himself from saying before Flash called the waitress over and asked her if they had a highchair for this two-year-old.

Lightfoot noticed that his fascination with the bomb was the one thing that could darken Flash's mood. Every time he brought it up Flash swore and lost his patience. Finally, one night after they'd driven through the Mojave and had stopped in Bakersfield, he told Lightfoot he didn't want to hear another goddam word about it.

There's something you're not telling me about the way they died and I'm not going to participate in your goddam fiction of it anymore, he told him.

—what do you mean, *something I'm not telling you?*—like what?

Well I don't *know,* do I, Sherlock? I wasn't *there* . . .

Lightfoot looked as if he were about to cry so Flash ordered a beer so at least *he*'d feel better.

Sorry junior, he relented.

—it's okay, Lightfoot told him. Then added, I don't know if I can be the person you expect me to become. I just don't know how to get from *here* to *there.*

Flash sipped his beer, a rim of foam clinging to his upper lip.

You think you're out here hunting for the great white whale? Trust me. You're wrong. The future always finds you, kid. The whale is coming after *you.*

Is that supposed to frighten me?

—no, that's supposed to make you want to learn to swim.

—*that* I can do.

Flash raised the glass and said, Well—here's to tomorrow, then.

Lightfoot raised his glass of water.

To tomorrow, then. And to a swim in the Pacific Ocean. Before he fell asleep that night Lightfoot tried to string all the places they had seen like beads in his memory, as if the journey west had been a straight unbroken line. He tried to piece their conversations—Flash's monologues—together into one long comprehensible trajectory, but his memories of places and of Flash's spoken words kept colliding, certain sights looming larger than the others, certain words resounding. *B-i-i-i-g-g-g country,* Flash had kept remarking as they'd journeyed west: *damn* big. How the hell did people do it before railroads? How the hell did people move across this goddam huge expanse on foot or on the backs of horses, and survive? On *hope,* he had decided. On greed. On dumb luck, or stupidity. The place was vast—and lonelier, in some stretches, than the inside of a prison or the Boys Home. They'd run into some truckers who swore it could be driven, coast to coast, in four days, but that kind of cutting of the distance didn't seem to Lightfoot like something that could aid in understanding what the country was, how it held together or, in places, came apart. Flash had kept returning to his single theme of shortening the distance between an object and the perception of it, but Lightfoot had to wonder what that had to do with daily life, with the lives of people in the plains of Texas where distances were gauged by railroad ties and the time it takes to drive between grain elevators. A person can't be in two places in the landscape all at once, no matter how small you tried to make the country, how many fast roads you built between the coasts. You can only be in two places at the same time—the past and the present, Tennessee and California—if you are there, in one of them, while *thinking* of the other. Or talking about one place while being in the other. Or reading about it. Or having someone read to you. Maybe Flash was right—maybe the key to an enriched life *is* being in two places at once, cutting the distance between the two down to absolutely nothing. Maybe the key to an enriched life is the life of the imagination, the places you can go to in stories held in books while you're still in your own room, the stories that reveal themselves through other stories or through conversations, or through talking to yourself out loud. He remembered doing that—talking to himself, talking to his whales before he fell asleep each night. He remembered the comfort it had given him to talk about the day out loud, pull it, through the spoken word, from the past back into the present. It was like being in two places at once, like having a story read to him, the story of the day he had just lived, the story of his life. But he hadn't spoken to himself that way for years—not since his first night in the Boys Home, and he doubted now, if he could ever find that voice again. It was a boy's voice, anyway, he thought—not the deeper voice he spoke in now. Not the voice that sounded like a man's. And wasn't that, really, the point of Flash's improvised Tutorials? To pull that voice out of his past into his future? The future is the one thing you can count on not abandoning you, kid, he'd said. *The future always finds you. Stand still, and it will find you.* The way the land just has to run to sea.

Drive west for long enough and you will run smack into ocean.

Just after noon the next day they came up over a rise, the sun in front of them, and Flash let out a whistle. At first, Lightfoot didn't recognize it as a great expanse of water, because from where they were, it looked like one great smooth expanse of *light*—peaceful, calm, *pacific*. But as they descended toward the shore the rocky coast exposed itself—and all the ocean's furious thunder.

Lightfoot had never seen an ocean, never experienced the relentless rhythm of the sea, which nothing on dry land approximates, except the ticking of Time's clock itself. He had never seen a pelican or the skittish water birds or heard the boom the weight of water makes when breaking. The shoreline, he realized, was somewhere that was never still—a place that shifted between two places at once. A place where you could stand or swim, or both, at the same time. He remembered Fos telling him that he'd grown up along a shore like this, how his father had made his living rowing boats against the surf out to the deeper anchorages of ships at sea. But if such a life was in his blood, Lightfoot didn't feel it stir. When Flash, exuberant, stripped down to his bare essentials and propelled himself into a wave, Lightfoot rolled his pant legs up, instead, and let the water come to him while he stood on solid ground and stared at the horizon.

South of Monterey, as the old abandoned sardine packing plants began to dwindle into desperate scrub and salt-encrusted boulders, they found a lazy village in a protected cove with a disused cannery behind it. It had a single narrow pier with only two sardine boats left—there were a few clam boats and some dinghies moored haphazardly around the bay, and a bar beside the little harbor, a gas station, general store, and scattered clapboard houses nestled on the hill along the shoreline. Flash went to explore among the fishing shacks while Lightfoot filled the car with gas and in a little while Lightfoot was surprised to see him climb into a motor dinghy with another man and start to chug across the peaceful bay out toward the spit of land that curved around the harbor. Flash waved an arm at Lightfoot and pointed toward the spit and Lightfoot followed the dinghy's course along the shore. When he reached the point, Flash and the other man had beached the boat and were standing by a structure that could only be described as an ocean-going captain's nightmare. Half marooned sardine boat, half tin shack of odds and ends of corrugated steel with a black chimney pot balanced on its slanted roof like a jaunty top hat, the thing looked like what it was: a shipwreck.

—what do you think? Flash wanted to know.

Well I wouldn't put to sea in it, Lightfoot told him. Unless you want a Viking's funeral.

I just bought it.

The man he had just bought it from looked about as smug as a prize fighter when he knows the fix is in.

—for *what?* Lightfoot needed to determine.

—for living in. That was the plan.

—that was the *plan?*—since when?

Since when we started.

Lightfoot didn't dare to look inside, if you could call it that—there was a gaping hole through the port side of the fo'c's'le as if it had sustained a cannonball broadside, and some kind of bird whose shit looked like spilled paint had recently been nesting there. He couldn't start an argument with Flash that he could ever win—the older man had age and cunning and superior vocabulary on his side. But he thought "the *finca,*" as Flash immediately christened it à la his role model Hemingway, was a nutso idea and wasted no time saying so.

This so called town isn't Havana, in case you haven't noticed. Does this so-called *pueblo* even have a name—?

Flash City. *San Flash-cisco.* First place in the United States to elect an ex-con mayor.

It doesn't even have a place to buy a book or get a paper.

Good thing, too, because there isn't any way to put out fires.

No church, no bank, no government, no Pepto-Bismol—they had to drive twelve miles back into Monterey to buy provisions to restore the *finca* to the minimum requirements for human habitation. They could barely get the Olds down the overgrown sand track that ran out to the point. For the next four days they worked from sunrise to sunset putting in a woodstove, installing the water tank, the head, and outdoor shower.

Lightfoot had put up his tent and they cooked on his Coleman stove, but by the fifth day Flash had built an outdoor fireplace and went at low tide to collect shellfish for supper while Lightfoot finished caulking seams and papering the roof. Flash came back with a bucket of clams, a bag of ice, some beers, a loaf of bread, some garlic and tomatoes, and a present that he gave to Lightfoot.

This is for you, kid. Little token of my gratitude.

He handed Lightfoot a smooth object carved in wood.

Lightfoot took it in his hand, surprised, and immediately asked, Where did you *get* this—?

On the pier. Couple so-called artists up there, and some Mexicans with gourds and starchy blankets. Old blind geezer sits and carves these. —and you're welcome, by the way.

Lightfoot disappeared inside his tent, reappearing with two other smooth carved objects.

Spot and Rover, his two whales.

Identical, he said.

He held all three out to Flash.

Feel, he said.

Flash stared at the three objects.

They're carved by the same person, don't you think? Lightfoot maintained.

—*so?*

These were my toys—I played with these with Opal. Upstairs, in my room. There were hundreds of them, I remember.

"Hundreds of carved whales," Flash verified.

—yes.

You played with them. Instead of playing with yourself. No wonder you're the way you are.

Don't you think it's strange? They're identical! Maybe the man on the pier is the one who carved all three.

And maybe the tree he carved them from grew in your backyard because Life just hands out lucky stars like that to me and you each day, don't it, kid. They're *whales,* junior. Classic shape, just like an egg. Round and sort of pointed on one end. Odds are any one-eyed moke could carve you one.

Well I'm going up there. Find this guy. Maybe he can tell me something.

You're gonna hafta leave this thing you've got about your past. That ship has sailed, my friend—how many times are we gonna hafta have this conversation—?

But Lightfoot was already headed toward the pier across the sand.

The breeze was coming off the water, carrying the scent of brine, and plains of gold shimmered on its surface. Beyond the inlet he could see a big ship toiling north toward San Francisco, trailing smoke. He balanced the three whales in one hand and picked a shell up and turned it over. Along its inner curve, suggestive of a source of warmth, it had the colors of an opal and he slid it in his pocket as a keepsake, realizing as he did, how few things he'd ever owned. Like a sailor, like the former creature in the shell inside his pocket, he could carry everything he owned slung on his shoulder, and he wondered what it felt like to have so many things you had to build a larger residence to house them.

He wanted things, he did, he wanted clothes and shoes that fit, he wanted money in his hand to buy the things that pleased him—food and books and entertainment—but he wanted things that money couldn't buy him, first. There were three kinds of orphan in this world, he had learned: The one whose deprivation fuels his acquisitions, whose fate is written like Jay Gatsby's. The one like that Russian writer Gogol that Flash talked about, whose disgust with the artificiality of riches drives him into madness. Or the one like Flash, who says, For fuck sake, fold or cheat but play the hand you're dealt as if it were the only time you'll get to play the game. Because it is.

The sun was in his eyes as he walked onto the pier but he could see a solitary figure sitting on the edge not far away, leaning against a tilting stanchion, figures carved in wood surrounding him.

Excuse me, Lightfoot said, approaching. Are you the man who carved these whales?

The man looked up, but not at Lightfoot, out to sea. He wore an old shirt, old pants, and threadbare slippers. His hair was white and long, unruly as a tattered rope, and his hands were brown and veined and ropy, too. On his wedding finger, there was the thinnest of gold rings.

Lightfoot moved around to intercept the figure's gaze and only then perceived the old man's eyes, pearly, glaucous as two saucers of thin milk.

I think you must have carved all three of these, Lightfoot said.

The old man sort of sniffed in his direction and then turned away, pulling all his whales around him for protection.

—*he doesn't talk!* somebody shouted, and Lightfoot looked toward the voice.

There was a woman painting at an easel farther down the pier.

—*boom hit him!* she called. *Years ago—can't see or talk—!*

Lightfoot gave the old blind man a last look, then headed toward the woman.

Standing at her easel, she was backlit by the lowering sun and her loveliness increased with every step he took toward her.

By the time he was beside her he was speechless. She was about his height, about his age and about the prettiest girl he'd ever seen.

—hi, she said. Your dad was up here earlier.

She pointed a long paintbrush toward the *finca* on the spit.

We've all been watching you out there with fascination.

She smiled.

—or at least *I* have.

Still, he couldn't speak.

His mind worked furiously over things that Flash had told him about women, his Tutorial on how to flirt.

I like what you've done with your hair, he finally blurted out. It must have taken you a lot of time, he noted, and she stared at him.

She was wearing a ponytail.

He blinked, and for the first time looked at her canvas, hoping something painted there could help him out.

There was nothing on it.

Where are you from? she asked, to ease his awkwardness. And because, he saw, she was sincerely curious.

Tennessee.

—oh, no kidding. That's where Tenner's from.

—Tenner?

The man back there who carves the whales.

—he *is?*

Well, I think so—that's the way the story goes, at least. He came out here before I was born so you'll have to ask my dad or some of the other older men who used to take him in their boats. But the story is he showed up one day out of nowhere claiming he was from Tennessee. Never told anyone his name—so they called him Tenner, short for Tennessee. Only told people all he wanted was to learn to be a fisherman.

Lightfoot looked back up the pier at the strange disheveled figure.

Problem was—he was a disaster at it. Like one of those cartoon characters who keep falling into manholes or running into walls. Every time he went out he'd come back with an injury—like that boom that swung around and hit him. Lost his hearing, lost his eyesight, fell overboard a couple times—never, once, in his whole lifetime, caught a fish.

She wiped her paintbrush on a rag and Lightfoot watched her hands.

He caught a whiff of turpentine—and something sweeter. Perhaps her skin.

But here's the part of Tenner's story that I know you'll like, she mentioned, as if she understood what he would like or wouldn't like, and with a rush of pleasure, Lightfoot realized she had employed the first rule that Flash had taught him about flirting—*implied understanding.*

Every boat that he went out on, she continued, came back with the biggest catch that day. *Every* time. He would never catch a thing and he might cause some serious damage to himself, but as a charm, he was lucky. Which is how he's managed to survive here. Everybody takes him in and feeds him and takes care of him. But you should come to Doc's one night and talk to the old boys—maybe someone can remember more about him.

—what's 'Doc's'?

She pointed to the harbor bar.

—where I work. My dad owns it. That's his old sardine boat you bought that ran aground out there. So now he just tends bar.

Is he the man who sold it?

—no that was Rickets. He owns the deeds above the waterline to most land around the harbor. Fairly worthless, since the cannery went bust. This used to be a *town*. Now . . . well. There's nearly nothing.

Is that why your canvas is a blank?

Who says it's blank?

There's nothing on it.

She tilted her head, then lifted up the palette and dipped a clean brush into what seemed to be some greenish pigment, and made a few quick strokes in the lower corner of the canvas.

Lightfoot watched, transfixed, as nothing—not a thing—materialized.

What are you painting with? he asked.

He touched his finger to the greenish mixture and brought it to his nose.

—what is this stuff?

Fish hearts, she told him.

He couldn't move.

There's phosphorus in fish hearts when you grind them up and when you mix that in a medium, say, turpentine, then you can make it fluid, almost like an ink—

Please don't tell me that you're married, Lightfoot interrupted.

She smiled as if she'd heard a private joke and answered, Okay, I won't tell you that I'm married. —is this a riddle?

Does that mean . . . you *are?*

I just promised not to tell you.

I have to buy this painting.

—you 'have' to?

—yes. I have to give it to someone.

—well, you *do* know it's going to shine in the dark, don't you?

—yes, I know that. —how much is it?

He started going through his pockets. —I've got . . . three dollars . . . and . . . a shell.

I'll take the shell.

—no, you have to let me pay you for it.

Please, she said. Let me give you this one. You can buy the next one.

Implied futurity! he recognized.

Let me pay for this one and you can give me the next one, he counteroffered, implying a futurity, himself.

Okay, she smiled, taking one of his three dollars. But come in for a drink tonight—on the house.

I'm Lightfoot, he told her.

Ramona, she said. I signed it, right there, in the corner.

She took the canvas off the easel and handed it to him.

Who are you going to give this to, if you don't mind my asking? It's not your dad, is it?

—you mean Flash? He's not my dad—he's . . . an old friend . . . of the family's. —why?

Lightfoot studied the blank canvas, thinking she was shy about her work.

I'd rather that you keep it for yourself.

Okay, he assured her.

But when he got back to the *finca* carrying an empty canvas, Flash would not let up.

—a *dollar,* he teased Lightfoot, you've been *had.*

—you'll see, Lightfoot rejoined, and hung it on a nail in the trunk of a screw pine while they waited for the coals to heat to boil the water for the clams, and for the giant crimson sun to set into the bright blue water.

Lightfoot had taken the shell he'd found out of his pocket and was fingering its edge along the curve that bound its ends together into one.

—so tell me more about her. Flash made chitchat the way a hawk might ask a chicken, What's for supper?

She paints with fish hearts.

—oh, my Aunt Sally. We-are-joking.

I mean, what are the odds of *that?*

Gigantic odds.

That's what *I* think.

Flash went over to the canvas and looked at it more closely, then said, I still think that you've been had.

Lightfoot stared out at the ocean and nursed a Coca-Cola.

I didn't know what to say to her—how to talk, he confessed.

You don't know how to talk to anyone. Not even to yourself.

—*that's* true.

Start with yourself, the chorus shows up later.

I *used* to talk to myself—I used to be a real good talker.

Isolation shuts the trap.

Isolation didn't seem to shut up *yours.*

Flash opened his beer bottle on the table edge and threw the cap into the fireplace. He raised the beer and toasted his companion.

I only speak these days because of you, Plato. Without you—I'm just another Ishmael alone in just another final chapter.

He drank.

Lightfoot watched a line of cormorants rake the wavelets in the bay.

Are you going to be all right when I take off?

—hell yes. That's the problem with us readers—too many books to read.

I mean with no one here to talk to.

You'll be back.

You think so?

Guaranteed.

He took a sip of beer and wiped his lips.

What's her name, by the way? —your fish heart goddess.

Ramona.

I'm in love with her already. I mean—vicariously. You know I had my flower sewn back on.

Yeah I know—but why?

—why what?

Why aren't you interested in women anymore—since you talk about the goddam benefits of love so much?

—listen to *you.*

Well it just seems hypocritical.

Penance, Flash explained.

You were in a prison twenty-three years, Lightfoot reminded him. And now you've gone all the way across the goddam country just to build another kind of solitary confinement—

What's your point, Voltaire?

If love is such a wonderful thing, why aren't you seeking it?

Because I already found it. Once.

But you make it sound like there's just a single chance for it.—*one* chance. —*one* love. —*one* woman. And I guess what I'm saying is, how did you know? How did you know she was the *one?* How did Fos and Opal know? How does anybody ever know for certain?

One person never does. Two almost always do.

Lightfoot turned the shell over in his hand and wondered if the curve that binds two ends together ever comes apart once it has been formed.

A little miracle occurs, Flash tried to explain to him. You feel it happening and you see it happening for the other person, too—and, bingo. Simultaneity. The birth of jazz. The perfect omelette. —what happened with the whale guy, by the way?

He's from Tennessee.

—christ, they're going to think we're taking over. A Communist plot.

The water in the pot was boiling and Flash got up to toss the clams in, and a minute later he put the steaming pot between them on the table as the sun balanced for a moment on the horizon, as if it could reverse the world, then dipped into oblivion. Venus shot up and half a dozen egrets, trailing their legs like bridal trains, flew laconically over the tidal pool, their wings reflecting gold against the sunset colors.

It's nice here, Lightfoot reflected. Especially this time of day.

Steinbeck calls it the Hour of Pearl.

Opal Hour.

—even better.

The sky deepened overhead and one by one the constellations flickered on, like house lights in a village, and when Flash turned to get a beer from the ice bucket he said, what the *hell?* What the hell is *that?*

Lightfoot followed his gaze to the canvas hanging on the tree, blue, now, in the twilight, and etched with otherworldly lines.

Fish hearts, he elucidated.

I know it's fucking fish hearts, surgeon, but I mean what *is* it? Is it what I *think* it is?

Lightfoot went to stand beside him by the canvas.

Neither of them spoke for what seemed like an eternity to Lightfoot, although he was grateful for Flash's forced discretion.

Finally, Flash asked, I wonder . . . is it . . . a . . . *self-portrait?*

Well it looks like her. The parts I saw. Lightfoot admitted, and for the first time in their acquaintanceship, Flash put an arm around his shoulder.

Son, he said. I think you better go and *find* this woman.

If it hadn't been for Flash, Lightfoot might not have ever seen the inside of a bar, but thanks to him, he was at least prepared for the etiquette of bar life—how to enter, how to make an entrance, how to walk into the room, how to choose a seat and what to say once you're seated. But nothing he had learned from watching Flash in bars and diners while they were on the road prepared him for the entrance that he had to make at Doc's because, first, everybody there was curious about the two strangers living on the spit—and, second, everybody there knew everybody else, except him—and, third, everybody there was several decades older than he was, male, and already slightly drunk.

He walked to the bar and a man rose from one of the tables and snapped a tea towel on his shoulder and stepped behind the bar and drew a slow beer from the tap. He set it down in front of Lightfoot.

—*on the house,* he said.

Lightfoot knew he had to drink it because everybody in the house was watching him, so he lifted the glass and turned around and raised it to the room and took a sip.

He had grown used to the smell of it from being around Flash so the taste was no surprise, although not particularly enjoyable. He put the glass down on the bar and looked at the bartender and asked him, Is Ramona here?

—*who?*

Ramona, Lightfoot repeated, and he could feel everybody's eyes on him again.

Ra-*mo*-na! the bartender called.

Everybody sort of laughed.

Ra-*mo*-na! There's someone out here asking about *you—!*

She came around the corner from the kitchen wearing a white apron, tucking a strand of hair behind her ear and blushing as the guys in the dark corners catcalled *Ramona . . . ooooh!*

When she saw him he could tell that she was pleased and she untied the apron strings and said, Come on, let's go outside—

Her hand slipped into his, he didn't know how it had happened, but it seemed entirely natural, and just as they were stepping off the porch into the night, the screen door opened behind them and the bartender stuck his head around and asked, Pat, you comin back again or should I shut the stove down?

—oh turn it off, they're finished eating for the night, she told him and he waved and told her, Seeya in the morning—*Pat.*

My name's not really Ramona, she explained to Lightfoot.

My name's not really Lightfoot, either. But it's what my parents called me.

I call *myself* Ramona—there's a difference.

They walked along the sand until they found a place to sit.

One day a yacht sailed in—I was nine or ten, never saw anything like it. It was on its way to San Francisco and it came in here in weather and it had more teak and brass than any Spanish navy and I fell in love with it. You know—you live in a place like this, a backwater, you wait for the day a boat like that sails in to carry you away. Except it didn't carry me away—it sailed and left me here. So I pretended it had left its name behind for me—*Ramona de la Luz.*

Pat's a good name, too.

Neither one's as pretty as my mother's name—Pearl.

He told her his was Opal then they smiled at one another, members of the same gem family. Then she asked him if the picture had *developed.*

—ooh yes, he said.

Did you like it?

—ooh yes, he said again.

There was an awkward moment when he should have told her she was beautiful or that the painting was a masterpiece of irresistible erotica but instead he sifted sand through his fingers and eventually asked, How did you learn about the fish hearts shining in the dark?

She smiled and said, You grow up in a fishing village, there's no part of a fish that you don't learn about one way or another. But I'll tell you how I learned about the phosphorus in fish hearts, even though I didn't know enough about it then to understand what phosphorescence was. I must have been about three or four years old, the canneries were booming, running double shifts and my mother—Pearl—was working graveyard for the extra money. And she would come home in the morning in the dark before the sun was up and before she changed out of her clothes she'd come into my room to check on me and one morning I woke up and she was standing there, a constellation in the dark. Bits of bioluminescences from the fish parts she had handled had become embedded on her skin, her arms, her overalls, her hair, and every little bit of it was shining. And from that morning I would try to stay awake until she came into my room. Because she carried her own galaxy.

Lightfoot touched her hair and said, Tell me more about her—where is she? There doesn't seem to be too many women around here.

Fishing's hard on women. Women don't last long in fisheries.

How come?

—the work's too hard. The elements. This kind of life takes its toll on all the men.

Come to think of it, there are never any women in the novels about fishing . . . in the tales about the sea. There are only two or three in *Moby-Dick* and they're all unimportant.

—are you a novelist?

—on golly no. Why do you ask that?

Because you're . . . quiet. Serious.

—oh, he answered, trying not to prove her point, but unable to come up with anything to *dis*prove it.

So . . . where do the women go? he finally asked.

Well while the canneries were up there were plenty women here—plenty jobs for everyone. Then when the sardines were fished out and the packing companies folded a lot of families moved north to other waters with the fleet. Some stayed. A lot of families broke up. Women left to go find work. Hard to live someplace where there's no way to make a living. Pearl stayed, though. She had fishing in her—her brothers and her father had had boats. She had one, too—one of the few. And one morning she took the boat out on her own . . . and never came back.

Lightfoot held her hand and said, I'm sorry.

—me, too.

How can you bear to . . . doesn't it bother you to look at the ocean? Everytime you look out there—?

Well, it's not *my* ocean, she told him.

—but I mean . . .

There are hundreds of stories out there, she gestured, sweeping her hand over the expanse of water before them. —*thousands.* I can't turn the whole ocean into a sad story for just me. That would be like turning the sky into my own little mirror—I look out at the ocean and think my god, what a miracle, my mother might be a part of all that glory—

She leaned her head against his shoulder and pointed to a quadrant high above them and said, Look—a falling star!

They sank back into the sand and she kept her head against him and rested her palm over his heart.

It's the Perseids, she announced.

—it *is?*

It happens every August at this time.

—my father used to show me this. He loved the sky at night.

—yeah, it's good entertainment. Scary for us in the war, though.

—why?

Well Japan is just the other side of all this water, don't forget. And they were telling us the Japanese were going to bomb us the way they did Pearl Harbor. Maybe that was something that you didn't have to think about in Tennessee, but here in California we were pretty scared of what might come at us some bright day from the sky.

That must be horrible.

—what?

Being afraid of something from the sky.

Sailors are always more frightened of things that come out of the sky than of things that come out of the ocean. Storms. Gales. Hurricanes. Typhoons.

My father said the sky was where man first encountered God.

Pat/Ramona rose up on her elbow and looked Lightfoot in the face.

I think man . . . first encountered God . . . right here, she said, and kissed him.

They counted fourteen falling stars that night and thirty-two the next.

It's my birthday in two days, he told her late that second night. And . . . I've got to go somewhere.

He felt her eyes on him and he felt her heart pound through his skin.

All the time that I was growing up here, he heard her say, I would wish on falling stars on nights like this, for some escape from here. Living by the sea you feel the land behind you, but it never beckons and you think some day you'll sail away—*Ramona de la Luz* will sail into your harbor and some solemn handsome man will come ashore and come into your life. I used to dream you—someone like you—would come into this town and we would meet and spend the night under the stars and you would turn to me and say I'm leaving on the morning tide and I would tell you *Take me with you* and you would.

She moved her hand across his brow and smoothed his hair back from his forehead.

And it's going to be very hard for me not to ask you that, but I'm not going to. Because wherever you are going, Lightfoot—I believe you have to go there on your own.

You know I think you're out of your lint-picking mind to do this, don't you? Flash reminded him for the hundredth time when they were standing by the loaded Olds at dawn the morning Lightfoot was leaving.

—yep.

I don't do good-byes, I gotta warn you. I fuck 'em up so bad they oughta lock me up and throw away the key any time I threaten to perform one.

This isn't good-bye.

—what is it, then?

Lightfoot didn't want to spoil the moment with a clever answer. And besides, he couldn't think of one.

I once saw Fos off on a morning such as this, Flash remembered. He was going on a quest, too, even though he didn't know it at the time.

What was he looking for?

—some cockamamie thing. The question is, what found him?

Okay. What *found* him?

—*love.*

Lightfoot had packed the tent in the trunk, and all the camping paraphernalia and Fos's picture of the Guntersville spillway, Pat/Ramona's painting, the Box of Clues and his three whales and the leather case of Opal's letters. And right before he drove away, Flash handed him the Leica.

You never know, he said. You may see something worth remembering—

And now as he made the turn at the junction of the sand track and the state road, he could see a figure coming toward him from the village carrying a blank white canvas.

She was in her bare feet, her face fresh, her hair wet.

I painted you a present, she said, leaning in to kiss him.

He took the canvas from her and propped it on the seat beside him.

I'll be back, he told her.

She stepped away and threw her arms into the air like a semaphorist out at sea and he could see her in the rearview mirror till the curve around the harbor stole her from his line of vision.

It was different driving on his own than it had been with Flash beside him—his thoughts ranged more freely over the scenery, uninterrupted by Flash's running commentary. By noon he had breached the ancient seabed of the great Imperial Valley and the miles and miles of cultivated fields baking in the August sun rewarded him with alternating wafts of oranges, strawberries, and celery. From the valley floor he could see the Sierra Nevadas and Mount Whitney in the distance and he decided not to try to drive over the range through Yosemite or Sequoia, but to skirt around the mountains in the south and drive along their eastern slopes, north, into

Nevada. But at Bakersfield the gas attendant told him he could save some time by going east across the Mojave, south of Death Valley on the Las Vegas road, then north. The testing grounds weren't marked on any map—in fact, he thought there must have been a printing error in the Nevada map he bought when he first looked at it because no map that he had ever seen, except the map of oceans that he'd seen in books, had ever looked so empty. On the map, in the light, Nevada was an empty mystery place like Ramona's canvas—a large white nothing.

By late afternoon he was doing speeds he hadn't done with Flash but still the dusty scrub and pancake-colored mountains seemed to crawl along past him at a snail's pace.

He stopped for groceries and a jug of water on the outskirts of Las Vegas and then, as the sun was going down, on an empty stretch of shiny rocks and undistinguished tumbleweed and cholla, he drove off the highway down an unmarked road that seemed to lead to nowhere, and stopped.

He put up the tent, dug a pit and laid some rocks down for a firepan, gathered scrub for kindling, then started a small flame, just as the first coyotes started howling. He put his bedroll on the ground outside the tent next to the fire and stretched out and let the hard ground realign his spine from all the hours driving. Just when he was comfortable, he remembered Ramona's birthday present and stood up—and even twenty feet away he could see it shining in the front seat of the Oldsmobile.

It was a likeness of the two of them, or the likeness of two lovers, or the likeness of all lovers in an embrace which curved their bodies into one. The lines, themselves, were like the lines a ship's lights cast on water. Lightfoot took the canvas in his hands and then for a fleeting, shocking moment, thought the lovers on the canvas looked like Fos and Opal on their bed where he'd last seen them. He looked away and then looked back again and there they were—as bound together by their love in this depiction as they had been in the final moments of their lives. He propped the painting up against the tent and lay back on the ground and looked up at the sky. *All these years,* he thought. For all these years all he had held onto was that morning of their dying, his failure to revive them with his breath and its sense of loss—but now, suddenly, he could feel the sense of who they were in their *lives,* not only in their dying . . . he could feel the sense of who they had always been in their love for one another.

A star fell overhead, and then another.

Of all the things the sky can hold, he thought—anthropomorphic pictographs. Constellations. Imaginary ancient gods . . . an imaginary modern One. A dread of storms. A ray of hope. Fear of attack. The Bomb.

Fos would not have seen The Bomb as a puffy soft-shaped cloud, a pretty picture subject for a photograph. He realized the moral degradation in its creation, and he would have wanted to protest its use against mankind.

Janet had said *suicides*—he hadn't forgotten that she'd said it. He simply refused to think she could be right.

She could be right, he now thought.

What if it were true?

Was that so bad?

To have created love like that out of absolutely nothing—it was a sort of miracle, wasn't it? To have set that kind of example for their son—for Flash—for everyone who saw them fumbling along together, walking, talking, marveling at life. It was a kind of glory, if he thought about it, he realized. A common uncontested outright glory for mankind, he thought. Like each and every unnamed, uncontested, unsung star up there, coupling with the dark for us to contemplate in silence. Glory was the word that Flash had used to describe the ultimate point where the past meets the present. And glory was the word that Pat had used when she described her mother being a part of the ocean—and in a sudden jolt of recognition he heard a voice speaking to him in the desert solitude, a man's voice, kind and strong and confident, recounting these thoughts and murmuring out loud. *Glory,* Lightfoot told the stars. *Glory,* he wished his parents. He glanced once more at the painting, then drew a curve across the sky like the one she'd drawn, a binding curve of energy between the stars connecting *then* and *now,* describing the impossible. It's not how long it glows, he needed to describe to Fos. It's *not* how long the light lasts, he needed to explain to him. It's what it says while it's still visible.

He put his hands behind his head and smiled. If he left at first light in the morning he could be back on the shore with her tomorrow night and they could count these falling stars together.

Glory, he heard his own voice saying.

"Glory," he repeated.

Halleluiah.

notes

The law prohibiting teaching Darwin's Theory of Evolution in the State of Tennessee was repealed in May 1966.

In 1966 a bill was introduced in the State Legislature to limit teaching evolution as "theory" only, not as fact. The bill lost by twenty votes.

I quote James Russell Lowell's poem "Voyage to Vinland." The full stanza is this:

> *Fate loves the fearless;*
> *Fools, when their roof tree*
> *Falls, think it Doomsday;*
> *Firm stands the sky.*

about the author

Marianne Wiggins is the author of six novels, including *John Dollar, Almost Heaven, Eveless Eden,* and *Separate Checks.* She has won a Whiting Award, an NEA award, and the Janet Heidinger Kafka Prize. She lives in California.